RUINING MISS WROTHAM

EMILY LARKIN

www.emilylarkin.com

Publisher's Note: This is a work of fiction. Names, characters, places, and incidents are a product of the author's imagination. Locales and public names are sometimes used for atmospheric purposes. Any resemblance to actual people, living or dead, or to businesses, companies, events, institutions, or locales is completely coincidental.

Ruining Miss Wrotham / Emily Larkin. -- 1st ed.

ISBN 978-0-9941443-7-9

Cover Design: The Killion Group, Inc

❀ Created with Vellum

A Baleful Godmother

Novel

It is a truth universally acknowledged, that Faerie godmothers do not exist.

Chapter One

July 15th, 1812
London

NELL WROTHAM HAD TWO GODMOTHERS. One had given her a bible when she was christened and a copy of Fordyce's *Sermons for Young Women* when she turned twelve. Her father had insisted that Nell read the sermons and she had dutifully obeyed.

Nell's second godmother hadn't given her a gift yet and Nell's father hadn't known about her, because *that* godmother was a Faerie and her existence was a deep, dark secret. Her name was Baletongue and she would only come once, on Nell's twenty-third birthday, and when she came she would grant Nell one wish.

Nell was wishing as the stagecoach she sat in rattled towards London. She was wishing that her twenty-third birthday had been yesterday, or perhaps today, or at the very latest, tomorrow. But it wasn't. She still had a week to wait.

She sat on the lumpy seat, pressed close by a stout widow on one side and an even stouter attorney's clerk on the other. Nell's fingers were neatly folded over her reticule, her expression calm, her agitation hidden. *A well-bred lady never shows her emotions*—one of the many maxims drilled into her by her father. Her father, whose rigid, unforgiving righteousness was at the root of this disaster.

Nell clutched her reticule more tightly and wished for the thousandth time that her birthday was sooner—and prayed that when her Faerie godmother finally came it wouldn't be too late.

Chapter Two

Mordecai Black reached London as the clocks were striking noon. The streets were dusty and the traffic sluggish. The air trapped between the buildings had a fetid undertone. He drew the curricle to a halt outside the Golden Cross Inn, thrust the reins at his groom, and jumped down.

The inn's yard thronged with porters and passengers, all of them hot and sweaty and irritable, but Mordecai had no difficulty traversing the crowd. People looked at him and prudently stepped aside.

The taproom was busy, the coffee room slightly less so. "Your master?" he asked a serving-man.

Mordecai followed the man's directions and found the innkeeper in a stuffy back office, bent over a ledger, tallying rows of numbers.

"The stagecoach from Bath that arrived this morning . . . are any of the passengers putting up here?"

The innkeeper looked up with a scowl on his brow, clearly annoyed by the interruption. He opened his mouth, took in

Mordecai's size—and thought better of what he'd been about to say.

"A woman arrived this morning from Bath," Mordecai said. "Traveling alone. Is she staying here?"

"There was a woman." The innkeeper put aside his quill and reached for a smaller ledger. Not accounts, but room allocations. He ran his finger down the entries and halted at one.

Mordecai's heart began to beat faster, a drumbeat of hope and nervousness. He was acutely aware of the document tucked into his breast pocket.

"Mrs. Webster," the innkeeper said. "Yes, she's putting up here."

"Mrs. Webster?"

"Yes."

"It's Miss Wrotham I'm looking for."

The innkeeper closed the ledger. "Then she is staying elsewhere."

W, Mordecai thought. *Wrotham. Webster.* "What does she look like? Young, slim, dark brown hair?"

"I wouldn't call her young," the innkeeper said. "Or slim."

Mordecai's hopeful nervousness evaporated. In its place was a feeling that was part unease, part worry. He went outside to speak with the porters. Half a crown each and a glance at his face bought him their full attention.

Some days it annoyed him that his appearance intimidated people; today it was useful, but only one porter had noticed Miss Wrotham. None of them had seen her leave the inn's yard.

MORDECAI DROVE TO GROSVENOR SQUARE, avoiding the other carriages by habit, scarcely noticing the landmarks. How the devil was he to find Miss Wrotham in a city the size of London?

The curricle rattled into the great square and there, on the far side, was his townhouse, a towering edifice with columns and a Palladian pediment and four rows of windows rising one above the other. Lord Dereham's house until eight months ago, and now Dereham's bastard's house. He'd heard the linkboys call it that—Dereham's bastard's house—not as a slur on his character, but merely acknowledging the truth of his birth: Dereham's natural son. Dereham's bastard.

Mordecai drew the curricle to a halt and clambered stiffly down. The hours he'd spent on the road were catching up with him: the journey to Bath, the journey back again, no rest in between.

"Take it round to the stables," he told the groom. "Have the rest of the day off."

The curricle clattered away over the cobblestones, but Mordecai didn't climb the steps to his front door.

Miss Wrotham was somewhere in London. Alone.

Mordecai stripped off his gloves and rubbed his face, felt grit and sweat and stubble. He needed food, a shave, a cold bath, fresh clothes. And maybe a nap.

He turned on his heel and stared across the square, seeing tall buildings, hazy rooftops, chimneys. The city seemed suddenly full of dangers. He felt a twinge of fear—an emotion he was unused to. He stood six foot five and weighed two hundred pounds and he knew how to fight, he was *good* at fighting, but Miss Wrotham was none of those things. And she was female, and alone in London without friends or protectors, and she had no experience of abbesses and cutpurses and bullyboys.

The sense of fear became stronger, laced with anxiety. *Where the blazes is she?*

Behind him, he heard his front door open. Mordecai looked around. His butler peered down the steps at him. "Sir?"

"I'm going for a walk."

HE WENT TO HALFMOON STREET, five minutes' fast walk from Grosvenor Square. The Dalrymples' house was closed and shuttered, the knocker removed from the door—they were away, but Miss Wrotham *must* have known that; the Dalrymples were her cousins and she knew as well as anyone that they spent every summer in the country. So why had she come to London, and how the devil was he to find her?

Mordecai hesitated on the doorstep of the shuttered house, sweating, tired, worried. God, it was warm in London, the air close and still and sticky, no breeze to ease the heat.

He loosened his neckcloth and rubbed his face again, stubble rasping under his hand. There was one other person Miss Wrotham knew in London.

Mordecai strode around to Berkeley Square telling himself that he was a fool, that the last person Miss Wrotham would visit was Roger—the man had jilted her, for God's sake!

Halfmoon Street to Berkeley Square took all of two minutes. Mordecai's pace slowed when he neared Roger's house. It was a handsome building, but not as handsome as his own townhouse, nor as large.

He wondered what the linkboys called it.

Mordecai halted at the foot of the steps. *A fool's errand, this. Roger won't know, and if he did, he'd delight in not telling me.* And then he felt the prickling anxiety again. He touched his fingertips to the marriage license in his breast pocket, took a deep breath, and climbed the steps of the new Lord Dereham's house.

The butler opened the door.

"Afternoon, Bolger. My cousin in?"

The butler's lips tightened at the word *cousin*, a tiny spasm of distaste. He looked as if he wished he had permission to close the door in Mordecai's face. "Lord Dereham is at home, sir," he said woodenly.

"I'll see him."

The entrance hall was similar to Mordecai's own: the high ceiling molded and painted by Robert Adam, the long stretch of marble floor, the doors to dining room, drawing room, and library on either side, the staircase at the end. There the resemblance ended; Mordecai didn't decorate his entrance hall with footmen. Vases were decoration, a Robert Adam ceiling was decoration, but his footmen were not. Roger's footmen were, poor sods. Four of them stood in their curling wigs and gold-braided livery, two on either side of the hall, backs to the wall, chins up, eyes staring blankly ahead. Human statues. Mordecai almost snorted. *Why in God's name must he have one standing here all day, let alone four?*

But he knew the answer: the footmen were because Roger liked to flaunt his wealth, and there were four because Roger liked symmetry. Two footmen would have been too few, and three or five unacceptable.

"Lord Dereham is momentarily occupied," the butler said, his expression dyspeptic, as if Mordecai's kinship to his master pained him as much as it pained Roger. "If you will step into the library, I shall inform him of your arrival." He gave a stiff-necked nod, and one of the footmen sprang to open the library door.

Mordecai had taken half a dozen steps towards the library, wondering how long the butler and Roger would choose to keep him waiting, when the drawing room door opened abruptly and a young lady strode out. "—hiding behind excuses. A *hen* has more courage than you!"

Mordecai halted.

He'd been truly and deeply surprised twice in his life. Once, when his father had come to claim him, and the second time when Henry Wright had stood up for him at Eton. This moment qualified as the third. He was so astonished that he gaped. Eleanor Wrotham was here? In Roger's house?

"If you won't help me, I'll find someone who has the gumption to do so!" Miss Wrotham was magnificent in her scorn, eyes flashing, voice ringing, cheeks flushed.

And then he saw the tears trembling on her eyelashes. She wasn't merely angry; she was upset.

Miss Wrotham didn't see him. She crossed the entrance hall briskly, flung open the door before Bolger could reach it, and marched outside.

Roger emerged from the drawing room—red-faced and righteous, his blond hair sleek with pomade. Mordecai ignored his cousin. He strode after Miss Wrotham and shut the door firmly in Bolger's face. "Miss Wrotham!" He took the steps two at a time.

Miss Wrotham halted on the flagway and glanced back. He saw surprise cross her face—a brief, wide-eyed flare of astonishment—and then the surprise snuffed out and she was once again her father's daughter, haughty and aloof.

Mordecai stared down at her and knew in his bones that she was the one woman in all the world whom he was meant to marry. Not because of her appearance and her breeding—those had been Roger's reason for offering for her—but because of what lay beneath those things: the clear-eyed intelligence, the suppressed passion, the spirit bursting to be free.

He trod down the last three steps. "I'll help you," he said. "Whatever it is, I'll help."

Miss Wrotham's eyebrows lifted slightly. She looked him up and down.

Mordecai was suddenly acutely aware of what he must look like: sweaty, hulking, unshaven, dressed in clothes that had been elegant yesterday, but today were wrinkled and travel-stained.

He resisted the urge to tighten his neckcloth and brush the dust from his coat, but it was impossible not to feel embarrassed. Of all the ways he'd imagined meeting Miss Wrotham again, this wasn't one of them. He felt a faint blush creep into his cheeks—and when was the last time he'd blushed? Years ago.

Mordecai endured her scrutiny, and wished he knew what Miss Wrotham thought of him. Not what she thought of his appearance—it was obvious what anyone would think of his appearance right now—but what she thought of *him*. Mordecai Black. Earl's son. Bastard.

Society accepted him—his father's sponsorship had seen to that—but not everyone liked him. Roger certainly didn't. Miss Wrotham's father—a high stickler—hadn't either. He'd thought Mordecai unworthy of his daughter's hand, but the man was dead now and the only opinion that mattered was Miss Wrotham's. What did *she* think? Did those astute eyes see past his reputation as a rake? Did she see who he truly was?

Perhaps she did, because instead of turning away from him as a prudent and respectable young woman should, Miss Wrotham said, "I need to go to Seven Dials, but none of the jarveys will take me—they say it's no place for a lady."

Seven Dials? Mordecai stared at her in astonishment. "They're correct."

"Will you take me there, Mr. Black?"

"No." He shook his head emphatically. "Absolutely not. If you have business there, allow me to go in your stead."

"I have to go myself."

"Seven Dials is little more than taverns and brothels," Mordecai told her bluntly. "It's not a place you should visit."

"My sister's there." Miss Wrotham's aloofness slipped. Desperation and urgency were clear to read on her face. "She's in terrible trouble. She needs my help."

Mordecai's eyebrows lifted. The sister who'd plunged the Wrotham family into disgrace? Who'd ruined Miss Wrotham's marriage prospects and caused Roger to jilt her? "Is this the sister who, er . . ." *Ran off with a soldier.*

"I have only one sister."

And whatever that sister had done, Miss Wrotham obviously still cared about her.

Mordecai hesitated. If Miss Wrotham's sister was in Seven Dials, then her fortunes had sunk very low. "I'll bring her to you. It's best that you don't—"

"I'm going with you."

"Miss Wrotham—"

"Mr. Black, you would terrify her!"

Mordecai felt himself flush. "I assure you that I'll treat your sister with respect," he said stiffly.

"It's not that," Miss Wrotham said, with an impatient wave of her hand. "Oh, don't you see? You look *dangerous,* and she's scared enough as it is . . . and I *have* to go with you. She's my sister!"

Mordecai looked down at her and saw fierce determination on her face and stubbornness in the set of her chin—the spirit he'd admired last year, no longer suppressed but burning brightly. And then he thought of trying to persuade a frightened young woman who didn't know him from Adam to trust him enough to get in a carriage with him. He grimaced inwardly.

"Please," Miss Wrotham said, and she reached out and touched his arm, a gesture that was somehow both reckless and cautious at the same time, as if she thought that merely laying her hand on his sleeve might ruin her.

Mordecai's awareness of her flared. The last of his resolve crumbled. He gave a reluctant nod. "We'll go together."

Relief and hope illuminated Miss Wrotham's face—and then the urgency returned. She gripped his arm, her fingers digging deeply into his sleeve. "Can we go now? Where's your carriage?"

"In the stables. A hackney will be quicker."

"They'll refuse—"

"They'll not refuse me."

Chapter Three

Miss Wrotham made no attempt at conversation. She sat alongside him, gripping her reticule, staring ahead, as if she could make the hackney go faster by sheer force of will. Mordecai had the disconcerting sensation that the clocks had lurched back a year and that now wasn't now any longer. Miss Wrotham was even wearing an outfit she'd worn during her Season: the ivory-white walking dress with the vandyked hem, the navy blue spencer that matched her eyes, the chip straw bonnet with the blue riband. An outfit that had been elegant last year but looked slightly shabby now.

It felt as if time had turned back, but also as if it *hadn't*, because this Miss Wrotham wasn't quite the young woman he remembered, even though she wore the same dress. This Miss Wrotham had the cool, aloof composure of last year's Miss Wrotham—but beneath that composure she radiated tension.

She turned her head and caught him looking at her.

"How far is it to Seven Dials, Mr. Black?"

"A mile or so."

Miss Wrotham gave a jerky nod and opened her reticule. She pulled out a folded letter. "Sophia wrote that she didn't know exactly where she was, but it's above a tavern. She could see the Seven Dials crossroads from her window. She says . . . she says that when she arrived in London she had no money and she didn't know where to go, and a woman took her in and fed her and gave her a bed for the night and then . . ." She gripped the letter tightly, crumpling it in her fist. "And then she said that Sophia owed her five shillings in return and that she must work to pay it off—and Sophia says it's a *brothel*."

Mordecai nodded, unsurprised. "It's a common ploy. The abbesses use it to catch young girls from the country, those who don't know any better."

"Well, it caught Sophia," Miss Wrotham said bitterly. "She says Mrs. Harris has locked her in a room, and she can't get out." She looked down at the letter, and smoothed it out on her knee. "But she had paper with her, and a pencil—she can draw, you see—she says she sometimes earns a little money from her drawings . . . and she says the girl who came to empty her chamber pot was friendly, and she was going to ask her to post this for her."

"She obviously succeeded." Mordecai tried to make his tone reassuring. "Miss Wrotham, your sister will be all right."

Miss Wrotham looked at him gravely. "I received this letter only yesterday, but Sophia wrote it four months ago."

Mordecai let out his breath slowly.

"Four *months*." The tears were back in Miss Wrotham's eyes.

Mordecai couldn't bring himself to say *She'll be all right* again.

Miss Wrotham dashed the tears away and lifted her chin. She held the letter out to him. "Sophia sketched what she could see from her window. I thought it might help me find her."

Mordecai took the letter. Sophia Wrotham had written fast. Her words were a rough, hasty scrawl, almost illegible. He resisted reading them and focused on the sketch at the bottom. It was neither rough nor hasty; Sophia Wrotham had taken pains with it.

His gaze drifted up to the final line of the letter—*I pray that you get this letter, Nell, for I know you will help me, whatever Father may say.*

Nell. Miss Wrotham's sister called her Nell.

He jerked his gaze back down to the sketch, studied it for a moment, fixing the details in his mind, then looked at Miss Wrotham. "It will help."

SEVEN DIALS HAD ONCE BEEN a respectable neighborhood, although no one would call it that now; each of the seven streets radiating from the crossroad boasted a public house on the corner. But there was more to the Dials than merely taverns. There were gin shops and chophouses and brothels and tenements and shops selling goods that were third or fourth hand, and hawkers loudly advertising their wares, and children playing in the gutters, and men and women of all ages afflicted with the same condition: poverty. A good many of them were afflicted with a second condition: drunkenness.

If Halfmoon Street had been uncomfortably warm, Seven Dials was sweltering. The air was thick, stifling, choking with foul smells. He and Miss Wrotham stood on the filthy flagway, buffeted by the heat and the noise, the stench, the people.

Mordecai kept a firm grip on Miss Wrotham's elbow. She pressed close to him, showing a calm face, but he felt her tension, felt the faint trembling of her arm. He glanced down at the sketch, and back at the scene before him. "Over there. You see it? That's where she drew this from."

Miss Wrotham followed his gaze. The building was shabby, its mortar crumbling, one of its upper windows boarded over. "I see it."

Mordecai handed her the letter and tightened his grip on her elbow—not because he was afraid she'd try to pull free, but because he wanted there to be no mistake. *To get to her, you have to go through me.* Together they crossed the road and gained the far side. The loiterers and the passersby paid them little attention; Mordecai scanned their faces, saw nothing that alarmed him, then looked down at the children playing in the gutter. He reached down and took one of the boys by the ear. "Which is Mrs. Harris's bawdy house?"

The boy yelped and screwed up his face—playacting; Mordecai's grip wasn't cruel. But the pretense of pain was earning the boy the wide-eyed attention of his companions.

"Which door?"

The urchin pointed.

Mordecai released him and tossed him a coin. The boy caught it, grinning widely.

The door had seen better days, but it was stout enough. Not a door a young woman would be able to break down if it were locked. It wasn't locked today. Mordecai pushed it open. A staircase led upward, steep and dark and malodorous. No bullyboy waited at the foot of the stairs, but Mordecai was certain there'd be one at the top.

He thought of his pistols in their silk-lined case, back in Grosvenor Square, and wished he had them with him. But if he didn't have pistols, he had his fists—and he'd wager he was a better fighter than any bullyboy.

Unless the bullyboy had a knife.

Mordecai glanced at Miss Wrotham. *She shouldn't be here.*

He imagined her shrieking and fainting—and dismissed it as impossible; and then he imagined her picking up a vase and smashing it over a bullyboy's head. *That* wasn't impossible, not if she was the woman he thought she was.

"If there's a fight, don't involve yourself," he said firmly. "Leave it to me."

Miss Wrotham nodded.

Mordecai didn't believe the nod; if it came to a fight, if she thought her sister's life was in danger, Eleanor Wrotham would plunge into the fray. Therefore, there must be no fight.

He set his foot on the bottom stair—then turned back and bolted the door behind them. Now their backs were safe.

Mordecai climbed the stairs, Miss Wrotham following closely behind him. At the top was a narrow corridor with doors opening off on either side. Here was the bullyboy, slouching in a chair, his chin sunk on his chest, half-asleep.

The man jerked awake when Mordecai loomed over him, staggered to his feet, and stood swaying. Mordecai revised his assessment: not half-asleep; half-drunk.

"Mrs. Harris," Mordecai said brusquely. "We wish to speak with her."

The bullyboy was shorter and heavier than Mordecai, with a fighter's face: broken nose, scarred eyebrows. "An' who might you be?" he said, bluster in his voice.

"Mrs. Harris," Mordecai said. "Now."

The bullyboy squinted at Mordecai's face while he worked through his options, then he made the wisest choice: he turned and headed down the corridor.

Mordecai and Miss Wrotham followed.

The bullyboy halted at the third door along and pushed it open. "Some'un to see you," he said.

Mordecai stepped into the room on the bullyboy's heels. It

was a parlor. There was only one occupant: a woman on a settee, a teacup in her hand. The settee had once been a handsome piece of furniture. Its lines were still good, but the fabric was thin in places, stained and greasy in others.

Apart from the settee, the room was sparsely furnished. There were no vases for Miss Wrotham to smash over the bullyboy's head. But there was a sturdy oak stool that would be easy to wield, and by the fireplace was a set of tools: poker, tongs, shovel, brush. Mordecai eyed the poker briefly, and then looked back at the woman.

Mrs. Harris was in a similar condition to her settee: she'd once been handsome, but was no longer. She looked as tough as her bullyboy, a woman on the wrong side of fifty with tight lines bracketing her mouth.

Miss Wrotham stepped into the room alongside Mordecai, so close that her arm brushed his. Mrs. Harris's gaze swung to her, sharp and assessing, like an auctioneer looking over a prime horse.

"Mrs. Harris?" Mordecai said.

The woman put down her teacup. "Who are you?"

"We're here for Sophia Wrotham."

"Never heard of 'er. Joe, show 'em out."

"No," Mordecai said, closing the door and standing with his back to it. "Sophia Wrotham. You offered her a bed for the night, gave her some food—and then told her she was in your debt. That she had to work for you to pay it off."

Mrs. Harris lifted her chin. "What if I did? I ain't a charity."

"Where is she?" Mordecai said, his voice hard and flat and full of menace.

"Joe," Mrs. Harris said shrilly. "Stop standing there like a fool! Get rid of 'em."

The bullyboy hesitated. His gaze traveled from Mordecai

to Miss Wrotham and then to the fireplace, coming to rest on the poker. He took a lurching stride towards it.

Mordecai took two quick steps forward, scooped up the stool, and threw it.

The stool hit the bullyboy solidly in the head—*crack-thud*. He collapsed bonelessly.

Mrs. Harris scrambled to her feet. She snatched up her teacup and held it like a weapon.

"Sophia Wrotham," Mordecai said again. "Where is she?"

"I don' know who you mean!"

"She was here four months ago," Mordecai said.

"Four months?" Mrs. Harris's expression changed. She looked as if she wanted to spit. "Girl with yeller hair? Pretty?"

Mordecai glanced back at Miss Wrotham. She nodded.

"A viper, she were. Broke a winder and run off. Took one of me girls wiv 'er."

"She's gone?"

"Are you deaf? I just tole you! She run off."

Mordecai surveyed the woman through narrowed eyes. "I want to see inside every room in this building."

MORDECAI SEARCHED FROM cellar to attic, his hand wrapped tightly around Mrs. Harris's upper arm, Miss Wrotham following silently. Sophia Wrotham wasn't there, although they found the room where she'd been kept. The window was broken and boarded over.

Mrs. Harris had five girls working for her, all asleep at this time of day. Mordecai shook them awake and asked them the same questions: Did they know where Sophia Wrotham had gone? Did they wish to leave themselves? They all answered *No* to the first question; three of them said *Yes* to the second.

Half an hour after he and Miss Wrotham had entered the bawdy house, they left it. The bullyboy was still out cold on the parlor floor.

Mordecai unbolted the door at the foot of the stairs and stepped out onto the street. Nothing had changed; the air was still thick and hot and stinking, the same urchins still played in the gutter.

"Is there somewhere you'd like to go?" he asked the three girls.

"Home," one of them said. She looked about eighteen years old, a thin, drab creature, pale-skinned and lank-haired. All her belongings fitted into one shabby carpetbag.

"Where's that?"

"Near Stevenage."

"I'll take you to a coaching inn," Mordecai said. "Get you a place on the stagecoach." He looked at the other two girls. "You?"

"Putney," one of them said. "Ma lives there. She'll 'ave me back."

"Mine won't," the last girl said. She looked like a farmer's daughter, strong-boned and ruddy-cheeked, but for all her sturdiness she also looked fragile and forlorn. Her gown was soiled and wrinkled, her hair disheveled, the remains of a bruise gray on her face.

Mordecai knew his duty. He'd have to employ her. A scullery maid? A housemaid? Perhaps a milkmaid on his Devonshire estate?

"Come wiv me, then," the second girl said. "Ma's a laundress. She'll be glad fer the extra 'ands."

MORDECAI SAW THE two girls into a hackney and paid their

fare to Putney. He gave them each a banknote. "Look after her," he told the girl from Putney, with a nod at the farmer's daughter.

"I will, sir."

He hailed a second hackney, handed the last girl into it, and found himself confronted by a dilemma. "Ah, Miss Wrotham?"

She glanced at him, and then at the girl in the carriage, and he saw that she understood both his dilemma and his unvoiced question: *Do you object to sharing a carriage with a prostitute?*

She responded by stepping up into the hackney.

Miss Wrotham's father would have turned over in his grave in horror; Mordecai was simply relieved. He directed the jarvey to take them to the Saracen's Head in Holborn, from where the coaches north departed, and climbed into the carriage.

It was a silent journey to the Saracen. The only sound was the clatter of the hackney's wheels. Miss Wrotham sat clasping her hands. She looked remote and haughty—and beneath the haughtiness, exhausted. Mordecai wondered if she'd slept at all on the stagecoach from Bath, and when she'd last eaten. And then he tried to remember when he'd last eaten. Too long ago, his stomach told him.

The Saracen's Head wasn't the inn Miss Wrotham had arrived at that morning, but it was just as busy. Miss Wrotham didn't appear to notice the press of people; her gaze was unfocused, her attention directed inwards.

Mordecai paid the girl's fare to Stevenage and ordered a meal for her. "Are you hungry?" he asked Miss Wrotham. "Would you like to dine here?" But she merely shook her head.

Mordecai gave the girl ten pounds. He could tell from her

expression that it was more money than she'd ever seen in her life. "Good-bye," he said, and turned to go.

"Sir?"

Mordecai turned back. The girl stood clutching the ten-pound note in her dirty fingers.

"I don' know where your friend is, but I know where Lizzie'll be."

Miss Wrotham's gaze became suddenly sharp. "Lizzie?"

"The one who run off wiv 'er."

Miss Wrotham took a step forward, her eyes fixed intently on the girl's face.

"Lizzie said she knew some'un who'd take her in, if she could get back to Exeter."

"Who?"

"I don' know 'er name, ma'am, but Lizzie said she's a godly woman who 'elps the fallen."

"Fallen women?"

The girl nodded. "Lizzie said she didn' like bein' preached at, but anything'd be better than whoring."

"Exeter?"

The girl nodded again. "That's where Lizzie will 'ave gone. And prolly your friend wiv 'er."

Chapter Four

NELL HURRIED OUT to the street. The hackney that had brought them was gone. She looked left and right, searching for another one, her mind racing ahead. Exeter. How soon could she get there? "Where's the nearest hackney stand?"

"Around the corner," Mr. Black said.

Nell set off for the corner. Her father would have rebuked her for her unladylike haste; Mr. Black merely lengthened his stride, keeping pace with her.

"Do you know where the stagecoaches to Exeter depart from?" Nell asked him.

"From here."

Nell stopped.

Mr. Black took hold of her elbow. "You are not going to Exeter by stagecoach."

"I can't afford a post-chaise." The admission should have embarrassed her, but Nell was past caring what people thought of her. She tried to tug her elbow free.

Mr. Black tightened his grip. "I *can* afford a post-chaise." And then he asked, "When did you last eat?"

Nell couldn't remember, and she certainly didn't care. She stamped her foot. "Let go of me! I need to put my name on the waybill."

"I can get you to Exeter faster than a stagecoach," Black said. "When did you last eat?"

Nell stared at him. Emotions warred in her breast: gratitude for his help in Seven Dials, annoyance at his highhandedness now, and hope that he'd help her get to Exeter. A hackney rattled into view.

Mr. Black hailed it, and of course the jarvey saw him and of course the carriage stopped. Black wasn't a man people could easily overlook, not merely because of his towering height and striking looks, but because of the indefinable aura of danger that clung to him. He stood out in ballrooms and dining rooms and assembly rooms, he stood out at the opera and in Vauxhall Gardens, he stood out riding in Hyde Park, and he most certainly stood out in Holborn. Nell didn't think she'd ever seen Mordecai Black in a situation where he *didn't* stand out, a fact that Roger had deeply resented.

Black handed her into the hackney. "Where are you staying?"

"The Earnoch, off Piccadilly."

Black spoke to the jarvey and climbed in after her. The door swung shut and she was alone with him. Alone with Mordecai Black.

Awareness of him swept through her, the same unsettling mix of attraction and fear that had plagued her Season. Her pulse fluttered and her skin tightened and her breath came a little shorter. *Don't be silly,* Nell told herself tartly. *You don't want him and he most certainly doesn't want you.*

She took a deep, steadying breath and turned her attention

to Sophia. How long would it take to reach Exeter? Dare she accept Mr. Black's assistance to get there? *Should* she accept it?

Nell gripped her reticule tightly and wrestled with her conscience. She ought not allow Black to pay for a post-chaise to Exeter. She could never repay him, therefore it would be wrong of her—and quite apart from that it would be grossly improper. She was an unmarried lady; he was Mordecai Black. Scandal clung to him. Any association with him would tarnish her.

But she was already tarnished. Scandal clung to *her*, too, and what did her reputation matter anyway? What mattered was finding Sophia as soon as possible, and if Mr. Black could help her, she would accept anything he offered. Even if it was improper of her to do so, and even if it put her in his debt.

Nell stole a glance at him and felt the familiar response: the fluttering pulse, the shiver. *I want him. I fear him.* Foolish, conflicting emotions. Emotions she ought to have mastered a year ago.

There was no denying that Mordecai Black had a memorable face—the dangerous angles of cheekbone and jaw, the eyes so dark they were almost black, the Dereham nose. That nose had overpowered the late earl's face, but it didn't overpower Black's face. It was in keeping with the rest of him: striking, strong. An assertive nose with a high and prominent bridge. The sort of nose a Roman emperor would have had. The nose stopped Black being pretty, as Roger was. It stopped him being classically handsome, despite his chiseled cheekbones. But it didn't stop him being beautiful, because Mordecai Black *was* beautiful, in a way that was purely and aggressively masculine. He had a face that drew the eye. A face women looked at twice. A face that made other men's faces appear soft and feminine by contrast.

Roger had resented that, too.

Nell looked down at her hands gripping the reticule. Mordecai Black's face was irrelevant. What mattered was his character. *Can I trust this man?*

The hackney halted. Nell looked up, surprised. Had they reached Piccadilly already? She peered out the window. The street wasn't one she recognized. She glanced at Mr. Black.

"We're eating here," he said.

"But—"

"We need to talk. We need to eat."

Nell peered out the window again. The neighborhood didn't look particularly genteel. "Here?"

"If we dine in Mayfair, someone's bound to see us. Here, we'll be anonymous." Black climbed down from the hackney and held out an imperative hand to her.

Nell dubiously descended. The hackney had drawn up outside a public house patronized by working men. Not down-at-heels laborers, not pale clerks who spent their days scribbling in ledgers, but men somewhere in between. Men who would have made her nervous if she wasn't in Black's company. "Have you ever been here before?" she whispered as they entered.

"No, but the jarvey says the pies are the best this side of the Thames."

The coffee room smelled strongly of ale and sweat, but beneath those smells was the tantalizing aroma of roasted meat. Nell's stomach clenched painfully, reminding her that she hadn't yet eaten today.

Black spoke to a serving-man, who led them out into a corridor and up a flight of stairs. "Where are we going?" Nell asked.

"I asked for a private room."

Everything she'd ever heard about him came flooding back: Mordecai Black was a womanizer, a libertine, a

25

dangerous rake. Nell felt a moment of pure fear. She halted on the stairs. Black was going to help her, but he was going to take payment in *flesh*.

"What?" Black said, glancing back at her. She saw his blank incomprehension—and then his sudden understanding. His face tightened, the muscles flinching as if she'd slapped him, and then he became utterly expressionless. "We can eat in the coffee room if you prefer." His voice was stiff, wooden, offended.

Nell flushed. "I'm sorry. I didn't . . . I mean . . ."

What did she mean? That she hadn't just thought he was about to force himself on her?

She *had* thought it, and he knew she'd thought it.

Her flush grew hotter. "I'm sorry," Nell said again, and she *was* sorry—and more than that, she was ashamed of herself. Mordecai Black had shown her nothing but kindness—and in return she'd treated him as if he were the vilest of men. "A private room would be nice. Thank you."

Black stared down at her, thin-lipped, taut-faced, offended, and for a moment she thought he was about to rescind his offer of help, that he'd walk out of the tavern and leave her—and then he gave a stiff nod and followed the serving-man to the top of the stairs.

Nell trailed behind him, along a corridor, into a small room furnished with a dining table and six chairs. The servant left with promises of food. Black went to stand near the window. Nell clutched her reticule and watched him. She'd offended him deeply. She saw it in the way he held himself, as if his ribcage was made of iron, not bone. The muscles at the hinge of his jaw were tight, the sinews standing out. He stood only a few yards from her, and yet it felt as if a gulf a mile wide lay between them.

"I'm sorry," Nell said again. "I wasn't thinking. I just . . ." *I'm tired and I'm worried and I'm afraid.* "I'm sorry."

Black's mouth compressed. He was huge, a giant of a man, made of strong bones and hard muscle, tougher than any of the men downstairs, a man no one could possibly hurt—and yet she *had* hurt him, without even meaning to.

How do I make this right?

Nell moistened her lips, and took a deep breath. "When I first came to London my father pointed you out. He told me to stay as far from you as I could, that you were dangerous, that you'd ruin a woman as soon as look at her."

Black's jaw clenched even tighter. He turned his head from her and looked out the window.

"But my aunt, Lady Dalrymple, said that was nonsense, that you'd never ruined anyone and I shouldn't believe half of what was said about you. She said that while she'd heard a great deal of gossip about your affairs, she'd never heard anything that made her think badly of your character."

Black stood absolutely motionless for several seconds, and then turned his head and looked at her. The impact of those dark eyes made her chest tighten, made her heartbeat speed up.

Lady Dalrymple had also said that she thought Black's lovers were to be envied, and Nell had privately agreed—but that wasn't something she wanted to tell him. "I'm sorry," she said again firmly, meeting his eyes. "I remembered what Father and Roger said, not what my aunt said."

Black unclamped his jaw. After a moment he said, "What did Roger say about me?"

Nell turned away from him. She put her reticule on the table. "Oh, not a lot." But what Roger *had* said was poisonous. "He's jealous of you, you know."

"He has no reason to be."

Nell glanced at him. Even rumpled and unshaven, Black was magnificent. "Alongside you, he looks . . ." She searched for a word and came up with: "Effeminate."

Black grunted. "I can hardly help that." He crossed to the table, tossed his hat on it, and raked a hand through his hair. It was thick and disheveled and as black as a crow's wing.

"No." But jealousy wasn't a rational emotion—which was why she'd forgiven it in Roger. It had been the only fault she'd seen in him. *How blind I was. How eager to marry and escape Father.* Nell grimaced. She stripped off her gloves and undid her bonnet and laid them on the table.

The serving-man returned and set two places. "Somethin' to drink, sir? Ma'am? Pot o' tea?"

"Ale," Black said. "A tankard."

Nell hesitated. She wanted something cool, something thirst-quenching. "Do you have lemonade?"

"No, ma'am."

"Water, then," Nell said.

"She'll have a half-pint of ale," Black said, and when the servant had gone, he said, "I wouldn't trust the water here. Ale's safer."

"But we're *eating* here."

"The food will be cooked and the ale fermented; the water . . ." He shrugged. "It could come straight from the Thames for all we know."

Nell pulled out a chair and sat, annoyed by Black's high-handedness. He was just like her father, telling her what to do. *God save me from overbearing men.*

And then she remembered Seven Dials. Mordecai Black was under no obligation to help her—and yet he had. And he was offering to help her get to Exeter.

He might be overbearing, but he was also a good man. A better man than Roger.

Nell sighed, and rubbed at the frown on her brow. She looked at her gloves lying limp and wrinkled on the table. *All of me looks like that.* Bedraggled and slightly grubby after more than a hundred miles in a stagecoach. And she'd thought Black had asked for a private room because he wanted to bed her? She snorted under her breath. *Vanity, Nell. Vanity.*

Black pulled out the chair opposite her and sat. He looked as tired and sweaty as she was, as if he had spent the last twenty-four hours on the road, too. Nell looked at his weary, stubbled face and felt a pang of guilt. "I can find my own way to Exeter, Mr. Black. You've helped me more than enough." *More than I deserve.*

"I have no intention of allowing you to travel to Exeter on the common stage," Black said.

Allowing? Nell's guilt evaporated. "Why not?"

"Respectable young ladies do not travel alone by stagecoach."

"Governesses do it all the time," Nell said, an edge in her voice. "And I could easily be a governess."

"But you're not."

"None of the other passengers would know that. If I tell them I'm a governess, they'll *think* I'm a governess."

"You're not a governess, and you're not traveling by stagecoach."

Nell drew breath to tell him that she was an adult and could do as she pleased—and the serving-man entered, bearing a laden tray. On it were three pies, each as large as a dinner plate, and two tankards, one large, one small.

"Pies 'n ale," the man said cheerfully, thumping the tray down.

Nell abandoned her annoyance. Her mouth watered. She was suddenly ravenous.

The jarvey had been correct; the pies were quite possibly

the best this side of the Thames. The pastry was light, flaky, golden, buttery, and the meat was tender and flavorsome. It was impossible to eat slowly, impossible to be ladylike, to take dainty mouthfuls, to lay down her fork while she chewed. All Nell could do was eat one hasty, delicious mouthful after another.

She had eaten half a pie before she was able to lift her eyes from her food and glance across at Black.

Her pulse gave its familiar, treacherous little flutter. Nell ignored it. She laid down her knife and fork, reached for the half-pint of ale, and took a cautious sip. The ale was slightly bitter. Not a pleasant taste, but adequately thirst-quenching. She took a larger sip. A tiny bubble of laughter rose in her throat. How vastly improper this was: to be in a tavern, to be alone with Mordecai Black, to be drinking ale. And then she thought of Sophia, and the laughter quenched. She put down the tankard. "How long will it take to get to Exeter?"

Black looked up from his pie. "It's nearly two hundred miles. Less than three days, if we travel fast."

"We?"

"We." He returned his attention to his plate.

How was it possible to be annoyed and relieved at the same time? "There is no need for you to come with me to Exeter," Nell said.

Black glanced at her again. "Do you know anyone there?"

"No."

"Then I'm coming."

That statement put her hackles up. Father had used to speak to her like that, as if she was incapable of making her own decisions. "There is no reason at all for you to accompany me."

Black put down his knife and fork. "Do you truly think I'd allow you to go to Exeter alone? With very little money and no acquaintances there? Exeter has slums, too. Places just as bad as the Dials."

"I'm sure the godly woman lives somewhere safe."

"Almost certainly," Black said. "But is your sister with her?"

Nell inhaled to retort *Yes, of course*, and then paused.

Black's expression softened fractionally. She saw sympathy in his dark eyes. "Lizzie and your sister left London four months ago," he said, and his voice was almost gentle. "They could be anywhere now. Quite likely with the godly woman, but perhaps not. Perhaps somewhere as bad as the Dials."

Nell's gaze dropped to her plate.

"You must see that I can't let you go alone; it wouldn't be safe."

Nell glanced across at him. An aggressively masculine face, but also a kind face. Unexpectedly kind. Stinging tears welled in her eyes. She looked hastily back at her plate and blinked fiercely.

"I'm coming with you," Black said, and the autocratic note was back in his voice. "The problem is how to do so without damaging your reputation."

"My reputation is of no matter. I was ruined the day Sophia ran away."

"Nonsense."

"Of course I'm ruined!" Nell said tartly. The urge to cry receded. She was able to look him in the face again. "Why else did Roger choose not to marry me?"

"Because he's a fool," Black said. "Your sister is ruined; you are not."

"I'm ruined by association."

"Did you run off with a soldier? No? Then you're not ruined." Black picked up his knife and fork again. "But if it becomes known that you've traveled to Exeter in my company, you *will* be ruined."

He spoke as if the decision had been made: he was coming to Exeter and she had no say in the matter. Nell bit her lip, and felt annoyance and relief. The relief won easily. Going to Exeter with Mordecai Black would be wrong in so many ways. It was wrong to inconvenience him so vastly, wrong to fall into his debt, wrong to be in his company at all—but it would also be much, *much* safer. A task that had been daunting suddenly seemed doable. With Black's help, she would find Sophia without having to wait for her Faerie wish. "If we tell no one, then no one will know of it."

"People notice me," Black said. "And if you're with me, they'll notice you, too."

And they'd think she was his latest paramour.

Awareness of him surged through her again, stronger than ever. She was aware of Mordecai Black's size and the way he loomed on the other side of the table, aware of his over-whelming masculinity and the indefinable hint of danger that he carried with him, aware of his untidiness—the stubble, the loose neckcloth, the rumpled clothes—and most of all, aware of his sheer physical beauty.

Her awareness of him was disturbingly visceral. It made her lungs tighten and her stomach tie itself in a knot and her pulse beat even faster, and it pushed aside everything else—hunger, worry, annoyance, relief, guilt, gratitude. And if her lungs were tight and her heart beating fast, her vision was suddenly much sharper. Details leapt to her eye: the taut planes of his cheeks beneath the dark stubble, the softness of his lower lip, the surprisingly long eyelashes.

Black's loose neckcloth gave her a glimpse of his throat—and that glimpse made Nell's own throat constrict. She jerked her gaze down to his plate . . . and found herself staring at his hands. Large, strong, shapely hands. She noted the grain of his skin, the shapes of bone and tendon and sinew, the long fingers, the clean nails. A little shiver ran up her spine.

Nell dragged her attention back to her own plate. *For heaven's sake*, she told herself sternly. *What on earth are you doing? Swooning over a good-looking man as if you're a foolish schoolgirl?*

She gave herself a sharp mental shake, picked up her cutlery, and embarked on the second half of her pie. This time she ate slowly, turning Black's words over in her mind. It was astonishing how much value he placed on preserving her reputation, given *his* reputation. But almost everything he'd said and done today had been surprising. Her aunt, Lady Dalrymple, had been correct: the gossip about Black was hot air and farradiddles.

Although he *was* dangerous. He'd lived up to that much of his reputation. Nell had a brief flash of memory: Black hurling a stool, the brothel watchman pitching to the floor. A moment of violence that was over before she'd even realized it had started.

"Would you like some of this last pie?" Black asked.

Nell shook her head. She finished what was on her plate, then sat sipping her ale, wondering how much to tell him. By the time she'd decided, he'd finished the final pie. She took a deep breath. "Mr. Black."

He glanced at her over the rim of his tankard.

"I appreciate your concern for my reputation, but I must tell you it's unwarranted. I don't intend to return to Society. Once I find my sister, we shall live quite anonymously. The polite world will never see us again."

Black frowned, and lowered his tankard.

"You see . . . I haven't told you it all."

Chapter Five

NELL TOOK SOPHIA'S letter from her reticule and spread it on
the table, smoothing the creases, not looking at Black's face.
She took a deep breath. "When Sophia wrote this she was
pregnant. Her baby will be a month old by now."

Black made no sound of surprise. In fact, he made no
sound at all. He didn't say, *Well, what do you expect when a woman
behaves as your sister has?* Or, *We can only pray that the child has died.*
Both of which were statements her Great Aunt Wrotham had
made yesterday. Nor did he say, *I understand why you're so anxious
to find her. Of course she must be helped!* which she half expected
him to say, which she *waited* for him to say. And which he
didn't say.

Finally, Nell looked across at him. His expression was grim.

"The baby needs a home," she said.

"And you intend to provide that?"

"Yes."

"How? My understanding was that your portion is small."

"Very small. Two thousand pounds. But invested in the

four-percents it will give me eighty pounds per year. If Sophia and I are frugal, we can live on that."

Black looked even grimmer. "Where will you live?"

"I shall buy a cottage somewhere, where no one knows us."

"How will you purchase this cottage?"

"My mother left me a few pieces of jewelry." Nell pushed the letter aside. "So you see, your scruples over my reputation —although they do you justice—are quite unnecessary. It doesn't matter what anyone thinks of me, because I shan't be returning to Society."

Black looked at her for several seconds. "You're determined on this course of action? After what your sister did?"

"She was only fifteen. A child! She didn't know what she was doing."

"Fifteen? Then how did she meet her soldier?"

"Oh . . ." Nell looked down at her plate, and pushed it to one side. "Father said Sophia was too young to come to London. He left her in Lincolnshire under the chaperonage of a friend." Poor chaperonage, as it had turned out. She looked up and met Black's eyes. "Sophia made a mistake, but I don't see why it should be allowed to ruin her life. And most especially not her child's life."

"What about *your* life?"

"I wish to be reunited with my sister." Her throat tightened. Nell paused, swallowed, took a steadying breath. She was *not* going to cry in front of Mordecai Black. "Once you meet her, you'll understand."

Black looked unconvinced.

"You think that because she ran off with a soldier, she's headstrong and shameless. Well, she's *not*. She's . . ." Nell frowned, and tried to find the right words. "Sophia has the sweetest nature of any person I've ever known. She loves everyone, and everyone loves her. Even Father loved her. She could make him smile, when I never could." *And then he stopped loving her and disowned her.*

Rage at her father kindled in Nell's breast. How could any man turn his back on a beloved child? "If Sophia has a fault, it's that she believes the best of people. She sees something to like in everyone. She trusts where she shouldn't trust. *That's* why she ran off with her soldier: because she trusted him. Not because she's a lightskirt."

Black still looked skeptical.

"You of all people should know not to judge a person by their reputation," Nell said with asperity. "And quite apart from what you may think of Sophia's character, there's the *child* to think of. It needs a safe home!"

"Is it illegitimate?"

"What does that matter?" Nell said tartly. "I've never understood why children should pay for the sins of their parents. They don't ask to be born out of wedlock and yet they're punished for it their whole lives." And then she remembered who she was talking to.

Her words echoed loudly in the room, and then silence fell. Black's illegitimacy seemed to loom between them, an invisible third person. His expression was no longer skeptical. He looked taken aback. After a moment, he said, "Your father held different views."

"I am not my father."

Black huffed a faint laugh. "No." She saw him relax. He reached for his tankard and sipped.

The atmosphere in the room eased. It felt as if they were almost-friends instead of almost-strangers.

Nell leaned urgently across the table. "So, you see, my reputation is of no consequence—"

The serving-man banged cheerfully in through the door. "Finished yet?"

Nell sat back and bit her tongue while the man gathered up their plates with a merry stream of conversation. Had they liked the pies? Did they want more? Would sir like a second tankard? Oh, sir hadn't finished his first one? No rush, then, take yer time—and shout down the stairs if yer want more. Finally the serving-man departed. In the silence that followed, Nell looked across at Black. He was sipping the last of his ale, his expression thoughtful, introspective, almost brooding.

He looked up and caught her gaze, and her pulse gave its familiar, foolish little flutter.

Black put down the tankard. "Miss Wrotham . . . there is a way we can travel together without damaging your reputation."

"How?"

He hesitated, as if weighing up his words, and then said, "If I may ask . . . why did you accept my cousin's offer of marriage?"

Chapter Six

NELL'S FACE STIFFENED. Responses leapt to her tongue: a cold and haughty *I beg your pardon?* A tart *That's none of your business.* But Black didn't strike her as a man who asked irrelevant questions.

The silence lengthened, and lengthened some more, and then Nell made herself reply in a tone that was neither cold nor tart, but merely neutral. "I didn't have many choices, Mr. Black. As you noted earlier, my portion is exceedingly small. Only three men offered for me, and I judged Roger to be the best of them."

"Three?" Black's eyes narrowed slightly. After a moment he said, "Roundhay?"

Nell nodded.

"Old enough to be your father."

Nell nodded again.

Black's eyes narrowed further, but he wasn't looking at her, he was looking *through* her. He seemed to be making a mental calculation, his eyelids twitching slightly as he thought. "Hislop," he said finally.

Nell nodded a third time.

"Very wealthy," Black said. "Good-looking. Extremely respectable."

"Domineering," Nell said.

Black's eyebrows lifted slightly, and then he gave a nod of agreement. "A man of decided opinion." He paused, and amended this statement: "Decided and *narrow* opinion."

Nell nodded again.

"I can see that given those choices, you'd choose Roger." Black leaned back in his chair. "But did it never occur to you that more than just those three men offered for you?"

"Of course not. Father would have told me."

"Would he?"

"Of course!" Nell said, and then, uncertainly, "Why wouldn't he?"

Because he liked to control your life, a little voice said in her head. Nell chewed on her lower lip. "Are you saying that other men offered for me?"

Black nodded.

"Who?"

"Colonel Brownlow and Reginald MacPherson most certainly, and at a guess . . . George Montescue and Sir Walter Prentiss."

Nell frowned at him. "But why did Father not tell me? They're perfectly respectable men!"

Black shrugged. "You knew your father better than I did."

Nell turned the names over in her head. Anger built in her chest, and alongside the anger was a stab of regret. She'd liked both Montescue and MacPherson. "Father didn't like soldiers. Or Scotsmen. Or Whigs."

Black opened one hand, a *there's your answer* gesture.

It was her father she was angry with, not Mordecai Black,

but he was in the room and therefore she scowled at him. "What has this to do with going to Exeter?"

Black gave a faint, ironic smile. "I offered for you, too."

Nell sat back with a jerk, almost a recoil. The anger snuffed out; astonishment took its place. "Me?" Her voice squeaked on the word. She stared at him in shock, in disbelief —and then shook her head decisively. "No, you didn't."

Black said nothing, he just watched her.

"You *didn't*!" The anger came boiling back. How dare he play with her like this? "You didn't even know I existed! You *never* look at débutantes."

Black's eyebrows lifted. "Who told you that?"

"My aunt, Lady Dalrymple. She said your mistresses are always older women. Diamonds of the first water." And *mistress* was a word she shouldn't utter in a man's presence, or indeed, anyone's presence, but she was too angry to care. "They're always beautiful and sophisticated and wealthy and *experienced.*"

"Your aunt is correct," Black said. "But the qualities one looks for in a mistress are quite different from those one looks for in a wife."

Nell suddenly found it difficult to breathe. The room seemed to not have enough air, and it was nothing to do with the summer heat; it was purely because of Mordecai Black, sitting opposite, watching her.

The skin-tingling, chest-tightening awareness of him flared again. It became even harder to breathe.

Mordecai Black wants to marry me?

She stared at him, hulking and unshaven and impossibly beautiful, and for a moment she felt an intense yearning to accept his offer. Common sense came to her rescue. Nell swallowed, and found her voice. "I could not marry a . . . a philanderer, Mr. Black."

"You're making an assumption, Miss Wrotham. An understandable one, I grant you—but incorrect nonetheless." He held her gaze for a moment. "You assume that if I were to marry I'd continue to take lovers."

Lovers. What a dangerously sensual word, a word that was a thousand times more erotic than *mistress*. Nell felt herself blush. Her awareness of him intensified sharply, almost making her shiver. She lifted her chin and tried to take refuge in haughtiness, but it was difficult to be haughty when one's cheeks were hot and every hair on one's body seemed to be standing on end. "You wouldn't?" Her voice, which she'd intended to sound cool and disbelieving, came out sounding uncertain.

"The foundation of a strong marriage is fidelity."

Fidelity. It was an absurd word to come from Mordecai Black's mouth—and yet he spoke it as if he meant it.

Nell lowered her chin. She stared at him, and listened to her heart beating loudly in her ears. Mordecai Black believed in the sanctity of marriage? "But you've had affairs with married women!"

"No," Black said. "I had the *appearance* of an affair with a married woman. Once."

Nell frowned at him.

"Wolverhampton was parading his mistresses quite publicly. His wife decided to show him that what was sauce for the gander was sauce for the goose." Black smiled suddenly, and it was a dangerous smile, sharp-edged. "Wolverhampton didn't like it at all."

"You pretended to have an affair with a married woman in order to punish her husband?" There was censure in Nell's voice.

"That's one way of looking at it," Black said. "Mary's view was different. She was trying to save her marriage."

Nell wrinkled her brow. "By pretending to have an affair?"

"She loved Wolverhampton. She wanted him back."

Nell turned this answer over in her mind. "Did he give up his mistresses?"

"He did. And then he took Mary off to America. She saw it as a new beginning. Personally, I think he'll be back to his old tricks by now." Black shrugged. "The world is divided into two types of people: those who stray, and those who don't. Wolverhampton's a strayer; Mary's not. It's not a foundation for a happy marriage."

Nell pondered this statement.

"And in case you're wondering, Miss Wrotham, I don't stray."

The sound of her heartbeat became even louder. Her throat was tight, her mouth dry, her skin prickling. "You have affairs," she whispered.

"Not nearly as many as Society credits me with," Black said. He paused, and then said, "Five, in case you're wondering. Five in eleven years. And I was faithful to each of them. And when I have a wife, I shall be faithful to her."

Nell heard the truth in his words. Mordecai Black meant exactly what he said. She sat back in her chair, shaken.

Black watched her for several seconds, and then said, "Will you marry me, Miss Wrotham?"

For a few seconds Nell found it literally impossible to breathe. She felt light-headed with disbelief. Mordecai Black was asking her to marry him? Mordecai Black was promising to be faithful to her?

Part of her *wanted* to marry him, the part that was intensely aware of his striking good looks—the cheekbones, that autocratic nose, the soft lower lip, the powerful body. *And he's kind,* a voice whispered in her ear. But another part of her—the sane part—told her that Black's nature was as imperious as his nose and she *couldn't* marry him.

Nell inhaled a shaky breath and shook her head. "I'm sorry." She felt a pang of regret as she uttered the words.

Black looked at her for a long moment, his face expressionless. "May I ask why not?"

It was an impertinent question, a question a gentleman wouldn't ask—but Mordecai Black was no ordinary gentleman. In fact, some people would argue he wasn't a gentleman at all.

Nell eyed him.

Black's posture was casual, leaning back in his chair—and yet . . . she thought he wasn't as nonchalant as he appeared.

Nell had never wondered what it must feel like for a man to propose marriage. She'd only ever thought about it from her own point of view: the awkwardness of turning down an offer one didn't want, the relief of accepting one that one did. Suddenly she found herself wondering what it felt like from the *man*'s viewpoint.

It would take courage, she realized. Courage and hope and a dream of the future.

Mordecai Black had just asked her to share the rest of her life with him—and she had refused. Rejected him. For all his apparent indifference, that nonchalant pose, he must feel humiliated and angry. Did he think she didn't believe his statement of fidelity? Did he think his illegitimacy disgusted her?

"My decision has nothing to do with your reputation," Nell told him firmly. "Or your birth."

His eyebrows lifted faintly, as if he didn't believe her. "What, then?"

Nell clasped her hands together, fingers interlinked, thumbs neatly alongside one another, and ordered her thoughts. "Mr. Black, I have spent my entire life being told what to do. My father was a dictatorial man, and if you will forgive me for saying so, so are you."

The nonchalance vanished. Black's eyebrows snapped down. He straightened in the chair. His expression was clear to read: affront.

Nell met his gaze steadily. "I cannot marry a man who will tell me what I may and may not do."

"Dictatorial?" He pronounced the word with distaste.

"Yes."

Outrage gathered on Black's face. He drew breath to argue.

"In the past hour you've told me that I may not travel to Exeter by stagecoach. You've told me that you're coming with me, whether I wish it or not. You've told me that I'm to drink ale, not water. You haven't discussed these things with me. You haven't asked for my opinion. You have *told* me."

Black closed his mouth.

"I am not a child," Nell said. "I'm an adult, and I will not marry a man who tells me what to do."

Black didn't reply to this statement. His mouth was tight and his cheeks were faintly flushed, but whether that tinge of color was due to anger or mortification, she couldn't tell. She rather thought it might be both.

Nell looked away. She'd made her point, but she felt no triumph in it; instead, she felt sad. She pushed back her chair. "Thank you for your help today, but I think it best if I find my own way to Exeter."

"Nonsense," Black said.

The sadness evaporated. Nell's temper sparked. "I can take care of myself."

Black pushed his own chair back with a harsh scrape of wood on wood. "I'm coming with you."

"You're telling me what to do again."

The muscles in Black's jaw bunched. She thought he was grinding his teeth together. "Yes," he said. "I am. Because you haven't the faintest notion of how dangerous it might be!"

"I am not a child," Nell said, coldly.

"No, you're an *innocent*, which is just as bad!" He flung out his hands, a gesture eloquent of frustration. "What do you think would have happened if you'd gone to Seven Dials by yourself? *What?*"

That last word was almost a shout, and it shocked Nell into silence. Her father's rages had been cold and quiet; Black's loud, hot anger was utterly outside her experience.

"What if you'd found Mrs. Harris? What if she'd refused to let you leave? What would you have done then?"

Nell eyed him uncertainly.

"I'm trying to *protect* you, damn it. And if that means I have to tell you what to do, then I *will*. Whether you like it or not."

They matched stares across the table. Black's expression was fierce, his nostrils flared, and he looked magnificent and terrifying at the same time—but Nell discovered that she wasn't afraid of him. She wasn't even angry anymore. Somehow, while his rage had escalated, hers had dwindled to nothing.

"I'm coming with you," Black repeated, his eyebrows meeting across the bridge of his nose in an intimidating scowl, but Nell wasn't intimidated.

"All right," she said, and then she smiled wryly at him. "You're a good man, Mr. Black. Tyrannical, but good."

Black lost his scowl. He went pink, and for a brief second he looked taken aback—and then he gave a stern nod. "That's settled, then."

"It is." Nell reached for her bonnet. She had capitulated, and yet it didn't feel like a defeat. It felt like a compromise. *I get what I need and he gets what he wants.*

And then she remembered his offer of marriage. No, Mordecai Black hadn't got everything he wanted.

"We'll leave at dawn tomorrow," Black said.

"Can't we leave today? Please? There's still several hours' daylight left."

Black shook his head. "We both need a good night's sleep."

Nell opened her mouth to protest, and then bit the words back. Black did look weary. Weary and disheveled and quite unlike his usual immaculate self. What had he been doing to make him look so unkempt? Traveling? And then she wondered why he'd come to Roger's house in all his dirt. His reason must have been urgent. *And yet he put it aside to help me.*

She felt a fresh pang of guilt. "Have you been traveling, Mr. Black?"

"Bath," Black said, pulling on his gloves.

Nell blinked. "Bath? What a coincidence. I just came from there."

Black gave her a sidelong, sardonic glance. "No coincidence. I was looking for you."

"Me? Why?" And then she remembered his proposal. Heat rose in her face. Nell looked away, flustered, and pulled on her own gloves. "You do me a great honor, Mr. Black, but I think you must see that we don't suit."

Chapter Seven

MORDECAI HAILED A HACKNEY, told the jarvey to take them to the Earnoch Hotel, and climbed into the carriage after Miss Wrotham. He sat alongside her on the shabby seat. Dictatorial? Tyrannical? The accusations stung. How could she compare him to her father? He wanted to set her *free*, not cage her.

Frustration stewed in his chest. He forced his muscles to relax. He was used to people saying things that hurt; he'd trained himself to keep an impassive face when the barbs struck home, to not show any reaction except perhaps mild amusement. And yet today he'd shouted. Shouted and raged and waved his hands and generally behaved like a great lummox. A great *dictatorial* lummox.

He closed his eyes in a wince. *It's tiredness,* he told himself. Tiredness was why she'd managed to make him lose his temper—something he hadn't done in years—and tiredness was why he wasn't going to continue arguing with her now, even though—God damn it—he *wanted* to.

He exhaled a long breath, filled his lungs again, and opened his eyes. "If we're going to travel together, you should choose another name."

"I appreciate your concern for my reputation, but I truly don't care if people know I'm in your company."

"*I* care," Mordecai said.

"But—"

"Regardless of what people say about me, I've never ruined a woman. I've taken great pains *not* to ruin any women." And, even though he tried to prevent it, an edge of anger vibrated in his voice.

Miss Wrotham bit her lip. He saw that she wanted to argue, and he saw her decide—as he'd decided—that now wasn't the time.

"Very well," she said. "I shall be Miss Smith."

"Mrs., not Miss. And not Smith. An unusual name would be better. If people notice you, it should be for your name, not your face."

Her eyebrows rose slightly. "I doubt they'll notice my face. It's quite ordinary."

Mordecai almost snorted. *If you think your face is ordinary, you've been looking in the wrong mirrors.* But he didn't tell her that; instead he said, "What name would you like?"

Her brow furrowed thoughtfully.

"Trussell-Quimby?" Mordecai suggested. "Polkinghorn?"

"Ramsbottom."

"Ramsbottom?"

"My father's man of business was named Ramsbottom. I always thought it an unfortunate name."

Mordecai gave a reluctant grunt of laughter. "Very unfortunate. And no, *not* Ramsbottom." Then he reviewed his words. He did sound a little dictatorial. He tempered his comment with: "It doesn't suit you."

Miss Wrotham eyed him for a moment, and then said, "Trussell-Quimby."

Mordecai gave a nod. "Do you have mourning clothes with you? If you could be a widow, that would be even better."

She shook her head. "I left them in Bath. And no—" as he opened his mouth, "please don't buy me any. I've worn black since my father died, and I won't wear it any longer."

Mordecai listened to the edge in her voice and noted the stubborn set of her chin. "Very well," he said. *See? Not dictatorial.*

They traveled the length of the Strand in silence. When the hackney turned into Haymarket, Mordecai said, "How about a wig and spectacles? Would you wear those if I bought them for you?"

He saw on her face that she thought disguises unnecessary. "Mr. Black—"

"Please," Mordecai said.

They stared at each other for a long moment, while the carriage lurched and swayed, and then Miss Wrotham colored faintly and looked down at her lap. She studied her gloves, smoothed away a wrinkle in the kid leather, and said, "If you think it necessary."

MORDECAI LET MISS WROTHAM down from the hackney at the Earnoch Hotel, promised to pick her up at dawn, then directed the jarvey to the nearest *perruquier.* He inspected the available wigs and selected two made of chestnut horsehair, one done up in a chignon, the other in a braided bun.

"Hairpins?" he asked, and the *perruquier* sold him two dozen, along with boxes to carry the wigs in.

Next he went to the oculist his father had patronized,

bought a pair of gold-rimmed spectacles, and had the man fit plain glass lenses into the frames.

His purchases made, Mordecai returned to his house in Grosvenor Square, where he issued a series of orders. As a result of those orders he had a cold bath, dressed in clean clothes, drank a glass of chilled white burgundy, and had an interview with his coachman and another with his house-keeper. To the former, he said, "Prepare the traveling chaise, Phelps. I'm going to Exeter tomorrow, fast. No livery; I want to keep a low profile." To the latter, he said, "I need a footman for several days, perhaps longer. His duties will be to help Phelps and act as my valet. Tell him not to wear livery."

"Yes, sir."

"I'll need a housemaid, too. Someone who's waited on a lady before—and has a discreet tongue in her head."

His housekeeper didn't bat an eyelid. "The new girl has experience as an abigail."

"New?" Mordecai said. "Another one of Roger's?"

The housekeeper nodded.

Mordecai sighed, and rubbed his brow with hard fingers. "Damn him."

The housekeeper said nothing, but Mordecai had a pretty shrewd idea what she was thinking. It was exactly what he was thinking himself: that Roger ought to be castrated. "Is she all right?"

"Yes, sir. He didn't do her any harm."

"Good." He blew out a sharp breath. "Very well, I'll take her. Send her to me, will you? I'll be in my study."

The new housemaid was a thin girl. Not the type to normally catch Roger's eye, but clearly she *had* caught it, because here she was in Mordecai's household, like many housemaids before her.

Mordecai leaned back in his chair and surveyed her across the broad expanse of his desk. "What's your name?"

"Bessie, sir."

"I understand you were in my cousin's employ."

"Yes, sir." Her gaze was fixed the desktop, not him. She was almost shaking with nervousness.

Mordecai stood abruptly and strode to the window, increasing the distance between them fourfold. He looked out at the square, then turned to face her. "You'll find that I run a very different household from my cousin. If you have any of *that* sort of trouble, you're to tell my housekeeper immediately." He might not be able to castrate Roger, but he'd sure as hell castrate any of his employees who attempted to force themselves on a woman.

"Yes, sir."

"And if she isn't in the house, you may come directly to me."

Bessie bit her lip, and cast him a timid glance, and nodded. "Yes, sir."

Mordecai leaned back against the windowsill and tried to look as unthreatening as possible. "I'm traveling to Exeter tomorrow with an acquaintance. A lady. I understand that you have some experience as an abigail?"

"Yes, sir."

"Do you become ill in a coach?"

"No, sir."

"The lady will be traveling incognito," Mordecai said. "But you may call her Mrs. Trussell-Quimby. I've purchased two wigs and a pair of spectacles for her." He nodded at the items on his desk—the wig boxes, the spectacle case. "Please see that she wears them."

"Yes, sir," Bessie said.

"We'll leave at dawn."

"Yes, sir."

"You may go."

Bessie bobbed another curtsy, and gathered up the wigs and spectacles. At the door, she glanced back at him. Her glance was scared and shy and yet at the same time almost worshipful, as if he were half ogre, half hero. The door clicked shut quietly after her.

Mordecai stayed where he was, leaning against the windowsill, while the sky slowly darkened. Then he sighed and rang for a footman. He ate a silent, lonely dinner, went upstairs, and stripped out of the clothes he'd put on only a few hours before. "Your portmanteau and valise are packed, sir," his valet said.

"Thank you."

"Are you certain you don't wish me to accompany you?" Tompkin's voice was almost—but not quite—neutral.

"You think me cruel to leave you behind? Console yourself, Tompkin; it's likely to be an uncomfortable journey."

"I wouldn't mind, sir," the valet said earnestly.

"Of course you wouldn't. You're a prince among valets."

But, prince or not, there'd be no space in the carriage for Tompkin once they found Sophia Wrotham.

Mordecai rubbed eyes that were gritty with weariness and climbed into his high, wide, empty bed. "Wake me at four, please."

Chapter Eight

NELL WENT TO bed with her thoughts a jumbled confusion of
Seven Dials and Mrs. Harris, the nightmarish journey from
Bath, the urgency of Sophia's letter, Roger and Great Aunt
Wrotham and her father, all mixed together. And Mordecai
Black. Mordecai Black throwing a stool at the brothel watch-
man. Mordecai Black asking her to marry him.

She'd thought it would be impossible to sleep, but it wasn't.
She woke to a chambermaid's knock on her door. Yesterday's
exhaustion was gone. The confusing jumble in her head had
distilled to two crystal clear questions: Why on earth did
Mordecai Black want to marry her? And—far more impor-
tantly—where was Sophia?

Nell dressed with the chambermaid's help, ate a hasty
breakfast, packed her valise, and hurried downstairs. Five
o'clock found her standing outside the Earnoch Hotel in the
gray light of dawn. The heat trapped between the tall London
buildings had eased only slightly overnight.

A coach-and-four drew up with a clatter of wheels and

hooves. Not a hired post-chaise with yellow paintwork and two postilions, but a private traveling carriage. A servant sat beside the coachman on the box. When the coach halted, he leapt down, lowered the steps, and opened the door with a flourish. The flourish told her he was a footman, despite the lack of livery.

Black stepped down from the carriage. Gone was yesterday's grime. He was clean-shaven and perfectly turned out. "Is that all the luggage you have?"

"Yes."

The footman sprang to take the valise. Nell climbed up into the carriage, Black followed, the door swung shut. She settled herself on a seat of soft squabs upholstered with velvet.

Two hundred miles alone with Mordecai Black.

Awareness of him prickled over her skin. This wasn't the familiar pulse-fluttering combination of fear and attraction; this was something close to panic. Her stays seemed to lace themselves tighter. It was suddenly extremely difficult to breathe.

Nell busied herself arranging her skirts, smoothing the wrinkles from the muslin, pulling composure around her like armor.

"I took the liberty of bringing a maid for you," Black said. "This is Bessie. Bessie, Mrs. Trussell-Quimby."

Nell glanced up. There on the backward-facing seat was a maid. Young, bashful, and painfully neat. The maid ducked her head. "Ma'am," she said shyly.

A maid. Two hundred miles with Mordecai Black and a maid.

Nell's panic fell away. Breathing became easy again. "Good morning, Bessie." She smiled at Black with gratitude. "Thank you."

He nodded.

The carriage swayed slightly as the footman climbed aboard, and then they were off.

BLACK HAD BEEN QUITE serious about the wig and spectacles, Nell discovered. The first time they halted to change the horses, he requested a private room and sent her and the maid upstairs to alter her appearance. Bessie produced two auburn wigs and a pair of spectacles. "Which wig would you like to wear, ma'am?"

Neither, Nell thought. "The chignon, please."

She put on the spectacles while Bessie removed the wig from its box. A small mirror hung above the mantelpiece. Nell crossed to it and looked at herself. The spectacles weren't much of a disguise; anyone who knew her would recognize her instantly.

"If you'll sit for a moment, ma'am?"

Nell removed the spectacles and obediently sat.

Bessie positioned the wig carefully, anchoring it with hairpins, then she stepped back. "All done, ma'am."

Nell stood and looked in the mirror again.

It was astonishing what a difference the wig made. That warm, autumnal auburn made her look quite unlike herself. Nell put on the spectacles again. Now she looked like another person entirely.

Nell stared herself in the mirror, unsettled. She had the same face she'd always had—eyes, nose, mouth, chin—and yet she was no longer Eleanor Wrotham.

How could a wig and spectacles make so much difference?

They hurried downstairs again. Black scrutinized her for a long moment, and then gave a curt nod. "Good."

The coach-and-four maintained a breakneck pace for most

of the day. They passed through Frimley, through Basingstoke, through Andover, and came into Salisbury as daylight was fading from the sky. The coach drew up in the courtyard of an inn. Black handed her down from the carriage. He had lost his immaculateness. His clothes were wrinkled and stubble shadowed his jaw.

Nell felt stiff, weary, hot, and slightly headachy. Ostlers and porters bustled around them, unloading the luggage, leading the horses away.

"Would you like to dine now?" Black asked.

She wanted to remove the wig, but even more than that, she wanted fresh air and to stretch her legs. "What I should most like is to take a walk."

Black turned to the innkeeper, attentive at his elbow. "Two of your best rooms, one for Mrs. Trussell-Quimby, one for myself. Rooms for our servants. A private parlor. Hot water in our bedchambers in an hour, and dinner fifteen minutes after that."

"Yes, sir."

"Walter?"

The footman snapped to attention. "Sir?"

"I leave you in charge here." Black gave Nell his arm. "Have you been to Salisbury before?"

"No."

"There's some very fine architecture."

Yesterday, walking with her hand on Mordecai Black's arm would have made her heart beat wildly, but Nell had spent a full day in his company and her pulse gave only the faintest flutter before settling down. She was becoming inured to Black's striking looks and magnetic presence.

They walked for an hour, and Black was correct: Salisbury was a handsome city. Nell passed through St. Ann's gate and the High Street gate, viewed the cathedral with its towering spire, and saw the ornate Poultry Cross. The evening was sultry, the air thick and humid. Walking didn't make her feel any cooler, but it rid her of the stiffness and the headache.

Back at the inn, Nell removed the wig and spectacles, washed her face, and changed her gown for dinner.

"Which wig would you like wear, ma'am?"

Neither. "The braided bun. Can you please brush out my hair first?"

"Of course, ma'am."

Nell sat at the dressing table. "Have you been with Mr. Black long?" she asked, as the girl unpinned her hair.

"Two days, ma'am."

"Two days?" Nell said, startled.

"Yes, ma'am." Bessie reached for Nell's brush.

"Oh," Nell said. "Well . . . I'm sure you'll be happy in his service."

"He's a good master, he is. None better."

Nell sat silently while Bessie brushed her hair, wrestling with curiosity. "In what way is he good?" she asked, when Bessie laid the hairbrush aside.

"He don't touch the maids, and he don't let anyone else touch us neither. Not the menservants, not his guests, no one."

"Oh," Nell said again.

Nell's hair hung down to her waist, nut-brown and straight. Bessie tied it back into a low ponytail, wound it around Nell's head, and set to work pinning it in place.

Nell watched in the mirror. Questions hovered on her tongue. "Did you know Mr. Black was a good master before you entered his service?" she finally asked.

"Yes, ma'am."

"How?"

"When the old lord died, Mr. Black let it be known that

he'd find places for as many of us maids as wanted to leave." Bessie removed the wig with the braided bun from its box.

"The old lord? You mean . . . Lord Dereham?"

"Yes, ma'am."

Nell blinked. "You were in Lord Dereham's household before this?"

"Yes, ma'am," Bessie said again. "Mr. Black don't have to take us in, he's got no obligation, but he always does."

"Always?" Nell said. "How many maids have gone to him?"

"Dozens." Bessie carefully placed the wig on Nell's head. "Most of them went as soon as the old lord died—they knew how it would be—but I stayed. I didn't think he'd notice someone as homely as me. But in the end he did." Bessie's lips tightened in the mirror.

The bedchamber was warm, the day's heat lingering despite the open window, but Nell didn't feel hot; she felt cold. "You mean . . . this man who noticed you, he *touches* the maids?"

"He does a lot more than that, ma'am."

Nell felt even colder. Bessie wasn't talking about unwanted caresses; she was talking about *rape*.

She sat numbly while Bessie fastened the wig with hairpins. Thoughts spun in her head. One of Roger's menservants was preying on the maids? Raping them? And then her numbness turned to outrage. "But why doesn't someone tell Roger? He'd put a stop to it!"

"Roger?" Bessie slid the last hairpin into place.

"The new Lord Dereham. He'd turn the man off at once!"

Bessie stared at her blankly in the mirror, and then said, "But it's the new Lord Dereham I'm talking of, ma'am."

"What?"

"It's Lord Dereham as is after us."

Nell shook her head, rejecting the words. "No! Not Roger!" She twisted in the chair to look the girl in the face. "He *wouldn't!*"

Bessie's lips tightened. She said nothing. The truth was clear to read on her face.

"Oh, my God," Nell said. She pressed her hand to her abdomen. She felt ill. "Roger raped you?"

"He tried," Bessie said. "But I hit him on the nose."

"I hope you made him *bleed*," Nell said savagely.

Bessie gave a sudden grin. "Blood everywhere. All over his clothes."

"Well done," Nell said, and wished she could hit Roger, too. Or better yet, skewer him with a sword. She turned back to the dressing table. Her face stared at her from the mirror, pale and shocked beneath the auburn wig.

Roger was a rapist?

SHE PUT ON the spectacles and joined Mordecai Black in the private parlor. Serving-men bustled around, placing dishes to best advantage, pouring wine into crystal glasses. Black pulled out a chair for her. Nell sat, and stared at her table setting. Roger raped his maidservants?

The serving-men departed. Silence fell. After a moment, Mr. Black said, "Miss Wrotham?"

Nell blinked, and realized that he was waiting for her to start. She served herself at random and then looked at the food on her plate. She hadn't the faintest desire to eat.

"Miss Wrotham . . . are you quite well?"

"I beg your pardon. I'm a little distracted." She managed a smile, and picked up her knife and fork.

"You're naturally worried about your sister." There was a note in Black's voice that her ears recognized as compassion.

Nell gazed across the table at him. Mordecai Black knew about Roger.

How did he know? *What* did he know?

"Miss Wrotham, if you don't mind me asking . . . how did you come to receive your sister's letter?"

Nell's thoughts changed track with the abruptness of a carriage overturning. "What?"

"You said she sent it four months ago," Black prompted.

"Yes." She looked down at her plate again, and laid down the knife and fork. "My father opened all my mail—I knew that—but what I hadn't realized was that he destroyed the ones he didn't want me to read." She glanced up. Black had laid down his cutlery, too.

"That particular letter arrived the day Father died. In fact, it may have precipitated his death. Hitchcock—his valet—says that Father had a seizure while going through the mail. Hitchcock found the letter on the floor afterwards."

"He kept it? The valet?"

Nell nodded. "Hitchcock was very loyal to Father. He knew Father would have burned the letter, but he also felt that, as a servant, it wasn't his place to take such a step himself."

"He should have taken it to you immediately."

"He knew Father wouldn't have wished it."

Black uttered a contemptuous snort. "He sounds like a fool."

"A ditherer. It took him four months to decide what he ought to do."

"He brought the letter to you?"

Nell nodded.

"It must have been a great shock." Again, she heard compassion in his voice.

"Yes." Nell picked up her knife and fork, cut a piece of chicken, and put the cutlery down again with a sharp clatter. "When I went to live with my Great Aunt Wrotham she opened my mail, too—she said Father had asked her to do it— and since I was living on her charity, I felt I had no right to argue with her. I wish I had! She *burned* letters from Sophia. She *admitted* it, not three days ago!" Rage vibrated in her voice. "Insufferable! Unforgivable!"

Mr. Black met her gaze steadily, and said nothing.

"When I told her Sophia was pregnant, she said it was nothing less than Sophia deserved, and she hoped the baby died."

A muscle twitched in Mr. Black's jaw.

"I slapped her," Nell said. "And I know that's unforgivable, too, but I was so *angry.*" She looked down at her food. Her rage congealed; shame took its place. "It's the worst thing I've ever done in my life."

"It sounds to me as if your great aunt deserved it."

Nell glanced up at him.

"Miss Wrotham, why didn't you go to live with the Dalrymples when your father died?"

"Oh . . ." Nell sighed. "They did ask me to, but I felt that I couldn't. Not after what happened with Hubert."

Black's brow wrinkled slightly in incomprehension. "Hubert?"

"Hubert Cathcart. Georgiana's fiancé. The one who went missing up in Scotland."

"Wasn't that years ago?"

"Four years," Nell said. "He's dead. Everyone knows that —even Georgiana." She sighed again. Poor Hubert. Poor Georgiana.

"I fail to see why Cathcart's disappearance should prevent you from living with the Dalrymples."

61

"Because I'm ruined, and Georgiana's still not married and I don't want to damage her chances of making a good match."

"You are *not* ruined," Black said forcefully.

Nell smiled wryly. "Thank you, Mr. Black, but in the eyes of the polite world, I *am* ruined. No respectable man would wish to marry me." And then she remembered his proposal.

She'd thought the day's travels had inured her to Black; they hadn't. Awareness of him rushed suddenly through her. Her pulse did its familiar, foolish, agitated, little dance. Heat bloomed in her cheeks.

Nell fixed her eyes on her plate, mortified with herself for blushing, mortified that Mordecai Black must be able to see it.

There was a few seconds' pause, and then Black said dryly, "Yes, but we both know I'm not entirely respectable."

No, he wasn't entirely respectable, but he was kind and good. Whereas Roger, who *was* respectable, was neither.

The mortifying warmth faded from her cheeks. Nell stared down at her plate and thought about what Bessie had told her, then she looked up and met Black's eyes. This time her pulse almost stayed steady. "Bessie told me that Roger forces himself upon his maids."

Surprise crossed Black's face. "She told you that?"

"Is it true?"

Black hesitated, and then said, "Yes."

"But he's such a gentleman."

"Quite a number of gentlemen practice *droit de seigneur*."

Nell frowned at him.

"It happens more than you might realize. Female servants are in a vulnerable position."

"But . . . *Roger*."

"Count yourself lucky you didn't marry him." Black

picked up his fork, pointed imperatively at her plate, and said, "Eat."

"How long have you known about Roger?"

"Eat, and I'll tell you."

Nell hesitated, and picked up her own fork. The piece of chicken still sat on the tines. She ate it—and discovered that she was hungry. Ravenously hungry.

After she'd consumed two mouthfuls Black began to speak. "Father's seat was in Derbyshire. I stayed there often with him. Roger used to visit, as his heir. One summer he made the mistake of accosting one of the maids. She screamed, a footman came running, there was a bit of a brawl."

"When was this?"

"Five or six years ago."

So he'd known—Mordecai Black had *known* that Roger forced himself on maidservants when she'd accepted Roger's offer.

"Roger insisted that the maid and footman be dismissed. Father kicked him out instead." Black grinned, showing a flash of white teeth. "And then he altered his will. Before then, everything had been split equally between Roger and me. Afterwards, it all came to me—except for what was entailed."

"Your father must have felt very strongly about it."

"Yes." Black's brief flash of humor vanished. His eyebrows drew together. "Whatever you may have heard about my mother, she entered their liaison willingly."

Nell shook her head. "I know nothing about your mother."

Black grunted, and looked down at his plate. "She was a governess in Father's household."

"Oh." Nell bit her lip. Dare she ask him about his mother?

"When Father died there was some consternation among his servants, so I told them I'd employ anyone who didn't wish to enter Roger's service. There were rather more than I'd anticipated."

"How many?" Nell asked.

"Upwards of fifty," Black said. "And not just maidservants. The footman, for example—the one who stopped Roger—several housekeepers, a couple of butlers."

"However did you employ them all?"

"With difficulty," Black said. "In the end I bought another estate. The problem is, they keep coming. Bessie's the second girl this month."

Nell looked down at her plate. Her appetite had waned. She laid down her knife and fork. "I almost *married* him."

Black said nothing.

"Why didn't you say something? Why didn't you *tell* me?"

"Miss Wrotham, what Roger does is no more or less than what many respectable men do. It doesn't mean he'd be a bad husband. He behaves to his wife one way, his mistresses another, and his maidservants another."

"Roger has a mistress?"

Black ignored this question. He looked at her plate and the abandoned cutlery. "Eat," he said.

"Roger has a mistress?"

"*Eat.*"

Nell sighed, and picked up her knife and fork again. She cut herself another piece of chicken, and ate it. "Roger has a mistress?"

"He has several."

Nell put down her cutlery. She couldn't equate the words *Roger* and *mistresses*. "Several? Are you certain?"

Black looked pointedly at her plate, and didn't reply.

Nell ate three more mouthfuls, and then said, "Who are they?"

"The usual. Actresses. Opera dancers."

Nell frowned, and ate some green peas, and then said hesitantly, "Does he have a *lot* of mistresses?"

Black shrugged. "Roger likes variety."

"But . . . how many?"

Black eyed her over a forkful of meat. "Do you really want to know?"

"Yes."

Black chewed, and swallowed, and thought for several moments. "Maybe half a dozen mistresses a year."

Nell's eyebrows rose. "Six different women a *year*?"

"Oh, more than that. He frequents . . . er, other places."

"You mean brothels?"

Black glanced at her and said nothing.

"How many women a year?" Nell asked.

Black laid down his cutlery. "Miss Wrotham, this subject is hardly—"

"I nearly married him," Nell said fiercely. "I thought he was a *decent* man. How many?"

Black hesitated.

"Please?"

Black let out his breath in a sigh. "I don't know. At a guess . . . he's at the brothels two or three times a week."

Nell digested this statement. Two or three times a *week*. "And he has mistresses?"

Black nodded.

"And he preys on his maidservants."

Black grimaced fleetingly, and nodded again.

"But . . . but that's *scores* of women every year!"

Black shrugged and picked up his cutlery.

Nell watched him eat. Black had told her how many mistresses he'd had. Five. Five in eleven years. His words rang in her ears: *I was faithful to each of them. And when I have a wife, I shall be faithful to her.*

"Why don't people talk about Roger's affairs instead of yours?" Nell burst out. "He's had *dozens* of mistresses and you've only had five!"

Black glanced up from his food. "Roger's liaisons are with women of a lower class."

"They don't count?"

"Not to most people."

"Well, they *should* count!"

Black shrugged, and then pointed at her plate with his fork. "Eat."

"You may have better morals than Roger, but he has better manners," Nell told him tartly.

Black shrugged again. "Roger and I are very different."

Nell gave a choke of laughter. "That's an understatement."

He grinned briefly, and Nell's breath caught in her throat. God, he was beautiful. Those dark eyes, that autocratic nose, the structure of his bones.

"Eat," Black said again, and his tone was every bit as autocratic as his nose.

Which was why she couldn't marry him.

Chapter Nine

THEY FINISHED THE meal in silence. Nell turned the conversation over in her head while she ate. *I very nearly married a man who rapes his servants.* The private parlor was warm, but even so, she shivered. Black noticed. His eyebrows went up. "Are you cold?"

Nell shook her head. She wasn't cold; she was chilled. Chilled by how close she'd come to making an appalling mistake.

She sipped her wine soberly, and made a silent toast. *Thank you, Sophia. But for you, I would have married Roger.*

And then she felt shame.

If slapping Great Aunt Wrotham was the worst thing she'd ever done, then being angry at Sophia for eloping was the second worst. For months after the elopement she'd felt nothing but bitter rage. She'd blamed Sophia for ruining her marriage prospects, for ruining her life. She'd been consumed by the consequences of the elopement to *herself,* not to Sophia.

The rage had eventually faded to resentment. Resentment

that she'd carried in her breast while her father sickened and died, resentment that she'd taken with her to her great aunt's house in Bath—and then three days ago she'd received Sophia's letter and learned that her sister wasn't living blithely with a soldier but was pregnant and penniless and trapped in a brothel. The resentment had vanished instantly. Sickening, stomach-knotting worry had taken its place.

But if she was honest with herself, a faint, shameful trace of resentment had lingered beneath the worry. It had taken this conversation with Mordecai Black to realize that in not marrying Roger she had been phenomenally *lucky*.

Sophia had ruined her, but she'd also saved her.

But if *she* had escaped the fate of being married to Roger, another woman had walked into it blindly. Nell had read the notice in the newspapers this spring—Roger Lockwood-Smith and Julia Seddon. At the time, she'd felt bitterness. Now, she felt a pang of sympathy. Poor Julia. Did she know yet about Roger's proclivities?

And then another thought intruded. *Has Roger sired any illegitimate children?*

"More wine?" Black asked.

Nell shook her head again.

She thought back to Roger's proposal, to the pretty speech he'd made. She had listened to his words and tried to judge his character. Would he try to control every aspect of her life? Would he let her voice her own opinions? Let her make her own decisions? At the end of his speech, she had agreed to marry him. Not because he was heir to an earldom, but because she'd thought they could have a congenial marriage.

She had thought her choice sensible and well-reasoned and mature. *Hubris, Nell.*

"He's not worth thinking about," Black said.

"I beg your pardon?"

"Roger. He's not worth thinking about. Forget him."

"Actually, I was thinking about hubris," Nell said. "*My* hubris." She put down her glass. "I thought myself a tolerable judge of character, but clearly I'm *not*. I considered Roger a pleasant man. A little pompous, to be sure, but it never occurred to me that he was a . . . a philanderer and a rapist!"

"I doubt Roger would consider himself either of those things," Black said.

Nell ignored this comment. "I thought I was making a sensible choice. A *good* choice. But my decision was just as bad as Sophia's was—for all that I was twenty-one. Old enough to know better!"

"Twenty-one isn't old."

"It's old for a début," Nell retorted. "I was practically on the shelf."

"An ape leader," Black agreed, with a glimmer of amusement.

"Yes," Nell said. "And it's all very well for you to laugh, but I *was* an ape leader. My cousin Georgiana was betrothed at eighteen, and I wasn't even *out* then."

Black leaned back in his chair. He didn't point out that while Georgiana Dalrymple had been engaged at eighteen, she was still unmarried nearly five years later. Instead, he said, "You were a little older than the average débutante."

"A *lot* older."

Black shrugged again, and reached for his wineglass. "Why did your father not bring you out earlier?"

"Oh . . ." Nell rubbed her forehead. "When I was eighteen, he said I was too young and silly—and he was probably correct. And the next year, my stepmother fell ill, so of course I couldn't leave her. And the year after that, she died. And by the time we were out of mourning, I was twenty-one. Almost twenty-two. An ape leader. It didn't surprise me at all that I only had three offers."

Black lifted his eyebrows briefly, but said nothing. He didn't have to. She heard his words as clearly as if he'd uttered them aloud: *You had more than three offers.*

To Nell's annoyance, she blushed. She looked down at her empty plate and rearranged her cutlery, acutely conscious of him seated across from her. Mordecai Black, with his striking good looks and dreadful reputation. People spoke of his wealth and his illegitimacy, his flagrant *affaires,* but never of his kindness.

A woman could lose her heart over Black's kindness.

The silence between them grew longer. Nell struggled to think of something to say. "Does Roger have any illegitimate children?" she blurted.

"Almost certainly. I doubt he's taken precautions to prevent it."

"Precautions?" Nell risked a glance at him. "What do you mean?"

"It's fairly easy to avoid siring children," Black said. "If one can be bothered."

Nell stared at him, astonished. "It is? How?"

"This is hardly an appropriate topic for conversation, Miss Wrotham."

No, it was shockingly *in*appropriate. But Nell didn't care. She was gripped by an intense curiosity. "I should like to know."

Black folded his lips together.

"Why should men know about this and not women?" Nell said sharply. "It's women who bear the children!"

Black looked away from her. He stared at the fireplace for a moment, blew out a breath, and then looked back at her. "There are a number of ways." His voice was brusque, dispassionate. "One can provide one's lover with a sea sponge to place inside herself. One can wear a sheath. One can tailor one's lovemaking to the occasion. Or one can withdraw before completion—if one has enough control."

Nell frowned at him. "I don't understand any of that."

"I'd be astonished if you did," Black said.

The door opened and the serving-men returned. Nell sat silently while the table was cleared, puzzling through Black's words. She thought she might understand what he meant about the sea sponge, but surely it would be very uncomfortable, so maybe she was wrong? And perhaps a sheath covered a man's procreative organ, as a scabbard covered a sword? But since she had no clear idea what a man's organ looked like, she couldn't imagine what a sheath looked like. Was it made of metal? Wouldn't that hurt?

The serving-men withdrew.

"What's a sheath?" Nell said, once the door had closed. "Is it made of metal?"

Black winced. "No."

"What, then?"

"Dried sheep intestines," Black said. "And I am *not* going to discuss this any further with you."

"But—"

"No."

Nell recognized finality when she heard it. She subsided into silence.

Black eyed her warily, and then leaned back in his chair. "What time would you like to start tomorrow?"

"As early as possible." She leaned back in her chair, too, and studied him. "You're a great deal more virtuous than gossip paints you. Does it not bother you?"

"My virtue?" Black said dryly. "Yes, it bothers me a great deal."

"Your reputation," Nell told him, equally dryly.

"My reputation doesn't bother me at all," Black said, with a shrug. "Why should it?"

"Because it isn't true."

"What isn't true? I'm a bastard. I'm a rake."

Nell studied him for several seconds. Black shifted in his seat. He checked his pocket watch.

"You do it on purpose, don't you?"

"What?" Black said, returning the watch to his pocket.

"Why?"

"Why what?"

"Why do you make yourself out as worse than you are?"

"I don't know what you're talking about," Black said. He pushed back his chair and stood. "If we're leaving at dawn, we should retire."

Nell stayed seated. "Why do you want people to think the worst of you?"

"I don't."

"You flaunt your affairs—"

Black looked at her down his magnificent nose. "I do not *flaunt* my affairs."

"You don't hide them."

"Of course not. Why should I?"

Nell frowned, and pondered this question. Why would a man choose not to hide his love affairs? A dislike of subterfuge? A desire for notoriety? Or was there some deeper reason?

Black checked his watch again. "If we're to leave at dawn—"

"Yes." Nell pushed back her chair and stood.

Black escorted her to her bedchamber. "Goodnight."

"Goodnight," Nell said. "And thank you." She touched his

sleeve with her fingertips, lightly, daringly, a gesture of gratitude. "You're a good man, Mr. Black."

The corridor was dimly lit, but she thought his cheeks
reddened. He took a step away, and then turned back to her.
"Will you marry me?"

Nell's throat tightened. Her heart began to beat faster. She
thought of Black's physical beauty, his chivalry, his kindness,
his odd morality—and then she thought of his tyrannical
nature. *Eat*, he'd told her, as if she were a child. "No," she said.
"I'm sorry."

Black said nothing. He gave a nod and turned to go.

"Mr. Black?"

He turned back to face her.

Nell gripped her hands together and took a deep breath.
"*Why* do you wish to marry me?"

Black was silent for almost half a minute. Finally, he said,
"Do you remember the Moorecombs' ball, when we danced
together?"

Nell remembered it vividly. It had been the most exhilarating
twenty minutes of her Season—and the most terrifying. She'd
been excruciatingly aware of the warmth and strength of Black's
gloved hand, excruciatingly aware of her body's response to him
—the tingling heat, the breathlessness—and excruciatingly aware
of her father's cold disapproval from the edge of the dance floor.

"I remember," she said.

"Didn't you feel the connection between us?" Black asked.
"That spark? I was certain that you did."

Spark? It hadn't felt like a spark; it had felt like an inferno,
as if she'd been precariously balanced on the edge of a
flaming pit. But however strongly she'd been drawn to
Mordecai Black, Nell had known what that flaming pit
held: ruin.

She'd thought that the primitive, visceral pull of attraction had been one-sided. Black was telling her it wasn't.

Finally, unwillingly, Nell said, "Yes. I felt it."

Black took a step towards her. "Then why won't you marry me?"

Because her physical attraction to him hadn't robbed her of her wits. Because even if she was an innocent, she knew that good marriages required more than sparks or infernos; they required compatibility of character.

Nell looked him in the eye. "People do not marry because of a single dance, Mr. Black."

"No?"

"No," she said firmly.

Black stood motionless for a long moment, his face shadowy. Nell braced herself for argument, but instead he gave a short nod, as if acknowledging her point, and said, "Good night, Miss Wrotham."

"Good night."

Nell watched him go. *I do not understand this man.*

Chapter Ten

July 17th, 1812
Hamptonshire

MORDECAI LEANED BACK in his corner of the coach. Salisbury was fifty miles behind them, Exeter fifty miles ahead. He stared out the window and pondered how best to find a godly woman who took in fallen women. Would it be quicker to ask at the churches or among the prostitutes? The prostitutes, he decided. He'd venture out this evening, find some whores, ask questions. By tomorrow, Miss Wrotham might be reunited with her sister.

The coach swung around a bend—and stopped so abruptly that Mordecai was almost thrown from his seat.

"Is it highwaymen?" Bessie cried.

Mordecai wrenched open the door and jumped out. Not highwaymen, but an accident. He took in the overturned phaeton at a glance. "Walter," he snapped. "Run back and stop any carriages, else the next one will run into us."

The footman obeyed, his coattails flapping.

Miss Wrotham climbed down from the carriage. "Someone's overturned?"

"Yes? Are you afraid of horses? No? Then I need you to hold ours. Phelps, give me the reins and run up ahead, see what you can do to help them."

The coachman obeyed, handing Mordecai the reins, jumping down from his box.

Mordecai spent a moment explaining to Miss Wrotham how best to hold so many reins, then he hurried ahead himself. Phelps was trying to soothe the panicked horses, so Mordecai turned his attention to the phaeton's passengers, two young bucks who'd been cast into the ditch. One had a copiously bleeding nose, but it was the second man, white-faced and wheezing, his face twisted with pain, who snagged Mordecai's attention. He went down on one knee. "What it is? Ribs?"

Ribs and an arm and quite likely a collarbone, too, in Mordecai's opinion. A farm cart trundled up, and a gig. He sent the gig for the nearest doctor. When he turned back to the injured men, he discovered that Miss Wrotham was staunching the bleeding nose with the victim's neckcloth. He glanced at his traveling carriage; Bessie sat on the box, clutching the reins, a look of nervous determination on her face.

Mordecai turned his attention to the phaeton's horses. Phelps had managed to untangle them from their traces. "The gray has a strained hock," the coachman said. "Otherwise they're all right."

"Good man." Mordecai crossed to the farm cart. "Give me a hand getting this phaeton off the road?"

It was easier said than done, but they had the road cleared by the time the gig returned with the doctor. Five minutes after that, Mordecai was back in his carriage. He looked at his pocket watch. "We should still make Exeter by dark."

His words were not prophetic. At Crewkerne they were held up by a funeral procession, just past Chard they were delayed by a farmer moving his sheep, and five miles short of Honiton, one of the leaders went lame.

They proceeded the rest of the way to Honiton at walking pace, arriving as the remnants of sunset were fading from the sky. Fortunately Honiton possessed a posting-inn. "I'm sorry," Mordecai said, when he handed Miss Wrotham down from the carriage.

"It can't be helped. Are we putting up here for the night?"

"If there's room for us."

Thereafter, the day improved, because not only did the landlord have room for them all, he also had an excellent wine cellar.

Mordecai dined with Miss Wrotham in a private parlor that was rustic, rather than modish. The beamed ceiling was so low he had to duck his head when he stood.

"How shall we find the godly woman?" Miss Wrotham asked, once they'd eaten.

"Ask at the churches," Mordecai said. The chestnut wig and spectacles that had so disconcerted his eye yesterday had become familiar today. He was able to see past them, to see Eleanor Wrotham beneath Mrs. Trussell-Quimby.

"If she helps fallen women, should we not ask among them?"

"*We* will not ask any fallen women anything," Mordecai said firmly. "*I* will ask them—if we fail to learn anything at the churches."

Her eyebrows lifted slightly, and Mordecai remembered the accusation she'd made in London. Dictatorial. He gritted his teeth and prepared for an argument, but Miss Wrotham said nothing.

Relieved, Mordecai reached for his wineglass. "Do you wish to leave at dawn again?"

"Exeter's only three hours from here, isn't it?"

"Less than that. Unless another horse goes lame."

"Eight o'clock, then." Miss Wrotham folded her napkin and laid it beside her plate.

Mordecai sipped slowly, savoring the wine, and thought of the marriage license in his breast pocket. And then he thought of Miss Wrotham's refusal yesterday, and her refusal the day before. *How many times should I ask before giving up?*

"Good night, Mr. Black." She pushed back her chair and made as if to stand.

"Miss Wrotham, will you marry me?"

She paused, then sat again. "Why do you keep asking me that?"

Because I have to.

"This isn't one of Beaumont's faerie tales, Mr. Black. I'm not Beauty and you're not the Beast."

Mordecai disagreed. Miss Wrotham *was* a beauty—even with the red hair and spectacles—and he'd always been an outsider, an outcast, and what was the Beast if not an outcast? He summoned a smile and a careless shrug. "That's a matter of opinion."

Miss Wrotham didn't smile back. She frowned. "Why do you wish to marry me, Mr. Black? And don't tell me it's because of one dance!"

Mordecai fumbled for an answer, and came up with, "Because I do."

She rolled her eyes—actually rolled her eyes—and Mordecai's heart missed a beat and he almost said, *That's why I want to marry you.* Because beneath that cool exterior existed a kindred spirit.

"Please be more specific," Miss Wrotham said, with her perfect, clipped diction.

Mordecai sipped his wine again, stalling. He couldn't tell her that he thought of ballrooms as hen yards, filled with débutantes clucking and pecking and jostling for the best places, and that Eleanor Wrotham had stood out as if she was a hawk with clipped wings, watching the fuss but not part of it, distant and aloof. He couldn't tell her that if her wings weren't clipped she'd fly far and wide. He couldn't tell her that he wanted to be the person who set her free. Miss Wrotham would laugh at him, think him a fanciful fool, a besotted idiot.

"You were kind to Arabella Knightley," he came up with, because that *was* one of the things he liked about her: her kindness to someone who was as much of as outcast as he was.

Her eyebrows lifted. "Arabella Knightley?"

"You didn't talk about her behind her back. At least, not that I heard."

"Of course I didn't!"

"Most people did," Mordecai said. "They were polite to her face—she's an earl's granddaughter after all—but what they said behind her back was . . . not nice."

Miss Wrotham snorted, and the sound made Mordecai's heart skip another beat. *See? Kindred spirit.* "Not nice?" she said tartly. "It was *cruel*. Especially after what that idiot St. Just said about her!"

Miss Smell o' Gutters. Yes, a cruel epithet to attach to a débutante.

Miss Wrotham leaned back in her chair, crossed her arms, and eyed him through the gold-rimmed spectacles. "That's why you wish to marry me? Because I was kind to Arabella Knightley?"

Mordecai shrugged. "Why not?"

"I didn't notice *you* being kind to her."

"Me?" Mordecai put down his glass. "Good God! Can you imagine what people would have said if I'd paid any attention to her?" Like calling to like. The soiled heiress, the bastard son. "She would have been crucified."

Miss Wrotham gazed at him for a long moment, her eyes narrow, as if she looked inside him. "It must be lonely," she said slowly. "To be notorious through no fault of your own, people talking *about* you instead of *to* you."

Very lonely. Mordecai shifted uncomfortably in his chair. "She had a difficult début."

"I'm not talking about Miss Knightley," Miss Wrotham said. "I'm talking about you."

What? Mordecai froze.

"Is that why you don't hide your affairs? You want to give people something to talk about other than your parentage?"

Mordecai felt like a moth skewered on a pin. No, not merely skewered; cut open, his innermost self bared to the world. "Of course not!" he said, with a laugh.

Miss Wrotham looked as if she didn't believe him.

Eleanor Wrotham's intelligence was one of the reasons he wanted to marry her, but at this moment, Mordecai wished she wasn't *quite* so perceptive. He groped for another topic, something to head her off. "Do you know why Roger offered for you? Because of your face."

Her eyebrows lifted.

"He told me once that you had the face of a duchess." Mordecai remembered the smug pride in Roger's voice—and the almost overmastering urge he'd experienced to hit him.

"A duchess? What's that supposed to mean?"

"Patrician," Mordecai said. He reached for his glass again. "Roger thought you'd be the perfect Society hostess. He said you had a most pleasing reserve."

"That doesn't sound like a compliment."

"It was, coming from him."

Miss Wrotham eyed him while he sipped, and she did look patrician. It was stamped on her face, something she had no control over. There was aloofness in the curve of her nostrils, hauteur in the set of her eyelids. Her father had had the same cast of feature, and it had matched his character. But in Miss Wrotham he thought the aloofness went no deeper than her skin.

"A perfect Society hostess." Her tone gave the words a caustic inflection. "Is that why you wish to marry me, Mr. Black?"

Mordecai almost choked on his wine. "Me? Good God, no."

"Then, why?"

Mordecai put down his glass. He took a deep breath and told the truth: "Because I think that beneath that face is someone who *doesn't* want to be a duchess. Because I think that given half the chance you'd be as unconventional as your aunt, Lady Dalrymple."

Miss Wrotham stiffened. Her expression became utterly blank.

Mordecai plowed on. If he was going to burn his bridges, why not do it thoroughly? "I think there are times when you want to pick up your skirts and run, even if it isn't ladylike. I think you'd like to ride *ventre à terre* and laugh loudly and do a great number of things that a lady *shouldn't* do."

Miss Wrotham said nothing. He'd shocked her, that was evident. She was gazing at him with the cold hauteur of a thousand duchesses.

"But I may be wrong," Mordecai said. "I may have misjudged your character."

Her gaze lowered. She subjected her table setting to an

intense, frowning stare that should have made the plate and cutlery cringe.

Mordecai sat silently, and hoped.

Finally, Miss Wrotham looked up. Her expression was unsmiling, somewhere between stern and perturbed. "You're not wrong."

Mordecai released his breath. He felt muscles in his shoulders and chest uncoil themselves.

She eyed him warily. "How did you know?"

"I saw you in Richmond Park once. You were riding with the Dalrymples, not quite *ventre à terre*, but close." She'd been flushed and laughing and vividly alive, and she hadn't looked at all like the cool, aloof débutante he'd seen at Almack's the night before.

She grimaced faintly. "I remember. I shouldn't have ridden like that."

"Why not?" Mordecai said. "Why shouldn't you gallop if you want to? Although personally I think it would be easier if you rode astride."

Shock flashed across her face. "Astride?"

He shrugged. "Why not?"

She stared at him for a long moment, and then said, "I couldn't possibly use a man's saddle." Resolute words, but her tone was uncertain, doubtful.

Mordecai let the silence grow, let her words drift there, then said, "Not in London, perhaps, but on a private estate you could do whatever you wanted."

She looked away. "I don't have a private estate."

"I have four of them," Mordecai said. *And if you marry me you'll be mistress of them all.* He didn't say the words aloud, but Miss Wrotham seemed to hear them. She colored faintly and pushed back her chair and stood, not haughty and aloof, but almost flustered. "Goodnight, Mr. Black."

Mordecai stood, too. The marriage license seemed to burn in his pocket. "Will you marry me, Miss Wrotham?"

She halted, her head turned away from him.

"Your sister and her child would live with us," Mordecai said. "That goes without saying. Our home would be their home."

Miss Wrotham turned slowly and looked at him, no longer flustered, but wholly serious. No, more than serious; frowning.

Mordecai reviewed his words in his head. "That wasn't a bribe," he said. "Absolutely not! I just . . . want you to know how it would be."

The frown faded. Miss Wrotham surveyed him silently, her gaze searching. Mordecai experienced the same sensation that he'd had a few moments ago, that he was an insect split open for inspection, helpless and exposed. Seconds ticked past in his head. He discovered that he was holding his breath.

"If you took Sophia into your home, you would lose your entrée to Society, Mr. Black."

She was almost certainly correct. Liaisons with members of the *ton* were one thing; taking a fallen woman into one's household was quite another. Doors that were open to him now would probably slam shut in his face.

Mordecai shrugged. "If that happened, it wouldn't bother me."

More seconds ticked past. Miss Wrotham's expression was troubled. "Perhaps it would bother me," she said at last.

"Miss Wrotham—"

"Thank you for your offer. You're very kind, but I cannot marry you. Goodnight, Mr. Black." She turned and almost ran from the room.

Chapter Eleven

NELL'S FATHER HAD disliked displays of emotion. Nell had learned at an early age to swallow her laughter and her anger, to suppress her tears. She wasn't a crier. She told herself that as she climbed the stairs to her bedchamber—*I am not a crier*— but as soon as she'd closed the bedroom door, the tears came.

Bessie fussed over her, dismayed. "What is it ma'am? Shall I fetch Mr. Black? Are you ill?"

Mr. Black was why she was crying, but she couldn't tell Bessie that. "My sister is missing," Nell said, removing the spectacles and mopping her eyes with a sodden handkerchief. "That's why we're going to Exeter."

Bessie gave her a fresh handkerchief. "Mr. Black will find her for you."

Nell blew her nose and wiped her cheeks. "She may not even be in Exeter."

"He'll still find her," Bessie said, and her faith in Mordecai Black should have been ludicrous—except that it wasn't. Black had earned Bessie's faith. He *deserved* Bessie's faith. And that made Nell's eyes fill with tears again. She blinked them back. *I am not a crier.*

But when Bessie had gone and Nell was tucked up in bed, alone in the dark, the urge to cry came again. She told herself it was because she was desperately anxious about Sophia, because she was exhausted, but she knew that the real reason was Mordecai Black.

Mordecai Black and his proposals.

She had told him this wasn't a faerie tale, that she wasn't Beauty and he wasn't the Beast, and while she'd been right, she'd also been wrong, because in this tale Black was both the Beauty *and* the Beast.

The *beaumonde* was Black's playground. He navigated its waters with careless confidence. Men envied him, women wanted him. He had lovers, wealth, notoriety. On the outside, a charmed life. But on the inside . . .

He is a very lonely man.

Last year she'd imagined what it must be like for Arabella Knightley—damned for something her mother had done—but she'd never imagined what it must be like for Mr. Black.

Tonight she had.

She'd looked at Mordecai Black and experienced a wave of such intense sympathy that she'd been tempted to accept his offer. But sympathy wasn't love. She must *not* confuse the two. If she married Black, she would resent his masterful nature. She'd be miserable—and that would make *him* miserable, and while Black deserved many things, an unhappy marriage wasn't one of them.

Nell blew out a breath, and shifted restlessly beneath the bedclothes, too warm, too agitated, too uncomfortable.

Black had offered Sophia and her child a home. *Just for that, I ought to marry him.* A sensible woman would. There could be no comparison between the life she planned and the one

Black offered. She wouldn't have to count every penny. She wouldn't have to sew her own clothes and do her own housework. She would live a life of luxury, comfort, ease, safety. And so would Sophia. And Sophia's child.

But Black would lose his place to Society, and she couldn't do that to him. Could *not* do it. The *beaumonde* was his *milieu*, and if he was torn from it he would come to resent her, just as surely as she had resented Sophia.

Nell sighed again, shifted restlessly again. She thought of Arabella Knightley. She thought of Mr. Black. She thought of herself. *We are all damned because of things others have done.* Miss Knightley's mother. Black's parents. Her own sister.

But there the similarities ended. Black and Miss Knightley had been accepted into Society—stared at, gossiped about, but still accepted. Black's father and Miss Knightley's grandparents had *fought* for that acceptance.

Her father hadn't. He'd fled Society, buried not just himself, but her as well. Made the choice for them both: hide, not fight.

The maxim her father had lived by was *Virtue above all*, but if Black had a maxim, it must surely be *I'd rather be damned for my lovers than for my birth*. And why not? Why not give people something to gossip about? Something *real*. Something one had actually *done*. What was the point in being virtuous when one was already tarnished through no fault of one's own?

Nell stared up at the ceiling in the dark, even further from sleep than she'd been ten minutes ago. That last thought reverberated in her head: *Why be virtuous when one is already tarnished?*

Chapter Twelve

July 18th, 1812
Exeter, Devonshire

THEY REACHED EXETER BEFORE NOON. Mordecai didn't direct his coachman to the hotel he usually patronized; he wanted somewhere he wasn't known, where he could keep a low profile. The inn he finally selected was a modest establishment more used to solicitors and country squires than the wealthy bastard sons of earls. "Remember: I'm plain Mr. Black from nowhere in particular," he told his servants. "I am *not* related to the late Lord Dereham."

"Yes, sir."

After a light luncheon, he and Miss Wrotham set out to visit churches. Exeter was as oppressively hot as London had been. Mordecai's shirt-points drooped. He sweated beneath his layers of clothing and envied the half-naked urchins begging for coins. They drew a blank at the first three churches, but at the fourth the churchwarden said, "A godly woman who takes in fallen women? That'd be Miss Pender."

"Can you give us her direction?"

"Why, she's just around the corner, sir."

Miss Pender did indeed live just around the corner, in a dour street that had the church at one end and a tavern at the other. Mordecai glanced at Miss Wrotham. A stranger would think her calm, but he saw suppressed excitement in the way she clutched her reticule and dampened urgency in her stride. She wanted to run, but was forcing herself to walk.

But where her steps quickened, his slowed. He wanted to stop the clock, halt time itself. He had a strong sense of doom approaching. *She will have no further use for me after this.*

Miss Pender's house was halfway down the street, tall and narrow and thoroughly respectable, its front step scoured clean, its door knocker polished until it shone.

They halted at the scrubbed doorstep. Mordecai unwillingly glanced at Miss Wrotham. Behind the spectacle lenses her eyes were bright with hope.

Frustration surged in his chest. He wanted to take her by the shoulders and shake her and say, *Marry me, damn it. Can't you see we would suit?*

Mordecai blew out his breath. He rapped on the door.

The maid who answered was as neat as the house, her starched apron crisp despite the heat. She bobbed a curtsy and didn't meet their eyes.

"My name is Black," Mordecai said. "May we see Miss Pender, please?"

The maid bade them enter. The vestibule was warm and narrow and dark and scrupulously clean. The floor gleamed. Mordecai smelled camphor, polishing wax, and a sharp note of vinegar.

They followed the maid to a back parlor. As she turned to go, he saw that her hands were red and work-worn.

Mordecai and Miss Wrotham waited. The parlor was suffocatingly warm. It had the same camphor, polishing wax, and vinegar smell as the vestibule. It was also the most precise room Mordecai had ever seen in his life. The chairs and the little tables, the candlesticks on the mantelpiece and the religious prints upon the wall were all rigidly aligned and perfectly spaced, as if someone had determined their placement with a ruler. The grate gleamed, the fender gleamed, the candlesticks gleamed. He would have been willing to bet his entire fortune that there was not one speck of dust in the room.

Around them, the house was silent. He listened for murmured voices, for a baby's crying, and heard absolutely nothing. Then his ears caught the sound of footsteps. Miss Wrotham heard it, too. She took a step towards the door. Her face was pale, taut with hope. Mordecai found himself fervently wishing that her sister and child were here—but he doubted they were. This didn't feel like a house with a baby in it.

The woman who entered the room was in her late fifties, tall and large-boned. Her face was square, her mouth wide, her lips thin. She couldn't help that gin trap mouth any more than he could help his beak of a nose or Miss Wrotham her haughty eyelids, but Mordecai took an instant dislike to her. He summoned a polite smile and a bow. "Miss Pender?"

"Yes." Miss Pender's graying hair was drawn back tightly from her forehead. Her eyes were blue. Not the deep navy blue of Miss Wrotham's, but a pale, icy color. Her appearance was as precise as the parlor, as if her hair didn't dare stray from its bun, her gown crease itself, or her starched cap wilt in the heat. She smelled strongly of vinegar.

"We're looking for my sister," Miss Wrotham said, with polite urgency. "Sophia. Did she come here?"

Miss Pender stiffened. Her resemblance to a gin trap became more pronounced. "There is no one named Sophia in my house."

There was a moment of stricken silence. Mordecai didn't look at Miss Wrotham's face. He couldn't. "Has she been here?' he asked. "We believe she was with a girl named Lizzie."

The thin lips compressed. "They left two months ago."

"Do you know where they went?"

"No."

"Why did they leave?"

"They didn't want to be saved."

Mordecai doubted that he'd want to be saved by Miss Pender, either.

"The integrity of the upright shall guide them: but the perverseness of transgressors shall destroy them," Miss Pender said forcefully, her esses hissing.

Mordecai felt a strong desire to step away from her. "Quite so," he said. "Ah, is there anyone in your household who might know where they went?"

Miss Pender's mouth tightened still further. Now she had no lips at all.

Mordecai took her silence for a *Yes*. "May we speak with them, please?"

Miss Pender had six reformed prostitutes in her household. The maid who'd answered the door was one of them. They were all dressed in starched aprons, they all had red, work-worn hands—and they all disliked Miss Pender. Mordecai saw it clearly in the way they averted their eyes from her.

He interviewed them one by one in the stuffy parlor, with Miss Wrotham standing silently at his side.

"Speak with righteous lips," Miss Pender commanded each girl, and they obeyed, whispering their answers, their eyes fixed on the floor.

Mordecai saw the second girl shrink back when Miss Pender stepped close, saw the fourth one flinch when Miss Pender raised her hand to open the door. He knew what those instinctive cringes meant; he'd shied away from blows often enough as a child. The muscles in his jaw tightened until he had a gin trap mouth, too.

None of the girls knew where Lizzie and Sophia had gone, although one of them said hesitantly that Lizzie had grown up in Stepcote Hill, so perhaps she'd gone there.

"Did Lizzie ever mention any names?" Mordecai asked. "People she knew in Stepcote Hill?"

The girl hesitated, and darted him a scared glance.

"Lying lips are an abomination to the Lord," Miss Pender said fiercely.

The girl fixed her gaze on the floor again. "Billy English," she whispered.

"Billy English?"

The girl shivered, and nodded.

"Who is he?"

"You don't want to go near 'im, sir. He's a bad 'un, is Billy."

After the final girl left the parlor, there was nothing to do but thank Miss Pender and leave. Mordecai did so with relief. He inhaled a deep breath as they stepped out into the street; the stink of an overwarm city was a thousand times better than the smell of camphor and vinegar and piety. He turned to Miss Wrotham. "We'll find your sister. I swear to you, we *will* find her."

"I know we will." Her voice was firm, but her eyes shone with unshed tears.

Mordecai's heart seemed to squeeze in his chest. He wanted to put his arms around her and hold her very tightly.

Miss Wrotham set out for the end of the street. Mordecai matched his step to hers. "Where is Stepcote Hill?" she asked.

"Here in Exeter. It's one of the poorest neighborhoods."

"Like Seven Dials?"

"Yes."

Miss Wrotham halted.

Mordecai braced himself for an argument. Even if she cried he was *not* taking her to Stepcote Hill. But instead, she turned and looked back at Miss Pender's. "I know I should admire her, but I don't." Her voice was troubled.

Mordecai turned, too, and looked at the grim, narrow house. "Miss Pender may be godly, but she hasn't an ounce of kindness in her."

"Then why does she help the fallen?"

Mordecai shrugged. "Duty?"

Miss Wrotham grimaced, as if *duty* was a word she disliked. "She reminds me of my Great Aunt Wrotham."

Mordecai gave a humorless grunt of laughter. "She reminds me of my mother."

Miss Wrotham glanced at him, her eyebrows lifting in surprise. "Your mother was very moral?"

"No," Mordecai said.

"She looked like Miss Pender?"

"No."

"Then in what way was she like Miss Pender?"

Mordecai hesitated, and then said, "Did you notice how

those girls flinched from her? She hits them. I'd say that's why your sister and Lizzie left."

"Your mother hit you?"

"Frequently." Mordecai began walking again, an attempt to halt the conversation. It didn't work.

"Father never hit us." Miss Wrotham's tone was sympathetic. "He just sent us to our bedrooms. I spent a large part of my childhood in my room."

Mordecai didn't tell her that he'd spent a large part of his childhood in the scullery because his mother couldn't bear the sight of him; instead he said, "I'll look for Billy English in Stepcote Hill this afternoon. And no, you may not come with me."

To his relief, this dictatorial statement distracted Miss Wrotham from further discussion of their childhoods. "But I came to Seven Dials with you."

"Didn't you hear what that girl said? Billy English is dangerous."

"But—"

"No," Mordecai said, in a tone that brooked no argument.

Chapter Thirteen

MR. BLACK WENT to Stepcote Hill by hackney, leaving Nell at the inn. She wasted no time being annoyed with him. She didn't have *time* to be annoyed with highhanded males. Her birthday was in four days, and her Faerie godmother would grant her a wish and she would know where Sophia was—but if four days was a short time, it was also a very long time if one was penniless and with a young baby. And even though Mr. Black had refused to allow her to go to Stepcote Hill, there were things Nell *could* do. Someone must have helped Sophia give birth. Had she been tended by a midwife? Gone to a lying-in hospital? Did Exeter even *have* a charitable lying-in hospital?

She posed that last question to the innkeeper, who told her that a very good lying-in hospital for poor women had recently been established, and that it would be quite safe for her to visit it. In fact, it was less than ten minutes' walk from the inn.

Nell went back upstairs at a pace too fast to be called ladylike. Her father would have scolded her for it. *A lady never runs, Eleanor. How many times must I tell you that?*

Bessie was in the bedchamber, checking Nell's few clothes, determining what needed washing, what ironing, what darning. "Bessie, you're to come with me."

"Where to, ma'am?"

"The lying-in hospital." Nell crossed to her valise, dug inside it, and drew out a thin package: two rectangles of pasteboard, bound together with ribbon. She hesitated, then untied the ribbon and parted the pasteboard, revealing the pencil sketch: herself and Sophia. Her throat tightened and for a moment she was unable to speak.

Bessie inhaled a reverent breath. "How beautiful."

Yes, Sophia was very beautiful. The pencil strokes couldn't show the golden hair and violet eyes, but they perfectly captured the loveliness of Sophia's features. She gazed out of the portrait and you could *see* who she was, could see her youth and her innocence, her capacity for joy, see that she was someone who always believed the best of people, who saw good in everyone.

Nell cleared her throat. "She drew this. Sophia did. That's her name: Sophia."

The sketch had been intended as a gift for their father, but it had never been given. And now never would.

Nell slid the sketch back between the pasteboard rectangles and briskly retied the ribbons. "Fetch your bonnet, Bessie."

———

THE CHARITABLE LYING-IN hospital was located in what had once been someone's mansion. A merchant's mansion, Nell thought, given its location amid Exeter's warehouses. The building had an imposing façade, but once inside it was oddly welcoming. Welcoming and clean and busy.

Nell spoke to the superintendent, a jovial man with spectacles and curling gray whiskers. She showed him the sketch.

"Within the last month, you say?" the superintendent said, peering at the sketch.

"June, I would think."

"I haven't seen her, but that doesn't mean she wasn't here. Come with me, Mrs. Trussell-Quimby. We'll ask my colleagues."

But no one within the lying-in hospital had seen Sophia either. Nell tried not to let her disappointment show. "Are there any other charitable lying-in hospitals in Exeter?"

"No," the superintendent said.

"Midwives, then. Do you perhaps have a list of midwives in Exeter?"

"I know a few names, but there'd be dozens more. Any woman may *call* herself a midwife, Mrs. Trussell-Quimby, but whether she actually knows what she's doing is quite another matter!"

"May I please have those names?"

The superintendent wrote them down for her. Six names, each with an address jotted alongside.

Nell examined the list. The addresses meant nothing to her. "Would it be safe for me to visit these places alone?"

The man hesitated, and then said, "I wouldn't advise it, Mrs. Trussell-Quimby."

"But none of them are as rough as Stepcote Hill, are they? None of them are actually dangerous?"

The superintendent made a movement of his head, neither nod nor shake, but something in between. "Not dangerous, no, but it would be best to take your husband with you."

Nell thanked him. Outside, on the steps of the lying-in hospital, she hesitated, unsure what to do next.

Across the street was a bakery. *Reid & Houghton,* said the sign. The bakery was doing a busy trade. Nell watched the customers come and go. Should she return to the inn? Or search for midwives?

She studied the superintendent's list again. Pinhoe. St Leonard. Heavitree. St. Paul. St. Mary Arches. Parishes she didn't know, in a city she didn't know.

Where are you, Sophy?

"To the devil with prudence," she muttered under her breath, and then she said, more loudly, "Come along, Bessie. Let's find a hackney." But when they found a hackney rank, caution made her hesitate. *I can't take Bessie somewhere that may not be entirely safe.* Nell glanced at the girl, and suddenly knew how Mordecai Black felt—and why he'd refused to allow her to accompany him. So instead of directing the jarvey to drive them to the nearest parish on the list, she asked him to take them back to the inn.

"Please wait here," she told the jarvey. "I shan't be above five minutes." And then she hurried inside in search of Black's footman. "Walter! Fetch your hat. You're coming with us."

THUS IT WAS that Nell interviewed three midwives that afternoon, in the company of her maid and a footman. One midwife lived in the parish of St. Mary Arches, the other two in St. Paul. Nell showed all three women the sketch of Sophia. None of them had seen her, but they gave her the names of four more midwives, one of whom was in Stepcote Hill.

Nell thanked the third woman for her time and went back

out to the street, followed by Walter and Bessie. The hackney she had hired was waiting, both horse and jarvey half-asleep.

Nell read out the address the third midwife had given her: Smythen Street. "Is this nearby?"

"Yes, ma'am."

"Take us there, please."

The jarvey hesitated. "It's in the West Quarter, ma'am."

"You think it's unsafe?"

The jarvey glanced from her to Bessie to Walter, and back again. "It ain't the safest part of the city, ma'am."

Nell looked down at her list. "Coombe Street, then. Or Preston Street."

"They're also in the West Quarter, ma'am."

Nell blew out a breath, and studied the list again. She skipped over Stepcote Hill. "St. Leonard? Is that also in the West Quarter?"

"It's a little ways outside the city, ma'am."

"Is it safe?"

The jarvey shrugged. "Safe enough."

But it was outside the city, and intuition told her that Mr. Black wouldn't be pleased if she ventured that far without him.

"How about Heavitree, then? How far is it?"

"Couple of miles past St. Leonard, ma'am."

"And Pinhoe?"

"Even further out."

Nell hesitated, and examined her locket watch. It was later than she'd thought. "How long would it take to get to St. Leonard and back?"

The jarvey shrugged. "An hour."

Which meant that she wouldn't be back at the inn until dusk.

Nell bit her lip, torn between wanting to find Sophia as fast as possible and the knowledge that if Mordecai Black returned to the inn and found her gone, he'd be worried.

She weighed the choices in her mind: Sophia's safety versus Black's worry. *But perhaps Black has already found Sophia in Stepcote Hill?*

"Very well," Nell said. "We'll return to the inn."

BLACK ARRIVED BACK fifteen minutes after Nell. He hadn't found Billy English, or Sophia and Lizzie. He looked disheveled and sweaty and slightly more dangerous than usual. Nell couldn't put her finger on *why* he seemed more dangerous . . . until she noticed that his right glove was split across the knuckles. "What happened?"

"Someone tried to rob me."

"Are you all right?"

"I am; they're not."

"They?"

"There were two of them." Black peeled off the ruined glove. Nell saw blood on his knuckles. "I need a wash. Dinner in an hour suit you?"

Nell nodded.

The next time she saw Black he was freshly shaved and impeccably dressed. He didn't look like a man who'd recently brawled with two thugs in a seedy part of Exeter—unless one examined his hands. His knuckles were faintly bruised, and one of them sported a tiny gash.

Black caught her glance. "Cut it on a tooth."

"Is Stepcote Hill *very* dangerous?" Nell asked, serving herself from the dishes laid before them.

Black shrugged lightly. "No more than Seven Dials."

"But we weren't set upon in Seven Dials."

"We weren't there long enough." Black helped himself to some beef olives. "If we'd been there for several hours, if we'd gone down every side street and alley, then I can guarantee you we'd have been set upon."

"But I thought pickpockets were *sly*, not violent."

"They weren't pickpockets. They were after more than my purse and my watch."

Nell frowned at him. "They were?"

"Look at my clothes," Black said. "How much do you think they cost?"

Nell's gaze jerked down to his chest—the blue superfine coat, the crisp, white neckcloth, the silk waistcoat—and then back to his face. "You think they would have taken your coat as well?"

"I think they'd have stripped me," Black said bluntly. "And probably put a knife between my ribs for good measure."

Nell stared at him, shocked. "You mean . . . murder? For your *clothes*?"

"My clothes cost more money than those people will ever see in their lives. It must have been like watching the Bank of England walk past. An irresistible temptation." Black shrugged again, and added some larded sweetbreads to his plate.

"I didn't realize Stepcote Hill was so dangerous," Nell said, aghast. "You could have been killed."

"There were only two of them. And they were half-drunk."

"But there could have been *four*."

"I would still have won. I learned to fight on the streets, not in Gentleman Jack's Saloon. I don't follow Broughton's rules."

Nell didn't know what Broughton's rules were, but she knew arrogance when she heard it. "You would have won a fight against four men?" she said dryly.

"Four men who were fuddled with gin? Yes."

But what if they *hadn't* been fuddled with gin? Or what if there'd been six of them, or eight? "I don't want you to go back there," Nell said.

"I have no reason to," Black said, serving himself from a dish of green beans. "Your sister isn't there. Nor is Lizzie. And Billy English has moved up in the world."

"Moved up?"

"He's left the West Quarter."

"Stepcote Hill is in the West Quarter?"

Black nodded.

Nell thought of the jarvey's reluctance to take her to the West Quarter, and silently blessed the man. "Where is Billy English now?"

"Down by the river. Cricklepit Street."

"Is it safer than the West Quarter?"

"Marginally. I'll go there tomorrow, see if I can find him."

Marginally. Nell pondered this word while she ate. It seemed to her that marginally safe was still very close to dangerous, and that Cricklepit Street might be a street where half-drunk men would try to rob Mordecai Black for his clothes and his purse. And stick a knife between his ribs.

I will know where Sophia is in a few days. I can't let him risk his life for this.

Nell laid down her cutlery. "While you were gone, I tackled the problem from another angle."

Black glanced at her.

"I went to the charitable lying-in hospital."

Black didn't move, but everything about him seemed to tighten—his shoulders, his jaw, the skin around his eyes, his grip on the knife and fork.

"It's in a perfectly safe neighborhood," Nell told him. "I checked with the innkeeper first. And I took Bessie with me."

Black didn't relax. He looked like a man trying to hold his temper in check.

"Sophia hadn't been there, but the superintendent gave me the names and addresses of several midwives."

Black closed his eyes in a wince. "Tell me you didn't—"

"I did," Nell said briskly. "And before you ring a peal over me, let me tell you that I took both Bessie *and* Walter with me."

Black opened his eyes and studied her for a long moment—jaw still tight, grip on his cutlery still tight—and then asked, "Where did you go?"

"St. Mary Arches parish," Nell said. "And St. Paul parish. Several of the midwives live in the West Quarter, but I didn't go there."

"The West Quarter?" Black put his knife and fork down with a loud clatter. "Good God! Do you have *any* idea how much danger you'd have been in if—"

"I'm not a fool," Nell told him. "I asked the jarvey whether he thought the West Quarter was safe, and when he said it wasn't I heeded his advice."

Black said nothing. He looked as if he was gritting his teeth.

"A number of the midwives live in parishes outside the city. I would like to visit them tomorrow."

Black's eyebrows lowered. He drew breath to argue.

"And I'd like you to come with me," Nell said.

Black processed these words. After a moment, he said, "What about Billy English and Cricklepit Street?"

"I'd like to try the midwives first."

Black thought about this for several seconds, and then said, "Very well." He visibly relaxed, the tightness of jaw, eyes, and shoulders melting away. "We'll go tomorrow." He gave a nod and returned his attention to his food.

He thinks he's keeping me safe. What he doesn't realize is that I'm keeping him safe, too.

They ate in silence. Nell had little appetite. She pushed her food around her plate. She knew what would happen once the meal was over: Mordecai Black would renew his offer of marriage.

He would sit there—or perhaps stand there—looking impossibly beautiful, and he'd ask her to be his wife, and she'd have to struggle with the urge to say *Yes,* because the more she grew to know him, the more she was drawn to him.

Yes, he was a man who publicly paraded his aristocratic lovers, yes, he was highhanded and masterful, but he was also kind and generous and, in his own way, very moral.

And he was lonely. As lonely as poor Arabella Knightley— and that knowledge made her heart ache.

Nell cast him a covert glance. Mordecai Black, the notorious rake, eating his dinner quietly.

Her pulse gave its familiar little flutter. It would be so easy to fall in love with him. Terribly easy. She was halfway there already—but if part of her yearned to accept what Black offered, the rest of her knew better than to take that step. Because Mordecai Black was as autocratic as he was kind, and she would *not* marry a man who told her what to do.

But if she were to cast aside her virtue, she wouldn't mind being his mistress.

Nell allowed herself to imagine it for a moment: being Black's lover, sharing his life but being independent in a way a married woman could never be. As Mordecai Black's mistress, she wouldn't have to obey him, she'd be able to make up her own mind what she would and wouldn't do—and she could walk away if his autocratic nature became too much. She'd be utterly ruined, of course, not merely tarnished as she was now

—but wouldn't being Black's mistress be *worth* being ruined for?

Her thoughts jammed for a moment, temptation and horror tangling together. How could she have thought such a thing? And having thought it, how impossible it was to *un*think it.

Nell looked blankly down at her meal, and knew she wouldn't be able to swallow another mouthful.

She carefully laid her knife and fork on the plate, and glanced at Black. God, he was beautiful. The strength and symmetry and dangerous angles of his face. The long eyelashes. The imperious nose. The soft lower lip.

Nell's throat tightened in a moment of pure physical yearning. Heat swept through her. Her pulse didn't merely flutter, it began an agitated dance.

She looked hastily away from him and set herself to examining the parlor instead—the sturdy green sofa, the little writing desk in the corner, the two armchairs by the fireplace. Even though the coffee room lay below, no hum of voices penetrated the floorboards.

The tightness in her throat eased. The heat faded. Her heartbeat steadied.

"Not hungry?" Black asked.

Nell glanced up and found his dark eyes on her. Her pulse gave a little kick. She shook her head.

"Tell me about the lying-in hospital," Black said. "And the midwives you visited."

Nell did, sipping her wine, but if half her attention was on her recital, the other half was very firmly focused on what would come next. Sometime between finishing his meal and bidding her goodnight Mordecai Black would propose again, and she would say *No* because it was the best thing for both of them, and then she'd go up to her room and cry because he was kind and lonely and her refusals hurt him and she didn't *want* to hurt him.

Black ate his last sweetbread. He laid his cutlery neatly on his plate. "And the parishes outside the city walls? Which ones are they?"

"Pinhoe," Nell said. "And Heavitree." Her stomach tied itself into a knot. "And . . . um . . ." She cast desperately for the third parish. "St. Leonard."

"They're not too far."

The knot in Nell's stomach became tighter as she watched Black fold his napkin and place it alongside his plate. "What time would you like to leave tomorrow?" he asked.

What time did midwives rise? "Eight o'clock," Nell said.

Black nodded, and reached for his wineglass. Her gaze fastened on his bruised knuckles.

"You said the other midwives are in the West Quarter?" Black said. "I'll visit them once we get back."

Nell's gaze jerked to his face. "No."

Black's eyebrows rose. "I beg your pardon?"

"I don't want you to go to the West Quarter. It's too dangerous."

"I'll be careful."

"You were careful today, and you almost got a knife between your ribs!"

Black put down his wineglass. "Miss Wrotham—"

"I don't want you going to the West Quarter any more than you want me going there," Nell told him. "And if I've heeded *your* wishes with regard to my safety, I hope that you'll heed mine."

They matched gazes for a long moment. Black's face was perfectly expressionless. Nell wondered what was going through his mind. Would he tell her that she was just a female, that he knew better than she did, that he'd do as he wished?

Black inclined his head slightly. "Very well."

Surprise held her motionless for a moment, and then she said, "You won't go to the West Quarter? Or Cricklepit Street?"

"I won't go unaccompanied. Will that set your mind at rest?"

Nell considered this for several seconds, and then nodded.

Black didn't pick up his wineglass again and relax back in his chair; instead, he stayed as he was, leaning slightly forward, his gaze intent on her face. "Miss Wrotham . . . will you marry me?"

Oh, God, not this again. Nell's thoughts scattered in panic. She put down her glass jerkily, almost knocking it over. She didn't want to hurt him. *If only he'd stop asking . . .*

An idea sprang into her head between one blink of her eyelids and the next. A shockingly scandalous idea—but one that she knew would work, because if there was one thing she'd learned about Mordecai Black it was that he would never ruin a woman.

Nell bit the inside of her lip. *Dare I?*

The knot in her stomach tied itself even tighter. She stared at Black. He stared back at her.

The silence between them grew, along with her panic.

"Miss Wrotham?"

If there was ever a time to put her idea into action, it was now . . . but Nell discovered that she hadn't the courage. "Why?" she blurted instead. "Why *me?*" And then she added: "And don't tell me it's because you saw me riding in Richmond Park or that we danced together once. Those aren't reasons to marry."

"Aren't they?"

"No!"

Black was silent for several seconds, then he leaned back in his chair. "I don't know if you recall, but last year, before the Season had fully started, you had an altercation with a jarvey."

Nell stiffened in shock. "I beg your pardon?"

"In Halfmoon Street," Black said. "Outside the Dalrymples' house. I imagine you'd just arrived in London."

Nell found herself unable to speak, unable to confirm his guess. She stared at him, aghast.

"The jarvey had almost run down a child, one of those urchins who peddle goods door to door. I was too far away to see what he had in his tray. Ribbons, perhaps. Or brushes."

Nell moistened her lips. "Blacking," she managed to say. "Blacking and bootlaces."

Black's eyes met hers for a long moment. "You remember."

Nell nodded.

"Then you know what happened next."

She nodded again. The jarvey had jumped down from his box in a fury of fright, grabbed the boy by the scruff of his neck, and given him a fierce thrashing.

"He was almost as large as me, that jarvey, a big brute of a man, and yet you marched right up to him and dressed him down as if he was no larger than a child."

Nell stared at him, transfixed with embarrassment that he'd witnessed that scene.

"I couldn't hear what you said—I was too far away—but I saw the jarvey's face when he drove past me. He looked quite chastened."

Nell felt herself blush scarlet. She looked down at her table setting.

"And then your father dressed *you* down, if I'm not mistaken."

Nell grimaced. No, Black wasn't mistaken. She could remember her father's exact words, his cold, low-voiced rage.

I've never been so mortified in my life. How could you? Brangling with a jarvey as if you were a fishwife, not a lady!

She'd protested that the child had needed help, that the jarvey was hurting him.

Then you should have requested a footman to intervene, her father had told her coldly. *That's what servants are for.*

"Your father didn't seem pleased."

Nell huffed a humorless laugh, and glanced at Black. "No, not pleased."

"What did he say?"

"Oh . . ." Nell pulled a face. "He said that I'd behaved like a hoyden and it was a blessing no one had witnessed it, that it would have given them a disgust of my manners. And he said that I'd proven I was too immature to go about in Society and he had a good mind to send me home."

But her father hadn't sent her home. She *had* had her Season, and Roger had offered for her, and she'd seen her chance at freedom and grabbed it with both hands.

"Disgust? Yes, Roger would certainly have been disgusted. I, on the other hand, was not."

Another blush rushed to Nell's cheeks. She fixed her gaze on the tablecloth, mortified with herself. She'd learned to control her expression years ago, to present a cool, aloof, lady-like face to the world; it seemed so unfair that Mordecai Black could make her blush like a schoolgirl.

"I never pay the slightest attention to débutantes," Black said. "But I paid attention to you after that . . . and I liked what I saw."

Nell's cheeks grew even hotter.

"Is that reason enough for you, Miss Wrotham?"

The question made her glance at him—and having glanced, she was caught. Caught by his dark, dark eyes.

"Will you marry me?" he asked.

Nell's panic came surging back, and with it was longing. An intense, foolish longing to throw caution to the winds and accept his offer. To marry Mordecai Black.

Her heart thumped loudly in her chest. She had the sensation she'd had once before—dancing with him at the Moorecombs' ball—that she stood on edge of a fiery pit.

It was tempting to throw herself in and burn in the pleasures that waited there. Very tempting. But while part of her wanted to make that leap, the rest of her *didn't*. Because she knew that if she flung herself into that fire, it would consume her. She would burn, and the flames would be bright and marvelous while they lasted, but once they died down she would be left with ashes. Because Mordecai Black was an assertive, masterful, highhanded man. A man who would control her life, who would tell her what to do. A man she would grow to resent, perhaps even to hate.

And that was no good future for either of them.

Knowing it didn't make it any easier to refuse. Each time he asked she wavered a little more.

I must stop him asking. Before it was too late. Before her common sense eroded and she made that fatal fall.

Nell swallowed.

It was time to put her idea into action.

Courage, she told herself. Her palms were damp with perspiration, her lungs tight. She moistened her lips, took a shallow breath, and said, "No, I won't marry you. But I'll be your mistress."

The shock on Black's face would have been comical under other circumstances. He physically recoiled, as if a jack-in-a-box had sprung open in front of him, and then sat like a man turned to stone, staring at her, his mouth half open, clearly speechless.

Nell gripped her hands together and hoped that her assessment of his character had been accurate. A knot tied itself tightly in her belly.

After a moment, Black closed his mouth. He blinked and swallowed, still looking faintly stunned, and then an expression slowly formed on his face. It was one she'd seen on her father's often enough: affront. "No!" he said, almost an explosive sound. "Absolutely not!"

She'd been correct in her estimation of him. Nell's panic subsided. The knot in her stomach unraveled. She tried not to let her relief show. "Why not?"

"Why not?" Outrage gathered on Black's face like storm clouds. "Good God, how can you ask such a question? You know why not!"

"Because it would ruin me," Nell said. "But in the eyes of Society I'm already ruined—or at least tarnished— because of Sophia, and I've decided that if I'm going to be damned, I want it to be because of something I've actually *done*."

It wasn't quite true—she'd thought about it, but not decided upon it—but her voice held a convincing note of conviction. Nell lifted her chin slightly and tried to look bold and devil-may-care, even though she was neither of those things.

There was a long moment of silence while Black digested her words. His expression told her he found them unpalatable. "You'll be my mistress, but not my wife?" he said finally.

The knot in Nell's stomach clenched tightly again. "Yes."

"Why?"

Nell flushed. She found herself unable to look him in the eye. "Because I like you," she said, directing her gaze to a button on his waistcoat. "But I don't wish to marry you."

"Because you think I'm dictatorial?"

She nodded, and glanced at his face.

Black's jaw clenched. His nostrils flared. He looked angry and offended in equal measure.

"I think you're a very good man," Nell said. "You're kind and generous and honorable, but you're used to having your own way, and if we were to marry I think we'd argue."

Black considered her words for several seconds, and then unlocked his jaw. "Perhaps we wouldn't argue. Perhaps we'd discuss things. Perhaps we'd compromise."

Nell ceded this with a nod. "Or perhaps we'd grow discontented with one another. Perhaps we'd come to regret our marriage."

His lips compressed. Muscles bunched in his jaw.

"We're both strong-minded, Mr. Black. We both like to make our own decisions."

"For heaven's sake!" he burst out. "Who do you think I am? I'm not like your father! I don't want to put you in a cage. I want to set you *free*."

Nell's throat constricted. *He truly means it.*

She looked down at her plate, shaken, and listened to Black's words ring in her ears—and for a moment the yearning to accept what he offered was so intense that she almost changed her mind. And then she thought, *But marriage is forever—and what if it doesn't work? What if we grow to hate each other?*

She raised her gaze to his face. "Right now I am free." Her voice was apologetic. "And I wish to remain that way."

Black's jaw clenched again.

"I'm sorry," Nell said. "I do like you very much."

"But not enough to marry."

"I like you *too* much to marry you."

He frowned at her.

"I like you too much to marry you," Nell said again. "Because I think I'd make you unhappy." And then she repeated her shocking offer, the one that would stop his nightly proposals: "I'll be your mistress if you'll have me, but not your wife."

Black stared at her for almost a full minute, while her heart beat high in her throat and she grew tense with fear that she'd misjudged him. "No," he said finally. "I won't ruin you."

Nell exhaled in shaky relief. Her tension melted away. Gratitude welled in her chest. She almost smiled at him. *Thank you.* "You're a good man, Mordecai Black." She reached across the table and touched his clenched hand lightly with her fingertips, and felt a pang of sorrow. *I'm sorry I can't give you what you want.* Then she pushed back her chair and stood. "Good night."

Chapter Fourteen

MORDECAI HAD HAD BETTER NIGHTS. His brain chewed on Miss Wrotham's words, gnawed them down to tiny fragments, spat them out.

Good. Kind. Generous. Dictatorial.

It wasn't the first time she'd called him kind. But *dictatorial* clearly outweighed *kind* in Miss Wrotham's lexicon. And—damn it—he *wasn't* dictatorial. He didn't want to control her life, didn't want to curb and constrain her; he wanted to help her spread her wings.

You're used to having your own way. I think we'd argue.

I like you too much to marry you.

I'll be your mistress if you'll have me, but not your wife.

Mordecai tossed, he turned, he threw off his sheets, he kneaded his pillow into a more comfortable shape. Finally he gave up trying to sleep and just stared at the shadowy ceiling.

I'll be your mistress.

Years ago he'd sworn an oath to himself: Never ruin a woman. It was one of the tenets he lived his life by. Every *affaire* he'd ever had had been carefully built around that rule. His lovers had become notorious, but they'd gained cachet from that notoriety.

Eleanor Wrotham didn't possess rank and wealth and social prominence. She wasn't an aristocratic widow with a string of lovers to her bow. An *affaire* with him wouldn't bring her cachet; it would bring her disgrace.

She was the woman he wanted to marry and she was inviting him to *ruin* her?

The irony of it should have made him laugh—but Mordecai had never felt less like laughing. Frustration bunched in his muscles. If he were in London, if it were daylight, he'd go to Gentleman Jackson's Saloon for a bout with the great champion and he'd fight until he was sweating and panting and barely able to stand upright. But he wasn't in London, it wasn't daylight, and there was no one he could spar with, no way of releasing the tension in his body. All he could do was lie in his rumpled bed and stare up at the ceiling and stew in his frustration.

He ran through the conversation in his head for the dozenth time: his offer of marriage, her counterproposal, his vehement refusal. He heard the words ring in his ears, saw Eleanor Wrotham's nervous bravado, the way she'd braced herself, shoulders and jaw tense—and then saw the tension melt away and relief light her face.

Relief that he'd *rejected* her proposal.

Mordecai's eyes narrowed.

Had she been playing him?

He thought about this for several minutes—Eleanor Wrotham's tension when she'd made her offer; her relief when he'd refused—and came to a conclusion: she *had* been playing him.

Mordecai stared up at the ceiling in stunned disbelief.

Eleanor Wrotham had played him? The disbelief was followed by outrage . . . and on the heels of outrage was admiration. She had *played* him.

His imagination gave him a glimpse of a chessboard—black and white squares, black and white chess pieces. He saw the white queen dart across the board in a bold bluff, saw the black king topple over, defeated.

Mordecai mentally picked up the king and set it back on its feet. They hadn't reached checkmate yet.

He kneaded his pillow meditatively and contemplated his next move.

He could do what she clearly wished him to do: stop proposing.

He could continue as he had been.

Or . . . he could call her bluff.

Such a move would cast the game into disarray, but it might win him what he wanted: Eleanor Wrotham as his wife.

The more Mordecai thought about it, the more he realized that he'd been handed an opportunity. A golden opportunity.

He could continue telling Miss Wrotham that they were meant for each other—or he could call her bluff and *show* her.

An affair. Sexual intimacy as a prelude to marriage.

He'd have to be discreet, damned discreet, because he'd rather cut out his organs than be the man who publicly ruined Eleanor Wrotham, but . . .

If he called her bluff—if she didn't back down—if she became his lover—if they spent time together—days, weeks—if he *proved* to her that he wasn't dictatorial, that he was prepared to compromise instead of argue, that they could be happy together—surely she'd change her mind and marry him?

Put like that, the decision made itself.

He would propose one last time. He'd call Eleanor Wrotham's bluff and *seduce* her into marriage.

HE MUST HAVE FALLEN ASLEEP, because all of a sudden it was daylight and his footman was in the room. Mordecai blinked his eyes drowsily and yawned—and remembered the decision he'd come to last night. He was suddenly wide awake.

"Good morning, sir."

"Good morning, Walter." Mordecai pushed back the bedclothes and sat up. The decision that had seemed so clear-cut in the middle of the night was less so now.

What if something went wrong? What if he somehow ruined Eleanor Wrotham?

I can't do it.

But he *had* to. This was his opportunity. Handed to him by Miss Wrotham herself.

Mordecai sat amid the tangled bedsheets, caught between conviction that he'd chosen the right move and an equally strong certainty that he hadn't—and then he thought of the endgame: marriage to Eleanor Wrotham.

How much was he willing to risk for that?

The answer was: everything.

Mordecai flung back the sheets and climbed out of bed, full of determination. *Tonight I call her bluff.*

THEY STARTED THEIR search for Sophia Wrotham's midwife in St. Leonard parish, then went to Heavitree and Pinhoe, back to Wonford, on to Topsham, trawling through Exeter's outlying parishes, each midwife giving Miss Wrotham more names to add to her list.

Midmorning became noon became early afternoon. They ate a light luncheon at a tavern, then went to Alphington, on the other side of the River Exe. Personally, Mordecai doubted Sophia Wrotham had found her way to Alphington, but he held his tongue.

Alphington was a pleasant little parish, with a village green and cottages with thatched roofs. The midwife wasn't at home.

A gnarled old man sitting on his doorstep said, "You want the rabbit catcher?"

Mordecai turned to him. "Yes. Do you know where she is?"

"Gone to help Missus Turpin, she has."

"Mrs. Turpin?"

"Farmer Turpin's wife."

The man was as wrinkled as a walnut, his eyes rheumy with age, but his directions were concise: Farmer Turpin lived half a mile out of Alphington, on the road to Shillingford Abbot.

Back in the carriage, Miss Wrotham said, "Rabbit catcher?"

"Midwife," Mordecai said.

"I *had* guessed that."

Mordecai glanced at her. She was looking at him with an expression halfway between curiosity and puzzlement.

"What?" he asked.

"It was cant, wasn't it?"

He nodded.

"Do most gentlemen know cant?"

Mordecai shook his head.

"How do *you* know cant?"

Mordecai shrugged. "I learned it as a child."

A crease appeared between her eyebrows. "Last night you said you learned to fight in the streets."

"I did."

"As a child?"

Mordecai nodded.

Miss Wrotham hesitated, and then said, "But your father was an earl and your mother a governess. I would have thought your childhood was as far removed from cant and streets as mine was."

Mordecai gave a snort of amusement. "No."

The crease on her brow deepened. "I don't understand."

It was Mordecai's turn to hesitate. His childhood was something he had never discussed with anyone.

Miss Wrotham colored faintly, and looked down at her lap. "I beg your pardon, I don't mean to pry. It's none of my business."

No, it wasn't her business, but if she was going to be his wife then she had more right than anyone in England to ask about his past.

"My parents' liaison was very brief," Mordecai said. "My mother was a handsome woman, but her nature was . . ." He turned words over in his head, and discarded *peevish* and *melancholy*. "Discontented. Father tired of her quickly, but she was pregnant, so he did the honorable thing and arranged for an annuity—two hundred pounds a year. As far as he was concerned, that was the end of the matter. He never expected to see my mother again—or to meet me."

Miss Wrotham nodded, her eyes on his face.

"My mother was very bitter about it. Father was a widower at that point and I think she'd half expected him to marry her—she was a vicar's daughter, so respectable, if not wellborn—but instead he removed her from his life." Mordecai shrugged. "I don't blame him for doing that; my mother was a difficult woman. It was her nature to be dissatisfied with everything."

"She was dissatisfied with you?"

"You could say that." He looked away from Miss Wrotham, out the carriage window, and remembered the time when he was six years old and his mother had said to him, *I wish you were dead.* Then he gave himself a mental shake and turned back to Miss Wrotham. "She blamed me. She said it was my fault she was ruined."

"*Your* fault?"

"If she hadn't fallen pregnant with me, she wouldn't have been ruined."

"But it was hardly *your* fault she fell pregnant!"

Mordecai shrugged. "No, but my father wasn't there and I was, so she blamed me."

"But she had a *choice,*" Miss Wrotham said hotly. "She *chose* to have a liaison with your father. She ruined herself!"

Mordecai shrugged again.

Miss Wrotham pressed her lips tightly together. She looked as militant as a woman wearing a chestnut wig and spectacles could look.

"Mother couldn't bear the sight of me, so I lived mostly in the kitchen. And when I wasn't in the kitchen, I was out on the street."

"You said she hit you. Your mother."

"Whenever she saw me—which wasn't often. I took care to stay out of her way."

Her lips compressed further.

"It wasn't a bad childhood," Mordecai hastened to assure her. "I may have looked like a street urchin, but I never went hungry and I had a warm place to sleep."

"You looked like an urchin?"

Mordecai shrugged. "The cook did her best. She made me

take a bath once a month, and whenever I grew out of my clothes she marched me down to the used-clothes shop and bought me larger ones."

"Used-clothes shop?" Miss Wrotham said, clearly appalled.

"Practical, for a child, don't you think? Why buy new clothes when they're just going to get torn and dirty?"

"I'd call it miserly, rather than practical," Miss Wrotham said tartly. "Your mother had two hundred pounds per annum. She could have afforded to dress you properly!"

That would presuppose that she cared enough to, Mordecai thought—but didn't say. "I preferred the used clothes. What boy wants to wear starched shirts and tight collars?"

Miss Wrotham didn't look as if she agreed.

Mordecai cast about for something to make her smile. "The cook was a good woman. She used to slip me treats and call me Ducks. I thought that was my name—Ducks—until I was old enough to know better."

Miss Wrotham didn't smile.

"I was quite happy," Mordecai said. "I enjoyed playing in the streets. I learned some very useful skills."

"Such as fighting."

"Such as fighting." He'd learned that hesitation was fatal, that you had to hit hard and fast—and that when you were outnumbered, you could still win through sheer ferocity. A lesson that had stood him in good stead at Eton.

Miss Wrotham regarded him gravely.

"And before you decide to pity me, remember that Father took me away when I was eight, and since then I've had more money—and more clothes—than any person needs."

Miss Wrotham considered this statement for several seconds, while the carriage rocked and swayed, and then asked, "Why did he change his mind about you?"

Mordecai grimaced, and glanced out the window again. A

hedgerow flashed past. "He changed his mind because his circumstances changed." He looked back at Miss Wrotham. "How much do you know about my father?"

"He had more than one wife. And his legitimate sons all died in childhood."

Mordecai nodded. "He had three wives, and four sons— legitimate, that is—and six daughters."

"How did the sons die?"

"Three of sickness, one by drowning."

"And his first two wives?"

"One died from fever, the other died in childbirth."

Miss Wrotham nodded. Her expression was somber. "Your father experienced a lot of loss in his life."

"Yes."

"He came for you after his fourth son died?"

"Yes."

She frowned. "He saw you as a substitute? A replacement?"

"No." Mordecai shook his head. "Not at all. He came for me because . . ." He frowned, too, and tried to find the right words. "Father was very patriarchal. He had no interest in his daughters. His sons were his pride and joy, his purpose in life."

Miss Wrotham's lips compressed slightly. She suddenly looked very like a duchess.

"I don't hold his views," Mordecai said hastily. "Absolutely not! A father should be as proud of his daughters as he is of his sons."

Miss Wrotham eyed him through her spectacle lenses, and said nothing.

"Daughters *aren't* less than sons," Mordecai said firmly.

She must have heard the sincerity in his voice; her expression relaxed fractionally. She was no longer a duchess.

"My father wanted a son—*needed* a son—and his third

wife proved barren, so . . . he came for me." He fell silent, remembering the first time he'd seen his father. A swell. Bang up to the knocker. A man as out of place on a Shoreditch backstreet as the Prince Regent would be in Seven Dials. "I was in the alley behind the house when he came, playing marbles in the dirt. He recognized me immediately." Mordecai stroked the bridge of his nose—the same great beak his father had had. "He came over and asked if he could play, too."

Miss Wrotham's eyebrows rose. "He did?"

Mordecai nodded. "He was good, too. Almost won. Kneeling in the dirt in all his finery." He grunted another laugh. "And the whole time he played, he asked questions. What was my name? How old was I? How had I got my black eye? Did I like school? By the time the game was over he knew me inside and out."

"How had you got your black eye?" Miss Wrotham asked. "Fighting?"

"Not that time."

"Your mother?"

He nodded.

She frowned, as his father had done. "What did he say when you told him that?"

"He said nothing to me, but he had a *lot* to say to Mother on that subject later. And about my schooling."

"What about your schooling?"

"I hadn't had any. Couldn't read or write."

"What?"

The shock on her face made him laugh.

"But . . . your mother was a *governess*. Surely she understood the value of education?"

Mordecai shrugged. "She didn't want me. Why would she educate me?"

Miss Wrotham stared at him, her lips parted, apparently speechless with indignation.

"Father was even more outraged than you are, believe me. He gave my mother a fine raking down."

"What did she have to say for herself?"

"Not a lot. It was midafternoon; she was rather ripe."

"Ripe?"

"Drunk."

Miss Wrotham's eyebrows climbed her forehead. "Your mother was *intoxicated*? In the middle of the afternoon?"

"She was disappointed with her life, so she drank." Mordecai shrugged again. "I don't know what your mother smelled like, but mine smelled of port wine."

Miss Wrotham was silent for a moment, while the carriage jolted and lurched over rough ground, then she said, "My mother died when I was six months old. I don't remember what she smelled like."

"I'm sorry," Mordecai said.

She shook her head, dismissing his sympathy. "My childhood was perfectly happy. My stepmother loved me as if I were her own daughter." She hesitated, and then said, "Your stepmother . . . Roger said she didn't like you."

Mordecai grimaced. "No, she didn't. Poor woman. She couldn't produce a child—which was grief enough in itself—and then my father dragged home a by-blow and expected her to look after him."

"Was she unkind to you?"

"Unkind? No. She was a very well-bred woman. She did her duty to me punctiliously."

"And your half sisters? I was given to understand that . . . that—"

"That they loathe me? Yes, they do. And quite frankly, I don't blame them. They were always second best because of their sex—and they knew it—and then their brothers died and Father brought *me* home—filthy and half-feral and illegitimate —and lavished all his attention on me."

"But that was hardly *your* fault."

Mordecai shrugged. "No, but I can understand why they hate me. Father had his flaws—and the way he treated his daughters was one of them. All children deserve to be loved."

"Your father loved you?"

"Yes." But his father's love had been tainted with guilt. In fact the very last words his father had spoken on his deathbed were *I'm so glad I found you,* and *I'm sorry it took me so long.* The twin emotions that had shaped their relationship: love and guilt.

"You must have been happy that he came for you."

"Happy? Not really."

Her eyebrows rose again. "But surely you were glad to leave your mother?"

"Shoreditch was all I knew. I didn't want to leave. And I most certainly did *not* want to become a gentleman."

"You didn't?"

"When I say I was half-feral, I'm not exaggerating: I *was*. I didn't want to wear clean clothes, I didn't want to mind my manners or speak properly or learn to read and write. It took a great deal of patience on Father's part to mold me into a gentleman."

"He succeeded."

"On the outside, yes. Inside . . . there'll always be a bit of Shoreditch in me."

The admission didn't appear to disgust her. She tilted her head to one side and studied him. Could those sharp eyes see the urchin in him?

"But it's not all your father's influence, is it?" Miss Wrotham said. "You went to Eton. And Cambridge."

Mordecai sat up straighter on the squab seat. "Eton? Good God, that just about undid everything Father taught me!"

Her brow creased. "How so?"

Dereham's bastard. A taunt he must have heard a thousand times at Eton.

"I didn't fit in," Mordecai said.

"No?"

"No." Mordecai repressed a grimace. "Father had to move heaven and earth to get me in, and I was almost expelled after the second week."

Her eyes narrowed slightly behind the spectacles. He could see that she wanted to ask about his near expulsion, but instead she said, "How did he gain entry for you? I understood one's name had to be placed on the register at birth."

"His four other sons *were* on the register. Father argued that he was merely replacing one name with another—and then he paid for an addition to the library—and I was accepted."

The carriage slowed, made a turn to the right, and halted.

They climbed down into a farmyard. Mordecai saw a few hens, a goose, and a pig in a sty. The house was old and modest and built of stone, but someone had planted flowers along its front. The door stood open. Several wide-eyed and bashful children stared at them from inside. Mordecai guessed their ages as two, four, and six. They had bare feet and were almost as grubby as he'd been as a youngster, but they were also plump and bonny and none of them had any bruises that he could see.

A man stepped into the doorway, shooing the two oldest children away good-naturedly, picking up the youngest and settling her on his hip. He was in his late-twenties, unshaven and weary, but cheerful. "Can I help you?"

"We're looking for Mrs. Williams."

"The midwife? Aye, she's here." The man's face split into a grin. "Just delivered us a new bantling, God bless her."

"Congratulations," Mordecai said. "A boy or a girl?"

"Boy," the man said, beaming.

Farmer Turpin fetched Mrs. Williams to the door, and she took one glance at Miss Wrotham's sketch and shook her head. "No, I've never seen her."

She gave them another midwife's name to add to the list, in St. Thomas parish.

Miss Wrotham thanked her and tucked the sketch away again.

Farmer Turpin walked across to the carriage, still carrying his youngest daughter, and gave the coachman directions to St. Thomas.

Mordecai slipped the man a folded banknote before he turned away. "For the bantling."

Farmer Turpin blushed and looked almost as bashful as his children, but he didn't try to give the banknote back.

THE COACH TRUNDLED out to the road again, turned north, and picked up speed. Mordecai settled back in his seat and looked at Miss Wrotham. She was gazing out the window, a thoughtful frown on her face. Was she worrying about Farmer Turpin's barefooted children?

Mordecai opened his mouth to tell her that children were very happy without shoes on, especially in this hot weather, when she turned her head and looked at him and asked, "Why were you almost expelled from Eton?"

Mordecai blinked, and closed his mouth. His thoughts made an abrupt about-turn. "Uh . . . for fighting."

"You started a fight?"

"No."

Her eyebrows lifted in a silent question.

Mordecai shifted on the seat and then adjusted his cuffs, stalling, deciding how much to tell her, and then he thought, *What the hell, tell her it all.*

"I was a bastard, and all the boys knew it. Some of them took it into their heads to be offended by it. They were fairly unpleasant." He grimaced in memory. "But I'd grown up in Shoreditch, so when they shoved me, I shoved back—harder."

Miss Wrotham frowned. "Did they shove you metaphorically, or literally?"

"Both."

Her frown deepened.

"One day, a bunch of them surrounded me in the schoolyard. They wanted to beat some humility into me." Mordecai reran the words in his head, and amended them: "Three of them wanted to beat it into me, the rest were going to watch."

"Three against one?"

"Yes."

"But that's hardly fair!"

Mordecai grinned. Not a cheerful grin like Farmer Turpin's, but a sharp, feral grin. "No, they hadn't a chance."

Miss Wrotham blinked. Confusion crossed her face.

"I'd been outnumbered before, in Shoreditch—so I won that fight."

Miss Wrotham's confusion became more pronounced. "But *how?*"

"Ferocity," Mordecai said. "And fighting dirty." And a desperate berserker rage. "I broke Milburn's nose, knocked out Stibbington's front teeth, and kicked Cranwell so hard in the, er, nutmegs that it was a week before he could walk again."

Miss Wrotham didn't ask what nutmegs were.

"It was all over in less than a minute—except that it *wasn't* over, because as soon as Stibbington, Millburn, and Cranwell were down, their friends stepped forward. Eight of them." Mordecai grimaced. "Three I could handle. But eight?"

He remembered standing there, panting, hands clenched, blood roaring in his ears, knowing that however hard he fought he couldn't win, knowing he was about to get hurt, badly.

"And then Henry Wright pushed his way forward and said 'Hardly sporting, is it?' And he stood alongside me and put up his fists and he was ready to fight *with* me, not against me." Mordecai's throat tightened for a moment. He swallowed.

"That was the end of it?"

"The fight, yes. But Stibbington laid a complaint, said I'd attacked him—unprovoked—and demanded that I be expelled."

Miss Wrotham's expression became indignant. "He *what*?"

"It came to nothing. Henry went to the headmaster and told him how it had been, and a couple of others did, too, and in the end it was Stibbington who left Eton, not me."

Miss Wrotham eyed him for a long moment, and then said, "Did the bullying stop after that?"

"Yes." There had been whisperings behind his back, but no one had dared say anything to his face—and they'd certainly not dared to touch him.

"Were you happy there?"

Mordecai shrugged again. "Is anyone happy at school?"

"Why didn't your father tutor you at home?"

"I asked him to. He came to Eton after the fight—there was a furor over Stibbington losing his front teeth—and I begged him to take me away, but he said that if I left Eton it meant they'd won, and he wouldn't allow that. He spun me a boxing metaphor about each bout being easier to win than the last, and he was right: I had to fight for my place in Society, and Eton was the first round."

Miss Wrotham compressed her lips. She didn't look convinced.

"Father fought for me as much as he could, but there were battles *I* had to fight—and that was one of them. The *beau-monde*'s just like the Shoreditch backstreets. The same rules apply. If you back down, you lose face. And Father wouldn't let me back down."

"But an *eight*-year-old—"

"I was eleven when I went to Eton. I had to learn to read and write, remember? And then there was the Latin and Greek and French." Mordecai pulled a face. "Father made sure I had a good grounding before he let me go. He wanted me to succeed, not fail."

She still looked dubious.

"He did the right thing," Mordecai said firmly. "Eton was difficult, but Cambridge was much less so, and by the time I was old enough to take my place in Society, I'd won all the battles I needed to win." And then he hastened to add: "Metaphorical battles, that is. Eton was the only time I ever fought literally."

Miss Wrotham still looked unconvinced. "But did you *want* to take your place in Society?"

Mordecai hesitated . . . and then hesitated some more. "Yes," he said, finally. "Mostly because Father wanted it, but partly because I wanted to *win*. I wanted to prove I could do it."

This answer made her frown again. "Do you actually *like* polite society, Mr. Black?"

"Not particularly. Now that Father's dead, I doubt I'll spend much time in London."

"No?"

"I prefer my Devonshire estate."

She glanced out the window. "We're in Devonshire now."

"Yes."

Mordecai waited for her to say *I'd like to see your estate,* but she didn't. Instead, she sank into thoughtful silence.

Mordecai examined her profile. Eleanor Wrotham, hidden beneath Mrs. Trussell-Quimby's spectacles and chestnut wig. And then he looked more closely at the wig.

"One of your hairpins is coming loose."

"Oh?" Miss Wrotham removed her bonnet and felt along her hairline.

"Allow me," Mordecai said. He shifted closer to her on the seat, so that their legs were almost touching, and peeled off one of his gloves. He reached out and removed the errant hairpin near her temple. His fingertips touched her skin. He saw a blush bloom in Miss Wrotham's cheek. "Hold still," he said, and shifted a little closer. Now their legs were touching.

Her blush deepened.

The carriage lurched and swayed. Mordecai carefully took hold of Miss Wrotham's chin with his gloved hand, steadying them both, and slid the hairpin back into place.

A single gleaming, nut-brown strand of hair had escaped from beneath the wig. Mordecai captured it and gently tucked it behind her ear. Then he released her chin and sat back. "All done."

"Thank you," Miss Wrotham said. Her voice was cool, but her cheeks looked very hot.

Mordecai suppressed a smile.

Eleanor Wrotham replaced the bonnet hastily. Her fingers fumbled as she retied the ribbons.

Mordecai pulled on his glove and settled into his corner. He gazed out the window and hummed silently to himself.

From St. Thomas parish they went to St. David's Down and then on to St. Sidwell. It was dusk by the time they returned to Exeter. The carriage rattled into the inn's yard. It was a relief to step down and stretch his legs. Mordecai inhaled deeply. The air was warm, and thick with smells.

"Dinner in an hour?" he asked Miss Wrotham.

She nodded.

Upstairs, Mordecai caught sight of himself in the mirror. His clothes were as creased as the marriage license in his pocket. Stubble shadowed his jaw. *You'll have to do better than that, old boy,* he told himself.

He washed and shaved. A jittery sense of anticipation built inside him while he plied the razor. He almost cut himself twice.

Mordecai donned fresh clothes, headed down one flight of stairs, and halted at the door to the private parlor. His scruples marshaled themselves like a bristling row of lancers on a battlefield, blocking his path, defending Miss Wrotham's virtue and reputation.

Mordecai ignored them. He was *not* going to ruin Eleanor Wrotham. He'd be discreet. No one would ever know of their affair. Moreover, his intent was honorable. This was seduction with marriage as the endgame.

Mordecai touched two fingertips to the license in his pocket, took a deep breath, and opened the door to the private parlor.

Chapter Fifteen

SEDUCTION WAS ALL VERY WELL, but first one had to dine. Mordecai ate with only part of his attention on his food—he noticed the ox rumps and the Rhenish cream, but little else. Each bite brought him closer to the end of the meal, to his offer of marriage and Miss Wrotham's counterproposal—and his reply.

He found himself growing nervous—which would have amused him in other circumstances. He was Mordecai Black. People were nervous of *him*, not the other way around. In fact, he couldn't remember the last time he'd been nervous. Eton, perhaps? And then he *did* remember: he'd been nervous when he'd asked Mr. Wrotham for his daughter's hand in marriage. He'd been nervous the first time he'd proposed to Miss Wrotham. And the second time. And the third. Last night he hadn't been nervous—he'd been fatalistic, already knowing what her answer would be—but he was nervous again tonight. His heart was beating faster than it usually did. He thought he might be sweating slightly.

"—tomorrow?"

Mordecai blinked, and dragged his attention to Miss Wrotham, seated across from him wearing her wig and spectacles. "I beg your pardon?"

"I asked about tomorrow."

"Tomorrow?" Mordecai tried to marshal his wits. "Uh . . . tomorrow I'll speak with the midwives in the West Quarter."

Alarm flickered across her face. "You promised you wouldn't go there alone."

"I shan't be alone. I'll take Phelps and Walter with me."

Miss Wrotham bit her lip, and then said, "If you take them, may I come, too?"

"No."

"But surely it would be safe—"

"No," he said again, firmly.

She frowned at him.

Mordecai laid down his knife and fork. "If I take you with me, I'd be placing us all at a disadvantage."

"How so?"

"It would divide my attention. I'd be worrying about you."

Miss Wrotham drew breath as if to argue.

Mordecai held up a hand to forestall her. "It's all very well to tell me that I needn't worry about you, but I wouldn't be able to help it. And if something happened—if it came to a fight and I was worried for your safety, if my attention was diverted for even one second . . ." He shrugged. "Hesitation can be fatal."

Miss Wrotham closed her mouth.

"I'm not being dictatorial," Mordecai told her. "I'm being *honest*. Phelps and Walter can hold their own in a fight; you can't. Having you with us would be a hindrance."

Her gaze lowered to her plate. She looked so crestfallen that Mordecai said, "And besides, it would draw more attention to have a lady with us. We'd more likely be targeted by pickpockets and cutpurses."

She glanced up. "If I were a man, would you take me?"

"If you were a man and you knew how to fight, yes."

Miss Wrotham's mouth tucked in at the corners. Mordecai interpreted that as frustration, or perhaps exasperation.

He waited a moment, but she made no further comment.

They finished their meal in silence, but it wasn't a brooding silence. He thought Miss Wrotham was sifting through her thoughts in much the same way that he was sifting through his.

"Is there anything I can do tomorrow to look for Sophia?" she said, when they'd both laid down their knives and forks.

Mordecai considered this for several seconds, and then shook his head.

"So I'm just to sit here while you go to the West Quarter?" Frustration was clearly audible in her voice.

"I'm sorry." He folded his napkin and placed it beside his plate. "I suggest you visit the cathedral and look at the shops on the High Street—but I must ask you not to go further afield than that. You don't know which parts of the city are safe."

"The cathedral." Miss Wrotham threw down her napkin; not in anger, but frustration.

"I'm sorry," Mordecai said again.

Miss Wrotham blew out a breath. "Oh, if only I were a man!"

I'm glad you're not, Mordecai thought.

"Once this is over, I'll teach you the fundamentals of boxing," he offered.

Miss Wrotham blinked. She was silent for several seconds, while the frustration on her face transformed into surprise. "You will?"

"If you'd like to learn."

She reached for her discarded napkin, smoothed it out,

and doubled it over once, then twice, then a third time, slowly and methodically. "It wouldn't be at all the thing," she said, once the napkin was perfectly folded. Mordecai thought he heard a wistful note in her voice.

"Who cares?" He leaned forward, his elbows on the table. "If you wish to learn how to box, why shouldn't you? If you want to ride like a man, why shouldn't you?"

Miss Wrotham hesitated. He saw the conflict on her face.

"I'll teach you how to fence, too, if you like. And shoot."

Her eyes narrowed. "Are you trying to bribe me into marrying you, Mr. Black?"

"What? No! I just thought you might like to learn. It has nothing to do with whether you marry me or not." He hesitated—should he charge ahead, or retreat? *Charge ahead.* "But since you brought the subject up . . . will you marry me?"

She pushed the napkin aside. "Must you keep asking me that?"

"Yes," Mordecai said.

Exasperation crossed her face. "I thought I made myself perfectly clear last night. I'm prepared to be your mistress, but not your wife."

"You did make yourself clear." Mordecai thought of the marriage license in his pocket. He took a deep breath and said, "I accept your offer."

Shock and astonishment chased themselves across Miss Wrotham's face before her expression congealed into frozen disbelief. "I beg your pardon?" she said faintly.

"I accept your offer."

Panic flared on her face.

"But if you wish to change your mind, that's perfectly all right," Mordecai said hastily.

There was a long, taut moment of silence. The panic on Miss Wrotham's face faded. She opened her mouth as if to speak, and then closed it again. Mordecai found himself holding his breath. Half of him hoped she would withdraw her offer—and the other half hoped she wouldn't.

The silence lengthened. And lengthened further.

Mordecai leaned back in his chair and tried to look neutral. This had to be Eleanor Wrotham's decision. He couldn't push her one way or the other, *wouldn't* push her.

She was thinking—thinking hard—her expression that of a person trying to balance a difficult equation.

Mordecai had a fairly good idea what the equation looked like. Propriety, prudence, and caution would be on one side; curiosity, recklessness, and a desire to thumb her nose at Society would be on the other. And somewhere in the middle —the unknown element in the equation—was physical attraction. How strongly was Eleanor Wrotham attracted to him?

If the answer was *very,* then she'd be more likely to risk an affair. If it was *not much,* she wouldn't.

She was a woman prepared to take risks. She'd never have left her great aunt's home otherwise—not with so little money, not with just a single valise—and the longer the pause drew, the longer it took her to decide, the more likely it was that she would decide to take another risk.

After nearly a full minute of silence Miss Wrotham said, "Very well. Let us have an affair."

Chapter Sixteen

MORDECAI FOUND HIMSELF caught between relief and dismay. His stomach made an odd seesawing motion, as if it lifted and fell at the same time. He opened his mouth—and closed it again as the door swung open.

Two serving-men entered the room and began clearing away the meal. Miss Wrotham's utterance seemed to hang in the air. *Let. Us. Have. An. Affair.* Mordecai wondered that the servants didn't feel the weight and magnitude of those words in the room, didn't sense the consequences gathering like thunderclouds over the table.

He sat in silence while the serving-men removed the plates and cutlery, removed the dishes, removed the tablecloth, refilled their wineglasses. He was acutely aware of Miss Wrotham seated across from him—and he knew she was equally aware of him. *Let us have an affair.* His stomach seesawed again.

The servants finally left the room.

"We'll be very careful," Mordecai told her, once the door had closed. "No one will find out."

Miss Wrotham lifted her chin in what he recognized as bravado. "I don't care if anyone finds out."

"I do," Mordecai said.

Her chin lowered.

"My father ruined my mother—and I promise I will *not* do that to you."

Her gaze was fixed on his face. "You said there are ways to avoid pregnancy."

An image flashed into his mind: he and Eleanor Wrotham making love, her pale legs wrapped around his hips. The image was so vivid that for a split second Mordecai actually *felt* his cock sinking into her smooth, soft, wet heat. The muscles in his groin tightened painfully. So did the muscles in his throat. Mordecai shoved the image aside. "You won't become pregnant." His voice came out slightly rough.

"Will you use a . . . a sheath?"

"No." He'd used one with Cécile until he'd learned to control his ejaculation, but not since. They were damned uncomfortable.

Miss Wrotham swallowed, and nodded, and glanced at the sofa, and Mordecai had a sudden flash of insight: it wasn't pregnancy Miss Wrotham was afraid of at this moment; it was physical intimacy between them—specifically, him tumbling her on the sofa and hastily relieving her of her virginity.

Mordecai leaned back in his chair, settling into it, slouching. He reached for his wineglass and sipped. *See? We're in no hurry.*

He thought Miss Wrotham's shoulders relaxed fractionally.

Mordecai didn't relax. Underneath the slouch, he was ridiculously tense. This wasn't how he usually embarked on an affair. He eased into his liaisons. There'd be days of circling each other, days of flirtation and laughter and growing attraction, so that when the moment came, when they found themselves alone in a dark alcove or secluded bower, the first kiss was spontaneous and natural and something they both wanted.

But he knew that when he kissed Miss Wrotham tonight, it wouldn't be spontaneous. It would be deliberate. Because while he most certainly wasn't going to deflower her on the sofa, he *was* going to kiss her on it. He wanted her to leave this parlor hungry for more—specifically, hungry for *him*. His kisses. His body in her bed. And given time, his ring on her finger.

Mordecai sipped his wine and wondered how to progress from sitting across the table from each other to kissing on the sofa.

The answer was: *Carefully.*

"I'd like it if you would call me Mordecai," he said.

Miss Wrotham moistened her lips, and nodded. She looked very like a duchess at this moment—and he had another flash of insight: when she was nervous, she retreated into haughtiness. "You may call me Nell."

Nell. The name her sister called her. A name that wasn't haughty at all. Giving him permission to use it seemed somehow terribly significant. An intimacy. Mordecai felt himself grow tenser. *Don't make a mull of this.* He searched for a light, smooth, reassuring comment—something amusing perhaps—and came up blank. He, whose skill with women was legendary, could literally think of nothing to say.

For a moment he debated telling her that, saying *I'm almost as nervous about this as you are*—and then he decided it wouldn't help matters. He and Miss Wrotham needed to get past this first kiss, and the best way to do that was to behave as if it was nothing to be nervous about. *Just get it over with,* he told himself. *Everything will be easier afterwards.*

"Why don't we sit on the sofa?" he suggested.

Miss Wrotham stiffened slightly.

"Just sit," Mordecai said, and then honesty compelled him to add: "And maybe kiss. But nothing more."

"Kiss?"

"Lovers generally kiss," Mordecai said mildly.

Miss Wrotham swallowed again, and cast a jerky glance at the sofa, and nodded.

Mordecai pushed back his chair and walked around the table to her, moving leisurely, trying to tell her with his movements that she had nothing to be afraid of.

Miss Wrotham became even more haughty. Her chin lifted slightly.

Mordecai tried not to loom over her, but it was impossible not to loom when one was six foot five inches tall. He held out his hand and gave her a smile that he hoped was both friendly and reassuring.

Miss Wrotham stood.

Mordecai led her across the parlor to the sofa. It felt . . . weirdly familiar, as if he was escorting her out onto a dance floor, not towards a settee to be kissed—and then he remembered: he *had* held her hand like this once before.

"Remember the Moorecombs' ball?" he said.

"Yes."

It had been the only time he'd ever asked Eleanor Wrotham to dance.

"I called on your father the next day, asked his permission to address you."

Her gaze flicked to him, and stayed there for a moment before lowering. She colored faintly. "He didn't tell me."

"No." But Mordecai didn't have it in himself be angry at

Mr. Wrotham anymore, not when he and Eleanor Wrotham were standing in front of the sofa they were about to kiss on.

He was no longer nervous, not now that he was *doing* rather than *thinking.* It was easy to tie oneself in knots if one thought too much. Eleanor Wrotham was still nervous, though. Her face looked very pale and haughty beneath the chestnut wig.

"Relax," Mordecai said. "I'm not going to do anything you won't like." And then he drew her down to sit on the sofa alongside him.

The sofa was a solid piece of furniture with sturdy lion-paw legs and a well-padded seat upholstered in green twill. It was wide enough for them both to sit on without touching.

"Let's get rid of these," Mordecai said, and reached out and gently removed the gold-rimmed spectacles that were perched on her nose. He folded them and tucked them in his breast pocket, alongside the marriage license.

Color rose in Miss Wrotham's cheeks. She didn't look haughty any longer; she looked like a woman about to be kissed for the first time, blushing, faintly flustered, too shy to look him in the eye.

"Did Roger never kiss you?"

Eleanor Wrotham's blush deepened. "He kissed me on the cheek once."

Mordecai repressed a snort. *Lord, what a fool Roger is.* He touched her cheek with a fingertip. "Here?"

"Yes," she said, and blushed even more deeply.

Mordecai trailed his fingers lightly over her skin—smooth, warm, soft—along her cheekbone and down the line of her jaw. He rested his fingertips under her chin, ready to tilt her face to him. "But never here?" He brushed his thumb lightly over her lower lip, and felt her quiver.

"No," she whispered.

"Has anyone else?"

Eleanor Wrotham stiffened. Her eyes lifted to meet his—navy blue and offended. "Of course not!"

Mordecai smiled at her. "I wouldn't have minded." But even though that was the truth, an atavistic part of him was rejoicing. He was the first. The first, last, and *only* man to kiss Eleanor Wrotham.

"Relax," he told her again, and then he tilted her chin up and laid his lips on hers, softly, lightly, fleetingly.

Eleanor Wrotham became very still. He thought she might have stopped breathing for a moment.

Mordecai kissed her lightly again—and a third time—and then he licked her lower lip, the barest touch of his tongue, teasing her, tempting her.

She shivered.

Mordecai bit her lower lip very gently with his teeth.

Eleanor Wrotham shivered again, almost convulsively.

Mordecai whispered, "Open your mouth."

Eleanor Wrotham hesitated, and then did as he bade, parting her lips slightly.

Mordecai nipped her lower lip again, licked where he'd bitten—and then let his tongue steal inside her mouth, not an invasion but a brief exploration, tasting her inner lip, feeling the smoothness of her teeth. He did it a second time, then drew back and looked at her.

Definitely not a duchess.

Eleanor Wrotham's cheeks were flushed, her lower lip sweetly red where he'd nipped it.

"Kiss me back," Mordecai said.

"I beg your pardon?"

"Kiss me back."

Shyness bloomed on her face. Her gaze dropped to the buttons on his waistcoat.

Mordecai laughed softly, and drew her closer, and whispered in her ear, "No one's watching."

For a moment she was stiff and shy in his arms, and he kissed her cheek—where Roger had once kissed her—and let his lips rest lightly alongside her mouth, and she turned her head and tried to kiss him. The kiss was clumsy and lopsided, mouths bumping awkwardly, and she drew back, flustered, blushing hotly, not meeting his eyes.

Mordecai gathered her closer. "Do it again," he whispered.

"I didn't do it right."

"Of course not. You've never done it before." He kissed her earlobe. "Did you dance the minuet correctly the first time you tried?"

She hesitated. "No. I had lessons."

"Consider this the first of your lessons. Don't worry if it starts out clumsy; we'll find our own rhythm." He pressed another kiss to her earlobe, took it in his teeth, bit lightly, and then kissed his way down her jaw to her mouth. "Try again," he whispered against her lips.

She tried again, and there were a few clumsy seconds when their mouths didn't fit, and then they *did* fit, as Mordecai had known they would. Because he and Eleanor Wrotham were meant for each other.

They kissed, their lips clinging together—and kissed—and kissed. His hand was on the nape of her neck, and she was leaning into him, no longer tense, but warm and pliant, and when her tongue fluttered shyly against his it felt *right*, as if every other kiss in his life had been a prelude to this one.

Slowly they learned each other's mouths, slowly they found the perfect rhythm, and he'd never experienced a kiss like this before, so virginal, so sweetly eager, and he never would again, because the next time Eleanor Wrotham kissed him she wouldn't be this shy. Mordecai wanted to hold on to this moment forever, wanted the kiss never to end . . .

They paused, catching their breaths. Eleanor Wrotham was blushing, trembling. *I love you,* Mordecai almost blurted. Instead, he gathered her in his arms and whispered, "That wasn't so difficult, was it?"

She shook her head, not completely relaxed, but not tense either, not trying to free herself. Still a little shy, a little self-conscious.

"It gets easier each time. Just like dancing. The more one practices, the better one becomes." He stroked the nape of her neck, and felt her shiver. "Shall we try again?"

Eleanor Wrotham hesitated, and nodded.

And so they did, and it was a little easier, the moment of awkwardness passing quickly, their mouths fitting together almost effortlessly. Eleanor Wrotham was less hesitant this time, more confident, daring to venture into his mouth, and Mordecai held her close, and simply existed in the moment, in the play of their tongues, the sweetness of her lips, the rising heat, the rhythm.

They kissed . . . and kissed . . . and kissed . . . and when Mordecai finally dragged his mouth from hers he was hot and panting and almost dizzy with arousal. He rested his cheek against her forehead and dragged air into his lungs. He wanted to go further, wanted to slide his hand beneath the hem of Eleanor Wrotham's gown and find her *centre de délices* and show her what he could do with his fingers.

For a moment, Mordecai allowed himself to imagine what she'd feel like—hot and damp and eager. He imagined sinking a finger into her tight, yielding heat, imagined her smooth muscles clenching around him.

His cock gave a sudden lurch inside his drawers and his balls tightened painfully.

Mordecai drew back and examined Eleanor Wrotham's face. Her eyelids were still haughty, but nothing else about her was. She looked as aroused as he was, and while it was possible that she *might* let him finger her to a climax—it was also possible that she would regret it afterwards. Too great an intimacy too soon.

Mordecai abandoned his fantasy. He wanted her to leave the parlor wanting more, not regretting what she'd done. "Let's catch our breath," he said. "Cool down a bit."

They did just that, sitting on the sofa, his arm around her shoulders, the heat fading from their faces—and then Mordecai realized that he hadn't locked the door.

His contentment evaporated abruptly. A servant could walk in at any moment.

Mordecai hurriedly stood, putting distance between them. "Time for bed."

Eleanor Wrotham stiffened. A flicker of panic crossed her face.

"Not together," Mordecai said hastily. "Absolutely not. Not yet."

The panic faded. He saw her relief—and her embarrassment that she'd misinterpreted his words.

"Come along," Mordecai said, holding out his hand to her. "Bessie will be wondering where you are."

Eleanor Wrotham let him draw her to her feet.

"Here." He fished the spectacles from his pocket and handed them to her.

She put them on, her fingers fumbling slightly.

Mordecai smiled down at her. "Goodnight, Nell." He bent his head and lightly kissed her cheek.

"Goodnight, Mordecai," she whispered, and fled the parlor, blushing.

Chapter Seventeen

July 20th, 1812
Exeter, Devonshire

To Nell's relief, Mordecai Black didn't act the lover at breakfast. He was friendly and polite, not amorous. He didn't mention their kisses, but memory of those intimacies hummed in the air between them. He had kissed her and she had kissed him, and it had been the most exhilarating experience of her life. She had felt alive in a way she hadn't realized was possible, as if she'd sleepwalked for twenty-three years and only been truly awake for that half hour on the sofa.

She understood now why Sophia had run off with her soldier. Who wouldn't run off with a man who made one feel like that? Who wouldn't choose ruin over respectability, if that was ruin?

After breakfast, Nell gave him the sketch and the names of the midwives in the West Quarter. "Be careful."

"I will." Black hesitated, and she thought he was going to forbid her to leave the inn, but all he said was, "Please don't take any risks."

"I won't."

Black didn't look entirely convinced.

"I shall visit the cathedral," Nell told him. "And perhaps look at some of the shops on the High Street. I'll take Bessie with me and I'll be everything that is prudent and respectable." An edge of tartness crept into her voice. "I know how to do that; I've been doing it my whole life."

"So you have." Black gave a nod of acknowledgment. "Very well, I trust your judgment."

EXETER'S CATHEDRAL WAS a handsome structure, but Nell had little attention for the immense vaulted ceiling or the astronomical clock; she was worrying about Sophia, worrying about Black. It was all very well for Black to tell her not to take risks today, but what if *he* took one?

After viewing the cathedral, she walked across the green to Exeter's High Street, Bessie at her heels, but she had no interest in shopping. She passed the haberdasher's without pausing and cast only a cursory glance at the bonnets displayed in the milliner's window. Even the bookshop failed to hold her attention; Nell picked up several volumes of poetry, flicked through them restlessly, placed them back. The only time she halted was at a bustling confectioner's shop. *Reid & Houghton,* the sign proclaimed. People were queueing for fruit ices. Nell's mouth watered. She heard her father's voice in her ear: *Respectable ladies do not eat in public.*

For a moment she was tempted to buy an ice just to defy

him—and then she thought of her little hoard of coins, and turned away.

She saved a few more pennies by returning to the inn on foot. It was yet another warm, airless day. By the time she and Bessie reached the inn Nell was hot enough that she wished she'd bought herself an ice. "Get this wig off me, please," she told Bessie. "I'm dying of heat."

It was a relief to be rid of the wig, even if it meant she couldn't leave her room. Nell sent Bessie down to the private parlor to fetch paper, ink, and a quill, and then sat at the little dressing table and wrote to her cousin, Georgiana Dalrymple.

Dearest Georgie

As you will see from the postmark, this letter comes to you from Exeter, not Bath. A lot has happened since I wrote to you last month.

She told Georgie about receiving Sophia's letter, about her hasty journey to London, about meeting Mordecai Black and all the help he'd given her—and their failure so far to find Sophia.

Baletongue will come in two days' time and I shall ask for the gift of finding people, so I shall shortly be reunited with Sophia. Once I am, I'll write again and let you know how she and the baby are.

We shan't come to stay with you, Nell wrote firmly. *So don't ask! We will be able to live quite comfortably on the interest from my portion.* That was almost a lie. By scrimping they should be able to live on eighty pounds a year; whether they'd be comfortable was debatable.

And then Nell remembered that she was Mordecai Black's mistress now, and that many men set their mistresses up in houses of their own.

Nell chewed on her lower lip and decided that if Mordecai Black *did* offer her a house, she would accept. For the sake of Sophia and the baby.

She continued with her letter: *Please tell your mother that I shall not be shortsighted in choosing my wish. It is not merely Sophia I shall be able to find, but anyone.*

Lady Dalrymple was scathing on the subject of poorly chosen wishes. *Don't squander your wish,* she had told Nell more than once. *Choose something that will last a lifetime.* Lady Dalrymple's favorite example of a well-chosen wish was Nell's great-great-grandmother, who'd wished that no ship her husband was on would ever sink—and throughout his forty-year career in the navy, her husband's ships had survived storms, reefs, waterspouts, and cannonballs. Twice his ships had sunk within minutes of his disembarking.

I know that Hubert's whereabouts is as important to you as Sophia's is to me, Nell wrote. *I promise I shall write as soon as I know where he is.* Which meant: where Hubert's bones lay. Because everyone knew that Hubert was dead, somewhere in the Scottish Highlands.

My love to you and your parents,
Nell

The letter written, Nell went through her few clothes, looking for something to darn, but Bessie had been before her and there was nothing. At the very bottom of her valise was a small jewelry pouch. Nell loosened the drawstring and emptied its contents into her hand.

Three brooches. One set with pearls, one with amethysts, one with rubies.

She carefully polished each brooch and returned it to the pouch. The pearl one first, since it was the one she liked least. Then the amethyst. And lastly, the ruby.

Her father hadn't liked the ruby brooch. He'd pronounced it gaudy and refused to allow her to wear it. But Nell loved the deep, lustrous crimson of the stones. Such a bold color, full of fire and warmth and life.

Nell spent a long time buffing each ruby with a scrap of

muslin. When she'd finished she held the brooch in the sunlight and watched the facets blaze. Glittering, barbaric, beautiful. *From my grandmother to my mother to me.*

Two things she'd inherited from her mother: brooches, and a Faerie godmother.

Chapter Eighteen

MORDECAI HAD TOLD Eleanor Wrotham that he trusted her judgment, and he *did*—but that didn't stop him being hugely relieved when he saw her waiting in the private parlor. "How was the cathedral?" he asked, as they sat down to eat luncheon.

"Very handsome," she said politely, serving herself from the platters laid before them.

He glanced at her face. "Were you bored?"

She glanced up, met his eyes, and nodded.

"I'm sorry." Mordecai served himself: slices of cold sirloin, mustard, bread-and-butter.

"Did you have any trouble in West Quarter?"

"Not much." Mordecai gave a grunt of amusement. "Walter fell victim to a fogle hunter."

Eleanor's eyebrows lifted. "A fogle hunter? What on earth is that?"

"A stealer of handkerchiefs."

Her eyebrows rose even higher. "There are people who make their living stealing handkerchiefs?"

"Among other things," Mordecai said, and applied himself to his food.

They ate for a moment in silence, and then Eleanor said, "I take it you had no luck with the midwives?"

"I found them," Mordecai said. "But none of them have seen your sister. They gave me four more names, though. That should keep me busy this afternoon."

"I'm sorry," Eleanor said.

"What for?"

She put down her cutlery. "It should be *me* looking for Sophia, not you. It should be *me* tramping all over Exeter finding midwives, not you. I hate that I can't and that you have to do it instead, and it's taking all your time and costing you money—"

"I'm happy to help," Mordecai said firmly. "I *want* to help." He reached across the table and took one of her hands. "There's nothing I'd rather do than help you find your sister."

He thought that her eyes filled with tears briefly, and then she blinked several times and looked down at his hand holding hers, and her fingers moved, so that she was holding his hand just as much as he was holding hers.

Mordecai's heart seemed to roll over in his chest. His throat tightened.

They sat in silence for several seconds, holding hands across the table, and then Eleanor raised her gaze to his face. "If I'd been betrothed to you and not Roger when Sophia ran away, would you have ended our engagement?"

"Of course not."

"Would you have helped me find her?"

"Yes."

"Would you have made the soldier marry Sophia?"

Mordecai shook his head.

Her eyebrows twitched together. "Why not?"

"A hasty marriage might have scotched the scandal, but I doubt it would have brought your sister happiness. No man of good character would run off with a fifteen-year-old."

"What would you have done when you found them?"

Castrated the bastard, Mordecai thought. "First, I would have married you. Then, I would have brought your sister to live with us."

"And brought ruin on yourself?" She shook her head. "Your father wouldn't have allowed it."

"He wouldn't have *liked* it," Mordecai corrected her. "But there's nothing he could have done to stop it."

"He could have disinherited you."

"He wouldn't have. He loved me."

"And it would have broken his heart to see you lose your entrée to Society!" Eleanor shook her head firmly, and removed her hand from his clasp. "I wouldn't have allowed it. I wouldn't have married you."

Mordecai recaptured her hand. "Then I would have found another solution. I would have . . . I'd have set her up in a house of her own, as Father did with my mother."

"In Shoreditch?"

"*Not* in Shoreditch," Mordecai said. "Somewhere more pleasant."

Eleanor was silent for a moment, studying him. "Do you think your mother would have been happier if she'd lived elsewhere?"

Mordecai considered this question, and shook his head. "I think that if Father had given her a house in Mayfair—even if he'd married her—she'd have been unhappy. Because it was her nature to be unhappy." He tightened his grip on her hand.

"But all this is irrelevant, Nell. It doesn't matter what might have happened, because it didn't."

"I know." Her gaze fell to her plate, where half a slice of cold sirloin lay uneaten. "I think Sophia would have been happy even in Shoreditch. It's her nature to be happy."

"Then she's very lucky."

"Yes." Eleanor's gaze lifted again. "I used to envy her," she said, with the air of someone making a terrible confession. "I used to wish I was happy all the time, too, and that people loved me as much as they loved her."

I love you just the way you are, Mordecai thought, tightening his grip on her hand.

"Sometimes I'd get so cross and so . . . so *impatient* with all the things I wasn't allowed to do—and I'd get cross with Sophia, too, for being so *amiable,* and for not being bothered by all Father's rules." She grimaced, a brief twist of her lips. "I'm not a very nice person," she said gruffly.

"I think you are."

Eleanor shook her head. "You'll like Sophia more than you like me. Everyone does."

"I doubt it," Mordecai said. "I've never placed much value on amiability. I much prefer spirit."

Eleanor looked at him uncertainly, as if she didn't believe him.

Mordecai smiled at her and released her hand. "Finish your luncheon, Nell."

Eleanor eyed him for a moment, then picked up her knife and fork again.

Mordecai thought about the special license in his pocket and wondered whether now would be a good time to ask Eleanor Wrotham to marry him. It felt as if it might be.

He took a deep breath, and said, "Will you marry me?"

Her gaze flew to him. She was silent for a long time, her

knife and fork poised above her plate, so long a time that he began to hope she'd changed her mind, and then she said, "I told you last night, no."

Mordecai released his breath, released his hope. "So you did."

But he didn't feel defeated as he picked up his own cutlery. One day when he asked, she'd say *Yes.* He knew it.

AFTER LUNCHEON, MORDECAI went up to his bedchamber and dug through his portmanteau, looking for the novels Tompkin had packed for him to read. One was called *Sense and Sensibility,* the other *Summer in St. Ives,* both bound in three volumes. Mordecai put *Summer in St. Ives* back; it was *not* the sort of thing one would offer to an innocent young lady. And then he took it out again. He'd told Eleanor Wrotham that he didn't want to cage her, that he wanted to set her free, which meant that he was not going to censor her reading.

He went down to the parlor. "Here," he said, placing the volumes on the table. "For you to read this afternoon if you wish. Novels."

"Novels?" Eleanor picked up the topmost book, opened it, found the title page. "The author is anonymous?"

"They're both anonymous," Mordecai said. "I've heard that *Sense and Sensibility* is a charming novel, whereas *Summer in St. Ives* is . . . well, let's just say that it's not something your father would have allowed you to read."

Eleanor gave a tiny snort. "My father never let me read *any* novels."

"What?" Mordecai said, incredulous. "You mean . . . you've never read a novel? Ever?"

"One, when I was staying with the Dalrymples."

"Did you enjoy it?"

Her lips tilted up. "Yes. It was quite absurd. Full of ghosts and fainting heroines."

"I don't think you'll find either of those in these novels," Mordecai said. "*Sense and Sensibility* is meant to be quite realistic, and *Summer in St. Ives* is, well . . . it's rather risqué. You won't find it in any bookshops."

She looked at him, her eyebrows lifting. "Then how did you purchase it?"

"Subscription," Mordecai said. "The publisher knows the kind of books I like. I haven't read this one yet, so I can't speak for its content, but the others by this author are . . . let's just say that she has a talent for writing novels that are amusing and titillating."

"She?"

"I believe the author is a woman."

"Oh," Eleanor said, her eyebrows lifting again. She looked down at the volumes on the table.

"You would be safest to read *Sense and Sensibility*," Mordecai said.

Eleanor glanced at him. "Safe?" It was one word only, but her tone held a hint of distaste.

"Read whichever novel you wish," Mordecai said, opening his hand in a *do as you will* gesture. "Just be aware that one of them may shock you." He picked up his hat and gloves. "I'll be off. Enjoy your afternoon."

At the door, he paused and looked back. Eleanor was examining the books, her lips pursed thoughtfully.

Chapter Nineteen

NELL RETREATED TO her room with the books. She rid herself of the wig and spectacles and sat down to read. Novels!

She most wanted to read *Summer in St. Ives,* but she glanced at the first page of *Sense and Sensibility* and found herself caught. This was a novel about a young woman like herself, of good breeding but little money. The heroine's name was even Elinor.

Nell read greedily. She knew she should have savored each sentence, but she couldn't. She turned the pages swiftly, gulping down the words, almost swallowing each paragraph whole with her eyes. She finished the first volume, finished the second volume. Dusk began to gather in the sky. Nell read even faster, skimming down each page. Names jumped out at her: *Elinor. Willoughby. Edward.*

When Bessie came to help her dress for dinner, Nell was on the final chapter. "One moment," she told the maid, holding up her hand.

Bessie dutifully waited.

Five minutes passed, during which time the fortunes of every character were resolved in a most suitable manner.

Nell closed the book with a sigh of contentment and hugged it to her chest. "Perfect," she said. "Simply perfect."

SHE WENT DOWN to the private parlor with her head full of the Dashwood family, but as she settled on the sofa the events of last night came flooding back.

The Dashwoods vanished abruptly from her consciousness. The parlor snapped into focus: the dining table, not yet set for dinner, the little writing desk in the corner of the room, the stout green sofa upon which she sat.

The sofa upon which Mordecai Black had kissed her.

Nell shivered in recollection. For a moment she tasted him in her mouth: heady, masculine, intoxicating.

Would Black kiss her again tonight?

She found herself hoping he would—but tangled with the hope and the anticipation was nervousness, because she knew that kisses were among the least of the intimacies that lovers exchanged. Once Black had tired of kissing her he'd want to move on to other things, and she had no real idea what those things might be. *I should have read* Summer in St. Ives *instead.*

But even though she wanted to find out what came after kissing, she was also a little afraid. Because intimacies were . . . intimate, and the thought of being intimate with Mordecai Black was as frightening as it was tempting.

Nell puzzled over that for some time. She wasn't in the least afraid of Mordecai Black. She knew she could trust him, she knew he'd do his best not to ruin her . . . so why did she fear physical intimacy with him?

Because being intimate with Mordecai Black meant having

no distance from him at all. He would come to know her better than any other human being. And that was frightening. *What if he doesn't like the real me?*

The door opened. Black stepped into the parlor.

Nell's heart gave a tremendous leap in her chest. She stood hastily.

Black closed the door. He stood for a moment, looking at her.

His gaze provoked the familiar chest-tightening, skin-tingling, pulse-fluttering response. Nell swallowed, and found her voice. "Any luck?"

Black shook his head. He crossed the room and took both her hands in his. "We'll find her, I promise," and his voice was so certain and so kind that Nell felt tears sting her eyelids.

She blinked them back, and gave him a smile. "I know we will," she said, and wished with all her heart that she could tell him about her Faerie godmother, because beneath the kindness he looked tired and worried.

Black released her hands and stepped back as the door opened again. Two servants came in to lay the table.

Black strolled across to the empty fireplace and stood there, leaning against the mantelpiece, an air of boredom clinging to him. He didn't look like a man who'd been holding her hands scant seconds ago; he looked like a man waiting for his dinner.

Nell took her seat again on the sofa and composed her expression into something genteel and respectable. She was good at genteel and respectable, she'd been practicing it her whole life—but it had rarely been so difficult. She didn't want to be respectable right now. She wanted Mordecai Black to hold her hands, whether there were servants in the room or not.

She glanced at Black, standing by the cold fireplace, looking bored and beautiful and ever so faintly dangerous. If she had spent her whole life smothered in respectability, he'd spent his bearing the stigma of illegitimacy. The path he'd walked had been far harder than hers, and yet despite that—or perhaps because of it—Black was a good man. Better than her father. Better than Roger.

The *ton* wouldn't agree. But birth didn't equate to character, and respectability didn't equate to virtue.

The late Lord Dereham had known his son's worth. In public he'd been as poker-faced as an earl should be, but Nell had once seen him look at his son when he'd thought himself unobserved, had seen raw love on Dereham's face, and deep pride. She'd wondered at it—wondered how on earth Dereham could be proud of so shockingly scandalous a son—but now she knew why: because Mordecai Black was as honorable as he was disreputable and as kindhearted as he was dangerous, and only the blindest of fathers could have failed to be proud of him.

Nell watched the servants place a roasted chicken on the table, a haunch of lamb, a gooseberry tart—and wondered whether Black had known how proud his father was of him.

Black pushed away from the mantelpiece. He politely held out a chair for her.

Nell sat and spread her napkin on her lap, genteel and respectable.

Finally the servants departed. She and Black were alone again.

Black carved the chicken, carved the lamb. Nell watched his movements—deft, confident—and thought about what he'd told her about Shoreditch, about Eton. She raised her eyes to his face. A strong, assertive face. A face that could have been cruel and sardonic on a different man, but wasn't.

There were so many men he could have become given his childhood, and yet he'd become this one.

Nell served herself, and then said, "I don't know if you recall the Epsoms' ball last year?"

Black reached for the dish of sautéed mushrooms, and shook his head. "I've been to a number of balls at the Epsoms'. Don't recall any of them in particular."

"Your father was there. I saw him watching you while you danced."

Black paused, a serving spoon full of mushrooms suspended above his plate.

"I've never seen a man so full of pride. Not in himself, but in you. He was bursting with it as he watched you."

Black looked down at his plate.

"I imagine you know how proud he was of you, but if you didn't . . . I thought you might like to know."

"Thank you," Black said. "I did know, but . . . thank you."

He blinked for a moment, and she thought he swallowed, as if his throat was constricted, and then he carefully placed the mushrooms on his plate. "He was a good father. There were things I did that he didn't approve of, things he did that *I* didn't approve of, but . . . he was a good father." He placed the serving spoon back in its dish and frowned. "A good father to *me*, that is. Not to my half sisters. That was his greatest flaw: he couldn't see the value in his daughters."

Nell wondered what the earl had done that Black didn't approve of. She could think of two things—aside from his lack of love for his daughters. The first was siring an illegitimate child, and the second was ignoring that child for the first eight years of its life.

Nell ate slowly, and thought about Black's childhood. "Did you ever see your mother again?"

"No. She died when I was fourteen. Father made me go to her funeral. I didn't want to."

Black's expression mirrored his voice—faintly pensive—

and then he smiled. "Mother's cook was there, so it was a good thing I went. I might never have seen her again otherwise. As it was, I asked Father to give her an annuity, and he did."

"Is she still alive? The cook?"

Black nodded.

"What's her name?"

"Dorothy Black."

"Black?" Nell said, lifting her eyebrows. "But that's *your* surname."

"I chose it because of her."

"You *chose* your own surname?"

"And my first name, too," Black said. "Mother only ever called me Boy, and Dorothy called me Ducks. I didn't know my real name until Father told me."

"What is it?"

"Bamber. Bamber Pew."

Nell stared at him. Mordecai Black's real name was Bamber Pew? She blinked, and blinked again, and then asked, "Why Mordecai?"

"Mordecai Schneider was a prizefighter, a thug of a man, ripped someone's ear off once with his teeth. The Jewish Mauler, they used to call him. I wanted to be as tough as him when I grew up, so I called myself Mordecai."

"Oh," Nell said, and then, "I'm surprised your father allowed you to keep such an unusual name."

"We had a few arguments over it, but even he could see I'm not a Bamber Pew."

No. The man seated across the table from her was definitely not a Bamber Pew.

"Father said that if I could spell Mordecai Black, I could keep the name. A tactic to make me learn my letters." Black grinned wryly. "It worked."

"Oh," Nell said again. "Pew? That's not a surname I've heard before."

"It's Welsh. Mother was Welsh."

Which explained his coloring, that black hair, those dark eyes.

They ate in silence for several minutes. Nell thought about Mordecai Black's childhood. If Black was a remarkable man, how more remarkable might he have been if he'd been loved from birth?

Or perhaps he'd have been *less* remarkable? Perhaps a childhood of wealth, privilege, and indulgence would have turned him into a man like Roger?

"I've been thinking about tomorrow," Black said.

Nell glanced up at him.

"There are several avenues we can pursue. It's possible that Lizzie and your sister somehow found enough money to pay for a doctor to attend the birth."

Nell nodded doubtfully.

"There's Billy English, who may know where Lizzie is."

Nell nodded again, even more doubtfully.

"And there are the newspapers. I'll insert advertisements in the *Flying Post* and the *Gazette*, offer a reward."

Nell's pulse quickened. "That could work."

"I'll do it first thing in the morning," Black said. "And then I'll look for Billy English."

"I'd rather you didn't. He's meant to be dangerous."

"I'll take Phelps and Walter with me."

Nell chewed on her lower lip. If anything happened to Black . . . "I'd rather you didn't," she said again.

"We'll be quite safe," Black said. "Cricklepit Street isn't the West Quarter."

"Then may I come with you?"

Black shook his head. "English is a criminal and I don't want you anywhere near him."

I don't want you anywhere near him either.

Nell stared at him helplessly, and wished she could tell him about Baletongue. *I'll know where Sophia is the day after tomorrow. There's no need for you to find Billy English.*

"If it makes you feel any better, I'll take my pistols with me."

"You have pistols?"

Black nodded. "Upstairs."

"All right," Nell said reluctantly. "But please be careful."

"I will." Black's smile seemed overly confident to Nell, but he *was* huge and he *was* dangerous, perhaps every bit as dangerous as Billy English, and he'd have Phelps and Walter with him. And he'd have pistols.

"I'll visit the doctors while you look for Billy English."

Black lost his smile.

"I'll be careful," Nell told him. "I'll take Bessie and I'll go by hackney."

Black didn't say anything. He sat, gripping his knife and fork. He wanted to forbid her, she could see it on his face. His cheeks were tauter than usual, his lips thinner, and there was a sharp little crease between his eyebrows.

"Doctors are expensive," Nell reminded him. "The neighborhoods they live in will be safe."

"I know," Black said. "I know. But—"

"Remember: I shall have Bessie in my charge, and even if you don't trust me to keep myself safe, at least trust that I'll keep *her* safe. It would be grossly wrong of me to expose her to any danger."

"It's not that I don't trust you," Black said. "It's just . . ." He blew out a breath and put down his cutlery. "You've lived a very sheltered life. Danger doesn't always look obvious. You may not recognize it when you see it."

"Bessie will. She hasn't lived a sheltered life."

Black pressed his lips together. The crease between his brows was sharper. Nell saw the conflict on his face.

"I promise I'll be careful. I won't take any risks. I won't venture into unsafe neighborhoods—and if I'm at all uncertain, I shall depend on the jarvey's judgment. You have my word."

Black stared at her for a long moment, lips tightly compressed, and then he blew out a breath. "All right, but for God's sake be careful!"

"I will," Nell said.

The sharp little crease still sat on Black's brow.

"You may select the jarvey, if you wish."

Some of Black's tension eased. "Thank you," he said. "I will." He gave a nod. After a moment, he picked up his cutlery again. After another moment, he resumed eating. He was still frowning. He wasn't completely happy about her visiting Exeter's doctors without him, but then *she* wasn't completely happy about him searching for Billy English.

We have both compromised.

Nell frowned at this thought, and picked up her own cutlery.

Compromise.

Black had said they would compromise rather than argue if they married, and she hadn't believed him.

FOR THE REST of the meal they discussed the advertisement, deciding on the wording, resolving on a reward of ten pounds.

Black refused to let her foot the reward. This time he didn't compromise.

"For heaven's sake, Nell," he said finally, an edge of exasperation in his voice. "You have eighty pounds in interest a year, I have eight *thousand.*"

At this point in the conversation, the servants came to remove the covers. Nell sat silently, and thought about the reward—that it was an excellent idea, that ten pounds would bring even the most reluctant of informers forward—and that it was unnecessary, because by the time the advertisements ran she'd know where Sophia was. Once again, she wished she could tell Black about Baletongue.

The servants departed, leaving her and Black seated across from each other at the empty table.

Nell stopped thinking about missing sisters and advertisements and Faerie godmothers. She was suddenly aware of the sofa. It seemed to loom huge in the room. Memory of last night's kisses flooded back. Her throat was abruptly dry. She swallowed and glanced at the sofa—and then at Black.

He was leaning back in his chair, loose-limbed and relaxed, watching her.

I won't be your wife, but I'll be your mistress. Did those words ring as loudly in his ears as they did in hers? Could he taste the memory of her in his mouth, the way she could taste the memory of him?

Black's gaze rested on her face. He was waiting for her to decide what happened next.

She could continue arguing with him about the reward. She could bid him goodnight. Or she could kiss him on the sofa.

Nell knew which of those three things she wanted to do.

Black waited, saying nothing. He wasn't going to push her in any direction, she realized. This was *her* choice.

Chapter Twenty

NELL'S HEART BEGAN to beat faster. Her throat became even dryer. She moistened her lips and said, "Shall we sit on the sofa?"

And then she blushed scarlet, blood rushing to her face.

Black smiled. "Yes," he said, and pushed up from his chair. But he didn't come around the table and take her hand; instead, he crossed to the door and locked it. Then, he turned to look at her.

They stared at each other for a long, long moment.

Nell's heart beat even faster. The blush stayed hot in her cheeks.

Black walked back to the table. He should have been intimidating, with that strong nose and those dangerous cheekbones and the sheer size of him, but he wasn't, because his lips were curved in a faint smile, and when he halted at the table and looked down at her, she saw that the smile was in his eyes, too. It wasn't a rake's smile at all—confident, arrogant, predatory—but something much more tender.

He reached down and gently removed her spectacles, folded them, and placed them on the table. Then he held out his hand and drew Nell to her feet. Emotions churned inside her. She felt shy and self-conscious and flustered and nervous and a little afraid, and yet every fiber in her body was taut with anticipation and expectancy and eagerness.

How could she be eager and afraid at the same time? It wasn't rational. She *wanted* to sit with Mordecai Black on the sofa, *wanted* to kiss him, so why was her heart beating so absurdly fast and why was she unable to look him in the eye as they both sat?

Black didn't release her hand. "Relax, Nell."

Nell tried to relax, but it was impossible. She was too tense, too shy, too eager, too nervous. She was certain her fingers were trembling in Black's clasp.

"You look very like a duchess right now," he said softly.

"I do?" Her gaze lifted to his—and was caught. Black truly did have beautiful eyes. Those dark, dark irises. Those long, long lashes.

He smiled at her. "There's no need to be nervous."

"I know," Nell said, and blushed even more hotly, and *why* was she blushing? *She* was the one who'd suggested sitting on the sofa. "I know," she said, more strongly. "But I can't seem to stop it."

"Perhaps I can help you with that." Black turned her hand over, exposing her palm, and brushed his knuckles lightly across it. Every muscle in Nell's body clenched. She shivered.

Black glanced at her, a smiling glance, almost a mischievous glance, and stroked his knuckles across her palm again. How could her skin be so sensitive? How could that light touch make her tremble so?

The gleam of mischief in Black's eyes became more

pronounced. He raised her palm to his mouth and kissed it lightly, his lips warm and soft—and then licked.

Nell's heart seemed to stop beating.

Black licked again, and his tongue was warm, soft, supple, marvelous.

Nell shivered convulsively. Dear Lord. How could a man's tongue do such things to her?

Black lowered her hand. "Kiss me, Nell," he said, and Nell didn't hesitate; she leaned closer and found his lips, and the shyness and nervousness evaporated and all that was left was eagerness, a desperate desire to taste him again, to reacquaint himself with his beautiful, sinful, *perfect* mouth.

When they finally broke for breath, Nell felt dazed and disoriented, as if Black was as potent as brandy. "Shall we take it a little further?" he asked, his voice low and slightly husky.

Nell blinked, and managed to focus on his face. His cheeks were slightly flushed, his lips rosier than usual, his eyes very dark. "How much further?"

"Not too much. Just a little."

"All right," she said, recklessly. "How?"

"Like this," Black said, and he took hold of her waist, his hands huge and warm, and lifted her effortlessly, and settled her sideways on his lap.

Nell tensed.

"Relax," Black said, and cupped the back of her head with one hand and kissed her.

After a moment, Nell did relax. It was impossible not to when Black kissed her so tenderly.

They kissed, and kissed, and then Black said, "A little more?" and Nell said, "All right," breathlessly, recklessly, and Black took her by the waist and lifted her again. "Knees on either side of me," he said, and she obeyed—and found herself sitting astride his knees.

Nell froze. "Is this sex?"

"No. It's just kissing. But you don't have to if you don't want to."

Nell hesitated. It felt very intimate to be straddling him like this. Alarming. Wanton. Her gown had ridden up to her knees, almost exposing her garters. She felt the same mix of emotions she'd felt when Black had led her to the sofa—shyness, nervousness, eagerness. There was a skip of excitement in her blood, a *frisson* of fear.

Black released her waist and when she didn't scramble off him, he took first one of her hands and then the other and lifted them to his mouth, kissed them lightly, and placed them on his shoulders.

Nell's heart began to beat very fast.

"Kiss me," Black whispered.

Nell hesitated, and then did as he asked, leaning towards him, her arms sliding around his neck. She kissed him shyly.

Black kissed her back, his hands at her waist.

They kissed like that for several minutes, and then Black drew her closer. Nell shivered with delight. Dimly, at the back of her mind, she was aware that she ought to be alarmed that her breasts were crushed to his broad chest, alarmed that her legs straddled his muscular thighs—such a *scandalous* way to kiss, so immodest, surely no respectable lady would ever kiss like this?—but she wasn't alarmed; she exulted in it, pressing closer, delving more deeply into his mouth.

A rhythm built between them, not just their mouths and their tongues, but their bodies, Nell swaying into him, Black gathering her closer. She felt aflame with heat, with sensation, with a strange, desperate, visceral *need*.

Black broke the kiss. He was panting. He looked at heated as she was. "Want to go even further?"

"Yes," Nell said, without any hesitation.

Black kissed her again. "Tell me if you want me to stop and I will."

Nell kissed him back, certain that whatever he did next she wouldn't ask him to stop, but the kiss seemed no different from before—just as sinful, just as perfect—and then she realized that it wasn't what his mouth was doing that was different, but what his *hand* was doing.

Black's right hand was no longer at her waist, but on her knee—and then it was under the rucked-up hem of her gown, skimming over stocking and garter before touching naked skin, climbing her thigh, moving slowly, his touch light and tickling, making her shiver, making her heart leap in her chest, making her *want* and *fear* at the same time.

Nell tensed and stopped kissing him.

"Do you want me to stop?" Black whispered against her mouth.

"I don't know," Nell whispered back.

"It gets better. A lot better."

His hand slid a few tickling inches higher and Nell shivered again and her heart leapt in her chest again and she didn't know what to do—so she stayed on his lap while his questing fingers crept up her thigh, tickling, making her tremble. They were no longer kissing, but their lips still clung together, and each breath she inhaled was his, and each breath he inhaled was hers—and Nell breathed him in, and trembled and quivered, while Black's hand stole higher, gliding over her skin, until his fingers brushed the little nest of hair at the junction of her thighs.

Every muscle in her body clenched, including muscles she'd not known she had—in her loins, in her womb.

"No drawers, Nell?" Black whispered against her mouth.

Nell squeezed her eyes shut, and struggled to breathe. "They're not respectable."

He laughed at that, softly, and kissed her, his tongue briefly in her mouth, and he didn't tell her that what he was doing was even more disreputable than wearing drawers; instead, his fingers feathered their way through the hair and found her nether lips.

Nell gasped, and stiffened.

"Relax," Black said. "Enjoy." And then his fingers began to move.

Nell lost the ability to speak, to think, almost to breathe. She should have been mortified that his hand was between her legs, but there was no space in her head for emotions like shame and mortification, no space even for incredulity, no space for anything at all. She was no longer a thinking creature but a *feeling* creature, her entire being focused on Black's skillful fingers and the extraordinary sensations they were evoking. She found herself gasping, found herself shifting helplessly as his thumb found a spot that was exceedingly sensitive, and then one of his long, wicked fingers was *inside* her, where she was hot and damp and pulsing.

Every muscle in her body clenched.

"Does that hurt?"

Nell couldn't speak; her throat was too tight. She shook her head.

Black slid a second finger inside her. "What about that?"

Nell trembled, and her body gave a great pulse of pleasure and seemed to clench around Black's fingers as if wanting to hold them there forever. Nell almost groaned with the sheer bliss of it. She managed to shake her head again.

"Relax," Black said again, and his voice was hoarse, slightly breathless, and he sounded as if he wanted to groan, too. "Enjoy it, Nell."

Nell didn't relax—it was impossible to relax while his fingers were delving inside her and his thumb was moving in small, tortuous, blissful circles. *Enjoy,* Black had said, and how could she not enjoy the sensations his clever hand was producing? *This* was seduction. *This* was what made a man a rake. This wonderful, shocking thing that Mordecai Black was doing with his thumb and fingers.

She shivered and trembled and struggled to breathe and shifted helplessly, her arms around Black's neck, her mouth pressed to his. Her whole body was tight, tense, pulsing, focused wholly on Black's fingers, on his merciless thumb, on the inexorable rhythm he was building. Tighter, tighter, like a bowstring about to break.

"Let go, Nell," Black whispered against her lips, and she didn't know what he meant—and then suddenly she *did* know, and the tension discharged in great jolts of pleasure, overwhelming and shocking and intense.

It was some time before she stopped shuddering and caught her breath, and even longer before she caught her wits. Slowly Nell's awareness expanded beyond her body. Mordecai Black's hand still nestled warmly between her legs, although his fingers were no longer inside her—but even as she noticed that, Black moved, withdrawing his hand, putting both arms around her. Nell closed her eyes and rested her cheek against his chest, feeling dazed and languorous and deeply, profoundly contented. More contented than she'd ever been in her life, as if every fiber in her body hummed with happiness. Black's chest was broad, his arms warm around her, his heart beating strongly beneath her ear. *I could fall asleep like this.*

But while part of her would have been quite happy to fall asleep, part of her wanted to know what on earth had just happened.

"Was that sex?" Nell asked.

"It's a sexual act," Black said. "But it's not what I'd call sex. I'd call it a prelude."

"There's more?"

"There's a lot more."

She wanted it. God, how she wanted it. "What's it called? What you just did."

"It has lots of names. My favorite is *pattes d'araignées.*"

Nell blinked. "Spider's legs?"

"If you're going to be literal, yes. But whenever I hear those words, I don't think about spiders, I think about sex."

Curiosity swamped her. Nell bit her lip, and then asked, "Do you hear them often?"

Black was silent for a moment. "Not for years." His voice sounded sad.

Nell sat up on his lap. "What?" she said. "What is it?"

For a moment she thought Black wouldn't answer, and then he said, "I call it *pattes d'araignées* because my first lover was French. That's what she called it."

"You miss her," Nell said.

Black nodded.

The warm contentment dissolved.

"You loved her."

Black nodded again.

Do you still love her? But Nell couldn't bring herself to ask, because she thought the answer might be *Yes,* and she didn't want to hear Black say it.

"Her name was Cécile," Black said. "Comtesse de Chevigny-le-Vieux. She was an émigré. A widow." His hands were at her waist, warm, holding her. His voice and his expression were faintly pensive. "She was thirty, I was eighteen."

Nell stiffened in outrage. "She seduced you?"

Black laughed. "No, I wouldn't put it like that."

"But she was *thirty,* and you were a boy!"

"No, I was a man," Black said. "With a man's desires and a boy's inexperience, and Cécile was exactly what I needed."

Nell shook her head.

"She didn't seduce me," Black said, firmly. "My interest in her was quite obvious."

"You approached her?" She couldn't imagine an eighteen-year-old earl's bastard approaching a thirty-year-old *comtesse*, but Black *was* assertive.

Black laughed again. "Heavens, no."

"Then how?"

Black looked at her, and hesitated, and then he seemed to give a shrug, not with his shoulders, but with his mouth, the tiniest movement, a faint compression of his lips, as if he said to himself *Why not?* "Cécile was the most beautiful creature I'd ever seen. *L'incomparable*, everyone called her, and she was: Incomparable." His eyes were smiling, as if he dwelled on a fond memory. "I'd never been intimate with a woman—although God knew I *wanted* to. Of course I had fantasies about Cécile. Every man who wasn't a eunuch was having fantasies about Cécile." His mouth twisted up at one corner, wryly.

"Father and I were invited to a house party—and Cécile was there, and one day I came across her in the rose garden, just her and me, and I was so *aware* of her." Black grimaced. "My body betrayed me, and of course she noticed. I couldn't speak I was so embarrassed, but Cécile just laughed and asked if I'd ever had congress with a woman, and then she offered to be my lover." Black grunted a laugh and shook his head. "The one woman in England that every man wanted, and she chose *me*. It was . . . unbelievable."

Nell didn't wonder why the *comtesse* had chosen him. Black would have been stunning as an eighteen-year-old, young and strong and vigorous, an edge of wildness to him. And also innocent and vulnerable.

"She didn't seduce me," Black said again, with heavy

emphasis on the *didn't,* as if he saw the disapproval on her face. "It wasn't like that at all."

Nell tried to keep her voice neutral. "What was it then?"

"We were outsiders, both of us, watched and whispered about, both lonely, both wanting companionship, and Cécile recognized that, she saw that we'd be good for each other, that despite the difference in our ages we'd make each other happy."

It still sounded like a seduction to Nell. A thirty-year-old woman and an eighteen-year-old boy? "What did your father think?"

"He was shocked, of course. Everyone was. And envious, I think, although he never said it. And I think . . . relieved."

Nell frowned. "Relieved? Why?"

"Because it was the scandal of the Season. *Everyone* was talking about it. My illegitimacy was suddenly far less important than the fact that I was sleeping with Cécile, that I'd succeeded where dozens had failed. I was no longer merely Dereham's bastard; I was the man who was having a liaison with the most sought-after woman in the *ton.*" Black grinned, a sharp, sardonic flash of his teeth. "Notoriety for *all* the right reasons."

Nell almost rolled her eyes at him. Men.

"The next year, we were less of a scandal, and by the third Season, we weren't much of a scandal at all. We were no more shocking than the Duke of Clarence and Mrs. Jordan."

"You were together for three *years*?" Nell said, taken aback. Perhaps Black was right: it hadn't been a seduction.

"Five years," he said.

"*Five* years?"

Black nodded.

"What happened?" Nell asked tentatively. "Why did it end?"

"Oh . . ." He shrugged with one shoulder. "Cécile was unhappy in England, wanted to go back to France—but of course that was impossible. So she chose to go to America."

"Did you want to go with her?" Nell asked, even more tentatively.

"What I wanted was to marry her, but she wouldn't have me, said she was too old for me, that I'd come to regret it."

Nell's eyebrows lifted. "You asked her to marry you?"

"Several times. I was quite desperately in love with her."

Nell looked at him soberly. *We were outsiders,* he'd said. *Whispered about. Lonely.* For five years the *comtesse* had made him happy. He'd loved her—desperately—and asked her to marry him . . . and she'd chosen to go to America instead.

How hurt he must have been.

"I'm sorry," she said softly.

Black smiled at her. "It was a long time ago. And Cécile was right: it was a young man's puppy love. I would have grown out of it."

"Even so." Nell tried to smile back at him, but her smile was crooked and for some reason there were tears stinging her eyes, so she put her arms around him and hugged him, partly to hide the tears, and partly because she needed to hold him.

Black's arms came around her, and they were so warm and strong and comforting that Nell's eyes stung even more.

Ten minutes ago it had felt debauched and wanton to sit astride Mordecai Black's lap with her arms around him; now it didn't feel like that at all. It felt purely comforting. Nell heard the clock ticking faintly on the mantelpiece, she heard Black's heart beat beneath her ear. Her eyes slowly stopped stinging.

She went back over everything Black had said about Cécile. Five *years.*

The woman had shaped him, just as surely as his childhood in Shoreditch had shaped him and his father's belated claiming of him had shaped him. The *comtesse* had taken an inexperienced youth and turned him into a lover that women flocked after, a man whose conquests other men envied.

Who would Black have become if he'd not met Cécile that day? If she'd not somehow noticed his interest in her, if she'd not proposed a liaison?

Curiosity flickered in her breast. "Mordecai? How did your body betray you in the rose garden?" What did that ambiguous statement mean?

Black gave a grunt of laughter. "Let's just say that I hadn't learned to control my desires."

"I don't understand."

Black inhaled, exhaled, seemed to consider his response. Finally, he said, "Nell, sit up."

Nell stopped hugging him and sat up on his lap. "What?"

"When a man wants to have sex, his body signals it very obviously."

Nell's brow creased. "It does?"

"Yes," Black said, and then his cheeks flushed faintly, as if he was embarrassed, and he said, "Nell, look," and he pointed, and she looked where he was pointing—and it was *very* obvious.

"It means I want to have sex with you."

Nell stared down at Black's loins. Something was tenting his breeches. Something that was evidently rather large and rather hard. Something that hadn't been there before.

"What is it?"

"It's my *bâton*."

"*Bâton*?" She glanced at Black's face. "Is that what Cécile called it?"

"It's one of the names she used."

"What are the others?"

"*Le brigadier. Braquemard.*" He flushed faintly again. "That's a type of sword."

"I know," Nell said. And a *brigadier* was a soldier. Interesting names for whatever was in his breeches.

"*Le membre virile.* That's probably the most accurate name," Black said.

Nell looked down at his lap again. That thing—soldier, sword, baton—was mere inches from her own loins. She must have almost been touching it when she kissed him. Perhaps she *had* been touching it and not noticed? But even as she formed that thought, she knew the answer: She hadn't touched it, because Black's *braquemard* was not something one could fail to notice.

Nell stared down at the strange, fierce shape beneath Black's breeches—and was gripped with the most intense curiosity she'd ever experienced in her life. The sort of curiosity that had led Pandora to open her box and Bluebeard's wife to unlock the forbidden room. She glanced at Black's face again. "May I see it?"

To her surprise, he blushed. Not a faint, self-conscious blush, as he had when he'd called his *bâton* a sword, but a full, deep blush that reddened his entire face.

Nell blushed herself, in response to his embarrassment. "I'm sorry," she said hastily, and tried to scramble from his lap, but Black caught her by the waist, stopping her.

"Nell . . . it's not that I don't want you to see it, it's just that I hadn't thought you'd want to tonight."

Nell averted her face, unable to meet his eyes. *Am I more wanton than he thought I was?*

"I don't want to rush you," Black said softly. "I don't want to push you into something you don't feel ready for. But if you truly wish to see my *bâton*, I'll gladly show you." One of his hands cupped her chin and tilted her face gently, brought her gaze to his. "Would you like that, Nell?"

Nell was too ashamed of her curiosity to give him an answer.

Black's thumb brushed across her lower lip, a feather-light caress, and then his hand slid around to her nape and he pulled her closer and kissed her, a kiss that was gentle and sweet and tender, a kiss that made her shame evaporate, that made everything all right.

"Would you like me to show you tonight, or would you rather wait?" Black whispered against her mouth. "Tell me truthfully, Nell."

At this moment, Nell wanted anything he was willing to give her. "I'd like to see it," she confessed, and felt her cheeks bloom with color.

"Then you shall." He kissed her again—lightly—and released the nape of her neck.

"Should I get off you?"

He caught her waist. "No, stay there." And then he frowned, and said, "I am *not* going to tumble you on this sofa. That's a promise, Nell. *Pattes d'araignées* is as far as it goes tonight."

Part of her was relieved to hear this, and part of her—the wanton part—was disappointed. "All right," she said.

Black released her waist and unbuttoned his breeches. He'd said he would gladly show her, but he blushed as he slid the buttons from their holes, a streak of color high on each cheek, accenting his strong, slanting cheekbones. Nell tried to imagine lifting her gown and baring that most private part of herself while he watched fully clothed. It would be beyond embarrassing; it would be mortifying. Her whole body tensed at the thought. "You don't have to," she said hastily. "Not if you don't want to."

His fingers stilled, his dark eyes met hers. "Oh, I want to," he said softly, and it was *her* turn to blush.

She blushed while he finished unbuttoning the breeches, blushed while he pushed the plackets aside exposing yet another layer of clothing—linen this time, soft and thin, straining tightly over his *bâton*, letting her see its shape more clearly—blushed as Black unfastened his drawers—two buttons only, swiftly done—blushed as he bared himself to her.

Nell stared. His *membre virile* was an eager organ, straining upwards like a soldier standing to attention. Strong and aggressively masculine, and yet at the same time oddly vulnerable—such naked skin, more naked than any skin she'd ever seen, pinker than any skin she'd ever seen. And large. Astonishingly large. It seemed impossible that an organ of such girth and length had ever fitted inside Black's breeches.

She didn't need to wonder what its purpose was; it was meant to go where Black's fingers had been earlier, inside her —and at that thought the muscles in her womb clenched in a spasm of desire.

What would his virile member feel like inside her? That bluntly rounded crest? The strong trunk that rose so vigorously from his drawers?

Her internal muscles clenched again.

He would be hot inside her, definitely. She could tell that just by looking. The smooth, vulnerable skin looked as if it burned with the fiercest of fevers.

She glanced at Black's face, and found him watching her. "Does it hurt?"

He blinked, and his eyebrows rose, and then he said, "You mean the first time? I believe it often does, but thereafter it shouldn't."

It was Nell's turn to blink. She wondered what on earth he

181

was talking about—and then she realized. "No, I don't mean that. I mean does it hurt *you* when it's like this?"

His eyebrows rose higher. "Me? No."

"It looks painful."

He laughed. "A little uncomfortable, but not painful."

"Are you certain it doesn't hurt?" Nell said dubiously, looking back at his virile member. It looked so *hot*.

"It aches a bit. But not in a bad way."

She understood what he meant, because she was aching, too. An ache deep inside her, as if her body lacked something it desperately craved.

"I can take care of it easily enough," Black said. "Don't worry about it, Nell."

She dragged her gaze from his virile member back to his face. "What do you mean, take care of it?"

"*Branlage, patinage*—whatever you want to call it. It's something anyone can do for themselves, man or woman."

"It is?"

"Of course," Black said, and then he hesitated and said, "You mean . . . you've never done it to yourself?"

Nell shook her head.

"Well, you can, you know."

"Oh," Nell said, and thought about that for a moment, and then she asked, "Is that what you'll do, to stop it aching?"

Black nodded.

Nell felt an intense surge of curiosity. *How* would he do it? He was shaped so differently from her. She bit her lip to stop herself asking, but her curiosity must have been evident on her face, because Black said, "Nell?" And then, cautiously, as if he wasn't certain whether he'd offend her or not, "Do you want to see me do it?"

Nell felt herself go scarlet. She didn't know where to look. Not at Black's face, not at his virile member, not anywhere.

"It's all right if you do," Black said. "There's nothing wrong with watching."

Nell glanced at him uncertainly.

"Cécile used to watch. I liked it when she did." Black blushed as he made this admission, high across his cheekbones.

Nell considered his words for several seconds. She rather thought that she disliked the *comtesse* intensely and that she didn't want to be at all like her—and then she thought, *What does Cécile matter? She's long gone.* What mattered was Mordecai Black, who'd shown her his virile member and who'd said that he didn't mind if she watched him deal with its ache—and she *did* want to watch, most desperately. She hesitated, and bit her lip, and said, "Are you certain you wouldn't mind?"

"I'm certain."

"I would mind," Nell confessed. "If it were me."

"Of course you would," Black said. "You've never done it before, let alone with an audience. But I've done it many hundreds of times, and, ah . . . an audience can make it more piquant." His blush deepened, as if this admission was something to be embarrassed about.

"Have you done it with all of your lovers?" Nell asked.

"All but one."

Which made the *comtesse* even less relevant. Nell felt happier. She gave a nod. "All right."

Black took his virile member in one hand, his long, strong fingers wrapping around the sturdy shaft—and seeing him touch it made Nell's internal muscles clench again.

"Are you certain?" Black asked. "Because this is a lot further than I'd intended to take it tonight."

Nell's throat was almost too tight for speech—not with fear, but with anticipation. She had to swallow before she could say, "Yes."

"All right," Black said, and he moved his hand in a slow

gliding stroke, all the way up to that blunt, rosy crest, and then down. He repeated it: up, then down.

The muscles in Nell's womb clenched again. She watched, transfixed, as Black's hand moved on his virile member—and then glanced at his face. He was watching her, not his hand.

Nell blushed hotly, but couldn't look away from his dark eyes. This was intimacy. *This.* Sitting on Mordecai Black's lap while he stroked away his ache, wanting him, feeling muscles clench helplessly inside her.

Nell realized she'd stopped breathing. She inhaled, and looked down at his virile member again, watched his hand glide up and down, heard the whisper of skin on skin, felt heat rise in her body and pulse in her womb.

Black was squeezing tightly now, his knuckles whitening, the strokes shorter, hard and fast, rough, almost brutal, as if he was pumping his virile member—and as if to complete that metaphor, pearly beads of moisture appeared on that straining red crest and spilled downwards, and his hand moved even faster and the shaft glistened in the candlelight, and the sound of skin on skin changed, became louder, more urgent.

Nell watched his hand move, feeling her body pulse in time with his strokes. A sense of tightness was building inside her. She snatched a glance at his face and saw the tension there, saw that his cheeks were flushed and his eyes half-closed—and then she looked down again and he was holding his member in both hands, his right hand pumping, his left cupped over the crest, and his whole body jerked, and her body did a little jerk of its own, a jolt of pleasure, not nearly as strong as when his fingers had been inside her, but still good.

She looked at Black's face. His head was tilted fractionally back and his eyes were closed. All the tension had drained from his body. He opened his eyes and caught her staring at him. His pupils were more dilated than she'd ever seen in a person before, but even as she watched they contracted again, the dark brown of his irises expanding.

Black blinked, and then his eyebrows and his mouth quirked slightly and he said, "What did you think?"

I think I want to see you do that again.

"It was interesting," Nell said, and felt herself blush. "It wasn't at all like what you did to me." Hard and fast and almost brutal. "Did it not hurt you?"

Black shook his head.

Nell looked down at his lap again, where he still clasped his virile member in his right hand. It wasn't as red as it had been, nor as stiff and upstanding, nor as large. She glanced back at his face. "What's it called at the end, when it feels so good?"

"There are lots of names," Black said. "*Jouissance. Spasmes amoureux.* And for men, *décharger.*"

"*Décharger?* You mean . . . like a pistol?"

Black opened his left hand. Cupped in his palm was a small amount of creamy liquid.

Nell stared at it. "Is that . . . ?"

"It's what makes a woman pregnant," Black said, and closed his left hand again. He released his virile member— much smaller than it had been, and quite limp now—and rummaged in his pocket.

Nell scrambled off his lap and straightened her gown, trying—and failing—to smooth away the creases.

Black located a handkerchief, wiped his palm, and then tucked his virile member back into his drawers, stood, and fastened his clothing. When he was finished, he looked the perfect gentleman again. There was absolutely nothing to show that five minutes ago he'd had a *braquemard* tenting his breeches. But then, there was nothing to show that ten minutes ago his fingers had been inside her.

Nell felt a strange sense of anticlimax.

"Well, Nell?" Black asked. "Tell me I didn't go too far?" There was a note in his voice that it took her a moment to recognize—uncertainty, a hint of anxiousness.

"You didn't. In fact, you may go further if you wish." And she blushed at her wantonness.

Black shook his head. "Not tonight. Our first time is *not* going to be on a sofa."

"I wouldn't mind," Nell said, still blushing.

"*I* would mind," Black said, and he took her hand and pulled her into a hug. "I want it to be good, Nell. I want it to be something you'll never forget."

Nell was certain their first time together would be unforgettable whether Black made love to her in a bed, on a sofa, or on the floor. But he was the expert, the rake. "All right," she said, and tried not to feel disappointed.

Black tilted her chin up with one finger and smiled at her with his eyes. "Tomorrow night, Nell, if you want." He kissed her lightly. "Or next week. Or next month. There's no rush."

"Tomorrow night," Nell said.

"If that's what you wish."

"It is," Nell said, feeling wanton and shameless and amoral —and her cheeks betrayed her again in a blush. *I ought to be ashamed of myself.* But she wasn't. Because she knew that sharing Mordecai Black's bed would be worth abandoning one's virtue for—and now that she'd made that decision, she didn't want to wait. "Or we could do it tonight."

She saw a tiny flare in his dark eyes and realized that even though Black was preaching slowness, he wanted to go fast just as much as she did—but then he shook his head. "Not tonight. I haven't had a bath."

Nell opened her mouth to protest that she didn't mind— and then closed it again. *She* hadn't had a bath either, and the day had been hot and sticky, and if she was going to share

Black's bed, she *definitely* needed to wash first—and on the heels of that thought, all her shyness and nervousness came tumbling back. To be intimate with Mordecai Black meant being naked with him, it meant being more exposed and vulnerable than she'd ever been in her life.

A faint flicker of panic kindled in Nell's breast. All Black's lovers had been beautiful, experienced women. Compared to them she would be gauche and ordinary and disappointing. *What if he regrets taking me to his bed?*

Black smiled down at her, and there was such tenderness on his face, such tenderness in his dark eyes, that the panic folded in on itself and was extinguished. It was impossible to feel gauche and disappointing when he was looking at her like that. Impossible to feel shy and afraid.

"Tomorrow night, Nell," he said, and she heard the promise in his voice.

Chapter Twenty-One

July 21ˢᵗ, 1812
Exeter, Devonshire

IN THE MORNING they visited Exeter's major newspapers and Black paid for advertisements to run in them—and then they went their separate ways, Black to look for Billy English, she to interview doctors. Black selected her jarvey, spoke to the man, and then bade Nell farewell. The muscles around his eyes and mouth were tight and he looked as if there was a lot more he wanted to say—warnings and advice, or perhaps even an outright refusal to let her go without him.

Nell understood his anxiety. She felt it, too. Words of caution crowded on her tongue. *Watch your back. Don't take any risks.* It seemed terrible that Black might endanger his life looking for Billy English today, when tomorrow it would all be unnecessary. She wished she could tell him about Baletongue, wished she could put off their search for the day—but he would wonder at her lack of urgency, so instead all she said was, "Be careful."

She and Bessie climbed into the hackney Black had selected. Nell settled on the seat and clutched Sophia's sketch in its pasteboard folder. *Surely I can trust him with my secret?*

And then she remembered Lady Dalrymple's warning: *Never tell a soul.* And she remembered that a witch had been hanged in Yorkshire only three years ago.

No. She couldn't tell Mordecai Black.

NELL RETURNED TO the inn at one o'clock. To her relief, Black was already there. He told her about his lack of success over luncheon. "Billy English has gone. He's no longer living in Cricklepit Street, or anywhere near it. And no one's willing to tell me where he is now."

"Was Cricklepit Street dangerous?" Nell asked. "Did you have any trouble?"

"We didn't, no."

Something in his tone made her lift her eyebrows. "But?"

Black hesitated, and then said, "There's a tavern at the end of the street, right on the corner, and the publican is missing. Last seen three days ago—when he had an altercation with Billy English."

Nell put down her knife and fork. "Do you think . . . ?"

Black shrugged. "I think there's a chance English killed him, but there's an equal chance the man is drunk in a ditch somewhere."

Nell considered this statement. "What do the residents of Cricklepit Street think?"

"Their money's on Billy English." Black said—and then he

added wryly: "Not that they have much money." He applied himself to his food again. "I take it you had no success?"

"No, but I still have two doctors to visit."

Black glanced up from his plate. "I'll come with you, shall I?"

Nell felt herself blush. "That would be nice."

NEITHER OF THE two doctors had seen Sophia, but Nell wasn't downcast. She felt buoyant, optimistic. By the end of tomorrow she'd know where Sophia was.

"Shall we walk back or take a hackney?" Black asked, as they stood on the final doctor's doorstep in Bampfylde Street. "Which would you prefer?"

"Walk," Nell said.

They strolled back along the High Street, and it was far too warm—and at the same time it was absolutely perfect: walking with Mordecai Black.

Black halted when they came to the confectioner's shop. "Would you like an ice?"

"I would love one," Nell said.

And so they ate ices together on a public street, and it was quite shockingly vulgar and at the same time blissfully marvelous: the oppressive heat and the jostling passersby, the clatter of carriages and clamor of street vendors; the coolness in her mouth and the sweet, tangy taste and Mordecai Black standing beside her.

"Good?" Black asked, when she'd finished her ice.

Nell smiled at him, feeling hot and sticky and happy. "Perfect."

Chapter Twenty-Two

BACK AT THE INN, Mordecai retreated to his bedchamber, where he stripped down to his shirt-sleeves. Damn, but it was *hot*. He wrote a number of letters—to his man of business, to his bailiffs—then had a cold bath. He sponged himself down and shaved carefully, while anticipation built in his blood. *Tonight I'm going to make love to Eleanor Wrotham.*

He went downstairs to the private parlor. Eleanor was already there. She was once again wearing the ivory-white gown with the vandyked hem. Mordecai had realized over the past few days that she had only three gowns with her. Three gowns, one pair of shoes, one bonnet, one spencer.

"Good evening," he said, and wondered if he dared offer to buy her a whole new wardrobe.

They sat at the table. Mordecai poured them both wine and carved the chicken. He could remember his own nerves before his first sexual experience. He'd been afraid Cécile would laugh at him, afraid that he'd be too fast, too slow, too clumsy, that he'd humiliate himself, that he wouldn't be good enough. Was Eleanor feeling some of that fear now?

He set himself to putting her at ease. "Have you looked at those novels yet?"

"Yes. I read *Sense and Sensibility* yesterday."

"What? All of it?"

Eleanor nodded. "And I read the first few chapters of *Summer in St. Ives* this afternoon."

"Did you now?" Mordecai hesitated, and then asked cautiously, "What do you think of it?"

"It's quite ridiculous," Eleanor said. "Very amusing. Shocking. But . . ." Her brow wrinkled. "I have the feeling that it has more layers than I'm aware of, that things are happening on the page that I'm not *seeing*."

Mordecai was certain of it.

"Take Mrs. Lightheel, for example—"

"Lightheel?" Mordecai said, and uttered a laugh.

Eleanor looked at him quizzically. Candlelight gleamed on her spectacle frames, gleamed on her chestnut wig.

"A lightheeled woman is one who, er, finds herself often on her back," Mordecai told her. "Because her heels fly up so readily."

"Oh." Eleanor blinked, and frowned slightly, as if trying to envisage this. "Then the name is well chosen. Mrs. Lightheel has already had an amatory adventure on a billiard table, and I believe she is about to have another one in a card room."

"You believe?" He reached for his wineglass.

"Yes. She has been playing cards with Mr. Readycock—"

Mordecai choked on his wine.

Eleanor looked blankly at him. "What?"

Mordecai put the wineglass down and caught his breath. "Cock is another name for a man's *bâton*."

"Oh," Eleanor said. "I thought the author was comparing him to a rooster."

Mordecai tried to suppress his laugh, and failed.

Eleanor wasn't offended. She smiled wryly. "You see what I mean? The book has layers that I'm oblivious to."

"I think perhaps we'd better read it together," Mordecai said.

Eleanor nodded. She sipped her wine, a thoughtful crease between her eyebrows. "Is flute another word for *bâton*?"

"Yes."

"Then Mrs. Lightheel is *definitely* about to have an amatory adventure. She's just lost at cards, you see, to Mr. Readycock, and rather than pay the twenty guineas she owes him she has offered to play on his flute." She frowned. "I couldn't understand why he agreed to it."

Mordecai couldn't help it: he laughed out loud again.

Eleanor gave another wry smile.

"What are the other characters called?" Mordecai asked.

Eleanor thought for a moment. "There's a Lord Tipvelvet. And a Lady St. George. Do those names mean anything?"

Mordecai nodded. "They're sexual acts." He paused, and then added, "Both of which I intend to show you."

Eleanor blushed vividly. She fixed her gaze on her plate, no longer wry but flustered.

Mordecai looked at her pink cheeks and changed the subject: "What did you think of *Sense and Sensibility*?"

They discussed *Sense and Sensibility* for the rest of the meal. It was much safer ground. It allowed them both to pretend that this was an ordinary evening, that they weren't intending to have carnal relations with each other shortly. Mordecai asked questions and listened to Eleanor's answers and ate his meal, while anticipation gathered beneath his skin.

When they'd both finished, Mordecai refilled their wineglasses. The evening stretched before them: shadows and heat and intimacy. His heartbeat sped up slightly.

"Tell me about the others," Eleanor said. "The ones who came after Cécile."

Her question caught him by surprise. Mordecai almost spilled the wine he was pouring. He glanced at her. Eleanor blushed faintly, but she didn't apologize for her words; she met his gaze straightly.

Her question was a direct one, and a bold one—and Mordecai admired her for it. "What would you like to know?" he said, putting aside the wine bottle.

"Who were they?"

Mordecai leaned back in his chair, rubbed the bridge of his nose, and thought about how to answer this question. "When Cécile went to America . . ."

When Cécile had gone she'd left a huge hole in his life. He'd been quite desperately lonely. Achingly lonely.

Mordecai rubbed his nose again, then reached for his wineglass. "When Cécile left I found myself rather more popular among the ladies of the *ton* than I'd anticipated. I'd acquired a reputation, you see. I must be a great lover, else Cécile wouldn't have stayed with me for so long." He sipped his wine. "An astonishing number of ladies threw their handkerchiefs into the ring. I should have been flattered, I suppose, but instead I was . . ." *Lonely.* "I wanted what I'd had with Cécile, you see. Companionship as much as sex. I wanted a kindred spirit."

Eleanor watched him silently.

"In the end, I realized I wouldn't find it again. Which left me with two choices: hiring a professional, or having an affair with one of the ladies lining up for me." He frowned at his wine. "Personally, I don't think sex should be a business transaction, so . . . the decision made itself." He shrugged. "I decided to treat it like Tattersalls."

Her eyebrows lifted. "Tattersalls?"

"If you want a horse, you go to Tattersalls, choose the one that best meets your needs."

"And what were your criteria?" Eleanor asked dryly.

"Not married," Mordecai said. "And not someone who wanted to be my lover merely to show me off—that narrowed the field considerably. And after that . . . someone whose company I'd enjoy, who had a sense of humor."

Eleanor Wrotham was eyeing him, a faint frown on her brow.

"I know it sounds calculating and . . . and *arrogant,* choosing a lover the way you'd choose a horse." Mordecai tried not to let a note of defensiveness enter his voice. "But I didn't want sex in exchange for money and I didn't want to play a game with someone who saw me as a trophy. I wanted to share my bed with a woman I actually *liked.*"

Eleanor looked at him for a long moment, her lips pursed, and then she said, "It doesn't sound calculating or arrogant, it actually sounds quite sensible. And . . . a little sad."

Mordecai stiffened with indignation. "Sad?"

"You're not a rake, Mordecai Black. You're a romantic."

Mordecai felt himself blush. Not a faint blush, but a deep blush that heated his whole face. He wanted to refute her comment, to deny it vehemently, but he couldn't. Because she was right. He *was* a romantic. He didn't want sex for the sake of sex; he wanted the dream. He wanted true love.

"Tell me about these ladies you selected," Eleanor said. "Four of them, am I correct?"

He nodded, his face still hot.

"Were they all widows?"

"All but one."

"Who was the first?"

"Annabel Wren."

Eleanor nodded. All of London knew Lady Annabel Wren. Duke's daughter. Duke's widow. Beautiful, wealthy, flamboyant, shocking.

"Why did you choose her?"

"Because I wasn't a trophy to her," Mordecai said. The heat was fading from his face. "And she made me laugh. Annabel has a very, um, interesting sense of humor." *Lewd* was the word he'd been about to utter. Lady Annabel could be as bawdy as a sailor when she chose to be, duke's daughter or not.

"And after her?"

"Mary Halliburton."

Eleanor nodded again. She clearly knew of Mary, too. Not quite as *outré* as Annabel. Fashionable rather than flamboyant, original rather than shocking. Earl's daughter, viscount's widow. A handsome, intelligent, assertive woman. A woman who knew what she wanted in and out of bed—and had the confidence to go after it.

"Mary was my mistake," Mordecai admitted. "She wanted more than one lover on her string. She wasn't faithful, so I ended it. And after her was Mary Wolverhampton." His second Mary, as different from the first as chalk from cheese.

"The pretend affair," Eleanor said, and then she quoted him: "What's sauce for the gander is sauce for the goose."

Mordecai nodded. "Mary and I played our game for almost two months, while Wolverhampton got crosser and crosser. I was hoping he'd call me out, but he didn't have the courage."

"You don't like him," Eleanor said. A statement, not a question.

"Remember that fight at Eton? How when the first three

went down, another eight stepped forward? Wolverhampton was one of the eight, so no, I don't like him."

Eleanor's eyebrows drew together in a sharp frown. "You said his wife loved him."

"She does."

"But how can she? He doesn't sound like a nice man at all!"

Mordecai shrugged. "Women don't always fall in love with good men—nor men with good women. Sometimes the heart makes decisions that aren't wise."

She looked at him for a long, frowning moment, and then said, "Do you count Mrs. Wolverhampton as one of the five?"

Mordecai shook his head.

"So that leaves two more?"

"Yes."

"Who were they?"

Mordecai sipped his wine. "Next was Véronique."

"Another Frenchwoman?"

"A creole. A *mulâtresse*." He observed her surprise. "Surely Roger told you? He was quite vulgar about her at the time."

Eleanor shook her head. "He spoke of your low tastes, but he never mentioned a *mulâtresse*."

Mordecai grunted, and drank some more wine. "Véronique was from Louisiana. Things are a bit different over there. Many of the wealthy men choose—I guess the closest word is concubines—from among the slaves. Véronique's mother was concubine to a Frenchman. A nobleman's son. After a time he freed her, and still later, he married her. When Véronique was born, her father saw that she was educated, had tutors sent out from France, taught her English, Italian, German. He settled a great deal of money and property on her and her mother.

"Véronique was legitimately born, she was wealthy, she

had aristocratic blood. She could have married a respectable man . . . but instead, she chose to be a mistress to a very *un*respectable man. Another French nobleman: Henri de la Rochelard, Comte de Pontillier." Mordecai shrugged. He didn't blame Véronique for her choice; Henri had been handsome, lighthearted, devil-may-care, *fun*.

"They were together half a dozen years. Henri brought her to London—she made quite a stir." As much of a stir as Cécile had done eight years earlier. "Henri was a gambler, he ran through money like water. He needed a wealthy wife, and Véronique wouldn't marry him, so he contracted a marriage with a sixteen-year-old heiress, a pudding-faced little thing. He thought he could have it all, you see: the beautiful mistress, the wealthy wife."

Eleanor's upper lip curled faintly in contempt.

"Véronique felt as you did. She left Henri to his poor little wife and took up with me instead. We got along very well."

"Was she beautiful?" Eleanor asked.

Mordecai nodded. Véronique had been even more beautiful than Cécile, in his opinion—the dusky skin, the lustrous dark eyes. "But more than that, she had *spirit*. She was her own person. She was quick-witted and funny and rebellious. She enjoyed shocking people." He gave a snort of amusement. "I remember once she tipped a bowl of punch over Henri. In front of half the *ton*. He had pink champagne in his hair, and orange peel."

"Why?"

Mordecai shrugged. "I can't remember. She used to fly into dramatic rages—then just as quickly be laughing again. She was . . . very alive."

Eleanor hesitated, and then said, "Did you love her?"

"Neither of us was in love. We just liked each other a lot."

"How long were you together?"

"Two years, and then Véronique went back to Louisiana. She hated England, hated the cold, the fog, the winters."

"You didn't want to go with her?"

He shook his head.

Eleanor considered this reply for a moment, and then said, "Who was after Véronique?"

"Sarah Tarleton."

Her eyebrows lifted. "Lady Tarleton?"

Mordecai nodded. Sarah Tarleton had been the opposite of Véronique. Their relationship had been comfortable, undemanding, restful. He'd enjoyed Sarah's even-tempered company as much as her voluptuous body. "We were together almost a year and then I met someone else, a kindred spirit, so I ended the affair."

"But you said you'd only had five mistresses."

"I have."

"But . . . who did you leave Lady Tarleton for?"

"You."

Eleanor Wrotham blinked, startled, and then a deep blush suffused her face.

"I've been faithful to you ever since," Mordecai said.

Eleanor moistened her lips and said, "How can you be so certain I'm a kindred spirit?"

"Because you helped that urchin in Halfmoon Street, when most other people would have looked away. Because you were kind to Arabella Knightley despite her past. Because you ride *ventre à terre* when no one's watching."

Eleanor looked down at her plate. "Georgiana rides like that sometimes, and she's kind to Miss Knightley, and she would have helped that boy if she'd been there. Perhaps you should marry her."

"Georgiana Dalrymple is a very nice girl," Mordecai

agreed. "But she and I have no spark. And besides . . . she doesn't have your eyelids."

Her gaze flew to him.

"I like your eyelids very much," Mordecai said softly.

A blush suffused her face again. She looked hastily back at her plate. After a moment she said, "You said one of your requirements for your mistresses was a sense of humor. You don't know that I have one."

"You have a sense of humor," Mordecai said. "You just don't let it out very often."

Eleanor glanced at him, a dubious frown on her brow. "How can you know that?"

"I've seen you make your cousin laugh."

"In public?" She shook her head. "I would never do that."

"At that balloon ascension in Hyde Park. I don't know what you said to her, but it sent her into whoops." Eleanor Wrotham had laughed, too, and she hadn't looked like a duchess at all, she'd looked full of mischief and merriment—and then her father had turned to look coldly at her and the amusement had wiped itself from her face as if it had never been there.

Eleanor grimaced and looked away. "Father was very displeased. He rebuked me afterwards."

"Of course he did," Mordecai said dryly. "Heaven forbid that anyone should ever laugh."

His tone made her glance back at him.

"What's wrong with laughing?" he asked her.

Eleanor considered this question for several seconds, and then said, "Nothing." Her chin lifted slightly, as if she was defying her father.

"Do *you* think you have a sense of humor?" Mordecai asked her.

She was silent for several more seconds. "I like to laugh," she admitted finally.

"Most people do," Mordecai said. "Your father probably would have enjoyed it, too, if he'd ever allowed himself to."

"Father? Laugh?" Eleanor shook her head. "I never saw him laugh. Not once."

This statement hung in the air for a moment, and Mordecai's only thought was: *How sad.*

Eleanor sighed. "Poor Father. He was so narrow."

"Yes." Mr. Wrotham had been very narrow in his views. "When I offered for your hand I wasn't at all surprised that he turned me down. I'd expected it." What he *hadn't* expected was for Eleanor Wrotham to accept Roger's offer. That had been a kick in the gut. He'd been consumed by a sick, helpless, hopeless rage. "When your sister ran away, when the scandal broke and Roger jilted you and your father took you back to Lincolnshire, I wrote to him and renewed my offer. His reply was . . . discouraging." Mr. Wrotham had penned a very unflattering summation of Mordecai's character, and ended his epistle with the vehement assertion that he would rather die than see his daughter marry a libertine.

"I addressed my next letter directly to you. I felt you should have the choice of refusing me yourself."

Eleanor's lips parted slightly. She shook her head. "I never received it."

"I realized that, eventually. I wrote twice more and did receive an answer in the end. From your father, telling me that I was wasting ink and paper, that no letter of mine would ever reach you."

Eleanor shook her head again. "I'm sorry."

Mordecai shrugged with one shoulder, and reached for his wineglass. "Not your fault." He sipped. "I was on the point of setting out for Lincolnshire, to make my offer face to face, when Father had his stroke. Naturally, I was unable to leave him." Six weeks, he'd spent at his father's bedside. And then he'd buried him. "After he died there was so much to do. It was . . ." He blew out a breath. It had been a nightmare. The estates being parceled out, Roger livid that so little had come to him, the servants in an uproar. He'd honored his pledge—that he'd find employment for anyone who felt unable to work for Roger—but it had been like the Great Flood. Not just housemaids and kitchen maids and laundry maids, but foot-men, butlers, housekeepers. He'd pensioned off the older retainers, but he'd still had too many servants. Far too many. In desperation he'd purchased Great Wynthrop, huge, long-neglected, gently decaying, and set them to the task of putting it to rights.

Every time he'd turned around a fresh problem had cropped up—the lawyers, the paperwork, the carpenters, the endless stream of defecting servants—and all the while he'd been thinking of Eleanor Wrotham, far off in Lincolnshire, guarded by her Cerberus of a father. He'd been aware of time slipping away, minutes, hours, days—and fear had taken root that she would marry someone else, someone her father approved of, someone who was prepared to overlook a ruined sister for the sake of a wife such as Eleanor Wrotham. There had been days when he'd barely been able to swallow his food, the fear had gripped his throat so tightly.

"And when I finally had everything under control, *your* father died."

Eleanor grimaced faintly, and looked down at her plate.

"Proposing to you at such a time would have been the height of ill-manners. But I did write, offering my condo-lences." He paused. "Did you get that letter?"

Eleanor shook her head. "My great aunt must have burned it." She squeezed her eyes shut for a moment, pressed her fingertips to her brow, and then opened her eyes again. "I'm sorry. It was unforgivable of them to destroy your letters. They had no *right*."

"They were trying to protect you."

"They were trying to *control* me," she said fiercely. "As if I were a child and completely incapable of making my own decisions! They opened your letters and then *burned* them. It was wrong. Grossly wrong!" She inhaled a sharp breath, and released it slowly. "I beg your pardon. I didn't mean to raise my voice."

"I don't mind," Mordecai said. "If you're angry, why shouldn't you shout?"

"I hope I wasn't shouting," she said stiffly.

Mordecai grinned at her. "Almost, but not quite."

Eleanor Wrotham looked down her nose at him, the picture of an offended duchess, and then smiled wryly. "I apologize for my father and my great aunt. Their behavior towards you was unforgivable."

"And their behavior towards your sister."

Her smile vanished. "Yes."

Mordecai put down his glass. "I should have waited longer, but I couldn't." Six months would have been proper. Five months, verging on disrespectful. Four months, too hasty . . . but four months had been all he'd been able to bring himself to wait.

Mordecai was suddenly aware of the special license in his breast pocket—wrinkled, dog-eared, precious—purchased at the Doctors' Commons the day before he'd set out for Bath and carried ever since, while his hopes rose and ebbed like the tide. The license seemed to burn its way through the fabric. He leaned forward. "Nell, will you marry me?"

She stiffened, and became a duchess again.

I shouldn't have asked. Mordecai sat back in his chair and resigned himself to yet another refusal, but Eleanor didn't say *No*. She didn't say anything at all. The silence grew—and grew—and optimism flowered cautiously in Mordecai's chest. "Nell?" he said at last.

"I don't know." Her voice was troubled, and so were her eyes.

Mordecai felt a leap of hope. *I don't know* was a thousand times better than an outright *No*. He leaned forward again, suddenly urgent. "Nell—"

The door opened: the serving-men coming to clear the table.

Mordecai experienced a burst of severe frustration. He sat back in his chair and tried to look relaxed not annoyed, but it was difficult when he'd just missed the perfect opportunity to press his advantage.

Then common sense reasserted itself. He didn't want to push Eleanor Wrotham into marriage. If she still had doubts, if she wasn't completely certain, then this *wasn't* the perfect opportunity.

It would come. Tomorrow, next week, next month. One day he would ask, and Eleanor wouldn't hesitate at all. She would say *Yes*, and she'd smile as she said it.

Mordecai sipped the last of his wine while the servants worked, and thought about what tonight would bring—the closeness, the physical intimacy, the deepening emotional connection between them. Anticipation stirred in his belly. And then he glanced at Eleanor. If an emotion was stirring in *her* belly right now, it would be nervousness. Or perhaps even fear.

Mordecai frowned. He wanted Eleanor to leave this parlor eager for what lay ahead, not nervous, and most definitely not afraid. He sipped his wine thoughtfully and eyed the sofa, and let an idea take shape in his mind.

When the servants withdrew, he said, "Run upstairs and fetch *Summer in St. Ives*, Nell. I'll read the first chapter with you now."

Eleanor hesitated, and then did as he bade.

When she returned, Mordecai latched the door. They sat on the sofa together. The sofa where he'd brought her to a climax last night. Where she'd watched him do the same to himself. His cock twitched at the memory. Mordecai opened the book to its first page, and glanced at her. "You may sit closer to me if you wish."

Eleanor blushed, and shuffled a few inches closer, until their legs were touching.

Mordecai put one arm around her, gathering her even closer, tucking her into his body. "There," he said, and then he turned his attention to the book. "Dear reader, between these covers you will find a true account of a house party that took place last summer. The characters who populate these pages are real, but you will recognize none of the names, for I have taken the precaution of altering them."

He read at a leisurely pace, his voice low. An atmosphere gathered around them, cozy and intimate. By the time he'd finished the second page Eleanor had relaxed, leaning warmly against him.

On the third page, Mrs. Lightheel and Colonel Everhard embarked on a game of billiards together.

"Does Everhard mean what I think it means?" Eleanor asked.

"It means that the colonel is a very priapic man," Mordecai told her.

"Priapic?"

"His *bâton* is constantly at a stand."

Eleanor nodded. "I thought so."

Mordecai continued reading. The prose was surprisingly

well written—and it reinforced his opinion that the author was a female. There was a subtlety to it that one didn't find in works such as *Fanny Hill*. The words themselves weren't actually sensual, but the way the author put them together *was*: the billiard cues were long, hard, smooth, powerful, and the pockets the balls dropped into were snug, dark, soft, warm. When Mrs. Lightheel lightly caressed the billiard balls while she positioned them on the table, Mordecai's own balls tightened. When she idly stroked her billiard cue—*her fingertips whispering along that sleek, rigid length*—he perfectly understood Colonel Everhard's comment: '*I beg you will cease that, ma'am. It's extremely distracting.*'

Mordecai explained all this to Eleanor. "A man's testicles are often referred to as his balls," he said. "And for a woman to fondle them is an extremely pleasant sensation." He stroked Eleanor's throat, just below her earlobe, a touch as light, idle, and *deliberate* as Mrs. Lightheel's caress of the billiard balls.

Eleanor shivered.

"And when Mrs. Lightheel strokes the billiard cue, the author clearly wishes us to imagine her stroking the colonel's *bâton*." He let his fingers whisper over Eleanor's skin again, making her shiver a second time. "The colonel imagines it, too, which is why he asks her to cease." Mordecai's fingertips drifted down her throat until they encountered the neckline of her gown. A prim neckline, as befitted Mr. Wrotham's daughter. "I can't say I blame the colonel. Seeing a woman touch a cue in such a suggestive manner would bring almost any man's *bâton* to a stand."

Mordecai's fingers wandered along the prim neckline, a light and tickling exploration that made Eleanor shiver again. He found the hollow of her throat. They were sitting together reading a book, a very sedate activity . . . but Eleanor's pulse was beating with great rapidity. Mordecai laid one fingertip over that betraying pulse and glanced at her face. Her cheeks were flushed a pretty pink.

Satisfied, Mordecai continued reading aloud. He kept his fingers at the hollow of Eleanor's throat, stroking lightly from time to time, feeling her shiver, feeling her pulse dance.

Mrs. Lightheel continued with her seduction of the colonel. She removed her gloves—to help her hold the cue more securely—and then, while awaiting her turn, she placed one fingertip between her lips and sucked on it. Mordecai's cock twitched again. "This is an allusion to a sexual act. You may imagine that Mrs. Lightheel's finger is the colonel's *bâton* —and you can be *quite* certain that this is what the colonel will imagine, too. If his *bâton* wasn't at a stand before, it will be now."

He laid the book down on his lap, took Eleanor's hand, and lifted it to his mouth, letting two of her fingertips rest on his lower lip. "Mouths are for more than just kissing," Mordecai told her. "They're tools for giving pleasure." He drew her fingertips into his mouth.

Eleanor shivered, a convulsive movement.

Mordecai sucked gently several times, letting her feel the heat of his mouth, the softness of his tongue, the rhythm he was building. He let his tongue roam over the sensitive pads of her fingertips, then bit lightly, and released her.

Mordecai picked up the book again. He glanced at Eleanor's face. Her pupils were dilated behind the spectacle lenses, her cheeks deeply flushed. He smiled to himself, and found his place on the page. "Mrs. Lightheel idly drew one rosy fingertip between her lips and sucked, an innocent gesture that wholly captured the colonel's attention. He missed his shot.

"'Oh, dear,' Mrs. Lightheel said, and sucked on her fingertip again.

"The colonel uttered an oath and cast aside his cue. He advanced on Mrs. Lightheel in a rampant state—"

"Rampant?" Eleanor asked.

"His *bâton* is erect," Mordecai told her. He continued reading: "He advanced on Mrs. Lightheel in a rampant state, gathered her up in his arms, and flung her upon the billiard table, an indecency to which she most eagerly submitted."

In a matter of moments Everhard had fought his way through the froth of Mrs. Lightheel's petticoats, exposing what the author called her "womanly bounty." That task accomplished, the colonel ripped open his drawers to display his own tumescent member.

"'Your yardstick is very large,' Mrs. Lightheel marveled.

"'All the better to pleasure you with,' Everhard growled."

Mordecai didn't pause to explain what *yardstick* meant; the context made it clear. He continued reading as Everhard plundered Mrs. Lightheel's bounty with single-minded vigor, an activity that propelled both participants to such heights of pleasure that Mrs. Lightheel gave a cry of ecstasy and swooned.

On this climactic note, the chapter ended.

Mordecai uttered a crack of laughter. "Good God. What utter nonsense."

Eleanor Wrotham giggled.

"I hope you're not expecting to be raised to such heights," Mordecai said. "If you are, you'll be sorely disappointed. I may be a rake, but my lovemaking has *never* made anyone swoon."

Eleanor giggled again. It was a very unduchesslike sound —and it warmed Mordecai's heart to hear it.

"It's a very silly novel, isn't it?" she said.

"*Extremely* silly." Mordecai closed the book and sat quietly for several seconds, savoring the moment: Eleanor leaning against him, soft and warm, the memory of her giggle in his ears, the hum of arousal and anticipation in his blood. He lightly stroked the hollow of Eleanor's throat, felt her pulse leap beneath his fingertips, felt her shiver, then he dipped his head and pressed his lips to her ear and whispered, "Tell me truthfully, Nell . . . do you still wish to make love tonight?"

Eleanor shivered again. "Yes." Her voice was low and faintly breathless.

The hum in Mordecai's blood became stronger. "Your room or mine?"

"I don't mind."

"Mine, then," Mordecai said, because that left the power in her hands. She could come to his bedchamber—or not. And she could leave whenever she wished.

Chapter Twenty-Three

WHEN CÉCILE HAD TAKEN him as her lover, the first thing she'd done was teach Mordecai about his own body. She'd shown him things he hadn't known about his balls and his cock, but also about parts of himself that he'd never associated with erotic pleasure before. She had let him conquer his virgin's shyness, his fear of being laughed at—and once he'd been completely confident she'd expanded his sexual education, introducing him to the more adventurous positions, challenging him to learn skills that required practice: *pattes d'araignées, langue exercée, faire postillion.*

That was how he intended to teach Eleanor Wrotham: confidence first, then skills.

But before that, he had to divest her of her virginity.

There wasn't a lot of preparation he could do—except for one very important task: If he was to have the self-restraint he needed tonight, he needed to dampen down his own arousal.

Mordecai took care of that task as soon as Walter had

gone, stroking himself briskly to a climax. That done, he washed his hands and waited.

Five minutes passed. Ten minutes. Mordecai was beginning to think that Eleanor had changed her mind when someone knocked quietly on his door.

His heart gave a leap in his chest. He crossed to the door, and opened it.

Eleanor Wrotham stood there, dressed in a nightgown. She wasn't wearing the spectacles, nor was she wearing a wig. She was herself, her hair drawn back in a simple braid.

It was a long time since Mordecai had seen her hair, and he suddenly realized how much he'd missed it: that rich brown with the mahogany glints in it.

Eleanor hesitated a moment, and stepped into his room. She looked paler than she usually did and even more like a duchess—and slightly taller, too, as if she was holding herself tightly upright.

She's nervous. And probably a little afraid.

"Nell . . ." Mordecai gently took her hands. The evening was warm, but her fingers were cool. "You can change your mind, if you wish."

Her chin lifted. Her shoulders braced. She seemed to stand even taller. "No."

He understood that the lifted chin and braced shoulders weren't aimed at him; they were aimed at herself. She was trying to conquer her nervousness.

Mordecai gave what he hoped was a reassuring smile. He locked the door and drew her across to the four-poster. "Sit," he said gently.

They sat on the edge of his bed, holding hands. After a moment, Mordecai turned her hand over, lifted it to his lips, kissed her palm softly—and then he licked, tasting her skin with his tongue, and felt Eleanor Wrotham shiver. He licked again, nipped lightly, then drew her closer and kissed her mouth.

The kiss started a little awkwardly, their mouths not quite matching, but then the awkwardness passed and their mouths *did* match and some of Eleanor's tension fell away. Mordecai kissed her—and kissed her—and kissed her, until she was warm and soft and pliant in his arms, and then he shucked his dressing gown and lay down on the coverlet and drew Eleanor to lie alongside him, their bodies not quite touching.

He kissed her again. Long delicious minutes passed. Their bodies eased closer. She was clutching his nightshirt, and their mouths were hot and hungry, and Mordecai slid his arm around her waist and drew her even closer, so that their bodies nestled intimately against each other, nothing but her night-gown and his nightshirt between them.

He felt her shudder with arousal, felt her stiffen with shyness and alarm. She broke the kiss.

Mordecai didn't let her draw away from him. He kept his arm around her waist, holding her close, letting her become accustomed to the heat and hardness of his cock pressed against her belly.

A minute passed. Mordecai moved his hips, rocked gently —and felt her quiver.

He did it a second time, a third time—and her hips instinctively rocked back.

Mordecai gave a low murmur of encouragement and slid his hand down from her waist and cupped one buttock in his hand, enticingly round beneath the nightgown. She stiffened slightly. "Relax, Nell," he whispered, and rocked against her, and after a moment's hesitation she pressed back.

They kissed each other, rocked against each other, slowly at first, and then more urgently, her body pressing eagerly to his, and he knew she was no longer alarmed by his hand on her buttock or his cock nestled against her belly.

Satisfied, Mordecai released her. He sat up and stripped off his nightshirt. Eleanor watched him in the candlelight. She had huge, dark eyes. Flushed cheeks. Well-kissed lips.

When he was naked he didn't reach for her, but stayed where he was and let her look at him. She did, an intent and wondering inspection.

His nipples tightened under that perusal. So did his balls.

"Your turn," Mordecai said softly.

She hesitated, and he saw a blush bloom on her cheeks, and then she sat up and undid the buttons at her throat, and pulled the nightgown over her head, her movements shy and self-conscious.

Mordecai's throat grew tight. He was extremely glad that he'd taken care of himself earlier.

Eleanor didn't have Sarah Tarleton's ripe figure or Véronique's dusky skin, but she was a beauty in her own right. Her curves were her own, the pale, smooth skin was purely hers, that patrician face, those haughty eyelids. She was unique, and perfect, and sitting on his bed, so close that he could reach out and touch her.

Mordecai did just that. He reached out and lightly touched her cheek, and felt her tremble, and then he slid his fingers down to the nape of her neck and leaned in and drew her to him and kissed her tenderly.

Their lips clung together and he was aware of her shyness, her self-consciousness, and also her eagerness.

Mordecai laid his hand carefully on her bare knee and felt her tremble and quiver—and then she placed her hand daringly on his knee.

They traded touches and kisses while the candle burned down in its holder. Mordecai explored Eleanor Wrotham from head to toe, showing her that every part of her body was made for pleasure, and he let her explore, too, let her acquaint herself with his chest, his thighs, his groin. The feather-light brush of her fingers as she examined his balls, the whisper of her fingertips over his cock—following the veins, skimming over the smooth, blunt head, outlining the slit—inflamed him more than Cécile's expert handling ever had. He came closer to losing control and spilling all over himself than he had in years. Mordecai clenched his jaw, gritted his teeth, felt the tendons in his neck stand out—and then the moment of danger passed, and he was in control of his body again.

He laid Eleanor on the bed and brought her to a climax with his fingers, delving into her tight, wet, fragrant heat. "*Pattes d'araignées,*" he whispered in her ear. And then he brought her to a second climax with his tongue. "*Langue exercée.*"

He let her catch her breath, then brought her to the brink again—and stopped.

"Oh, God, Mordecai." Eleanor's voice held a groan. She was almost writhing on the bed, flushed and quivering. The bedchamber was warm, shadowy, candlelit, fragrant with their arousal.

Mordecai laughed. It came out hoarsely because he was almost as mindless with need as she was. He settled himself over her. "It might hurt. First times can."

"I don't care." Eleanor clutched his arms, arching up, pressing against him, urgent and eager—and Mordecai had another moment when he almost lost control, when he almost spilled his seed before he'd even entered her.

He held himself still, didn't move, didn't breathe—and the moment passed—and he inhaled a shuddering breath and entered her carefully.

She was tight—exquisitely tight—and hot and slick and

eager. Mordecai pushed into her slowly and felt her body accommodate him, felt muscles tighten . . . and then ease to let him in.

"Does that hurt?" he asked when he was fully sheathed.

"Not much," Eleanor said breathlessly, and her hips moved, instinctively urging him on.

And so he did what her body craved, what *his* body craved, and withdrew and sank into her a second time.

"Does it hurt?" he asked again.

"No." Her hips moved again. Véronique would have said, *Stop talking and just fuck me,* but Eleanor Wrotham didn't have that vocabulary. Mordecai understood the language of her body, though, so he gave her what she wanted. What they both wanted. There was none of the awkwardness he'd anticipated. The rhythm built swiftly and naturally, a much faster rhythm than he'd intended. This was no leisurely lovemaking, but urgent and gasping, straining against each other. Eleanor climaxed quickly, and then almost immediately a second time.

Cécile had taught him that good lovemaking was about control and stamina, but Mordecai had neither control nor stamina tonight. He withdrew hastily. He didn't have time to reach for his handkerchief, but climaxed helplessly, fiercely, spilling his seed over his hands in great spurts—and when it was over he lay gasping on the bed, half-dazed. *Christ.*

Mordecai groped in his dressing-gown pocket for a handkerchief and cleaned himself. Then he gathered Eleanor Wrotham in his arms. She nestled close.

He stroked the damp tendrils of hair at her temple, pressed a kiss there, and felt ridiculously pleased with himself. He'd given her a night he knew she'd never forget.

Chapter Twenty-Four

July 22nd, 1812
Exeter, Devonshire

NELL WOKE KNOWING that the world was a different place and that she was a different person. The first twenty-three years of her life lay on one side of a great divide and the rest of her life lay on the other side.

She'd been so certain she could never love Mordecai Black —*determined* not to love him—but Black was no autocrat, and marriage to him wouldn't be a cage; it would be freedom and companionship and joy.

And love.

Because she loved him. She loved Mordecai Black.

It was a life-altering realization.

Everything had changed—and at the same time, it hadn't. Mordecai Black hadn't altered at all. He was exactly the same man he'd been in London a week ago, but she'd been blinded by his reputation, by his assertive nature, by his imperious nose. He hadn't changed; *she* had. She'd learned to see who he truly was, and that man wasn't the rake the gossipmongers painted him as. He was kind and tender, decisive and blunt-spoken, liberal, unconventional, moral. And romantic. And lonely.

Nell had once heard a sermon in which a good marriage was likened to a garden: the husband watching over his wife and children while they bloomed under his care, protected and sheltered and nurtured. The vicar had been talking of flowers, but Nell had seen an espaliered tree in her mind's eye, branches bound in place, lovingly forced to grow into a shape someone else wished it to.

Marriage to Black wouldn't be like that. She wouldn't be espaliered, she'd be like a great oak in the woods, able to grow into whatever shape she wished.

If I'm going to be free, I want to be free with him.

Nell flung back the bedcovers and climbed out of bed. She stood for a moment, trying to sense a change in her body, some physical reminder of last night's events, but there was no ache, nothing. Her virginity had been taken, her heart had been lost—or won, depending how one viewed it—and her body carried on as if nothing had happened.

What did you expect, you goose? Nell crossed to the window, drew the chintz curtain back, and stared out at the rooftops of Exeter. The sky was bright, hazy.

Today I will find Sophia.

"Hurry up, Baletongue," Nell said, under her breath. She turned and surveyed the room, but there was no Faerie concealed in the shadows of the bedhangings. She stood for a moment, listening, waiting, hoping. Lady Dalrymple had told her that when Baletongue arrived every hair on her scalp would stand on end—but her scalp felt completely normal.

The door swung open. Nell gave a great, convulsive start, but it was only Bessie, carrying a pitcher of steaming water.

"Good morning, ma'am."

"Good morning, Bessie," Nell said. "It looks as if we're in for another hot day."

SHE ATE BREAKFAST in the private parlor with Mordecai Black, and it felt awkward at first—he'd seen her naked, she'd seen him naked, he'd been *inside* her—and then Black met her eyes and smiled, and it no longer felt awkward, it just felt right. Deeply and profoundly right. *This is how it's meant to be: the two of us together.*

But as much as Nell wanted to spend the morning with him, she had to be alone in order for Baletongue to show herself. "I have a letter I need to write," Nell said, once they'd finished eating.

If Black was disappointed, it wasn't obvious on his face. He nodded, and said, "I'll go for a walk. May I take that sketch with me? I'd like to show it around, see if anyone recognizes your sister."

"Of course."

Ten minutes later, Black left the inn. Nell went to the window, watched him step out into the street, and felt a sharp pang of regret. She didn't want to wait for Baletongue; she wanted to be with him.

NELL WAS TOO RESTLESS to sit. Emotions churned inside her: a jittery, edgy impatience underlain by a prickle of fear. Baletongue was no benevolent Faerie godmother; she was dangerous. *An ill-chosen wish can ruin your life,* Lady Dalrymple had cautioned. *Don't let her trick you into something you'll regret.*

The church bells struck nine o'clock. Nell peered out the window again. Her impatience surged. Sophia was out there somewhere. "Hurry up, Baletongue."

She pushed away from the windowsill. Her father, if he could see her, would rebuke her. *Restlessness is a sign of an unregulated mind,* he'd told her more times than she could remember. *Go to your room until you can control yourself.* And Nell had conformed to the cage he'd built around her, had learned not to fidget, not to laugh, not to run, not to raise her voice, not to be anything but calm at all times.

She wasn't calm now. She was impatient for Baletongue to come, impatient to find Sophia, impatient to get on with the rest of her life.

Nell paced, and kept an eye on the clock.

The minute hand crawled around the face. And crawled. And crawled. And Baletongue didn't come.

"Oh, for heaven's sake," Nell told herself after twelve minutes of restless pacing. "Sit down and write Georgie another letter!"

She marched across to the little writing desk, located paper and ink and a passable quill, and started the letter: *Dearest Georgie.* The clock caught her eye again. Nell watched the minute hand make another creeping circuit—and then gave herself a sharp, mental shake. She bent her attention to telling Georgie about her decision to marry Mordecai Black. *I know you'll be alarmed by this news, but believe me when I tell you that his reputation as a rake is vastly overblown. He's a great deal more virtuous than anyone gives him credit for. More virtuous, certainly, than Roger Lockwood-Smith. (I'll tell you what I mean by that when we next meet face-to-face; it's too shocking to be committed to paper.) But until we meet you shall just have to trust me when I say that he is the kindest and best of men.*

I have no doubt that you'll think I've lost my wits! I assure you I haven't. And if you doubt my estimation of Mordecai Black, ask your mother for hers. I think you'll find that she approves of my choice.

Lady Dalrymple liked Mordecai Black. In fact, if Lady Dalrymple had been ten years younger and widowed, she would almost certainly have been one of Black's mistresses. The viscountess moved in the best circles, but there was nothing staid about her. She was everything that Nell's father had deplored: outspoken, original, open-minded. Viscount Dalrymple hadn't tried to mold his wife into the perfect lady, he'd let her be the person she was.

And Mordecai Black will let me be myself, too, Nell thought.

She glanced at the clock again. Three more minutes had passed.

Nell dipped the quill in the inkpot, and began a new paragraph: *I wish Baletongue would hurry! I am in a fever of impatience— but I confess I am also a little afraid. If your mother was frightened by her, then she must be terrifying indeed—but I take courage in the knowledge that even if she scares me witless, I will be reunited with Sophia shortly—and for that, I would face down the fiercest of Faeries.*

You'll see Baletongue for yourself next month, dearest cousin. Be stout of heart! Baletongue cannot be too terrifying, or else our ancestresses would all have died of fright on their twenty-third birthdays. Although perhaps fright is why some of them have chosen so poorly?

As soon as I know where Hubert is I shall seal this letter and send it to you.

All my love,
Nell

BALETONGUE HADN'T APPEARED by noon. At twelve thirty, the servants began setting the table for luncheon. At twelve thirty-five, Mordecai Black returned to the inn. He came up the stairs fast, taking the steps three at a time, and one glance at his face told Nell that he had news. She took a step towards him. "Sophia?"

"I found someone who saw her last month."

"Where?"

"Not far from here. We can go now if you like."

Nell did want to go—desperately—but she said politely, "Do you wish to eat luncheon first?"

Black glanced at the table and shook his head. "Food can wait."

Nell ran upstairs to fetch her bonnet. "Who's this person who saw her?" she asked, as she and Black clattered down the stairs to the street.

"A costermonger."

Outdoors, it was stiflingly hot. A bell pealed loudly nearby, *clang-clang-clang.*

Black set a brisk pace. "The costermonger says that Sophia was in the company of another young woman. Lizzie, I'm guessing. He thinks they were lodging in Turnagain Lane. He saw her several times."

"*Were* lodging? They're not there now?"

"He doesn't think so. But there's a good chance someone in Turnagain Lane will know where they went."

Another bell began pealing. *Clang-clang. Clang-clang. Clang-clang.*

"What sort of neighborhood is it?" Nell asked.

"Better than the West Quarter."

A third bell started ringing, and a fourth. It was as if every bell in this part of the city was suddenly clamoring. Nell heard steeple bells and a deep, booming workhouse bell and the brassy jangle of vendors' bells.

Black halted abruptly and turned on his heel, scanning the sky.

"What?" Nell said.

A coachman's horn sounded in the distance, loud and urgent blasts.

"Fire," Black said grimly.

Nell followed the direction of his gaze—and saw smoke rising above the rooftops. Not a thin plume, as from a chimney, but a thick pall.

Even as she watched, the column of smoke swelled.

"Back to the inn," Black said. "Now!"

They were only two hundred yards from the inn, but getting there was like swimming upstream against a river. It was as if a floodgate had opened, spilling people into the street.

Exeter's panic was a tangible thing. Nell heard it in the wildly clanging bells, tasted it sharp on her tongue, felt it buffet her on all sides. People elbowed her, shoved her, trod on her feet. Black kept a tight hold on her arm. She clung to him, glad of his formidable size, glad of his strength.

They tumbled breathlessly into the relative calm of the inn's yard. Walter crossed to them at a run. "Sir!"

"Tell Phelps to put the horses to," Black said. "I want us gone within three minutes."

"Yes, sir." Walter ran for the stables.

Nell could smell the fire now, a wild, acrid smell.

A cry of pain came from the street. Nell turned and saw a boy on the ground, rolling and scrambling, trying to regain his footing only to be knocked down again. She started forward, but Black moved even faster, shoving back into the crowd, scooping the boy up, hauling him to safety.

Black set the child on his feet in the yard. He was an urchin, scrawny and barefooted, no more than six years of age. "You all right, son?"

The urchin didn't reply, just darted back to the street, plunging into the crowd, heading towards the fire, not away. He made it two paces before he was knocked down again.

Black hauled him back into the inn's yard. This time he held on to the boy's arm. "You'll get trampled out there. Best stay with us."

"I gotta help me ma!" the urchin cried, straining to break free. His face was smeared with dirt, and beneath the dirt was pure desperation. "She can't get down the stairs wi'out me!"

"Where is she?" Black asked.

The boy kicked at Black with his bare feet. "Lemme go!"

Black shook him sharply. "Where is she?"

"There!" the boy said, tears spilling from his eyes. "She's there!"

There was no doubting where *there* was, just as there was no doubting what needed to be done.

"We'll come with you," Nell said, catching up her skirts, taking an urgent step towards the street.

"No," Black said.

"This boy's mother—"

"*I* will find his mother. You're getting out of Exeter."

"But—"

"*You're leaving*," Black bellowed, and then he inhaled a deep breath and said in a more moderate tone, "You've got two minutes. Go and get Bessie."

"I'm not a child," Nell told him. "I can make my own decisions."

"This is one decision you're not going to make. Either you get in that carriage, or I'll damned well *put* you in it myself!"

Nell's temper sparked. She drew breath to tell him what

she thought of overbearing men who treated women as if they were helpless idiots—and saw the implacable determination on his face and knew that it didn't matter what she said or did: Black was going to make her get in the carriage, and if he had to abandon the boy and his mother to their fates in order to do it, he would.

Nell looked at Black, and then at the boy—small, dirty, desperate, straining to break free. She swallowed her anger. "All right," she said. "You have my word I'll get in the carriage. Go."

Black rocked back on his heels as if he'd expected argument not capitulation. He frowned fiercely. "You promise you'll leave?"

"I promise," Nell said. "Now go!"

Black swung the urchin up on his shoulders, took a step towards the street, and looked back at Nell. She saw the conflict on his face: he didn't want to leave her.

"I'll be safe, Mordecai," she said. "Now go. And be careful!"

He gave a curt nod, and stepped into the street. The crowd didn't knock him down; it parted around him.

Nell watched him stride out of sight—a giant of a man with a grubby child on his shoulders—then she turned and ran across the inn's yard. "Bessie!" She thudded up the stairs and hurtled into her bedchamber. "Bessie!"

The maid was standing at the window, wide-eyed and pale-faced.

"We're leaving in two minutes. Go grab your things."

Bessie nodded and ran from the room.

Nell snatched up her valise, threw her clothes into it, and hurried across to the window. The sky was dark with smoke. She tried to guess how far away the blaze was. Three streets? Four?

A prickling shiver crept up her spine. *People are dying right now.*

Bells rang wildly and voices rose from the street below, high-pitched and urgent.

Nell leaned out to see more clearly. The thoroughfare was choked with people, a great throng that surged and heaved yet seemed at a standstill—and then she saw why: a cart had locked wheels with a wagon.

In that instant she realized that they'd not get the carriage out of the yard. There were too many people, too much panic.

Nell glanced at the rooftops again. Was that a glow of flames, writhing and orange, beneath that black pall of smoke?

A shiver prickled up her spine, up the back of her neck, crawled over her scalp—and Nell suddenly realized what it meant.

She spun around.

A woman stood behind her, silent and unmoving. Nell recoiled against the windowsill. Her brain seemed to freeze. *Baletongue.*

The woman's gown was the color of blood, her face as pale as white marble, and her eyes were black. Pure black.

Nell's heart began to thud loudly.

"Eleanor Margaret Wrotham?" Baletongue said, and her voice was light and sibilant and cruel.

Nell moistened her lips and swallowed. "Yes."

Baletongue said nothing more, just watched her with those terrible black eyes, waiting for her to make her wish. The shiver crawled up Nell's spine again, not because of Baletongue's eyes or the inhuman perfection of her face but because of the cruelty that clung to her.

This was a creature without mercy.

Nell suddenly understood why so many of her ancestors had chosen poorly. Not just terror, but because Baletongue had no compassion, no kindness. *She'll feel no remorse if my wish leads to my destruction.*

Nell took a shallow breath. She heard the clanging of bells and the cries of people in the street, inhaled the smell of smoke. For days she'd known what she would wish for—but that certainty had evaporated. *People are burning to death at this moment.*

Baletongue's lips quirked, as if she saw inside Nell's head and understood her dilemma—and was amused by it.

Oh, God, what should I wish for?

Nell listened to the bells and smelled the smoke. Mordecai Black would have reached the blaze by now.

What if he burned to death? What if Sophia did?

Nell opened her mouth, heard Lady Dalrymple's voice —*Choose something that will last a lifetime*—and blurted: "I wish for control over fire."

"Done," Baletongue said, and between one blink of Nell's eyes and the next, she vanished.

Nell spun round and stared out the window. In the distance, a rooftop was in flames. "Stop!" she told it firmly.

The rooftop didn't stop burning.

Nell gripped the windowsill, leaned out, and screamed, "Stop!" as loudly as she could.

The flames didn't quench. The rooftop stilled burned.

I have to be closer.

Nell wrenched open her bedroom door and ran along the corridor, down the two flights of stairs, across the yard, and plunged out into the crowded street. "Out of my way!" she cried. "Move!" And she pushed and shoved with all her might, using her elbows, not caring if she stepped on people's feet, battling her way towards the fire quite as desperately as the young urchin had.

She fought her way forward fifty yards, sixty yards, and

then suddenly broke free of the crowd. The street was much emptier, only a few laggards in her way: the elderly and the lame. Nell picked up her skirts and ran as hard as she could. *Stupid! Stupid!* She should have told Baletongue to quench the fire. A one-time wish. Lifetime wishes didn't matter when people were dying *now.*

The air was thick with smoke. Charred scraps of paper and cloth spun in the currents like thousands of black moths. She reached the end of the street and turned the corner, chest heaving, lungs straining—and there was the fire. Not flames on a far-off rooftop, but three buildings at the end of the block, tall and half-timbered and well ablaze, flames pouring from their many windows.

Nell halted, gulped a breath, and shouted, "Stop!"

The buildings went on burning, flames cascading from the windows and bending upwards to the sooty sky.

Nell ran again. The street wasn't empty; people were frantically hauling possessions from their homes and businesses. Half a dozen men were wetting down the front of a shop—yet another *Reid & Houghton* bakery—throwing buckets of water in what even she could see was an act of futility. The whole street was half-timbered; if one building burned, they would all burn.

If Black died because she'd chosen the wrong wish . . .

Nell ran even harder, until it felt that her lungs might burst, until the fire's fierce heat beat at her, until she heard its roar in her ears, until it seemed her clothes would catch alight—and then stumbled to a halt. "Stop!"

Her voice was weak and breathless, and the fire took no notice.

Nell staggered to the nearest house and slapped her hand against the rough, hot plaster. The building was shuddering, as if the timbers inside had already succumbed to the flames. She inhaled a gasping, sobbing breath, and cried: "*Stop!*"

The world stood still for a moment—and then came a sound like a vast thunderclap. There was an instant of intense heat, when Nell felt as if she burned from the inside out, and then the heat vanished as abruptly as it had come—and all her strength vanished with it. The fire collapsed inwards on itself, sucking back into the windows, and Nell collapsed, too. Her heart stopped beating, her lungs stopped working, and she experienced a moment of sharp clarity—*I'm going to die*—and on the heels of that realization came a brief burst of emotions —disbelief, despair, rage—and then they snuffed out, too, and she felt nothing but a strange, detached calmness. She had the sensation that she was floating above herself, gazing down at her crumpled body, and she felt nothing, not even sorrow— and then Nell suddenly fell back into herself. Her cheek was pressed to the hot, gritty flagway and she was coughing and gasping and alive.

Chapter Twenty-Five

A MAN HELPED Nell to her feet, a stranger dressed in a baker's apron. He took her back to the inn. She walked leaning on his arm, feeling stupidly weak. It wasn't until they were nearly there that she realized the baker was limping, and that beneath his apron he had a wooden leg.

Black's traveling chaise was in the inn's yard, a grim-faced Phelps on the box. Bessie rushed towards her, crying, "Ma'am! Ma'am! Where have you been?" and Walter was behind her, looking no less distraught.

"The fire's out," Nell said, still leaning on the baker's arm, but her voice was weak and Bessie and Walter didn't hear her. They detached her from the baker and tried to herd her into the carriage.

"The fire's out," Nell said again. She stretched a desperate hand towards the baker. "Tell them, sir."

"Fire's out," the baker confirmed. His voice was a deep, authoritative bass.

Bessie and Walter stopped trying to bundle Nell into the carriage.

"Fire's out," the baker said again. "Snuffed out in an instant. Miracle, it were. God's work." He gave a decisive nod and turned and left the yard.

Nell stood with Bessie on one side and Walter on the other, feeling weak to the point of fainting. It took all her effort to stay standing. "Has Mr. Black returned?"

"No, ma'am."

"Walter, can you please go and look for him?"

Walter hesitated, and then said, "Yes, ma'am," and followed the baker out into the street.

"Phelps, you may put the carriage away."

Phelps hesitated, too, and then said, "Yes, ma'am."

Nell sagged against Bessie.

"Ma'am, are you all right?"

"I need to lie down," Nell said.

Bessie helped her up the stairs. Nell's head swum and bright stars danced across her vision. When she reached her bedchamber, she half-collapsed on the bed. Bessie bundled her briskly out of her clothes. "Ma'am, all your seams are charred," she said, a note of horror in her voice, and "Ma'am, the soles of your shoes are burned through!"

"Please wake me if the news about Mr. Black is bad," Nell said, crawling under the bedcovers. "If he's injured, or . . . or . . ." *Or dead.*

"Yes, ma'am."

Nell pressed her face into the pillow and discovered that she was wearing the spectacles. She fumbled them off. A wig was still pinned to her head, but she didn't care. She closed her eyes and was asleep in an instant.

IT WAS EARLY evening when Nell woke. She lay and listened to Exeter's church bells tolling six o'clock. The echoes died away. Silence returned. Not complete silence—a murmur of far-off voices drifted in the open window, a clatter of wagon wheels, a dog's faint bark—but those were safe, ordinary, everyday sounds. She heard no panicked shouts, no cries of alarm and warning.

Nell sat up. She felt only a little tired. When she pushed back the bedclothes and climbed out of bed her legs didn't buckle and her head didn't swim.

She crossed to the window and looked out and saw a hazy, smoke-tinged sky. The distant rooftop where the flames had leapt was a charred and blackened shell.

She had slain Exeter's fire, but in return the fire had almost slain her.

Nell turned away from the window. She fumbled at her hairline, pulling out the hairpins, and removed her wig. It smelled strongly of singed horsehair.

The door opened behind her. She turned, and saw Bessie peeping in.

"Ma'am! You're awake."

"Has Mr. Black returned?"

"Just now, ma'am. He and Walter were helping with the fire. Walter says it's a dreadful mess, buildings falling down, some of 'em with bodies still inside." Bessie gave a shiver.

"He's all right? Mr. Black?"

"Dirty as a chimney sweep, but quite safe."

"Thank God," Nell said.

"How do you feel, ma'am? Would you like a bath?"

Nell most definitely did want a bath. She washed the soot from her skin and the stink of the singed wig from her hair. Dressing was problematic, though, because everything she'd been wearing was ruined. Not just her gown, but her petticoat and chemise and stays. The gown disintegrated when Bessie held it up, the bodice parting company from the skirt, the little cup sleeves falling off.

"But why only the seams?" Bessie said, perplexed. "Why didn't the whole gown catch fire?"

Nell could have answered that question: Because it hadn't been the inferno that had burned the seams; it had been magic. *Her* magic.

The blue kidskin shoes had fared no better than the gown. Each sole had great charred holes in it.

"Are you certain your feet aren't burned, ma'am?"

"I'm certain." Nell examined the white cotton stockings she'd worn. They were speckled with tiny holes. "My garters?"

The garters were ruined, the pretty embroidery charred and flaking.

"Look at your bonnet." Bessie held it out, a bedraggled object with a scorched brim. The smell of burned straw clung to it. "It's a miracle your wig didn't catch on fire."

The wig looked like the pelt of a long-dead animal. When Bessie picked it up, a great hank of horsehair fell off.

Nell gazed at the pile of clothes. Everything she'd worn needed to be replaced. *What on earth am I going to wear tonight?* She had two more gowns and one more pair of stockings, but no spare petticoat or chemise, no stays, no garters and shoes.

She thought of her reticule with its shrinking hoard of funds. Thank God she'd been in such a hurry she'd forgotten to wear her spencer and her gloves. "Bessie, tomorrow morning you must go shopping for me. I'll stay in my room until then."

"I have these for you, ma'am," Bessie said, and folded on the chair were a petticoat and chemise. "You can borrow them for now."

"Whose are they?" Nell asked, astonished.

"They belong to one of the servants here." Bessie hesitated, and then said anxiously, "You don't mind, do you, ma'am?"

"Mind? Of course not!"

Bessie looked relieved. "I couldn't find any stays for you to borrow, ma'am."

"I shall be quite happy without stays," Nell said.

She donned the borrowed chemise and petticoat, and then her own gown and stockings. Bessie gave her two mismatched ribbons for garters, and then produced a pair of yellow silk slippers.

"Whose are these?" Nell asked.

"The landlady's. They might be a little too long, but they're the best I could find, ma'am."

"Does she not mind me wearing them?"

Bessie shook her head.

The slippers were almost a perfect fit. Nell looked at herself in the mirror, and then turned to Bessie and impulsively hugged the girl. Her father would have scolded her for such a gesture, but Nell didn't care. "Thank you, Bessie. You're a marvel."

Bessie blushed pink with pleasure. "It's nothing, ma'am." And then she glanced at the clock on the mantelpiece. "Mr. Black ordered dinner for eight o'clock. Shall I do your hair?"

Nell glanced at the clock, too. Twenty to eight. "Yes." She crossed to the dressing table and sat.

Bessie combed out Nell's damp hair and pinned it up, then she fitted the second wig in place. She chattered while she worked, telling Nell everything she knew about the fire. "A whole street of houses burned to the ground, ma'am, and three more streets started to burn and then stopped. Walter says there are houses that are half burned and they look like the fire ate a great bite out of 'em and then just snuffed right out, and the walls and the furniture and everything is half ash and half not. He says there's no understanding it, ma'am, except that it's a miracle."

"Did many people die?" Nell asked. "Do you know?"

"Walter says there are a score or more dead," Bessie said, deftly placing a hairpin. "That's what he and Mr. Black was doin' all afternoon: helping get the bodies out. But Walter reckons there are some folk as are ash and will never be found."

Nell grimaced and looked down at her hands, clasped in her lap. How many people had died while she'd run? *I chose my wish badly.*

"Walter says there was lots of folk helping, but there was also some as were looting. He says Mr. Black gave one young devil a right hiding." Bessie's busy fingers stilled. Her expression in the mirror was suddenly flustered. "Begging your pardon for the language, ma'am."

"Young devil sounds a perfectly accurate description for such a person," Nell said. "I'm sure he deserved his hiding."

Bessie gave a relieved smile and resumed her placing of the hairpins.

"Do you know what happened to the boy Mr. Black went to help? The one whose mother couldn't get down the stairs?"

Bessie shook her head. "No." She slid a final hairpin into place and stepped back. "Finished, ma'am."

Nell looked at herself in the mirror. There was nothing to show that she'd been face to face with an inferno only a few hours ago. Her skin wasn't reddened in the slightest. If anything, she looked a little pale . . . but perhaps that was because she'd almost managed to kill herself that afternoon. "Thank you, Bessie."

A glance at the clock showed it was ten minutes to the hour. Nell went down to the private parlor. The luncheon they'd not eaten had been cleared away. The table was now set for dinner.

The letter to Georgie lay where she'd left it, on the little writing desk, folded and addressed, but not yet sealed. She'd have to rewrite it, have to tell Georgie that she had no way of knowing where Sophia was—or Hubert—but she couldn't face that task tonight.

She wouldn't mention Mordecai Black in the new letter, wouldn't tell Georgie that she planned to marry him . . . because she no longer did.

Nell sat on the sofa and clasped her hands in her lap. The last time she'd been in this room she'd been so certain she knew what the day would bring: meeting Baletongue, finding Sophia. And she'd been certain in her feelings for Mordecai Black. Certain that she wanted to marry him.

And then the day had tipped upside down and everything had changed. She had a wish she hadn't intended to ask for. She didn't know where Sophia was. And she no longer wanted to marry Black.

This is one decision you're not going to make, Black had told her. And he'd meant it. There had been no discussion, no question of compromise. He'd overridden her bluntly and emphatically, ignored her objections, treated her as a child to be told what to do.

Nell clasped her hands tightly and stared down at the toes of the borrowed yellow slippers. She still loved Mordecai Black —but she didn't want to marry him.

One couldn't walk away from a marriage, but one *could* walk away from a liaison.

Chapter Twenty-Six

ELEANOR WROTHAM WAS SITTING on the sturdy green sofa when Mordecai entered the parlor. She rose to her feet.

Mordecai closed the door and examined her. She looked particularly haughty, and perhaps a little wary. *My fault.* He'd made a bad misstep this afternoon. He wasn't sure how to retrieve his footing, or if it was even possible. He took a deep breath. "Nell . . ."

The door opened behind him and two serving-men entered bearing dinner.

Mordecai swallowed the words he'd been about to utter— *I'm sorry I shouted at you*—and stood silently while the food was placed on the table. Thank God none of the dishes was roasted pork. He didn't think he could eat pork tonight. In fact, he wasn't sure he'd ever be able to eat it again. His memory gave him an image of a half-charred body and the smells that had accompanied it: scorched hair, burned clothing, roasted flesh. Mordecai shook his head sharply, banishing the memory, and crossed to the table. He held Eleanor's chair out for her. She silently sat.

Mordecai took his own seat and unfolded his napkin.

"Will there be anything else, sir?" one of the serving-men asked.

"No, thank you."

The servants left.

Mordecai took a deep breath and prepared to launch into his apology, but Eleanor said, "Did you find the boy's mother?"

"Uh . . . yes. I did."

"Was she in danger?"

"Yes." He poured her some wine, and then himself. "The house next door was burning."

"You got her out?"

"Yes."

He looked at her face and saw that she wanted more than a mere *Yes*.

"It was an attic room," Mordecai told her. "The boy's mother is lame. She couldn't get down the stairs without his help."

Eleanor's eyebrows lifted slightly. "She shouldn't be in an attic."

Mordecai shrugged. "She'd rather live in an attic in a respectable neighborhood than a ground floor room in the West Quarter—and I can't say I blame her."

"Is the attic still livable?"

Mordecai shook his head. "She'll need new lodgings. As will a great many people."

"You rescued her just in time."

"Yes." He looked down at his plate, and then back at Eleanor—and saw again that she wanted more than just a *Yes*.

"There were four flights of stairs," Mordecai told her. He'd charged up them, the boy, Jemmy, scampering urgently ahead, and when they'd burst into the hot, cramped, smoky room at the top they'd found the boy's mother on the floor, half-hysterical with terror. "It was all right on the way up, smoke but no flames, but on the way back down . . ." He'd been less than a minute in the attic, just long enough to scoop the woman up and throw her over his shoulder—but in those few seconds fire had taken hold of the house. "I told Jemmy to run down the stairs and not stop until he was outside. I followed as fast as I could." The smoke had been hot, thick, choking, making him cough, searing his throat, making his eyes water, and he'd heard timbers popping and cracking in the walls. "The last flight of stairs was on fire, but there was no other way out that I knew of, so I went down them."

Eleanor was staring at him, her face pale and shocked beneath the chestnut wig.

"We were unharmed," Mordecai assured her. "The fire stopped just as I reached it. God only knows why, but it did." The flames had lunged at him—and then quenched, and he'd thundered down the smoky staircase and plunged out into the street, coughing and wheezing, his eyes streaming, and there had been no fire. Heat and smoke, but no flames. No flames anywhere.

Eleanor was still staring at him, aghast.

"We were unharmed," Mordecai said again, firmly.

"The boy?"

"He got down the stairs before they caught alight."

Eleanor swallowed, and then said, "If the fire hadn't stopped—"

"I think we'd have survived," Mordecai told her. "I think we'd have made it to the street. I was running so fast by that time the flames couldn't have stopped us." But they would have been burned. Perhaps badly.

His memory supplied him with images of the bodies he'd seen that afternoon. But for the grace of God . . .

Mordecai managed not to grimace. He smiled instead and gestured at the dishes, even though his own appetite was unenthusiastic. "Please eat."

There was a long pause, while Eleanor looked at him, then she transferred her gaze to the table. After another long pause, she served herself a small portion of peas.

"More than that," Mordecai told her dryly.

Her gaze lifted to him again and she didn't look haughty at all; she looked as if she was on the brink of tears.

"Nell . . ." Mordecai pushed back his chair hastily, walked around the table, pulled her from her seat, and hugged her. Eleanor hugged him back and inhaled a sobbing breath. She was tense, trembling.

Mordecai cupped one hand over the back of her head, the horsehair wig coarse beneath his palm. "Today has been a terrible day," he told her in a low voice. "People have lost their homes. People have died. But you and I have been lucky. We're safe, Nell. We're safe and unharmed. So if those tears are for me, wipe them away." He hugged her more tightly, holding her close. She inhaled another sobbing breath.

"We can't do anything for the people who died," Mordecai said quietly. "But we can help those who survived. There'll be a collection and you can be certain I'll give generously." He already had, emptying his pockets, giving young Jemmy and his mother money for new lodgings. "Life will go on, Nell. It always does."

"I know," she whispered. Her arms tightened around him. "I'm glad you weren't hurt."

"So am I. And I'm glad you weren't hurt. Or Walter or Bessie or Phelps. Or Jemmy and his mother. Or any of the people who could have been burned today but weren't. It's been a terrible day, but it could have been far worse. We have a lot to be thankful for, Nell. All of Exeter does."

"I know," she whispered again.

Mordecai stroked the nape of her neck comfortingly and released her. "Now, I need you to eat. All right?"

She nodded, and gave a wobbly smile, and Mordecai bent and kissed her cheek. "Sit down," he said gently. "Eat."

DESSERT WAS A GOOSEBERRY TART. Mordecai enjoyed the combination of sweetness and tartness. He had two pieces. When he was finishing the second one, Eleanor said, "Did Walter tell you that I went to see the fire?"

Mordecai almost choked on his last bite of tart. "No," he said, putting down his fork. "He did *not* tell me that."

"I went because . . . because I heard . . . because someone said the fire was out, and I wanted to see if it was true." She flushed, and didn't quite meet his eyes, and if she'd been anyone else he'd have thought her lying, but Eleanor Wrotham wasn't the sort of woman who would lie.

"It *was* out," she said, slightly defiantly. "So I told Phelps to put the carriage away and sent Walter to look for you." Now she met his eyes, and the defiance fell away. "I broke my word to you. I'm sorry. I know you'll be disappointed and . . . and angry."

Mordecai carefully placed his plate to one side, trying to decide how to respond. Anger wasn't the foremost of his emotions. Nor was disappointment. What he felt most was horror. He saw the burning stairwell in his mind's eye, saw the bodies he'd pulled from the blackened rubble.

Eleanor sat silently, watching him. She looked haughty and

contrite and slightly wary, her posture tense, her shoulders braced, her hands clasped tightly together.

She thinks I might yell at her again.

Mordecai inhaled a slow breath and released it. "I'm not angry," he said. "Or disappointed. But I do wish you'd left town—even if events proved it unnecessary."

She bit her lip, and then said, "I was afraid for you."

"Then you must understand that *I* was afraid for *you*."

"I do," she said. "But I'm as much an adult as you are, Mordecai, and if you can decide that you're going to help an urchin, then so can I."

"It was more dangerous for you than for me."

"The neighborhood was a perfectly respectable—"

"It had nothing to do with respectability," Mordecai said. "You're smaller than me. You're not as strong. People were being knocked over in that crowd, trampled on, and you could have been one of them. And there was a *fire*. You were wearing a muslin dress and a straw bonnet, for Christ's sake. You'd have gone up like a bloody candle!" He caught himself, took a steadying breath, spoke more moderately: "I beg your pardon. But you must see that it was much more dangerous for you than for me."

Eleanor looked as if she didn't quite believe him.

"We're both adults," Mordecai told her. "We're both capable of making our own decisions. But what's safe for *me* and what's safe for *you* are two completely different things."

Her lips pursed. She pushed her spectacles up her nose. She still looked as if she didn't fully believe him.

Mordecai decided to push his point home. He moved everything—plates, glasses, serving dishes, candelabrum—to one end of the table and folded the tablecloth back, baring a square of polished wood three foot by three foot. "Imagine this is England."

Eleanor's eyebrows lifted. She gave a short nod.

Mordecai took his linen napkin and spread it out, almost filling the square of cleared tabletop. "You and I inhabit different Englands," he said. "This is the England *I* live in—" He tapped the napkin. "Inside its borders, I'm safe. Outside them, I'm not." He ran a finger along the narrow strip of exposed wood. "These are places it would be dangerous for me to go. Back alleys in Whitechapel and opium dens down by the docks. Places where I might be beaten or robbed—or have my throat cut."

Eleanor frowned.

Mordecai pushed the napkin aside and pulled his handkerchief out of his pocket. Unfolded, it was a much smaller square than the napkin. "This is your England. Because you're a woman, there are a lot more cliffs for you to fall off and a lot more swamps—metaphorically—so the part you can move around in safely is smaller." He traced the edge of the handkerchief with a fingertip. "*I* don't define those borders; society does." He met her eyes. "You agree?"

Eleanor hesitated, and gave a reluctant nod.

Mordecai reached for the cutlery, selected the three cleanest pieces, and laid them in a small triangle in the middle of the handkerchief. "This is the part of England that your father let you inhabit. It's very restricted. Call it a cage, if you wish." He glanced at her. "Agreed?"

She grimaced, and nodded again.

Mordecai cleared away the cutlery. "The England you can safely inhabit is smaller than the one I can, but it's not a cage I've built for you. I don't want to put *any* cages around you." He leaned forward and held her gaze. "Go anywhere inside your England that you wish—but know that if you try to step outside it, I'm going to haul you back, because I don't want you to fall off a cliff and break your neck."

She met his eyes and said nothing.

"What happened this afternoon was a cliff. A neck-breakingly high cliff—and I don't just mean the fire. I mean the street, the crowd, the panic. If you'd come with me—if we'd become separated—you could easily have been knocked down and trampled. And if you *had* made it as far as that attic, I don't know you'd have got out alive." He could imagine it: the hot smoky staircase, the flames licking upward, her gown catching alight. A shudder ran through him. "It was a cliff, Nell—a really *high* cliff, and you could have broken your neck."

Her gaze fell. She was silent for a long moment. "But it was a cliff for you, too, wasn't it?"

Mordecai considered this question. "The streets weren't a cliff. Not at all. The attic . . . yes, but it was a smaller cliff for me than it would have been for you, because I'm stronger, because my clothes don't burn as easily."

Her gaze lifted. "You can pull me back from cliffs, but I can't pull you?"

Mordecai hesitated, and then said, "Yes, of course you can."

"You didn't let me today."

"No," he admitted. "I'm sorry, Nell. If you ever think I'm getting near a cliff, tell me, and we'll talk about it."

"We didn't talk today."

"I'm sorry I yelled at you," Mordecai said. "It will never happen again."

One corner of her mouth lifted up in a small, wry smile. "If you think I'm about to break my neck, you have my permission yell at me."

Mordecai said cautiously, "You're not angry at me?"

She shook her head.

Mordecai reached his hand out across the table. "I'm sorry I yelled," he said again, quietly.

"I know." Eleanor took his hand. Her fingers were warm and slender. "I forgive you."

Mordecai's throat constricted. *I haven't ruined everything.* "And I forgive you for risking your neck, but Nell . . ." He tightened his grip on her hand. "Please don't ever do anything like that again. I *beg* you."

She looked at him soberly, and then nodded. "No cliffs, either of us."

"No cliffs."

Mordecai released her hand. They'd just made a vow together—that neither of them would jump off any cliffs, metaphorical or otherwise—and he wanted to ask her to make another one with him. *Marry me, Nell.* But he knew the time wasn't right. You didn't propose to a woman the same day that you'd yelled at her, even if you'd been trying to save her life and even if she'd forgiven you.

Mordecai refolded the handkerchief and put it in his pocket. "We'll look for Sophia first thing in the morning."

"Thank you," Eleanor said. "But I can't come with you. I haven't any shoes."

"No shoes?"

"The soles burned through. I must wait for Bessie to buy me a new pair before I can leave the inn."

"Burned through?" Mordecai said, his pulse giving a leap of alarm. "What do you mean, burned through?"

Eleanor hesitated, and then said, "The cobblestones were hot and my soles were thin, that's all. My feet are unhurt."

At that moment the serving-men returned to clear the covers. If they wondered why the tablecloth was turned back and all the dishes pushed to one end, they made no comment. Mordecai held his tongue, and by the time the men had finished, he'd rethought the wisdom of giving voice to his alarm. *Let it rest,* he told himself. Eleanor had promised not to leap off any more cliffs. But even so, the soles of her shoes had *burned through.*

With effort he wrenched his thoughts away from that terrifying piece of information. He pushed back his chair and stood. "The sofa?"

They sat on the sofa, but neither of them was in the mood for caresses and kisses. Mordecai put his arm around her and they were simply quiet together. Mordecai felt weary. Weary in his body, weary in his mind. The events of the day were almost too great for comprehension. The fire, the heat, the smoke, the fear. The moment when he'd stared down that flaming stairwell and made the decision to keep running—and the moment when the fire had snuffed itself out.

He didn't understand it. No one did. It had been a miracle, pure and simple, and he'd witnessed it, and he still felt wonder and disbelief and sheer, utter, heart-stopping relief.

After the miracle had come the search for bodies. Grim work. Work that had made his soul ache. And now that the day was over, all he wanted to do was to hold Eleanor Wrotham and know that they were both alive.

Mordecai stroked her cheek with a fingertip. "Tired?"

She nodded silently. He thought she felt the same way he did: weary, subdued.

Mordecai released her and stood, drawing her to her feet. "We could both do with a good night's sleep."

He escorted Eleanor upstairs to the bedchambers, but when they reached her door he found himself reluctant to bid her goodnight. He didn't want to sleep alone tonight; he wanted to sleep with Eleanor Wrotham safely in his arms.

He thought that perhaps she felt the same way, for she made no move to open her door.

Mordecai took her hand. "Nell . . ."

Eleanor didn't say anything. She didn't look haughty, but sad and almost fragile.

Mordecai hugged her, right there in the corridor, where anyone might see them, and she made no move to pull away, but rested her head on his chest. "Nell, if you don't wish to be alone tonight, just tell me. We don't need to do anything, we can just be together. If you would like?"

She nodded against his chest.

"Are you certain?"

Eleanor nodded again.

Mordecai felt his heart lift. He released her, and cupped her face in his hands and gazed down at her. *I love you, Nell.* "Your room or mine?"

"Mine."

WALTER WAS WAITING in Mordecai's room, in his rôle of temporary valet. Mordecai sent him to bed. "I shan't need you tonight. Go and rest." And then, as the footman turned to go: "You did well this afternoon, Walter. Extremely well."

Walter colored faintly. "Thank you, sir."

Mordecai nodded—not a nod of dismissal, employer to servant, but a nod of acknowledgment, man to man.

Walter's cheeks became even pinker. "Goodnight, sir."

"Goodnight, Walter."

Mordecai stripped slowly and donned his nightshirt. When half an hour had passed he let himself out of his room and walked quietly down to Eleanor Wrotham's door. He listened for a moment, heard no murmur of voices, and tapped softly.

Eleanor opened the door. She was wearing her nightgown. Her hair was in a simple plait, and she was barefoot and solemn and more beautiful than she'd ever been before.

Mordecai's heart clenched in his chest. "You're certain?" he asked.

She nodded silently.

Mordecai stepped inside and closed the door. "We'll just rest, nothing more. You're tired, and so am I." He took her hand and led her across to the bed. "In you get."

Eleanor climbed in, and he did, too, and he pulled the covers up and drew her close. His whole body gave a silent sigh of contentment. The last of the day's tensions unraveled. "Some nights it's better not to be alone," he said, and laid a light kiss on her brow.

"I know," she whispered, tilting her face to him.

Mordecai kissed her gently and she kissed him back, and there was no heat in it at all, just comfort and tenderness, their mouths moving slowly together.

Time crept past while they kissed, and Mordecai's mood gradually changed. When he'd climbed into Eleanor's bed all he'd wanted was companionship and rest, but as the minutes slid by he found himself craving more. Not orgasm, but connection. Connection at its deepest and most profound. Eleanor felt it, too, he thought. She pressed close, not with urgency, but with need. The need to be together.

Finally he broke the kiss and whispered, "Nell?"

She understood the question. "Yes," she said.

Sex had many moods, and tonight it was gentle and slow. Mordecai peeled off his nightshirt, peeled off her nightgown, and made love to her. It was tender and quiet and perfect, and when she climaxed with a soft gasp Mordecai felt it deep inside himself, in his soul. He withdrew, then, and held her. Held her while she curled into him, naked and warm and trusting. Held her while she fell asleep. And even though he hadn't come to completion himself, he felt more complete than he'd ever been in his life.

He'd looked down that flaming gullet today and thought he was going to die, but he hadn't. Instead, he had this: Eleanor Wrotham, asleep in his arms.

Chapter Twenty-Seven

July 23rd, 1812
Exeter, Devonshire

Nell half-woke when Mordecai Black coaxed her back into her nightgown, but she didn't fully wake until much later. There was no sign anyone else had been in her bed; the second pillow, the one he'd lain on, was smooth. Nell reached out and turned it over. The fabric was rumpled and a single short masculine hair clung to it. She touched the creased linen with her fingertips, touched that hair. Mordecai Black's hair. Mordecai Black, who had held her for most of the night, who had dressed her in her nightgown again, who had turned over his pillow when he left.

I love you, Mordecai.

This time yesterday she'd been certain she was going to marry him—and then he'd ordered her from Exeter and her certainty had vanished—and now she was certain again. Utterly and absolutely certain. The certainty had come during dinner, when he'd looked at the peas on her plate, looked at her face, then come around the table and hugged her. Because he'd known she needed to be hugged. Black *could* be domineering, but she no longer minded. She loved him just the way he was, kind and generous and occasionally overbearing, perfect and imperfect at the same time.

We are all of us imperfect.

The door opened quietly. "Ma'am, you're awake." Bessie advanced into the room, her expression anxious. "How do you feel? Are you all right?"

"Of course I am. Why should I not be?"

"When you didn't wake earlier I thought you might be ill."

"What time is it?" Nell looked for the clock. "Good gracious! It's past ten o'clock."

"Mr. Black said to let you sleep as long as you needed. He said to tell you he's gone to Turnagain Lane and he'll be back for luncheon."

"Oh," Nell said. "Good. Thank you." She felt a little sleepy, and wholly disconcerted. Ten o'clock! She hadn't slept so late since her London Season, when the balls had gone on until two in the morning.

"I have a tray prepared, if you'd like your breakfast in bed."

Eating breakfast in bed was another thing Nell hadn't done since her Season, but she was hungry. Famished. "Yes, please."

Bessie brought in the tray—and a newspaper. "Mr. Black said you'd want to see it."

Their advertisement was on the front page. *£10 REWARD!* it proclaimed.

Nell read the newspaper while she ate, then she dressed in the mismatch of clothes, half her own, half borrowed. She carefully counted out the last of her shillings and sent Bessie to buy the items she lacked: chemise, petticoat, garters, shoes, a spare pair of cotton stockings, a bonnet, and the lightest stays the maid could find.

Bessie departed cheerfully. Nell went down to the private parlor, not at all cheerfully. She had to write a new letter to Georgie—and she wasn't looking forward to it. Not only did she have to tell her cousin that she had no idea where Sophia or Hubert were, she had to confess that she'd chosen her wish poorly.

Nell sat down at the little writing desk. Control of fire. What a singularly *useless* gift to have.

She laid out a fresh sheet of paper, uncapped the inkpot, dipped the quill in . . . and frowned at the paper until the ink dried on the quill.

A candle in its holder sat on the writing desk. Nell studied it warily. Could she make the candle burn? Would doing so almost kill her?

After a moment, she laid the quill down. Her heart began to beat faster. *It's only a candle*, she told herself. *One tiny flame.* Even so, she was conscious of a prickle of fear as she reached out and touched the wick with one fingertip.

I didn't die yesterday; I won't die today.

Nell inhaled a shallow breath and said, "Burn."

The candle sprang alight.

Nell jerked her hand back.

The candle continued burning, a bright little flame.

Nell conducted a mental survey of herself. There had been no sensation of heat. No sapping of energy, no faintness. Her heartbeat hadn't faltered, her lungs hadn't seized up. She examined her clothing. The seams weren't singed at all.

Encouraged, she touched the stem of the candle. "Stop."

The candle obligingly stopped burning.

Nell did it several more times. She discovered that she didn't need to touch the candle to set it burning. Snapping her fingers was enough. She imagined telling Georgie that. *My wish is extremely useful. I can light and snuff my chamberstick without needing to get out of bed.*

Nell pulled a face—and heard her father's silent admonishment in her ear: *Ladies do not make faces, Eleanor. It is uncouth. Go to your room.*

She shook her head, banishing his voice, and frowned at the candle and wondered just what control of fire *meant.* Obviously she could start and stop fires, but what else? Could she control what burned and what didn't?

Nell snapped her fingers. "Burn." Then she picked up the sheet of paper and held one corner to the candle. It flared alight.

"Don't burn the paper," Nell told the flame firmly.

The paper snuffed instantly, despite the merry golden flame licking at it.

Nell held the paper in the flame for a whole minute, but the paper didn't catch alight again. Thoughtfully, she laid it back on the desk. Then she said, "Don't burn me," and held her hand over the candle.

The flame didn't burn her either, not even when she brought her palm close enough to touch the wick. She felt no pain, no discomfort, nothing except a warm, tickling sensation. Her palm, when she inspected it, was no pinker than usual.

"Hmm." Nell turned to look at the fireplace. A fire was laid in the grate.

Dare I?

Nell pushed back her chair and went to kneel in front of the hearth. She looked at the lumps of coal for a long moment, considering her next move. One, or all? *Prudence,* she told herself. She focused her attention on one coal at the top of the pile and said imperatively, "Burn."

The coal burst alight.

Nell stared hard at the flames and told them they weren't to spread. They obeyed her.

She sat back on her heels and observed what she'd done: a whole fireplace filled with lumps of coal, but only one was burning.

She imagined demonstrating this feat to Georgie—*Look at this impressive gift I've chosen. Ta-da!*—and imagined Georgie's giggle.

Nell snorted under her breath. No, impressive wasn't the word for it. Absurd, perhaps?

She worked with the single coal for several minutes, quenching the flames, reigniting them, making them burn hot and high, damping them to a gentle glow. Then she allowed the flames to spread, first to one coal, then two, then half a dozen. Finally she set every coal in the fireplace burning, coaxed the flames to roar high up the chimney, then to sink low, then to snuff themselves altogether.

Nell conducted a mental survey of herself: she didn't feel breathless or faint and her heartbeat was quite steady. She examined her gown. The seams were perfectly fine.

She set all the coals burning again. "You will not burn me," she told the fire firmly, and then she reached her hand towards the flames.

Nell tensed for stinging heat, but all she felt was a warm, pleasant sensation on her outstretched fingertips. She warily immersed her hand in the fire. The sensation spread along her fingers and thumb, across her palm, up her wrist. When the flames were licking almost to her elbow, Nell stopped.

Her heart was beating rather fast, not because it was a strain to do this, but because it looked so odd, so *wrong*. Her flesh should be burning. She should be in agony. But instead she had this: a warm tickle as the flames murmured over her skin.

Georgie wouldn't giggle if she could see this. She'd be wide-eyed, silent, horrified.

Nell shivered, and told the fire to extinguish itself. It did instantly.

She climbed to her feet, a little shaken. There were more tests she should do—if she put her gloved hand in the fire, would the glove burn or not?—but she'd had enough for one morning.

Soberly, Nell returned to the writing desk. She dipped the quill in ink again, drew the sheet of paper with its singed corner towards her, and told Georgie about yesterday's events.

We will find Sophia soon, I am certain of it. The advertisement ran in the Flying Post *today and will be in the next issue of the* Gazette. *But that doesn't help you to discover what happened to Hubert. I am very sorry.*

As for this gift I have chosen, I can't see it being very useful. It's a trick, nothing more. If my gown were to catch fire, then I would certainly be able to put it out. I think it quite possible that I could walk through a burning house unharmed. But how likely is it that either should happen?

Nell frowned, and reread the last paragraph, and continued: *Do you remember what your mother told us about our ancestors who wished for healing gifts? How some were careful and shepherded their strength, while others tried to heal too many people and died. I think that control of fire is similar. I think the magic draws on my own physical strength, and the more I ask of it the more it takes from me. Yesterday's fire was huge, Georgie, and stopping it took everything I had in me. I had no strength left to breathe. My heart had no strength left to beat. And for several seconds I was actually dead.*

I think I was lucky. I think that if the fire had been any bigger, my heart wouldn't have started beating again. So I need to be careful. I have a gift that isn't really useful at all—but that could also kill me.

I know your mother has told you this countless times, but <u>be careful what you choose</u>.

I will write again when I have news of Sophia.
Yours,
Nell

Mordecai Black returned to the inn shortly after midday. He came into the parlor, huge, magnificent, and sweaty. "Hot out there," he said, stripping off his gloves and tossing them on the table.

"Did you have any luck?" Nell asked. She sealed her letter with a wafer and put it to one side.

"Your sister and Lizzie were lodging in Turnagain Lane until about six weeks ago, when Lizzie's finances suddenly improved. She took rooms just off the High Street. Sophia moved with her."

"Her finances improved?"

"Reading between the lines . . . I think Lizzie may have acquired a wealthy patron."

"A patron?" It took Nell a moment to understand what he meant. "Oh. She became someone's mistress?"

"I think so," Black said. "I have her surname now, and a good description. I spent the last two hours going up and down the High Street, asking after them both. I can't find anyone who remembers Sophia, but several people have seen Lizzie recently. She's well-dressed. Very fashionable. Shouldn't be too hard to find her."

After luncheon they took a hackney to the High Street. Once there, Black began halting people, showing them Sophia's sketch. "Have you seen this girl? What about a girl named Lizzie Wellsford? She's pretty, with brown curly hair, about eighteen years old." They worked their way along the street. Black talked while Nell scanned the flagway, looking for Sophia, looking for Lizzie.

Black spoke to shopkeepers and street vendors and urchins and all manner of people. In front of the *Reid & Houghton* confectioner's shop, he found a crossing-sweeper who'd seen Lizzie several times. "Good-lookin' lass. The sort yer notice, if yer know what I mean."

"Did you see where she came from? Where she went?"

The crossing-sweeper considered this question for a moment, leaning on his broom. "Came from over there," he said, with a nod of his head to show where.

"Thank you," Black said, and gave the man a coin.

They crossed the street. Nell examined faces while Black asked his questions. On the next corner, an urchin lounged, watching them intently. *Because he wants to pick our pockets? Or because he knows something?*

"Mordecai . . ." She touched Black's arm. "Over there."

He walked across to the boy. "Have you seen this girl?" he asked, holding out the sketch.

"No, sir." The boy had freckles and ginger hair and no front teeth.

"What about a girl called Lizzie Wellsford? Brown curls. Pretty. Lives around here."

"No, sir."

Black frowned down at the boy. "I've seen you somewhere before, haven't I? Cricklepit Street, wasn't it?" His eyes narrowed suddenly. "Do you know where Billy English is?"

The urchin didn't reply; he ducked his head and darted off.

Nell and Black exchanged a glance. Black shrugged. "I'm pretty sure I saw him in Cricklepit Street."

Ten minutes later, when Black was showing the sketch to a knife grinder, the urchin reappeared. Nell watched him watch them.

Next, Black spoke to a brisk woman carrying a basket. The boy sidled closer.

"You think you've seen Miss Wellsford in Gandy Street?" she heard Black say.

"Half a dozen times," the woman said.

Nell turned to look at her, but the woman was already bustling off.

"Did you hear that?" Black said. "Gandy Street."

"Where's that?" Nell asked.

"Just up there," Black said, and nodded at the next corner. "Come on."

The urchin darted forward and tugged at Black's sleeve. "Please, sir. I know some'un who's seen 'er."

Black halted. "Seen who?"

"The girl in the picture," the urchin said. "My frien' knows where she lives."

"Where's your friend?"

The urchin pointed.

"Gandy Street?"

"Yes, sir."

"Very well," Black said. "Let us speak to your friend."

THE URCHIN LED them to an establishment on the corner of High Street and Gandy that advertised itself as a silversmith's shop but which Mordecai's eye told him was merely an expensive pawn shop, selling a miscellany of trinkets and jewelry and silver plate that people had been forced to part with. Its custodian was a little man with sharp eyes and a wide smile.

Mordecai showed the man the sketch. "I understand you know where this girl lives."

"In this very building," said the man, and he opened a door at the back of the shop, revealing a dark corridor.

Mordecai felt suddenly uneasy. He didn't like the pawnbroker's welcoming smile and sharp, cold eyes—or that dark corridor.

He glanced at Eleanor. Her face was alight with eagerness and urgency. She gave a tiny, imperative nod, telling him to hurry.

Mordecai hesitated, and inspected the pawnbroker. He was a little fellow, a Jack Sprat. *I could swat him as easily as I'd swat a fly.* Even so, Mordecai slid the sketch back into its pasteboard folder, tied the ribbons, and tucked it inside his waistcoat. Now he had both hands free. "After you," he told the pawnbroker.

"Oh, no. Young Joe'll take you along. Show the lady and gentleman the way, Joe."

Mordecai felt foolish for his uneasiness. What had they to fear from a child? *Chickenheart,* he told himself. *Imagining dangers where there are none.*

He followed the lad along the shadowy corridor, down a flight of stairs, and then along another even more shadowy corridor. Mordecai's unease returned. "You, Joe. How far are you taking us?"

"We're there, sir," the boy said, and he rapped loudly on a door and opened it.

The room was not quite a cellar. Daylight came from a dirty window set high in the wall. Mordecai glimpsed a dark courtyard through the grime—which told him they were in the warren of backstreets and courts behind the High Street. The room was sparsely furnished, containing nothing more than a table and three wooden chairs.

He stepped cautiously inside.

The room had an occupant, but it wasn't Sophia Wrotham. It was a man, short and wiry, with sandy hair and weatherbeaten skin and a nose that looked as if it had been broken several times.

"There's been some mistake," Mordecai said. "We're looking for Sophia Wrotham and Lizzie Wellsford."

"No mistake," the man said. "Get goin', Joe. Shut the door."

Joe closed the door. Mordecai heard his bare feet scampering away.

"You know where Sophia Wrotham and Lizzie Wellsford are?" Mordecai asked.

"I know where the person yer lookin' for is."

"Where?"

"Right in front of yer," the man said, with a fierce, feral grin. "I'm Billy English."

This was Billy English? The criminal from the West Quarter that everyone was afraid of?

Billy English looked tough—a man who knew how to fight, who *enjoyed* fighting—but he was a foot shorter than Mordecai and nearly a hundred pounds lighter. To Mordecai's eye he wasn't intimidating at all. Even so, he didn't want Eleanor anywhere near him. He stepped in front of her, shielding her from the man's gaze. "Someone told us you knew Lizzie Wellsford. That true? You know where she is?"

"Never heard of Lizzie Wellsford," Billy English said. He laughed, a hoarse, barking sound. "An' if I knew, I wouldn't tell yer." His expression hardened. "Yer been askin' questions about me, an' I don't like that."

If he'd been alone, Mordecai would have knocked some manners into the fellow. With Eleanor Wrotham looking on, he couldn't. He merely gritted his teeth, turned to the door, and opened it.

The corridor was no longer empty. Two men stood there. Men as large as Mordecai himself.

Billy English barked his hoarse laugh again. "I tole you," he said. "I don't like folk askin' questions."

"Nell," Mordecai said quietly. "Stand back." His heart was beating fast. Every muscle in his body was taut. There was bright, razor-sharp clarity in his mind. He knew what he had to do.

No hesitation.

No rules.

Fight to kill.

Chapter Twenty-Eight

"YER KNOW WHAT I does to people who ask questions about me?" Billy English said. "I kills 'em, and buries 'em in the damps."

Nell had no time to be frightened by this threat. Black erupted into action. One moment he was blocking the doorway, the next he was in the middle of the room, striking Billy English, a massive backhand blow that sent the man flying, blood spraying from his nose.

There was a moment of ringing silence. Nell didn't breathe. Billy English didn't appear to breathe, either. He looked lifeless, sprawled on the floor.

Black spun towards the open door. The two men barreled into the room. One closed on Black but the other turned to Nell. Her heart stopped beating in sheer panic—and then Black was there, shoving her aside, clouting her assailant with his fist, a great blow that lifted the man almost off his feet.

Black swung to face their second attacker. The man he'd struck took a lurching step towards Nell and collapsed to his hands and knees. She scrambled away from him, but he paid her no attention. His eyes were wide and dazed. A string of bloody spittle hung from his open mouth.

Nell jerked her attention to Black.

He was locked in a fierce brawl with the other man, exchanging savage blows, striking hard and fast.

The table overturned with a crash.

Nell knew that Black had faced greater odds before and won. But his attacker was no Eton schoolboy. He was as large as Black, and as ferocious. A man from the backstreets. A man who'd grown up fighting.

Nell snatched up the nearest chair and swung it with all her might at Black's assailant.

The chair struck the man's back and fell apart.

Nell grabbed one of the legs and beat it over the man's shoulders, great blows that made her grunt with effort. *Whack. Whack. Whack.*

She caught a blur of movement out of the corner of her eye—the first man lurching to his feet. She swung to face him, striking out with the chair leg, but he caught it with one hand and jerked it from her grip. He came at her, the chair leg raised like a club—and Black was suddenly there, lashing out with a booted foot, kicking the man's knees out from under him, catching him across the temple with a short, brutal back-swing of his elbow.

The man's head snapped sideways. The chair leg dropped from his fingers. He collapsed bonelessly.

"Run," Black snarled at her. "Get out of here."

The second man punched Black in the head.

Black staggered and dropped to one knee, then surged upright again, swinging to face his attacker, grappling with the man.

Nell snatched up the chair leg again and raised it high.

Black and his assailant were wrestling for dominance, blundering past the upturned table, stumbling over the ruins of the chair, arms locked around each other, and it seemed to her terrified eyes that Black was dizzy from the blow he'd received —then Black struck the man's forehead hard with his own, a dull *crack*—and shoved the man violently from him.

The man staggered back several paces, thudded against the wall, and slid down it.

Black stood where he was, panting. He looked unsteady on his feet.

Nell lowered the chair leg. "Mordecai—"

An arm hooked around her throat from behind, hauling her against someone's chest, choking off her voice.

Nell dropped the chair leg. She clawed at the arm, struggling to breathe, struggling to keep her balance. She tried to kick backwards.

Something thin and razor-sharp pressed against her throat. "Don' move."

Nell froze. She knew what was pressed to her throat: the blade of a knife.

Mordecai Black swung around, almost losing his balance, and froze, too. His face stiffened in horror.

The man who held her wasn't tall, but he was strong. Billy English. She smelled him: sweat and blood. His breath rasped in her ear. "Don' move," he told Black. "Else yer lady dies."

Nell saw Black sway slightly on his feet, saw him blink as if trying to bring his eyes into focus, saw him gauge the distance between them and take in the obstacles—the upturned table, the broken chair. An emotion flickered across his face: despair.

I'm too far from him.

"Sykes, Fitch," English snarled. "Get up. Grab 'im."

The man Black had butted staggered to his feet. The other man didn't move.

"*Run,*" Nell told Black, her voice hoarse and urgent. But Black didn't move. He stayed where he was, swaying slightly, his gaze not quite in focus.

"Truss his hands, Fitch," English ordered. "Use his bib."

Fitch wrenched Black's neckcloth loose and bound his hands behind his back. Black made no attempt to fight. He stood looking at Nell, despair on his face.

When Fitch had finished, he clouted Black on the side of the head, making him stagger and almost fall.

"No," Nell choked out. "Don't hurt him!"

Billy English barked a laugh. "We ain't gonna hurt 'im— we're gonna kill 'im." His arm tightened around her throat. "Kill 'im, sell yer." He pressed his mouth to her ear and whispered, "But before I sell yer, yer an' me are gonna have some fun."

Nell's heartbeat became louder and more panicked, reverberating in her head. And then she remembered her Faerie gift.

Burn, Nell told the knife handle fiercely.

There was no flash of flame; instead, she heard a sizzling sound, smelled something scorch. English yelped and jerked back, dropping the knife, releasing her.

Nell snatched up her chair leg and charged at the man holding Black, swinging hard, aiming for his face, and Black was suddenly fighting, too, despite his bound hands, kicking out savagely—and then something struck her on the back of the head and her legs gave way.

There was a gray, amorphous moment when the world retreated and nothing made sense . . . and then slowly the room came into focus.

Nell was lying on the floor. She blinked, and blinked again, and saw Billy English standing over her, a chair leg dangling from his hand. He tossed it aside and dropped to a crouch alongside her. His nose was bloody, his chin stained red. He yanked the bonnet from her head, tore off the ribbons, and hauled her hands behind her back.

Nell struggled, but English was too strong. He bound her wrists tightly together, then sat back on his heels and looked at her. "Bitch," he said, and he reached out and plucked the spectacles from her face and flung them away. "Yer won't be needin' them where yer goin'."

The room rotated gently around her. Nell craned her neck, searching for Mordecai Black. He was on his knees, Fitch restraining him. He looked quite wild—blood streaking his face, teeth bared. Wild and helpless. Arms bound. On his knees. Blood dripping off his chin.

"Did yer hear me?" English took hold of her jaw, thumb digging under her chin, fingers crushing her lips, and hauled her head around, making her look at him. "I said——"

Nell bit his fingers as hard as she could.

Billy English screamed and reared back, trying to jerk his hand free. He tasted of salt and something sour—and then suddenly of blood.

English grabbed hold of her wig, trying to wrench her from him—and the wig came off Nell's head with a sudden, painful scattering of hairpins. English fell over backwards, a movement that jerked his hand free. The room tipped upside down for a moment—then it righted itself. She saw Billy English scrambling away from her like a crab.

Nell blinked, trying to bring everything into focus.

"Yer'll pay for that, bitch," Billy English said. He pushed to his feet, shaking his hand, spraying drops of blood, and crossed to where the first man lay sprawled. "Sykes, get up!" He toed the man sharply in the ribs, then bent and took his shoulder and hauled him over onto his back.

Sykes's eyes were wide open, staring, blank. He was quite clearly dead.

English straightened and turned to look at Black. "Yer killed one of me men." His voice was low and rasping, and the menace on his face made Nell shiver. She tugged uselessly at her bound hands—and remembered her Faerie gift. *Ribbon, burn.*

She felt brief warmth at her wrists, smelled scorched silk. This time, when she tugged, her wrists parted.

Billy English crossed to where Black had been forced to kneel and crouched so that they were eye to eye. "Yer goin' down in the damps." His lips spread in a bloodstained grin. He leaned closer. "I hope yer scared of the dark."

Nell pushed to her elbows, gathered her willpower, and prepared to set English's clothes on fire.

Black snapped his head forward—sudden, shockingly fast —catching English across the bridge of the nose with his fore-head. Nell heard the dull *crack* of impact, felt the floorboards shiver.

Billy English collapsed, his body folding limply backwards.

Fitch cuffed Black across the head. Black swayed on his knees and almost fell.

"Stop!" Nell cried. "Don't you dare hurt him!" She pushed furiously to her feet—and the room swung around her: the broken chair, the upturned table. Her legs seemed to dissolve. All of a sudden she was on the floor again.

Her vision grayed out for a moment. *Don't faint,* Nell told herself fiercely. *Don't faint.* She clung to the floor. The world felt as if it had tilted and she'd slide off it she moved.

Slowly the room stopped tilting. Vision returned. She saw Fitch crouch at English's side. "Billy? Yer all right?"

Mordecai Black didn't try to climb to his feet. He sagged. Blood was dripping steadily off his chin.

Fitch shook English's shoulder, then leaned down to check his breathing.

Nell struggled to her hands and knees again. *Mordecai!*

"Yer killed Billy," Fitch said. There was disbelief in his voice, and a note of awe.

Nell climbed carefully to her feet.

Fitch's head snapped around. His face twisted into an ugly snarl. He lunged upright and took a step towards her.

Nell set his left boot on fire.

Fitch took one more step—and noticed his burning boot. He recoiled back two paces and screamed, a high note of panic in his voice. He stamped frantically. The boot kept burning, golden flames curling across the cracked leather. Fitch screamed again, stamped again.

Nell crossed to Black with hasty, unsteady steps. "Mordecai?"

His head lifted. Blood streaked his face. She saw him blink, saw him try to focus.

Fitch screamed again. The sound drew Black's attention.

"Mordecai? Can you stand?"

Black didn't appear to hear her. He was staring at Fitch's burning boot.

Nell crouched and fumbled behind him for the neckcloth that bound his wrists together. The knot was too tight for her clumsy fingers. *Knot: burn,* she told it—and the knot did, flaring alight. Bright flames ate into the muslin. When Nell quenched them the knot disintegrated.

She hastily unwound the neckcloth from his wrists. "Can you stand?"

Fitch stopped screaming and stamping. Nell turned her head in time to see him tear the boot off and throw it from him. "Mordecai," she said more urgently. "Can you stand?"

Fitch turned towards them, panting heavily. His face was

flushed. He looked wild, half-maddened. His lips drew back from his teeth. His hands curled into fists the size of mallets.

Fear kicked within Nell's chest. She gripped Black's shoulder and stared at Fitch. *I may not be stronger than you, but I am more powerful.*

But Fitch didn't attack. They eyed each other across the ruins of the table, and Nell realized that he was afraid. Afraid of a female and an injured man.

Fitch bent and groped for something on the floor—Billy English's knife, the handle scorched black. He took a step towards them, the blade held out threateningly. "Yer goin' down the damps. Both of yer."

"No," Nell said. "We're not." *Burn,* she told the knife handle.

Fitch yelped, as Billy English had done, flung the knife away, and scrambled back several steps. She saw his chest rise and fall as he gulped for breath.

Nell set his right boot on fire.

Fitch gave a high, choked scream and recoiled instinctively, almost falling over. This time he didn't try to stamp the flames out; he ripped the boot off and flung it across the room. Then he turned to look at her. He was panting, shaking. The smell of burned leather was strong in the room. "Yer a witch," he hissed.

"Yes," Nell said cordially. "I am. And I shall burn you to death if you don't leave now."

Fitch took a step away from her.

"Get going," Nell said. "Before I burn you alive."

Fitch backed his way to the door, then turned and hurried out. He slammed it shut. Nell heard a bolt shoot home, and then another.

She rose from her crouch and crossed to the door. She

listened until she no longer heard Fitch's rapid footsteps and then tugged at the handle. The bolts stood strong.

Burn, Nell told the door.

The door flared alight.

Hotter, Nell told the flames. *Faster.* And then she cautioned: *But only the door. Burn nothing more than the door.*

She waited a moment to see that the flames were obeying, and then hurried back to Black. He was on his feet, swaying, his face streaked with blood. "Hurry," Nell said, reaching for his arm.

Black recoiled from her.

"Come on," she said urgently, grabbing his wrist.

Black jerked free and lurched back a step, staggering, almost falling. Nell saw disbelief on his face, but also fear, as if she'd transformed into a monster in front of his eyes.

"Come *on,*" she said, even more urgently. "I'll explain later."

Black tried to evade her, but Nell was faster than he was. She caught his wrist again and dragged him across the room. "Hurry."

The door had burned through. Nothing remained but the hinges. *Stop,* she told the last feeble flames.

They quenched instantly.

Nell stepped through the smoky hole, tugging Black with her.

They climbed the wooden stairs, Black stumbling, trying to pull his wrist free, but right now Nell was stronger than he was.

At the top of the stairs, Black stopped trying to free himself. He'd caught her urgency. To the left stretched a long, dim corridor. The corridor young Joe had led them along. To the right was a door. It was bolted on the inside. Nell drew the bolts and tried the handle cautiously.

The door swung open. Daylight flooded into the corridor.

Nell pushed Black hastily outside and shut the door behind them.

They were in a dark, grimy courtyard with buildings all around. "Come on," Nell said, taking hold of Black's wrist again.

They hurried across the courtyard. Fear tightened the back of Nell's neck. Where was Fitch? Was he fleeing Exeter—or gathering a mob to lynch her?

The yard opened into a backstreet. Nell turned left.

"No," Black said.

They went right. Nell's stride grew steadier with each step; Black's didn't. He lurched and stumbled, his legs buckling. Nell slung his arm around her shoulders. He tried to pull free, almost fell, and didn't try again.

They turned right again, down an alley—and suddenly they were on the High Street.

Nell halted. Black leaned heavily on her, his head hanging. Drying runnels of blood painted one side of his face from brow to chin. His eyes were closed. Beneath the blood his skin was gray.

Nell looked around desperately. A dozen yards from them, a hackney drew up. A man and woman alighted. The woman could almost be Lizzie Wellsford—brown curls, pretty face—but Nell ignored her. She hailed the jarvey loudly, urgently: "Hie!"

The jarvey lowered his reins.

Nell staggered across to him, her legs almost giving way under Black's weight. When the jarvey saw Black's face he looked as if he wished he'd driven on.

"He had a fall," Nell said. "He needs a doctor. Help me get him in."

The jarvey looked at Black mistrustfully. Nell saw him decide to refuse, saw him gather up his reins.

"Five pounds!" she said urgently. "Five pounds if you carry us."

The jarvey hesitated.

"Five pounds," Nell said again. "Help me get him in."

The jarvey climbed down from his box, opened the carriage door, and helped her to heave Mordecai Black inside.

Nell gave the name of their inn. "Hurry!"

She scrambled in after Black and closed the door with a slam. The carriage lurched into motion. Nell peered out the window. She saw no pursuers. What she *did* see was the silver-smith's shop. She fixed the name in her memory—Latham's—then turned to Black, gripping his arm, steadying him as the hackney picked up speed.

His eyes had been closed. Now, they opened. He stared at her for a long moment, and then said, "Did you burn Exeter yesterday?"

Nell released his arm. "No," she said. "Of course I didn't."

Black looked as if he didn't believe her.

"I *stopped* the fire," Nell said. "I *saved* Exeter."

His expression didn't alter. She saw suspicion and wariness. As if he no longer trusted her. As if he thought she was evil.

It was like being kicked in the chest. Her lungs drained of air. "Mordecai . . ."

Black turned his head away.

Nell sat there, feeling sick. *He doesn't believe me.*

Tears sprang into her eyes. She blinked them fiercely back. One of her hairpins dangled near her right eyebrow. Nell untangled it from her hair. Her fingers were trembling.

She checked the rest of her hairline, blinking, sniffing, trying not to cry, removing the few hairpins that remained while the hackney rattled towards the inn.

She glanced at Black again. He was sagging forward, eyes

squeezed shut. It wasn't mistrust she saw on his face, but nausea.

The hackney lurched to a halt outside their inn.

Nell flung the door open. "Help me get him out!" she said urgently.

Black's legs gave way as he descended from the hackney. He fell to hands and knees on the flagway and vomited.

Nell left him with the jarvey and ran into the inn's yard. "Phelps! Walter!"

When she returned with the coachman and footman, Black was still retching weakly. The jarvey stood several feet away, disgust on his face.

"Sir!" Phelps cried, and went to his knees beside Black.

Nell crouched, too. "He was struck on the head. He needs a doctor."

"He needs a bed, is what he needs." Phelps took Black's arm and helped him to his feet as tenderly as if Black were a child.

Chapter Twenty-Nine

SHE HAD LOST her wig and spectacles and the new bonnet. Her navy blue spencer was ruined, the seams joining the arms to the bodice torn open. Nell stared at the damage blankly—and then realized what had caused it: wielding the chair leg. Her sprigged muslin gown was torn, too, across the knee.

There was a lump at the back of her head, but no blood. That lump, and the growing bruise on her throat where Fitch had half-throttled her, were her only injuries—but Mordecai Black hadn't been so lucky. "Quickly, Bessie—help me to change."

"Are you certain you don't wish to lie down, ma'am?"

"Mr. Black was hurt far worse than I."

Nell hastily changed into her sole remaining gown. Her throat ached and her head ached, but those things were unimportant. The injuries that mattered were the ones Black had sustained.

Memory gave her images: Black with blood dripping off

his chin. Black needing Phelps's help to stand. Black's legs giving way in the corridor outside his bedchamber.

She turned towards the door.

"Your hair, ma'am. We'd best cover it. Mr. Black wouldn't like you to be seen like that."

"But how?" One wig was burned, the other was in Billy English's den.

"Your shawl, ma'am."

Nell suffered to sit still for two minutes while Bessie fashioned the shawl into a turban. She kneaded her hands together, remembering the blows Black had taken to the head, remembering the blood.

Mordecai Black was so large and strong that she'd thought him invincible. But he wasn't invincible. He was a man made of flesh and bone, and he could be hurt, and he could die.

She leapt up from the chair as soon as Bessie was finished, hurried down the corridor to Black's bedchamber, and rapped on the door. The seconds it took Walter to open it were the longest of her life. "How is he?" she asked the footman urgently.

"Come see for yourself, ma'am."

Nell pushed past him and hurried to the bed. Black lay there, dressed in a nightshirt, the sheets pulled up to his chest. Someone had washed his face.

He looked dead, a corpse laid out for burial, perfectly still, eyes closed, skin bloodless, hands resting limply at his sides.

The impression of death was so strong that Nell reached out to touch his wrist. His skin was warm. His pulse beat steadily.

She inhaled a sharp breath, and managed not to burst into tears. "Have you sent for a doctor?"

"Nothing a doctor can do for him," Phelps said. "That cut

don't need stitching, and if his head's broken it's nothing a doctor can mend."

There was a cut on Black's brow, almost at the hairline. Nell examined it closely. The coachman was correct: it didn't need stitches. "That's what was bleeding?"

Phelps nodded. "Ain't nothing we can do now but wait, ma'am. Rest is what he needs."

"How much rest?"

"Don't know, ma'am. A day, two days, a week, a month. Depends how hard he was hit."

"Quite hard," Nell said. "And more than once."

Phelps grimaced, but said nothing.

"What happened, ma'am?" Walter asked.

"Billy English," Nell said.

"Shall I send for the parish constable?" Walter asked.

"He's dead. English, I mean. Mr. Black killed him."

Phelps gave a satisfied grunt.

Nell thought about the silversmith, smiling so affably as he invited them to their doom, and she thought about the damps, where Billy English buried his dead. "But there are things the constable needs to know." She released Black's wrist reluctantly. "I'll write a note. You can take it to the constable, Walter."

"Yes, ma'am."

Nell crossed to the door and opened it, and looked back at Black, lying still and pale in the bed. *Live, Mordecai.*

NELL DECIDED TO write her letter anonymously—partly because she didn't want to hang for witchcraft, and partly because Mordecai Black had killed two men today. Those deaths had been justified, but she didn't want him accused of murder.

She thought hard before committing ink to paper. Had she and Black left anything in English's den that might identify them?

The spectacles and bonnet were unexceptional items; no one could trace her through them. The wig was more unusual. Had the *perruquier*'s label been stitched into the welt?

She couldn't remember.

Black's hat must be in that room, too. He'd been wearing it when they arrived and not when they left. Could he be identified by it?

Nell almost decided not to write the letter—and then she realized she was worrying needlessly: if her wig and Mordecai Black's hat brought a constable to their doorstep, they could simply claim the items had been stolen. English *was* a known criminal, after all.

Nell laid out a fresh sheet of paper and uncapped the inkpot. *I wish to draw your attention to a murderer's den in Exeter. Go to Latham's on the corner of High Street and Gandy. The proprietor is in league with a criminal by the name of Billy English. The door at the back of his shop will lead you to English's den.*

English and his men are murderers. By his own admission English has killed people and buried them in a place he calls the damps.

Nell described everything she'd seen in as much detail as she could: the long corridor, the stairs descending, the room at the bottom. She hesitated, uncertain whether to tell the constable that English was dead or not. After careful consideration, she decided to let the constable discover that for himself.

She described the men she'd seen—Billy English, Fitch, Sykes, the silversmith. She didn't mention the urchin, Joe.

When the letter was written, Nell gave it to Walter. "Impress your urgency upon the constable, but don't say who you are or who employs you. I don't wish Mr. Black to be involved in this. He doesn't deserve to be called a murderer."

Walter's jaw firmed. "I shan't tell him anything, ma'am. You can trust me on that!"

Nell went back to Black's bedchamber. Nothing had altered. He still looked like a man laid out for burial, but when she touched his wrist she found his pulse beating steadily.

She wanted to stay at his bedside, but her head ached and her body shook with exhaustion. "I need to lie down, Phelps. Will you please stay with him?"

"You can be certain of it, ma'am."

Nell crawled into her own bed and fell asleep almost instantly. When she woke, it was late evening.

She ate a little soup sitting up in bed, then draped her shawl around her head and shoulders and went to Mordecai Black's room. Like hers, it was lit by candles.

"Has there been any change?"

"No, ma'am."

Nell touched Black's wrist and was reassured to feel his pulse. "Should we try waking him? Perhaps *sal volatile*?"

"Best to let him sleep, ma'am. His head'll heal of its own accord and there's nothing we can do to hurry it along."

Nell stared down at Black's face. How could a face be both strong and vulnerable at the same time?

"Don't be too worrit. He's not the first man to get hit in the head and he won't be the last. Rest is what he needs. He'll wake in his own good time."

"Do you think he'll be all right?"

"Most likely. Strong as an ox, Mr. Black. Mind, he mightn't remember everythin' that happened today."

Nell stared down at Black—and found herself hoping that he *did* forget what had happened. "Will you stay with him until he wakes?"

"I'll be here all night, ma'am."

Nell glanced at him. Phelps's tone hadn't been that of a servant doing his duty; he sounded as if he *cared* about Mordecai Black. "Have you been with him long?"

"Since he were eight years old," Phelps said. "It was me as taught him to ride, and to handle the ribbons."

Nell nodded, and looked back down at Black. She touched his wrist again, felt the warmth of his skin, the steady beat of his pulse. *Get better, Mordecai. And forget what happened today.*

Chapter Thirty

July 24th, 1812
Exeter, Devonshire

IN THE MORNING Nell no longer had a headache, although her head was tender where Billy English had struck her. She fingered the lump and thanked God for the wig she'd been wearing. "Has Mr. Black woken, Bessie?"

"Yes, ma'am. For a few minutes." Bessie placed a pitcher beside the washstand, then opened the chintz curtains. Daylight streamed into the little bedchamber.

"How is he?"

"Mr. Phelps said he's a bit befuddled, but that's only to be expected. He said it's nothing to worry about and Mr. Black will be right as rain in a week, mark his words."

"I hope so," Nell said. "I hope so."

She climbed out of bed and washed. The bruise at her throat, where English had half-throttled her, had darkened overnight. When Bessie saw the size of it she was horrified. "Ma'am! You could have been killed."

"Very easily," Nell said soberly.

Bessie brushed out Nell's hair, pinned it up, and hid it beneath a turban. "Shall I buy another wig for you, ma'am?"

Nell thought about the few pennies in her reticule. "Not today."

"Or . . ." Bessie hesitated. "Perhaps we could tell the servants here that you decided to dye your hair brown?"

Nell turned to look at her.

"Only, I don't know if Mr. Black will like it, ma'am."

"He probably won't," Nell said. "But *I* like it." She touched the turban wound snugly around her head. A foolish fashion, and far too hot for this weather. "I'll speak to him about it." *If he will speak to me at all.*

She examined the clothes she'd worn yesterday, hoping the spencer and gown were repairable. They weren't. Nell rubbed her brow and sighed. She needed another bonnet, a new spencer, and at least one more gown, preferably two.

She hadn't enough money for even the bonnet.

I shall have to sell Mother's pearl brooch.

It was a task she didn't feel up to coping with today.

Nell went down to the private parlor for her breakfast. She detoured past Mordecai Black's door and hesitated for a long moment, gripping her hands together, unable to bring herself to knock. Would he remember yesterday's events?

Resolutely, she took a deep breath and knocked.

Walter opened the door.

"Is Mr. Black awake?"

"No, ma'am. But he was awake earlier."

Nell's heart gave a treacherous skip of relief. "How was he? Does he remember what happened yesterday?"

"I can't say as to that, ma'am, but Mr. Phelps reckons all

he needs is a few days in bed and he'll be good as new."

"Oh. Good." Nell turned away, and then turned back. "Walter? How did it go with the parish constable?"

"I handed over the letter, ma'am, said it was urgent, and got out of there as fast as I could. No one followed me back here. I made sure of it."

"Thank you, Walter."

Nell ate a desultory breakfast. She was sipping her tea when Bessie peeped in the door. "Mr. Black's awake, ma'am, if you're wishful to see him."

Nell put the cup down with a clatter. "He is? Oh. Good." She pushed back her chair and stood, feeling absurdly flustered.

She went up one flight of stairs and tapped on Black's door.

Walter opened it. He gave her an unfootmanlike grin. "He's awake, ma'am."

"May I see him?"

"Of course, ma'am."

Nell moistened her lips, inhaled a shallow breath, and entered the bedchamber. *Please don't let him remember.*

Black was sitting up in bed. He didn't look befuddled; he looked alert—and one glance at his face told her that he *did* remember. Those dark eyes were unsmiling.

Nell halted in the middle of the bedchamber. She felt cold, as if all the blood had drained from her body. She clutched her hands together and said awkwardly, "How are you?"

"Phelps insists I stay in bed today."

Phelps, at his post beside the bed, gave a nod. "You're not getting up 'til tomorrow at the earliest."

Black grimaced faintly, but didn't protest.

"How do you feel?" Nell asked. "Does your head hurt?"

"A little. But I've had worse headaches in my life."

"Oh," Nell said.

There was a moment of awkward silence. Black was looking at her with eyes that held wariness and suspicion and mistrust.

Whatever you're thinking, it's not true. I'm not a monster. I didn't set fire to Exeter. But she couldn't utter those words, not with Phelps and Walter in the room.

Nell swallowed, and clutched her hands more tightly together. "Do you need anything?"

"No, thank you."

Nell felt an urge to burst into tears—and an equally strong urge to run from the room, to put an end to this horrible, stilted conversation. She managed to do neither. She was a Wrotham, and Wrothams didn't cry in public or run from rooms like heroines in melodramas.

"Very well. I shall leave you, then." She inclined her head courteously. "I'm glad to see that you're almost restored to yourself."

"Thank you," Black said, equally courteously.

The urge to cry became stronger. Nell turned away, walking as her father had taught her: calm, unhurried, lady-like. Walter smiled at her as he opened the door for her.

Nell stood for several moments in the empty corridor, eyes closed, hands pressed to her face. She was trembling. She felt sick. She wanted to cry.

She raised her head at the sound of footsteps. One of the serving-men came up the stairs, carrying a tray. On it was a tea set and a plate of bread-and-butter. Invalid's food.

Nell retreated to her own bedchamber. Bessie was there, mending the spencer. She looked up from her task. "Do you want something, ma'am?"

Nell swallowed. "I don't think that spencer's repairable."

"I'm good with a needle," Bessie said cheerfully.

"Oh, well, if you wish to try." Nell backed out of the room and went down to the private parlor. Once there, she locked the door.

And then—safe in her privacy—she cried.

MORNING BECAME AFTERNOON. Nell had no appetite for luncheon. "You look pale, ma'am," Bessie said. "Perhaps you'd like to rest?" But Nell didn't want to sleep any more than she wanted to eat. What she wanted was something she couldn't have: for Mordecai Black to forget what had happened yesterday.

He fears me.

Tears welled in her eyes. Nell blinked them back.

"Are you certain you don't wish to lie down?" Bessie said anxiously.

"I'd like to wash my face," Nell said. *And I'd like for yesterday not to have happened.*

Bessie went downstairs for warm water. Nell stood at the window, hugging herself, looking out over Exeter, shrinking from what needed to be done.

She had to sell her mother's pearl brooch, leave the inn, and find lodgings somewhere else. But even though she knew it was necessary, she couldn't bring herself to it. It was too daunting, too frightening.

Bessie returned bearing a pitcher of steaming water, her face alight with excitement. "Oh, ma'am! Have you heard the news?"

Nell shook her head.

"They've found two dead men in a room off the High Street. Criminals!"

"Oh," Nell said.

Bessie poured water into the washstand bowl, and glanced at Nell. "They're the ones that attacked you, aren't they?"

Nell nodded.

"Mr. Black killed them, didn't he?"

Nell nodded again.

"I'm glad!" Bessie said stoutly. She put down the pitcher, hesitated, and then said, "Ma'am . . . they found four more folk buried in one of the old water tunnels. Three men and a woman. Murdered!"

So the constable had looked further. "I'm not surprised," Nell said.

Bessie handed Nell a cloth to wash her face with. Her expression was sober. "It could have been you buried down there."

"But it wasn't." Nell dredged up a smile. "Thanks to Mr. Black."

NELL WENT BACK DOWN to the parlor, where she sat and did nothing, hugging her misery to herself.

How quickly life could change. This time yesterday she and Black had been setting forth. She'd been certain the end of her search was in sight, certain she was about to be reunited with Sophia.

Nell stared at the cold fireplace, and as she stared she formed a resolution. She *would* find Sophia today.

She'd go to Gandy Street and ask questions of the passersby. She'd find Sophia, and then she'd sell her mother's pearl brooch and get on with the life she had planned.

Nell rose to her feet, full of determination, but before she reached the door one of the inn servants knocked. "Mrs. Trussell-Quimby? Visitors for you."

"For me?" Nell said blankly—and then she felt a stab of panic. Constables coming to interrogate her? "Who are they?"

"Two gentlemen and a lady, ma'am."

Not constables, then. Nell's panic faded. *Visitors? For me?* And then she realized who they must be: people who'd seen the advertisement in the newspaper and had come to claim the reward. People who knew where Sophia was. Her pulse gave a leap of excitement. "Show them up!"

"Yes, ma'am. Here's the gentleman's card." The servant handed her a small rectangle of white card.

She took it and glanced at it—and then stared. "The Earl of Cosgrove?" But the servant had already departed.

"The Earl of Cosgrove?" Nell said again, perplexed. Why on earth would an *earl* be coming to claim a ten-pound reward?

She hastily smoothed her gown. *Calm*, she told herself. But her pulse was tumultuous with hope.

The servant returned and ushered three people into the room. Both the men were tall, both in their thirties, both striking in their looks. The lady was striking, too. Not so much for her looks, but for her poise and her elegance. She looked almost regal.

Nell was suddenly aware of the shabbiness of her gown. The turban felt ridiculous on her head.

"Mrs. Trussell-Quimby?" one of the men said. "How do you do? I'm Lord Cosgrove."

Nell curtsied politely. "My lord." She frantically sorted through her memories. Had she met him during her London Season? She didn't think so; his was a face not easily forgotten —strong, stern.

"May I introduce you to Mr. and Mrs. Reid?"

Nell curtsied again.

"You *are* Mrs. Trussell-Quimby?" Cosgrove asked.

"Yes, sir."

The lady's eyebrows lifted slightly at this, as if she knew Nell was lying, but Nell knew she'd never met the woman before; she would have remembered that regal elegance.

Her father's lessons came to her rescue. Even if she looked dowdy, even if the turban were absurd, she knew how to behave as a lady. "Please be seated. Would you like refreshments?"

"No, thank you."

They settled themselves, the Reids on the green sofa and Cosgrove in an armchair by the fireplace. Nell perched on one of the dining chairs. "You've come about the advertisement, I take it?"

"Advertisement?" Cosgrove said. He looked as perplexed as Nell felt. "No. We're here about the fire."

Nell stiffened slightly. "Oh? What about it?"

Cosgrove glanced at Mr. Reid. So did Nell.

"I have a number of businesses in Exeter," Mr. Reid said. "Bakeries. One of them is on Alpers Street."

Nell had a sudden flash of realization. This was the man behind the *Reid & Houghton* bakeries.

Reid didn't look like a man who owned bakeries. There was nothing of the shop about him. His voice was well-bred, his manner quietly authoritative.

"My bakery escaped the fire, but it was a close call. Very close. The fire was only four buildings away when it went out." Reid looked at her. His eyes were a very light gray. Piercing. Nell had the sensation that he was able to see inside her head. "Odd that, don't you think? That a fire of such magnitude should just extinguish itself."

"A miracle," Nell said. She gave Mr. Reid a cool half-smile. It was an expression she'd perfected years ago. Courteous. Ladylike. Faintly aloof. Usually it masked boredom; right now it concealed alarm. What did these people want with her?

"My men were attempting to save the bakery from burning," Reid said. "One of them says he saw a young lady run up to the fire—to within touching distance, he says—and when she did, the fire stopped." He snapped his fingers. "Like that."

Panic took root in Nell's chest. She lifted her eyebrows slightly. "Oh?"

"He said it was like magic."

Nell permitted herself an amused smile. "Magic?" She was aware that Cosgrove was watching her keenly, and Mrs. Reid, too, that three pairs of eyes were focused intently on her face.

"Impossible, of course," Reid said.

"Impossible," Nell agreed.

"He said the woman fainted, so he helped her up and brought her to her lodgings." Reid made a gesture with one hand, indicating the inn. "Here."

Nell couldn't think of anything to say. She took refuge in her aloof smile again.

"Was that woman you, Mrs. Trussell-Quimby?"

"Me?" Nell managed a disdainful laugh. "Of course not."

Reid and his wife exchanged a glance. Mrs. Reid gave an infinitesimal shake of her head.

Reid looked back at her. "So, you didn't stop the fire, Mrs. Trussell-Quimby?"

"Of course not," Nell said again. She took refuge in cold hauteur. "Your man sounds as if he's been imbibing too freely, Mr. Reid. I wouldn't give any credence to his claims if I were you."

"Sergeant Ackroyd is a very reliable man," Reid said mildly.

"Sergeant Ackroyd?"

"I employ invalided soldiers," Reid said, and Nell suddenly

realized that Reid had been a soldier, too. Everything about him—that authoritative voice, the keen gaze, the military bearing—said that he'd been an officer.

"If I may?" Mrs. Reid said, and Reid sat back slightly on the sofa, ceding the conversation to his wife.

Mrs. Reid smiled at Nell. "So you don't believe in magic, Mrs. Trussell-Quimby?"

"No," Nell said. Her panic was growing. She remembered the way Mordecai Black had looked at her, as if she was a monster. She remembered Lady Dalrymple's warning: *Never tell a soul.* She remembered that a witch had been hanged in Yorkshire not three years ago.

Was that was Cosgrove and the Reids intended? To expose her as a witch? To see her hanged?

"Do you believe in Faeries, Mrs. Trussell-Quimby?"

"Of course not!"

"Or Faerie godmothers?"

"No," Nell said firmly. She rose to her feet. "Faerie tales have nothing to do with the real world. Now, if you will excuse me, I have business to attend to."

Her guests didn't rise. Nell was aware of a silent message passing between them—a glance, a nod.

Mrs. Reid looked up at her. "I have a Faerie godmother," she said, quite matter-of-factly. "Her name is Baletongue. She granted me a wish on my twenty-first birthday, and I chose to be able to hear truth from lies."

Nell stared down at the woman.

"Please sit, Mrs. Trussell-Quimby . . . and tell us your real name."

Nell fumbled for her chair, and sat. She felt quite numb with shock.

"It was you who stopped the fire, wasn't it?" Reid asked.

Nell stared at him. After a moment, she nodded.

"What's your name?"

Nell looked at the Reids uncertainly—*Dare I trust them?*—and then glanced at Lord Cosgrove. She heard Lady Dalrymple's warning in her ears. *Never tell a soul.*

Cosgrove smiled at her. "My wife had a visit from Baletongue, too. She chose metamorphosis."

Metamorphosis? The ability to change shape?

Nell felt a sudden, intense curiosity to meet Lady Cosgrove. She bit her lip, and then blurted, "My name is Eleanor Wrotham. Miss Wrotham."

"It's a pleasure to meet you, Miss Wrotham." Cosgrove leaned forward, his elbows on his knees, his gaze intent on her face. "Please, will you tell us what happened two days ago?"

Nell looked at the three of them, at the friendliness on their faces, the eager curiosity, and hesitated.

These people are my kin. They won't betray me.

She took a deep breath and said, "It was my twenty-third birthday, the day of the fire. I was waiting for Baletongue to come."

She told them about Sophia being missing, about seeing burning rooftops from her window, about Baletongue's arrival. "So I chose control of fire instead. What else could I do when people were dying? Only it didn't work as I thought it would. I had to get close to the fire to stop it, and it almost killed me." She told them how she'd collapsed, how her heart had stopped beating for a moment. "I think it's like the healing gifts. I think it takes *from* you, and if you're too ambitious, if you aim for too much, it can drain all the life from your body."

Mrs. Reid nodded. "One of us is a healer. Her husband is very careful how much she does."

Questions gathered on Nell's tongue. "She told her husband?" she said, and, "How many of you are there?"

"Three. Four, counting you. And yes, our husbands know

—although perhaps they wish they didn't." Mrs. Reid glanced at her husband, her expression wry. Reid returned the glance, equally wryly.

"Do you know of any others?" Cosgrove asked.

Nell bit her lip.

Mrs. Reid's eyes brightened. "You do!"

Never tell a soul.

But these people were *family*. "My aunt and cousin," Nell said. "But my cousin hasn't chosen yet. Her birthday is next month."

"For heaven's sake tell her to be careful!" Mrs. Reid said urgently. "There are gifts that can destroy a person."

Nell nodded. "I know. Being able to hear people's thoughts. It sends you mad."

"Foretelling, too," Mrs. Reid said. "My great-great-grand-mother wished for that—and killed herself because of it."

Nell blinked. "Why?"

"Because she knew the fate of every person she met. She knew when they would die, what catastrophes would befall them. She knew when her husband's heart would stop beating. She knew that her sons would both die young. Her gift drove her mad—and she *knew* it would, even before it happened, because she couldn't *not* know. Just as she knew she would commit suicide—and how and when." Mrs. Reid grimaced. "It sounds all very well to know the future, but it's a burden, not a gift."

Nell grimaced, too. "I'll write to Georgie today and tell her."

"Your sister will presumably receive a wish, too?"

Nell shook her head. "We're half sisters only."

"You said she was missing. Tell us about her."

So Nell told them everything. She left nothing out. She told them about her family's disgrace and her broken betrothal to

Roger Lockwood-Smith, the new Lord Dereham. She told them about receiving Sophia's letter and her frantic journey to London, about Roger's refusal to help—and Mordecai Black's unexpected assistance.

Cosgrove stirred when she mentioned his name.

Nell tensed. Was Lord Cosgrove one of Black's detractors? "You know him?"

"Very well," Cosgrove said. "I've often sparred with him."

Nell relaxed. Lord Cosgrove was a friend of Black's. She continued with her story: Seven Dials, the journey to Exeter, the disguise she had worn, the days searching. The only things she left out were Black's offers of marriage and their sexual intimacy. Lastly, she described yesterday's events: Billy English, Black's reaction to her magic.

The Reids and Lord Cosgrove listened intently. Reid's face revealed the least. He was focused on her words, but utterly expressionless. Cosgrove frowned while he listened, his eyebrows drawing together. Mrs. Reid's face was the most expressive. Her eyes widened and her lips parted in horror. "Goodness!" she said, when Nell had finished. "It sounds as if you're lucky to be alive."

"We are." Nell touched the bruises at her throat, hesitated, and then said, "If I hadn't been there, Mr. Black would have won. I distracted him. Slowed him down." The very reason Black had given for not taking her to the West Quarter—and he'd been right. She remembered the knife blade pressed to her throat, remembered Black standing unresisting while Fitch bound his wrists. *But for me, he would have fought his way free.*

"How is he?" Cosgrove asked. "You said he was struck in the head?"

"Several times," Nell said, and shivered in memory. "He's better than he was yesterday, but not well enough to leave his bed."

Cosgrove's frown returned.

"He saw you set fire to the boots?" Mrs. Reid asked. "And the door?"

Nell nodded, and clenched her hands in her lap.

"And his reaction was . . . not favorable?"

"He thinks I'm a monster," Nell said, and tears filled her eyes. "He thinks I started that fire two days ago. He thinks I'm *evil.*"

"Did you tell him about Baletongue?"

"How can I?" Nell cried. "He won't believe me. No one would!"

Both Reid and Cosgrove grimaced faintly. They exchanged a glance. Cosgrove pushed to his feet. "I'll have a word with him."

"What will you tell him?" Reid asked.

"The truth," Cosgrove said.

Reid frowned.

"I'll tell him about Baletongue, and Charlotte. But not about Letty or Merry."

"Is that wise?" Reid asked.

"Black's a good man. If he gives his word, he keeps it."

"You trust him enough to tell him about Charlotte?"

Cosgrove nodded.

"You may tell him about me if you wish," Mrs. Reid said.

Reid turned to her. "Letty—"

"I agree with Cosgrove." Mrs. Reid smiled at her husband and took his hand. "Black's a good man. Dreadful reputation, of course, but he's nowhere near as, ah, as *black* as he's painted. I've never heard him lie—and that's not something I can say about most members of the *ton.*"

Nell assimilated this statement. Mrs. Reid clearly moved in the best circles.

Reid frowned at his wife. He was holding her hand quite

tightly.

"I trust him, Icarus."

Reid sighed. His expression became resigned. "Very well. Tell him."

Cosgrove turned to the door. Nell stood. "Shall I come with you?"

Cosgrove shook his head. "Best not. Where's his room?"

Nell told him, and watched him leave the parlor. Desperate hope flowered in her chest. *Believe him, Mordecai.*

She sank back on the chair and forced her attention to the Reids. They were still holding hands. "Who are Charlotte and Merry?"

"Charlotte is Cosgrove's wife," Mrs. Reid said. "And Merry's her cousin. They'll be very glad to meet you. You must visit once you've found your sister."

Nell shook her head. "My reputation—"

"I agree with Black on this," Mrs. Reid said. "A runaway sister does not ruin a person."

Nell looked down at her lap. She pleated a fold of muslin. "I've been traveling with Mr. Black, and that *does* ruin a person."

"Mrs. Trussell-Quimby is clearly ruined," Mrs. Reid said. "Miss Wrotham, on the other hand, is not."

Nell glanced up at her.

Reid leaned forward. "You said you think your sister might be in Gandy Street?"

Nell nodded.

"I know the neighborhood well," he said. "I own the confectioner's shop on the High Street. Perhaps you saw it?"

Nell nodded.

"I'll ask my men to put out the word," Reid said. "I'd like to see that sketch of her. And tell me everything you know about the girl she's with. What's her name? Lizzie Wellsford?"

Chapter Thirty-One

MORDECAI LAY IN HIS BED, propped up on two pillows. He was bored, but an attempt to read had ended in failure; the letters had marched across the page in all directions, evading his attempts to decipher them.

Phelps had told him not to worry, that his head would be right before the week was out, but Mordecai *was* worried. What if he could never read again?

A knock sounded on the door. Phelps opened it. Mordecai heard the murmur of voices—and then a most unexpected person walked into the room. For a moment he thought his eyes were deceiving him—*I'm seeing things that don't exist*—and then the apparition spoke: "Hello, Black."

"Cosgrove?" Mordecai said, astonished. "What on earth are you doing here?"

"Came up to Exeter on business. Heard you'd been laid up. Took a few blows to the head, did you?"

"Yes."

Cosgrove came closer to the bed and stood looking down at him. "How are you? Truthfully."

"Truthfully?" Mordecai grimaced. "My head hurts like the devil and I'm unsteady on my pins." And then he blurted: "I can't read; the letters won't stop moving." The moment the words were out he wished them unsaid. His voice had been too high, too anxious, his fear audible. "But I have all my wits—and few days in bed will see me right."

Cosgrove took the chair Phelps had been sitting in. "If your head doesn't mend itself, I know someone who can help."

"It will mend itself," Mordecai said. *I hope.*

"Most likely," Cosgrove said. "But you must promise to let me know if it doesn't." He glanced at Phelps, standing unobtrusively by the door. "Would you mind stepping outside? I have something of a private nature I need to discuss with Black."

"Very good, sir," Phelps said, and exited the bedchamber.

"What's this about?" Mordecai said, groping for another pillow so he could sit up. "Something wrong?"

"Lie down, man. No, nothing's wrong. I just need to tell you something." Cosgrove eyed him for a moment, and then said, "I must have your promise that you won't repeat what I tell you."

"Of course I won't repeat it," Mordecai said. "My word on it."

Cosgrove nodded, and leaned forward, elbows on his knees, expression serious. "I'm going to tell you something that will sound very far-fetched. You won't believe it. *I* didn't believe it at first."

"What?" Mordecai said, baffled by Cosgrove's air of solemnity.

Cosgrove opened his mouth, closed it, grimaced. "It will sound ludicrous, but it *is* true. I swear it."

"What?" Mordecai said again.

Cosgrove hesitated. He removed his hat, ran a hand through his hair, grimaced again, said, "I don't know where to start."

"At the beginning," Mordecai said, slightly alarmed. Even at Jackson's boxing saloon, stripped half naked, sweating and panting, Cosgrove had never been anything other than self-assured. But right now the man looked awkward, uncertain.

"You won't believe it."

"Cosgrove, for God's sake, just *tell* me."

Cosgrove blew out a breath. "It's like this: there are Faeries."

Mordecai opened his mouth . . . and then closed it again. His alarm became stronger. *He's lost his wits.*

Cosgrove held up a hand, even though Mordecai hadn't said anything. "Just hear me out. All right?"

Mordecai nodded warily.

"Five hundred years ago—or maybe six hundred, I don't think anyone knows for certain—a woman won a wish from a Faerie, and her wish was that her daughters would receive wishes when they grew up, and their daughters in turn. You with me so far?"

Mordecai nodded, even more warily.

"My wife is descended from one of those daughters, and on her twenty-fifth birthday she received a wish. She chose metamorphosis, which means that she can change shape."

Mordecai looked away. *Oh, God, he's dicked in the nob.*

"The first time I saw it I thought I'd gone mad," Cosgrove said.

Mordecai unwillingly looked back at him.

"Whatever you're thinking right now is *exactly* what I thought then. I can guarantee it. When Charlotte tried to explain, I couldn't believe it, because it was so . . . so *impossible.*" Cosgrove leaned even further forward on the chair. His gaze was fierce, intent, earnest. "But here's the thing, Black: it *is* true."

Mordecai shook his head.

"You saw it yesterday. The door Miss Wrotham burned down, the boots she set on fire—that was magic. Faerie magic."

"How do you know about that?"

"She told me."

Mordecai grimaced. He looked away from Cosgrove, towards the end of the bed.

Cosgrove was silent for a moment, then he said, "Going back to the beginning again, there were three daughters. Three different lines of descent. My wife's line receive their wishes on their twenty-fifth birthdays; Miss Wrotham's receive theirs on their twenty-third." Cosgrove paused. "Do you know when Miss Wrotham's birthday was?"

Mordecai shook his head.

"The day of the fire."

Mordecai reluctantly looked at Cosgrove.

"You think Miss Wrotham started the fire," Cosgrove said. "But the truth is that she put it out. She was in her bedroom watching the roofs burning when the Faerie came—and so for her wish she chose control of fire. She put out that fire, Black; she didn't start it."

Mordecai stared at him, and remembered plunging into the fiery stairwell—and flames snuffing themselves out all around him.

"I know it goes against the laws of nature," Cosgrove said. "You don't need to tell me that: I *know* it. But the thing is, there *are* Faeries and there *is* magic."

Mordecai shook his head again.

"You *know* it's true. You saw it yesterday."

Mordecai couldn't deny that.

"There's magic in this world, and your Miss Wrotham possesses it. But it's not evil. *She's* not evil. She saved a lot of lives, including yours."

That was an indisputable truth: Eleanor Wrotham had saved his life yesterday.

He thought of the flaming staircase again.

"I know you're not in plump currant right now, so I won't talk anymore—but believe me, Black. I'm not lying on this."

Mordecai reluctantly nodded.

Cosgrove stood, and held out his hand.

After a moment, Mordecai took it.

Cosgrove's handclasp was firm and his gaze was as intelligent as it had always been. He *looked* sane.

"I meant what I said," Cosgrove said. "If your head doesn't mend, I know someone who can heal it for you." He released Mordecai's hand, nodded farewell, and left the bedchamber.

Mordecai stared at the door for a long time, deeply unsettled. Cosgrove was someone he admired—for his intellect, for his boxing prowess, for his vocal stance against the slave trade. And yet the man believed in Faeries and magic?

———————

Conversation halted when Lord Cosgrove returned to the parlor. "How did he take it?" Reid asked.

"Hard to tell. You know as well as I do that it's not an easy thing to believe." Cosgrove ran a hand through his hair. "I didn't tell him about Letty, if that sets your mind at rest."

"Thank you."

Cosgrove turned to Nell. "I'd leave him be. Give him time to think it over. He's pretty knocked-up."

"I will," Nell said. "Thank you."

The Reids stood. "I'll make enquiries in Gandy Street," Mr. Reid said. He examined her with those piercing gray eyes, and said, "I think you shouldn't go out today, Miss Wrotham. Allow yourself time to recover. I'll let you know the moment I have any news."

"Yes," Mrs. Reid said, taking one of Nell's hands in both of hers. "You look quite done in. I would rest, if I were you." She smiled wryly. "You may tell me I'm not your mother, if you wish!"

Nell was surprised into a laugh—and at the same time felt tears prick her eyes. "Perhaps I shall rest."

Mrs. Reid released Nell's hand. "I look forward to furthering our acquaintance." When she smiled like that, she didn't look regal, she looked like someone Nell would like to be friends with.

I think Letty Reid might be a kindred spirit.

Once they were gone, Nell stood for a moment in the parlor. She did feel tired. Exhausted. There was no doubting Reid's ability to look for Sophia and Lizzie; he would learn more in one hour on Gandy Street than she would in four. *Perhaps I will rest.*

Wearily she went upstairs. Bessie was in the bedchamber. "Look, ma'am," the maid said, and showed Nell the spencer.

"My goodness. It looks as good as new." Nell took the garment and examined it. Bessie had cut out the ripped seams and sewn in gussets of the same shade of navy blue. "Where did you get the fabric?"

"I took out some of the lining," Bessie said.

Nell turned the spencer inside out. Bessie had replaced the lining with scraps of ivory-white muslin.

"From your gown that was burned," Bessie said. "And look . . ."

Nell looked. Her two ruined gowns were spread side by side on the bed.

"If I take two panels from this one . . ." Bessie pointed to the vandyked walking dress with the burned seams. ". . . and cut them down, I can use them to replace this panel." She smoothed the torn sprigged muslin gown with her hand. "Do you see, ma'am?"

Nell did see.

"Of course, the fabrics won't match, but if I do the same to the bodice—add a strip of this muslin here—then it'll look as if it's *meant* to be that way." She glanced at Nell, looking hesitant and eager at the same time. "What do you think, ma'am?"

I think that you have guessed how little money I have. Nell swallowed the sudden lump in her throat. "I think it's a very clever idea." She gave a shaky laugh. "Can you conjure bonnets from thin air, too?"

Bessie grinned, and crossed to the dressing table—upon which sat a bonnet.

It was a very ugly bonnet.

"A lady left it behind last month," Bessie said. "None of the servants wanted it."

I can see why, Nell thought.

"I'll do it over," Bessie said. "Get rid of all them tassels and that wreath. It'll be much more the thing once I'm finished with it."

Nell believed her. "Thank you," she said, and then she hugged the maid—propriety be damned. "I don't know what I've done to deserve you, Bessie. You're the best maid in all England!"

Chapter Thirty-Two

July 25th, 1812
Exeter, Devonshire

IN THE MORNING, Mordecai insisted on getting up. A full day spent in bed was more than enough for any man. He walked across to the window. His head scarcely ached and his legs felt as if they belonged to him again. "I'll get dressed," he told Phelps.

Dressing exhausted him, but he tried to hide it. He didn't think Phelps was fooled. "You sure you're wanting to go down-stairs?" the coachman asked.

"Just as far as the parlor," Mordecai said.

He had no problem with the corridor, but the staircase was another matter. His head didn't like it, and nor did his legs. He halted after three steps, clinging to the banister.

"Back to bed with you," Phelps said, and Mordecai didn't argue.

He slept again, and when he woke it was nearly noon. For

the first time since the incident on the High Street, he was properly hungry. "Fetch me up a sirloin," he told Walter.

He ate a substantial repast, and once that was over he was bored. He didn't quite dare to open a book again; he was afraid that the print would still be unreadable. Which left him with two options: sitting here twiddling his thumbs, or getting dressed. Mordecai chose getting dressed. This time, it didn't exhaust him. He felt almost himself as he shrugged into his tailcoat.

He straightened his cuffs, smoothed his lapels—and hesitated. For weeks he'd carried the marriage license with him, carefully tucking it into his pocket each time he dressed.

"Sir?" Walter asked. "Is something wrong?"

"There was a paper in my breast pocket yesterday," Mordecai said.

"I put it in your portmanteau for safekeeping," Walter said. "Along with your pocketbook."

"Oh. Good."

"Would you like it, sir?"

"Uh . . . no. Thank you." Mordecai gave himself a mental shake and turned to the door. "I'd like to try the stairs again."

Phelps frowned, but said nothing.

Mordecai took the stairs slowly—and his head coped, and his legs coped—and he reached the private parlor with a sense of triumph. *I'll try reading next.*

"I shan't need you," Mordecai told Phelps and Walter. "I'll ring if I require anything." He opened the door and stepped inside—and there, sitting on the green sofa, was Eleanor Wrotham.

Mordecai froze, and wished he'd stayed in bed.

Eleanor stood. She wore an odd-looking turban on her head. Her expression was cool and aloof. "Mordecai. How are you?"

"Much improved, thank you," Mordecai said. "Uh . . . how are you?"

"Perfectly well."

An awkward silence fell. *I should have stayed in bed.*

"I'm waiting for a new friend to visit," Eleanor said. "Mrs. Reid. She says she knows you."

"Reid? I don't think I know a Mrs. Reid."

"She'll be here at one."

They both looked at the clock on the mantelpiece. Twelve fifty-eight.

"Uh . . . well . . . then I'll leave you," Mordecai said, turning towards the door.

"She may have news about Sophia and Lizzie."

Mordecai reluctantly looked back at her. Eleanor Wrotham. Who could burn down doors and set boots on fire.

He didn't know what to believe. Didn't know what to think. Didn't know how he felt about her anymore.

The door opened. Letitia Trentham, the great heiress, walked in carrying a hatbox.

Mordecai did a double take.

"I'm glad to see you on your feet, Mr. Black," Miss Trentham said. "How do you feel?"

"Uh . . . fine. How are you, Miss Trentham?" *And what the devil are you doing here?*

"Mrs. Reid now," Miss Trentham said with a smile.

"Oh? When did that happen?" And how had he missed it?

"Three and a half years ago."

"Oh," Mordecai said again. *I must have forgotten.* Which was more than a little disturbing.

Miss Trentham glanced past him to Eleanor. "No solid news, yet. But Icarus is hopeful. The countermen at the shop definitely remember Lizzie. The next time she shows up, they'll send her here."

Eleanor seemed to understand this cryptic utterance, but Mordecai was floundering. "Who's Icarus? What shop?"

"Icarus is my husband. He has several businesses in town. The confectioner's on the High Street is one of them."

"Oh," Mordecai said. It took several seconds for his brain to put her words together in a way that made sense.

Miss Trentham's brow creased. "Are you feeling quite well?"

"I'm sorry," he said. "My wits are rather slow. I think . . . if you'll excuse me . . . I think I'll lie down."

Mordecai retreated to his bedchamber, shaken.

"IS HE QUITE ALL RIGHT?" Mrs. Reid asked, frowning, as the door shut behind Black.

"I don't know," Nell said worriedly. "He's not usually like that."

"He needs to see Merry."

"Is she in Exeter?"

Mrs. Reid shook her head. "Thirty miles away." She hesitated, and then said, "Has he spoken yet about your magic?"

"No."

Mrs. Reid grimaced faintly, and then held out the box she was carrying. "This is for you. So you can get rid of that turban."

Nell took the box and opened it. Inside was a wig of coppery-red hair dressed in a Psyche knot, with pretty ringlets around the hairline.

"Mrs. Trussell-Quimby has red hair, didn't you say? I think that's an illusion we'd best maintain."

Nell hesitated. The wig looked very expensive. "I can't possibly accept—"

"Nonsense," Mrs. Reid said briskly. "Try it on."

Nell unwound the turban. With Mrs. Reid's help she soon had the wig on her head.

"Very nice," Mrs. Reid said approvingly. She folded up the shawl. "Personally, I've always hated turbans."

"So have I." Nell touched the ringlets gently. They felt very soft. Human hair, not horse.

"Do you have hairpins upstairs?"

"Plenty of them," Nell said.

"Oh, I almost forgot. Spectacles." Mrs. Reid rummaged in her reticule and produced a slender case.

"I can't—"

"Nonsense," Mrs. Reid said again.

The spectacles had tortoiseshell frames this time. Nell slid them onto her nose.

Mrs. Reid stepped back a pace and scrutinized her. "Goodness. You do look quite different. I almost wouldn't recognize you." She grinned suddenly, no longer regal but full of mischief. "I must try this on Icarus one day, see if I can fool him."

Nell found herself grinning back.

They sat on the sofa and talked—and talked. Very quickly they were *Letty* and *Nell*. Nell found herself telling Letty about Mordecai Black's proposals, about how much he'd come to mean to her, about her decision to marry him the next time he asked. "But perhaps he won't want to marry me anymore." She kneaded her hands together, realized she was doing it, and forced herself to stop.

Letty shook her head. "That doesn't sound like Black to me. I always enjoyed dancing with him. He never treated me as an heiress. I don't think my money meant anything to him. He . . ." She frowned, as if searching for words. "He judges people by a different set of criteria than most men."

Nell hoped she was correct.

"Give him time," Letty said. "Icarus didn't become comfortable with it until he met Cosgrove and Sir Barnaby." She shook her head again, and smiled wryly. "Poor Icarus. He would much rather *not* believe in magic, but he has a wife who can hear lies and a daughter who will one day receive a magical gift."

"A daughter?"

Letty's smile softened. "We have twins. A boy and a girl." Then she said, more briskly, "I suggest we all go to Woodhuish once you've found your sister. You can meet Charlotte and Merry, Black can talk with Cosgrove and Barnaby and Icarus . . . and I think you'll find that the issue resolves itself."

Nell hoped so. "What are Charlotte and Merry like? Can you tell me about them?"

They plunged into conversation. When Nell next looked at the clock she realized that an hour had sped past.

"Gracious! Is that the time?" Letty Reid exclaimed. "My poor children will be wondering what's become of me."

"You brought them to Exeter?"

"We always do," Letty Reid said cheerfully. She took her leave, hugging Nell. "We'll let you know as soon as we hear anything about your sister. I promise!"

MORDECAI TOOK REFUGE in his bed, where he lay and stared at the ceiling. How had he not known Letitia Trentham had married? He *must* have known.

He rummaged through his memory, trying to find gaps, and failing—and that worried him even more. Had he found no gaps because there weren't any . . . or because he couldn't recognize them?

In the middle of the afternoon, someone knocked on his door. It was Lord Cosgrove.

Mordecai was relieved. "Cosgrove," he said. "It's good to see you." He sat up and shoved several pillows between his back and the headboard. "Walter, fetch up some coffee, will you?"

Cosgrove took off his hat. "Letty Reid sent me. She's worried about you."

"I'm worried, too," Mordecai admitted. "I didn't remember she was married. I still can't remember it! And I should be able to, shouldn't I?" There was a note of anxiety in his voice.

Cosgrove pulled a chair across to the bed and sat. "It wasn't a Society wedding. A notice in the newspapers, nothing more."

"But I must have *known*."

"Probably, but it was several years ago now, and the Reids rarely go to London. It's only natural you'd have forgotten."

It was calming to talk with Cosgrove. They'd sparred often at Gentleman Jack's, and even though Cosgrove was eight years older and three inches shorter, Mordecai had lost as often as he'd won. Outside the boxing ring, they'd had little in common—Cosgrove was a peer of the realm and moved in political circles; Mordecai was a bastard with no interest in politics—but inside it, they were well matched, and because of that, they'd been friends.

When Cosgrove had remarried and moved to Woodhuish the sparring sessions had stopped. They'd seen each other rarely, and Mordecai had forgotten quite how much he liked the man. Cosgrove had an inner fire and strong principles and the courage to fight for what he believed was right.

They sat and drank coffee and the earl told him about the lying-in hospital Letty Reid had established in Exeter, about her husband's business enterprises. "Staffed wholly by invalided soldiers. He was a soldier himself. A major. You'd like him."

"They live in Exeter?"

"No, but they're here fairly often."

Mordecai's anxiety came surging back. "But surely I must have met them? I pass through Exeter several times a year."

"Why should you have met them?" Cosgrove asked. "I'm in Exeter as often as they are—and how many times have we met these past few years?"

"Not many." Mordecai paused. "At least, not many that I remember."

"A couple of times, that's all." Cosgrove put down his cup and reached across and gripped Mordecai's hand. "You're not losing your wits, man."

Mordecai's throat tightened. He found himself unable to speak.

Cosgrove picked up his coffee cup again. "Miss Wrotham said you went to the West Quarter. What did you think?"

Mordecai grimaced.

Cosgrove leaned forward and began telling him about his plans for the West Quarter.

Mordecai listened in astonishment.

". . . decided to start with the poorest of the children. The ones whose parents have abandoned them. Get them off the streets and into good foundling homes. Letty's helping me. Her mother had all those foundling homes in London. You remember?"

For a moment Mordecai was afraid that he didn't—and then he did: Miss Trentham's mother had been a philanthropist. She'd established a lying-in hospital in Holborn, and several foundling homes.

"We've set up two foundling homes and a charity school

already," Cosgrove said. "It's early days yet, but it's looking promising. Extremely promising."

"Be careful who you choose to run the places," Mordecai cautioned. "Sometimes children are safer on the streets."

Cosgrove hesitated, and then said: "Letty has a Faerie gift, too. She knows when people lie. You can be certain that anyone she selects to have charge of the children will have their best interests at heart."

Mordecai stared at him.

Cosgrove shrugged, and took another sip of his coffee.

Mordecai watched him drink, deeply unsettled. Had Cosgrove gone mad?

Cosgrove lowered his cup and met his gaze. His lips twitched faintly, as if he was amused. "Want to talk about it?"

Mordecai knew what he meant by *it*: magic. "Not really."

Cosgrove shrugged, and turned the subject. For the next ten minutes he talked about his wife and children, his face animated, his voice warm: a man who loved his family.

Mordecai listened, while Cosgrove's question nibbled away at the edges of his mind: *Want to talk about it?*

"Well," Cosgrove said. "I'll be off." He pushed to his feet and stood for a moment, looking down at Mordecai. "Don't worry, Black. If your skull doesn't mend itself I know someone who can do it for you."

"Magic?"

Cosgrove nodded. He didn't say *Want to talk about it?* again, but the offer hung silently in the air.

"I'm sorry," Mordecai said. "It's just . . . too much right now."

Cosgrove nodded. "It's a lot to get your head around. I know." He smiled, and donned his hat. "I'll be seeing you."

MORDECAI HAD A NAP, and then decided on a second foray down to the parlor. He was buttoning his waistcoat when a knock sounded on the door.

Walter went to answer it.

His guest was even more unexpected than Lord Cosgrove: Letitia Reid. Relief lit her face when she saw him. "Oh, thank God! You're up."

"What's wrong?"

"We've found Lizzie." She twisted her hands together. "Icarus is bringing her. He sent me on ahead."

Mordecai looked at Letitia Reid's anxious face, looked at her twisting hands, and felt a deep sense of foreboding. "What is it? Tell me."

"Sophia Wrotham's dead."

Mordecai held his breath for a moment, and then released it soundlessly.

"Will you come down to the parlor? Please? From the way Nell talks about you, I think she'd be glad of your presence."

"Of course," Mordecai said. "Walter, my tailcoat."

He shrugged into the coat and went down the stairs with Letitia Reid, and he didn't think about his legs or his head, didn't think about anything except Sophia Wrotham. *Please let this be a mistake,* he prayed silently. But he didn't think it was a mistake. Letitia Reid wasn't the sort of woman to make mistakes of this magnitude.

Eleanor Wrotham was seated at the writing desk. She looked up as they entered and stood hastily. "Letty!" she said with a smile, and then the smile faded and she said, a little uncertainly, "Mordecai. How are you?"

"Fine," he said. "Nell . . ." He floundered to a halt. Should he say anything? He glanced at Letitia Reid.

"Is something wrong?" Eleanor asked.

"We've found Lizzie Wellsford," Letitia Reid said. "But the

news about your sister isn't good. You need to prepare yourself."

"Not good?" Eleanor said. "What exactly—"

The door opened. A man Mordecai had never seen before stepped into the parlor. With him was a young woman.

The man was in his mid-thirties, tall and lean, with a soldier's bearing. *Reid,* Mordecai's brain labeled him. The woman was young, no more than eighteen. She had a pretty face and curling brown hair and was dressed very smartly. *Lizzie,* he labeled her.

There was a moment of silence, while they all looked at each other. Letitia Reid broke it. "Lizzie, this is Miss Wrotham. Sophia's sister."

Eleanor took a hasty step forward. "Where is she? Where's Sophia?"

Lizzie tried to smile, but it came out lopsided. She shook her head. Tears shone in her eyes. "I'm sorry."

"No," Eleanor said. All the color seemed to drain from her face.

Mordecai crossed to her and took her hand, gripping tightly. "Sit," he said, drawing her to the sofa. "And you, too, Lizzie."

Eleanor sat with none of her usual grace. She moved as if her limbs were rusty. Mordecai sat alongside her. He kept hold of her hand. He didn't consider that she was a woman who could set doors on fire, nor did he consider that holding her hand in public might ruin her. There was only one thought in his head: that she needed comfort.

Lizzie Wellsford chose one of the armchairs beside the fireplace. Letitia Reid took the other one. Reid stayed standing. He was carrying a slim package. Brown paper tied with string.

"We followed you from London to Exeter," Mordecai said.

"We found Miss Pender, and the lodging house in Turnagain Lane. What happened after that?"

"We moved to Gandy Street," Lizzie said. "I met a gentleman and he set me up with a place." Her cheeks flushed pink and she lifted her chin, ashamed and defiant at the same time.

"Needs must," Mordecai said mildly. "Anything would be better than Miss Pender, I should think."

Lizzie's chin lowered. She grimaced. "You're not wrong."

"Tell us," Mordecai said. "We're none of us here to judge you."

"We moved to Gandy Street," Lizzie said again. "Mr. Wheatley hired three rooms for me, and a maid's room in the attic. It's better than any lodgings I've ever had before! Sophy pretended to be my maid, and when Mr. Wheatley wasn't there she taught me how to read and write."

Mordecai smiled at her, and nodded encouragingly, aware of Eleanor's hand clinging to his.

"The baby was born two weeks after we moved. The sweetest little girl you ever saw. Sophy called her Felicity. Felicity Eleanor Elizabeth. And she loved her so much! We both did. But . . ." Lizzie bit her lip. "But the afterbirth didn't all come out, and the midwife had to come back, and after that Sophy caught a fever, and it got worse and worse . . ." Tears were bright in her eyes. She pressed the back of one hand to her mouth.

"When did she die?" Mordecai asked quietly.

"July second," Lizzie said, and sniffed, and wiped the tears away with her knuckles.

Mordecai glanced at Eleanor Wrotham. Her face was very like a duchess's, pale and haughty. He put an arm around her shoulders, drawing her close, not caring what the Reids thought.

"What happened to the baby?" Letitia Reid asked.

"I didn't know what to do." Lizzie sniffed again, wiped her eyes again. Reid silently handed her his handkerchief.

Lizzie blotted her eyes, blew her nose, took a deep, shuddering breath. "She needed a wet nurse, and I couldn't have one living in the rooms—Mr. Wheatley wouldn't have liked it! But I didn't want to give Felicity to a foundling home, so I asked the midwife to find someone to look after her. I thought that maybe one day I could take her back." Lizzie turned the handkerchief over in her hands, twisting it. "And the midwife found someone. A Mrs. Jellup. Only I didn't like her. Lushy, she was. She swore she never touched a drop of liquor, but I grew up in the West Quarter. I know drunkenness when I sees it." And then Lizzie corrected herself: "See it." She twisted the handkerchief more tightly. "I was going to move her, little Felicity, only Mr. Wheatley wanted to take me out of town." A tremulous smile lit her face. "He's right kind, Mr. Wheatley. Treats me very decent." The smile faded. "So I left Felicity where she was, and when we got back I went to fetch her away, only . . ."

There was silence while Lizzie wiped her cheeks, blew her nose. No one prompted her to speak. They all knew what was coming: the baby was dead.

Lizzie blew her nose a second time, and then said, "The wet nurse lived in Meacham Street, and it's gone. Burned to the ground. And everyone says Mrs. Jellup burned with it. She didn't get out."

Mordecai closed his eyes. *Oh, God.*

"So Felicity's dead, too. And it's all my fault!"

"Hardly your fault," Letitia Reid said. "You did the best you could. No one could have known what would happen."

Lizzie shook her head. "I should've done better. Sophy was the best friend I ever had." Tears filled her eyes again.

"It sounds to me as if *you* were the best friend she ever had," Letitia Reid said firmly.

"Yes," Eleanor said, her voice low and choked. "You were. I'm glad you were with her these last few months. That she had a friend, someone to look out for her. I'm glad she didn't die alone." Tears trembled on her eyelashes. One detached itself and slid down her pale, haughty cheek.

Mordecai watched it, and felt his heart break. *Nell.* He tightened his grip on her shoulders.

"Sophy knew you'd come for her," Lizzie said. "She said it over and over: 'Nell will come, I know she will.' She never stopped saying it."

Eleanor's face twisted.

Lizzie turned in her seat, seeking Reid. "Where's—?"

Reid silently handed her the package he was carrying.

"Here," Lizzie said. "Sophy gave me these for you." She crossed to the sofa and perched alongside Eleanor. "Keep them safe, she said. Give them to Nell when she comes." She untied the twine and peeled back the brown paper. Inside were two journals with cheap pasteboard covers, one stained crimson, the other yellow, and several sheets of loose paper. "This one's for you," Lizzie said, picking up the crimson book. "She said this was your color."

At that comment, Eleanor gave a muffled sob. She pressed one hand to her mouth.

Lizzie opened the book. The pages were full of writing. "She said she wrote letters to you, but after London . . . she weren't—wasn't—so certain you'd got them. She thought you were married, you see, and that your husband had forbidden you to reply. But she went to his house and it wasn't you as was his wife after all. Sophy didn't know what had happened to all the letters she'd sent, so she wrote this instead." Lizzie closed the book and held it out.

Eleanor lowered her hand from her mouth. She took the book.

"It's everything," Lizzie said. "From the beginning up until the very last day." She smiled crookedly. "She knew you'd come."

Eleanor didn't open the book. She pressed it to her breast.

"And this is the one she started writing for Felicity. Yellow, for happiness. She said she'd give it to Felicity when she was grown, but . . ." Lizzie's mouth twisted. "I think she'd want you to have it. There's a blue book, too, which she was using to teach me how to write, but I kept that."

"Of course," Eleanor said. Her voice was low, little more than a whisper. "Of course you must keep that one." She took the yellow book and slowly opened it. The first page held writing, but the second . . .

Eleanor inhaled a faint, soft gasp.

"That's Felicity," Lizzie said. "Beautiful, wasn't she?"

Eleanor touched the sketch lightly, reverently. "Very."

"And these are some of Sophy's other drawings." Lizzie handed over half a dozen sheets of paper. They were creased and dog-eared. "I kept the ones she did of me, and also one of Felicity. I hope you don't mind?"

Eleanor shook her head. "Of course not." She closed the yellow book carefully, almost reverently, and then looked at the drawings, one by one.

"Sophy had nothing else to leave, except a ribbon she said you'd given her. It matched her eyes. She never would sell it, even when she was hungry and had no money for food."

A spasm of grief crossed Eleanor's face. She closed her eyes tightly.

"I made sure she was buried with the ribbon in her hair," Lizzie said. "I knew she wouldn't want to be parted from it."

Mordecai expected Eleanor Wrotham to break down at

those words. He would have. He held his breath, waiting for it to happen, ready to comfort her, but she sat silent and unmoving, almost unbreathing, her head bowed, her eyes closed, one hand pressed to her mouth—and then she inhaled a shaky breath and lifted her head and opened her eyes. "Where is Sophia buried? I want to see her grave."

"Bartholomew's Yard," Lizzie said.

"Can we go there now? Please?" Her voice trembled, and Mordecai heard how close she was to breaking.

"Of course we can go now," he said firmly. "Lizzie? You'll take us?"

Lizzie nodded.

They all stood, Eleanor jerkily, clutching the books and the sketches to her breast.

"Where's your bonnet, Nell?" Mrs. Reid asked quietly. She held out her hand. "Come up with me to fetch it."

Eleanor let Letitia Reid lead her from the parlor.

There was a long moment of silence after the door closed behind them. Mordecai released his breath and turned to Lizzie Wellsford. "Thank you," he said, taking both her hands in his. "Thank you for everything you did for Sophia Wrotham. Thank you for being her friend. For keeping her safe. For being with her when she died. And thank you for coming here today."

Lizzie gave a watery smile, and nodded.

Mordecai released her hands. "Sophia Wrotham was fortunate to have you as a friend."

"It's me as was fortunate," Lizzie said, moping her eyes. "Sophy was the nicest person I ever met. Always had a good word to say about everyone. Even about Miss Pender." She gave a choked laugh, and then a sob. "Everyone loved her."

Mordecai said nothing. There didn't seem to be anything to say.

Reid stepped forward. "You must be Black. I'm Reid. Icarus Reid."

"Mordecai Black," Mordecai said, shaking the man's hand. "Thank you for finding Lizzie."

"You're welcome. I'm just sorry . . ."

The parlor door opened. Letitia Reid entered the room alone.

"Where's Nell?" Mordecai asked.

"Washing her face. Do you intend to come with us to Bartholomew's Yard?"

"Of course."

Letitia Reid looked him up and down. "Are you well enough?"

"Yes," Mordecai said, even though he wasn't certain of it.

Her eyebrows twitched up slightly, as if she didn't believe him . . . and he remembered Cosgrove's disclosure: Letitia Reid could hear lies.

"I'm coming," Mordecai said firmly.

Chapter Thirty-Three

THEY WENT TO Bartholomew's Yard burial ground in two hackneys. It was less than ten minutes from the inn. Which was fortunate, because the journey brought Mordecai's headache back.

He should have been first out of the hackney, should have helped Eleanor to descend; instead, he was last, and when he made it to firm ground he had to lean against the carriage for a moment, fighting dizziness, fighting nausea. Eleanor didn't notice. She looked numb with grief, blind with grief. Reid gave her his arm, and Mordecai blessed the man silently, and then closed his eyes for a moment and gritted his teeth. *I am not going to throw up*. When he opened his eyes, Letitia Reid was standing beside him.

"How do you feel?" she asked.

"I've had better days," Mordecai admitted. He pushed away from the hackney.

He walked into the burial ground arm in arm with Letitia Reid. To an observer it would have looked as if he was escorting her—but he and Letitia Reid both knew that she was supporting him. By the time they reached Sophia Wrotham's grave, Mordecai's nausea and dizziness had faded. Only the headache remained.

"There's no headstone yet, but I *will* get her one," Lizzie said. "A good one. Only I can't afford it, yet." She hesitated. "I could if I sold some of the dresses Mr. Wheatley bought me, only that doesn't seem right somehow."

"How did you pay for the burial, Lizzie?" Letitia Reid asked.

"Mr. Wheatley paid for it. He's very good to me." She gave a tremulous smile. "He probably would have paid for the headstone, too, only . . . I want to pay for it myself. I want it to have more than just her name on it. I want it to say something about her."

Eleanor stirred. She glanced at Lizzie. "Would you mind if I paid for it?"

"Of course not."

Eleanor smiled faintly, sadly. "You can help me choose the words."

THE JOURNEY BACK to the inn was even worse than the journey to the graveyard. Mordecai almost cast up his accounts. He descended hastily to the flagway and leaned against the hackney, eyes closed, breathing shallowly. When he was finally able to open his eyes he found that the person waiting silently beside him was Icarus Reid.

"Miss Wrotham?" Mordecai asked.

"Letty took her inside."

"Good." Mordecai shakily pushed away from the hackney.

Reid matched step with him. "You shouldn't have come."

"No." He'd been no use to Eleanor Wrotham. No use at all.

Reid discreetly took Mordecai's elbow, helping him up the stairs.

"Thanks," Mordecai said, when they reached the parlor door.

"I suppose it's no use telling you to go to bed," Reid said mildly.

"No."

Reid smiled, as if that was the answer he'd expected . . . and then the smile disappeared. He leaned close. "I'm going to Meacham Street," he said in a low voice. "I want to be certain about that wet nurse. Don't say anything to Miss Wrotham. Don't get her hopes up."

"I won't."

Reid gave a short nod. He opened the parlor door. Mordecai saw Eleanor and Lizzie and Letitia Reid seated on the sofa together.

"I'll be back in an hour or so. Sit down. Drink some tea." Reid clapped him on the shoulder and disappeared down the stairs again.

Mordecai sat in an armchair and drank a cup of tea, and then a second cup, and listened to Lizzie talk about Sophia Wrotham. The girl spoke eagerly, words spilling from her tongue, and Eleanor listened, no longer blind-eyed, but fiercely intent, as if Lizzie's words brought her sister alive again. Mordecai sipped the tea and felt his headache fade and watched. *They both need this,* he thought. Lizzie to talk about Sophia, and Eleanor to hear it.

It wasn't until he'd finished his second cup that he noticed the wig Eleanor was wearing. Mordecai stared at it, astonished. Where had the ringlets come from? And then he noticed that she was wearing a pair of spectacles that he'd never seen before in his life.

Mordecai looked away, blinked several times, looked back. Eleanor was still wearing the unfamiliar spectacles and wig.

He poured himself a third cup of tea, deeply unsettled. Where had she got the wig and spectacles from? And how on earth had he failed to notice that she was wearing them?

"If it wasn't for Sophy, I'd still be at Mrs. Harris's. I'd given up, you see. But Sophy didn't give up. She said we could get out of Mrs. Harris's if we put our minds to it, and we did. She used to say that tomorrow would be a better day than today, and the day after that even better. And she was right. Look at me." Lizzie gestured to the fashionable gown she wore. "I never would have guessed this would happen to me, not in a hundred years. And it's all because of Sophy. She taught me how to speak better and how to act refined, and Mr. Wheatley would never have looked at me otherwise."

Mordecai looked at Lizzie's pretty face and trim figure and thought that Mr. Wheatley would doubtless have looked at her however she spoke or acted. Any man would. And then he thought, *But Wheatley might not have treated her as well as he is now.* Lizzie wasn't a lady, but she was a long way from a tuppenny whore—which is what she'd been in London, and what she doubtless would have been if she'd returned to the West Quarter. And Sophia Wrotham was responsible for that change.

Mordecai sipped his tea, and thought about the annuity his father had given Dorothy Black. Would Lizzie accept an annuity for her care of Sophia Wrotham?

"She chose my surname, too, Sophy did. Because it sounds respectable. Wellsford."

Mordecai put down his teacup. "What's your real name?"

"Wix. Lizzie Wix."

No wonder Billy English hadn't recognized Lizzie's name.

Mordecai was contemplating a fourth cup of tea when Reid returned. The man's expression was thoughtful, frowning. Mordecai met Reid's eyes and lifted his brows, asking a silent question.

Reid grimaced faintly back. He poured himself a cup of tea and took the other armchair.

"Icarus?" Letitia Reid said. "Where have you been?"

"Meacham Street."

All attention focused on him.

"What did you learn?" Mordecai asked.

"Mrs. Jellup *did* definitely die in the fire, but she no longer had the baby with her."

"What?" Lizzie said sharply.

"I found one of Mrs. Jellup's neighbors, a widow who had the room next to her. She said Mrs. Jellup often took in babies, that she'd had one until two days before the fire, but at the time of the fire, she didn't. She was quite certain of it. Swore on it. Said the walls were paper thin and she could hear every scrap of noise, and there was definitely no baby with Mrs. Jellup the day of the fire."

"But . . ." Lizzie said, and then closed her mouth.

"My guess is that Felicity died and Mrs. Jellup had her buried," Reid said. "But there is a chance—a very slim chance —that she gave Felicity to someone else. I'll make some enquiries. Please don't get your hopes up. I think it most likely the baby is dead."

Lizzie nodded, but her eyes were already bright with hope. Eleanor Wrotham's face was less revealing. She sat still and taut, her hands clasped in her lap.

"If you don't mind, I'd like to take one of the sketches of Felicity with me," Reid said.

"Of course," Eleanor said.

"She had a ribbon tied around her wrist," Lizzie said

eagerly. "A yellow one. Mr. Wheatley gave it to me, and I tied it round Felicity's wrist so there could be no doubting who she belonged to. I told Mrs. Jellup not to take it off. Not ever!"

THE REIDS LEFT, taking Lizzie with them. Mordecai and Eleanor ate dinner together in the private parlor. It was a silent meal. Letitia Reid had said that Eleanor would be glad of his presence, and Mordecai hoped that was true, but he couldn't quite believe it. Eleanor had retreated into a silent, private grief. He didn't think she was aware of his presence at the table any more than she was aware what she was eating. Her movements were slow and slightly jerky, her gaze unfocused.

"Nell?" Mordecai said quietly once the meal was over. "Is there anything I can do to help?"

He thought she hadn't heard him, but after a moment she smiled at him, a faint, mechanical movement of her mouth, and shook her head.

Even though it was not yet nine o'clock, Mordecai escorted her upstairs and handed her into Bessie's care. Then he went to his own room. He went through the familiar routine—stripping, donning his nightshirt, cleaning his teeth, washing his face—but his mind was elsewhere.

"Good night, sir," Walter said.

"Good night," Mordecai said absently.

He stood looking at his bed for a long moment—the turned-back covers, the smooth sheets, the plump pillows—then he shrugged into his dressing gown and found his slippers and went down the corridor to Eleanor Wrotham's room.

Bessie answered his quiet knock.

"How is she?" Mordecai asked.

"She hasn't said a word, sir. It's like she's sleepwalking. I'm not sure I should leave her alone."

"Go to bed, Bessie. I'll look after her."

He saw shock flicker across Bessie's face.

"I won't do her any harm."

Bessie flushed. "I know you won't, sir." She hesitated for a moment, shifting her weight from foot to foot, then came to a decision. She dipped her head and stepped past him into the corridor. "Good night, sir."

"Bessie . . ."

She halted, and turned to look at him.

"I won't do her any harm," Mordecai said again.

She smiled at him, sudden and sweet. "I know, sir. Else I wouldn't be going now." She dipped her head again, not obedience this time, but acknowledgment. "Good night, sir."

"Good night, Bessie."

Mordecai watched her out of sight, then stepped into the bedchamber and closed the door. The room was dim, lit by the last of the fading daylight. Eleanor was in her nightgown, standing beside her bed, staring down at it as if she didn't recognize it for what it was.

Mordecai crossed to her. "Come on, Nell," he said gently. "Time to sleep."

He coaxed her into the bed, climbed in alongside her, pulled the covers up, and put his arms around her. She was more marble statue than woman, her body angles, not curves. She didn't speak, didn't nestle into him, just lay silently. *Does she even know I'm here?*

Darkness fell. Eleanor relaxed by slow increments. Mordecai drew her closer, tucked her into the curve of his body, stroked her hair gently, whispered in her ear, "Go to sleep, Nell."

She didn't go to sleep; she cried. Deep, wracking sobs that shook her body.

Mordecai held Eleanor Wrotham while she wept, and then held her while she fell asleep. And then he slept, too, and didn't wake until it was daylight. He blinked drowsily, turned his head, and saw Bessie standing by the bed.

Mordecai suppressed a groan. God. It was morning already.

Eleanor was fast asleep, wholly relaxed, curled into his embrace.

Mordecai disengaged himself carefully and slid from beneath the covers. Bessie handed him his dressing gown.

Don't wake her, Mordecai mouthed, and Bessie nodded, and opened the door for him, and her smile was just as sweet as it had been last night. She approved, he realized groggily. Bessie approved of him holding Eleanor Wrotham while she slept.

Once in his own bed, he fell asleep again. It was midmorning by the time he woke. Mordecai slitted his eyes open and watched Walter lay out his shaving tackle. The lad was quiet, but not as quiet as a valet. Walter looked around, saw he was awake, and snapped to attention. "Good morning, sir."

"Morning, Walter." Mordecai sat up. He rubbed his face, heard the scratch of stubble, and yawned.

Walter poured hot water into the washstand bowl and handed Mordecai a cloth for his face. He was attentive, conscientious, assiduous—and unusually poker-faced.

"Uh . . . Walter?"

"Yes, sir?"

"What time did you first check whether I was awake?"

Walter avoided looking at him. He fussed with the razor.

"What time, Walter?"

"Oh, um, . . . about seven o'clock it was, sir."

At seven o'clock Mordecai had been fast asleep in Eleanor's bed.

He squeezed his eyes shut for a moment. *Shit.* Had Walter guessed where he'd been?

Of course he had. Walter wasn't a fool.

Mordecai opened his eyes, took a deep breath, and said, "Walter, I would appreciate it if you didn't mention to anyone——"

"Of course I won't say anything!"

Mordecai looked at the footman's indignant face, and said, "I beg your pardon. I didn't mean to insult you."

Walter looked slightly less indignant. He nodded, much as Bessie had done last night—a nod that combined respect and complicity and approbation, all at the same time.

"She needed someone with her," Mordecai said, and that sentence was an admission all by itself, but Walter only nodded again and said, "I know, sir," and handed him his razor.

HE HAD A VERY late breakfast in the private parlor. Eleanor joined him. They ate without speaking. Mordecai kept an eye on her plate. She consumed very little. Her face was pale and aloof. She was holding her emotions tightly to herself.

"Nell?" he said, when they'd both finished eating. "Would you like mourning clothes?"

She stiffened.

Mordecai waited silently.

Eleanor looked down at her plate and pushed it away. "Not black," she said. "Not black for Sophia."

"Not if you don't want to."

"Crimson," Eleanor said, lifting her gaze to meet his. "We wore black when her mother died, and Sophia hated it. She said that if I died before her she would wear violet for me, and if she died first I must wear crimson. She made me promise." A spasm of grief crossed her face, and was almost instantly gone. "I'll wear crimson for Sophia—and I don't care what anyone thinks."

"I know of a good *modiste*," Mordecai said. Véronique had patronized her. "You can have a fitting this afternoon." He waited a moment, and then said, "What about a headstone?"

Grief spasmed across her face again. She looked away from him.

"You can visit the stonemason today if you like," Mordecai said. "Or it can wait."

Eleanor was quiet for a long moment, then looked at him. "Today. With Lizzie."

Mordecai nodded. "I'll arrange it." He hesitated, uncertain how much money Eleanor had. Not very much, he suspected. "May I pay for your mourning clothes? Please? My gift to you."

Eleanor stiffened again.

"I can't bring your sister back," Mordecai said quietly. "But I can give you the wardrobe she would like you to wear."

Eleanor bit her lip. After a moment, she nodded. "Thank you."

Mordecai exhaled a silent sigh, relieved to have cleared that hurdle. "May I pay for the headstone, too?"

Eleanor shook her head. "I want to pay for it myself."

"Can you afford it?"

Eleanor bit her lip, blinked several times, inhaled a deep breath. *She's very close to tears.* "I need to sell my mother's pearl brooch."

Mordecai shook his head. "Nell, please, let me pay—"

"I want to pay for it myself." Her voice was low and fierce.

Mordecai breathed in slowly, and then breathed out. "All right," he said. "Would you like me to sell the brooch for you?"

She bit her lip again, and nodded. Moisture brimmed in her eyes.

Mordecai reached across the table and laid his hand over hers. "Nell . . ."

She pulled her hand from beneath his. "Please don't," she said in a choked whisper.

Mordecai understood what those two words meant. It wasn't *Please don't touch my hand,* but rather, *Please don't make me cry.*

He pushed back his chair and stood. "I'll make those arrangements."

Eleanor nodded and blinked back the tears, trying to regain her composure. "Thank you." She stood, too, and crossed to the little writing desk, her steps jerky, hasty. "I need to write to the Dalrymples." Her hands fumbled as she opened the inkpot. She kept her face averted from him.

She's trying not to cry.

Mordecai's heart clenched painfully in his chest. He wanted to hug her, but knew if he did that she *would* cry. And she didn't want to. Not in daylight. Not in public. Eleanor Wrotham was clinging very hard to her composure, and the kindest thing he could do for her right now was to give her privacy.

So he did.

Mordecai sent Walter to arrange private fittings with the *modiste,* the milliner, the shoemaker, and the tailor—the latter to measure Eleanor for a riding habit—and directed Phelps to find the best stonemason in Exeter. Then he opened his writing case and sat down to write some letters of his own, but the words twisted and slid sideways. Just looking at them made his head hurt. By the time Phelps returned, he had the devil of a headache.

"Phelps. Finish this letter for me, will you?"

The coachman obediently picked up the quill.

"What have I written?"

"Please inform Tompkin that."

"That I wish him to come to Coombe Regis with all haste," Mordecai said, closing his eyes and rubbing his aching temples. "It's unlikely I'll return to London for several months, so he should pack whatever of my wardrobe he believes necessary for a long stay in Devonshire."

He scrawled his signature at the bottom of the letter and had Phelps address it to his housekeeper in London. Then he dictated a letter to his housekeeper at Coombe Regis, telling her to expect himself and at least one guest shortly, to air the Rose Suite, to prepare the nursery in case it was needed, and to send his curricle to Exeter with all haste.

Mordecai signed that letter, too. "Have them both sent express," he told Phelps.

"Yes, sir."

Walter returned. Mordecai sent him out again with a message for Lizzie Wellsford, inviting her to visit the stone-mason with them later that afternoon.

Eleanor Wrotham and Bessie departed for the fittings. Before they left, Bessie brought him a pearl brooch. "Ma'am said to give this to you."

"Thank you, Bessie."

Mordecai examined the brooch once she'd gone. It was demure little piece—which didn't surprise him. He couldn't imagine Mr. Wrotham allowing his wife to wear anything that would draw the eye.

He had promised to sell the brooch for Eleanor and he would keep that promise—but right now he didn't feel up to haggling with anyone, least of all jewelers. Mordecai tucked the brooch into his portmanteau, found his pocketbook, and counted out one hundred and fifty pounds in banknotes. Was that a fair price? After a moment's consideration, he added fifty more pounds to the pile.

Not long after that, Reid arrived. His shirt-points had wilted in the heat and his hair, when he removed his hat, was dark with sweat. "Damn this weather." He pulled out a handkerchief and wiped his brow. "As bad as India."

Mordecai ordered ale for them both and ushered the man into the private parlor. "Found anything?"

"No. As far as I can ascertain, no one buried Sophia Wrotham's baby."

"That's . . . not what I expected."

"Not what I expected either," Reid said.

The ale arrived. Reid took a long swallow, then a second, and then told Mordecai about his day. By the time he'd finished, Mordecai was ready to believe that Felicity Wrotham hadn't been buried in Exeter. At least, not legally.

"Either the baby died and Mrs. Jellup disposed of her somehow," Reid said. "Or she gave the child to someone."

"Where to, now?"

"Foundling homes first. And after that . . ." Reid shrugged. "Mrs. Jellup could have given that baby to anyone."

"An advertisement in the newspapers could be useful."

"Yes."

"Would you write it?" Mordecai asked. He felt himself flush. "I, uh, can't read or write at the moment."

"Of course," Reid said. "I'll do it today."

"Thank you," Mordecai said awkwardly. "You've gone beyond the call of kindness. We're little more than strangers—"

"Miss Wrotham is family."

Mordecai eyed him. Reid's expression was extremely neutral.

Mordecai hesitated, and then said, "Cosgrove told me about Letitia."

Reid grimaced faintly. "I know. He told me."

"I shan't tell anyone. You have my word."

Reid eyed him for several seconds, then gave a nod. It was more than a silent *Thank you;* it was a nod of kinship.

"You believe it?" Mordecai asked. "About the Faeries?"

Reid grimaced again. "Yes. Although I don't want to. It's . . ." He searched for a word and came up with: "Challenging."

Mordecai grunted a laugh. "It is."

Amusement gleamed briefly in Reid's eyes. The sense of kinship between them became stronger.

"It makes my head hurt, just thinking about it," Mordecai confessed.

"I'd say a lot of things make your head hurt right now."

Mordecai grunted another laugh. "You're not wrong." He rubbed his hands through his hair and sighed.

Chapter Thirty-Four

THE DAY PASSED. That was all that could be said for it: it passed. The hours followed one another, and at last it was evening and Nell could retreat from the world.

She undressed mechanically, bade Bessie goodnight, and climbed into bed. Her limbs were stiff, her heart aching, her eyes dry. She had never felt less like sleeping. She stared blankly at the ceiling.

Her door opened quietly, closed quietly. Mordecai Black came to stand beside the bed. He didn't say anything, just climbed under the covers and took her in his arms—and it was such a relief. Such a profound relief.

Nell rested her head against his chest and finally—finally—was able to relax. And to weep. And to sleep.

Chapter Thirty-Five

August 5th, 1812
Coombe Regis, Devonshire

FELICITY WASN'T IN any of Exeter's foundling homes. "We'll
have to hope the advertisements bear fruit," Reid said, and
they did, after a fashion. Six people came forward, each with a
baby that they claimed was the missing infant. But according
to Letitia Reid, all of them were lying.

So Mordecai took Eleanor Wrotham home to Coombe
Regis.

It was nearly two weeks since he'd taken the blows to his
head. He could read again, he no longer wanted to vomit
whenever he rode in a hackney . . . but even so, Mordecai
erred on the side of caution. He drove the twenty miles to
Coombe Regis in his curricle with a groom beside him ready
to take over if dizziness threatened, and the traveling chaise
trundling sedately behind. But dizziness didn't threaten, and
Mordecai was confident enough at Clyst St. George to take

Eleanor up beside him and relegate the groom to the tiger's seat. "Go on ahead," he told Phelps. "Tell Mrs. Putnam we'll be there shortly."

Three quarters of an hour later, they trotted slowly along a high-banked lane, and then the lane swung left and the view opened out and there was Coombe Regis—the parkland, the woodland, the house—and beyond those things, not visible from here: the coast, with its red cliffs and rocky islets.

"Coombe Regis," Mordecai said, bringing the curricle to a halt. "Home." He glanced at Eleanor. "You can take that wig off now, if you wish. And the spectacles. Unless you want to wear them? My servants won't gossip about you."

Eleanor hesitated for a moment, and then took off the tortoiseshell spectacles and placed them in her reticule. She unfastened her bonnet. She removed the hairpins holding the wig in place, and then the wig itself.

"Does that feel better?" Mordecai asked.

"Much better."

The wig went into one of the deep pockets of Mordecai's driving coat, the hairpins into another. He waited for Eleanor to tie the ribbons of her bonnet again, then lifted the reins and urged the horses into a slow trot. "When I was fourteen Father started teaching me how to manage Coombe Regis. He signed it over to me on my seventeenth birthday." He could still remember how he'd felt: alarmed and exhilarated, daunted by the enormity of his new responsibilities, determined to succeed, and—to his embarrassment—a little tearful. Holding the title deed had given him a strange feeling in his chest, a feeling it had taken him years to find a name for: security. The security of having a home—this soil, this grass, these trees, this house. *These things are mine. No one can take them from me. They belong to me and I to them.*

He had other estates, now, and the house in London, but Coombe Regis would always be home.

Mordecai wanted to extol every point of beauty, to defend every possible flaw. He bit the tip of his tongue in an effort to remain silent, but silence became impossible as the curricle swept into the forecourt. The house's façade was ornate, playful, exuberant. Mordecai wanted Eleanor to find the scrolls and volutes comical, not outlandish. "Baroque," he said unnecessarily. "A bit excessive, really, but I confess I find it amusing."

He drew the curricle to a halt in front of the steps. The groom jumped down and ran to the horses' heads.

Mordecai climbed down more carefully and gave Eleanor his hand. Sophia Wrotham had been correct: crimson was Eleanor Wrotham's color. It made her skin creamier, her hair darker, her eyes a deeper blue. She looked grave and sad and patrician and bold and wholly, utterly beautiful.

In that gown Eleanor Wrotham suited the house perfectly. Mordecai looked at her, and knew in his bones that she belonged here just as much as he did.

"Welcome to Coombe Regis," he said. *Welcome home.*

Mordecai's valet, Tompkin, had arrived from London before them. Mordecai greeted him with relief. Walter was a good lad, but he was a footman, not a valet; he sometimes had to be prompted what to do. Tompkin never had to be prompted. Tompkin knew what Mordecai needed or wanted before Mordecai did himself. Take now, for example: the steaming pitcher of water, the clothing laid out.

Mordecai washed the dust from his face and dressed in his country clothes, everything a little looser, a little more comfortable. Even his neckcloths had less starch in them here. Sometimes all he did was knot them casually, and sometimes he didn't bother to wear them at all.

Today he wore one, and tied it carefully.

In the dressing room, Tompkin was already unpacking Mordecai's luggage.

Mordecai checked his appearance in the mirror one last time, and headed for the door.

"Sir?"

He turned back.

Tompkin emerged from the dressing room, holding a folded piece of paper.

It was the marriage license. Its shape was so familiar by now that Mordecai thought he could tell it from a thousand other marriage licenses just by its creases.

"This was in your portmanteau. Do you wish to take it with you?"

"Yes," Mordecai said. Of course he did. And of course Tompkin had known. Tompkin always knew what was important and what wasn't.

He took the license carefully, but he didn't tuck it into his breast pocket. He hadn't placed it there for days. A license in one's pocket meant that one intended to propose marriage imminently, and he didn't. He *couldn't*. Not while Eleanor's grief was so fresh.

Another six months. Four, at the very least.

The license would have expired by then. He should tear it up and burn it, but Mordecai couldn't quite bring himself to do that. Instead, he took it down to his study and locked it in the top drawer of his desk—but that didn't feel right either. The license was a piece of paper, nothing more, but it was too imbued with hope to be locked in a dark drawer.

Mordecai took the license upstairs again, uncertain what to

do with it. Not a pocket, not a drawer. Where, then? Inspiration struck as he entered his bedchamber. His pocketbook. It was the perfect place. Neither hope*ful* nor hope*less*. Neutral. He tucked the license at the very back, behind the folded banknotes.

THAT AFTERNOON, MORDECAI took Eleanor walking along the clifftops. Devonshire had some gentle stretches of coast, and at first glance this looked like one of them—the lush, undulating pastures, the deeply wooded hills, everything green and fertile and well-tended—and then the cliffs came into sight and the impression of gentleness fell away and it was wild and dramatic—steep red bluffs and great pillars of red rock rising from the sea—nothing gentle about it at all.

Mordecai inhaled deeply. *God, I love this place.* He glanced at Eleanor, hoping that she liked it.

For days Eleanor Wrotham had been half woman, half statue, but right now, standing on the clifftop, dressed in crimson, the sea breeze tugging at her hair, she looked wholly human.

"What do you think?" Mordecai asked.

"Magnificent."

They walked further, not talking, taking in the view. Mordecai listened to the waves and inhaled the sea breeze and tasted the salt-tang on his tongue, and felt himself relax. This shore had always done that to him. Yes, the scenery was dramatic, but underneath the drama was serenity. There was something about the sea that was deeply restful. Here on the cliffs his troubles fell away and the world came into balance.

He thought Eleanor felt the serenity, too. She seemed to hold herself less tensely.

If her sister wasn't dead, if the baby wasn't missing, he thought she would have stood on the clifftop and flung her arms wide and laughed with sheer delight—and he would have lifted her off her feet and kissed her. But the spirited, passionate, slightly reckless Eleanor Wrotham was burdened with sorrow, so Mordecai didn't kiss her; instead, he took her hand.

Her fingers were slim and cool and fitted into his perfectly.

Marry me, Mordecai wanted to say, but didn't.

HE DIDN'T ASK her to marry him that night, when he lay in the great four-poster bed in the Rose Suite with his arms around her, or the next morning while they breakfasted in the sunny front parlor, but when he drew her attention to the ceiling, with its riot of garlands and cupids painted on a bright blue sky, she smiled, and it wasn't a polite smile, but a smile that touched her eyes, and if her sister had been alive he thought she would have laughed.

Later that morning he took her to where the cliffs dipped down to a sandy cove shaped like a half moon, and they peeled off their stockings and paddled in the sea, and he thought she seemed almost happy, as if the pure simplicity of sea and sky, cliffs and sand, gave her the same sense of deep serenity it gave him.

Afterwards they sat on a red boulder and waited for the sun and the breeze to dry their feet, and he saw the happiness slowly drain from her.

In the Greek myth, Galatea had been a statue turned woman; Eleanor Wrotham was a woman turned statue.

"Nell," he said softly. "If you want to talk . . ."

Her lips compressed slightly. She said nothing, just shook

her head. Mordecai gave a silent sigh, and put an arm around her.

For a moment, Eleanor resisted, and then she leaned against him, resting her head on his shoulder.

Minutes passed, while their feet slowly dried. Eleanor grew stiffer, and stiffer, until she seemed all angles and bones and misery, and then she burst out: "I was so *angry* with her."

"Of course you were angry," Mordecai said. "You would have been very unnatural if you hadn't been."

Eleanor said nothing. She was still angles and bones and unhappiness.

"Even a saint would have been angry," Mordecai said. "She destroyed your family's reputation and ruined your betrothal. Of *course* you were angry."

"Sophia said she didn't realize how it had been until she went to Roger's house looking for me." Eleanor uttered a choked sound that was half sob, half laugh. "She hadn't thought that I'd be ruined, too. How could she *not* have realized? How could she have been so naïve?"

Naïve was one word for Sophia Wrotham. Foolish was another.

"Oh, God. She was only fifteen. Why am I angry with her?" Eleanor's stiffness dissolved into despair.

"Because you're human," Mordecai said. He removed her bonnet and put both arms around her and pressed his face into her hair. "Because you're human and it's human to be angry when people do things that hurt you."

"But she didn't *mean* to hurt me."

"No, she didn't. Any more than you mean to be angry with her." He kissed her hair. "Your feelings are natural, Nell. Don't blame yourself for them." He rocked her gently, kissed her hair again. "When you discovered she was in trouble, you went looking for her. That's what counts."

She was silent. Did she doubt him?

"Being angry doesn't mean you didn't love her," Mordecai told her. "We can love people and be angry with them at the same time."

Eleanor sighed. "I know. And I forgive Sophia, I *do*, but I'm still angry. Not about Roger, but . . . oh, the *waste* of it. Her life!"

"Your sister made a grave mistake," Mordecai said. "But the mistake your father made was far worse. He could have saved her. Not from her initial ruin, but from everything that came afterwards."

"I failed her, too."

"No," Mordecai said, very firmly. "Listen to me, Nell. This is important. You did *not* fail your sister. You may have been angry, and perhaps even hated her at times, but you *didn't* fail her. The moment you knew she needed help, you came for her, and it wouldn't have mattered how fast you traveled because she was already dead. Nothing you did could have changed that. You did *not* fail her."

Eleanor was silent for almost a full minute. Mordecai listened to the *shush* of the waves on the sand and the cries of the sea birds.

"There have been times this past year when I did almost hate Sophia," Eleanor whispered, and he heard her shame. "I wish I could have spoken to her one last time. I wish I could ask her to forgive me for being so angry with her."

"Do you doubt that she would?"

"Sophia?" She uttered another choked laugh. "Of course not." Then she sighed. "She had so much faith in me. More than I deserve."

"No," Mordecai said. "Just the right amount, I think."

Eleanor was silent for even longer this time. "That book," she said finally. "The one Lizzie gave me . . . I thought it was a diary, but it's not. It's a letter, a . . . a *conversation*. It's as if Sophia's speaking to me. I just wish . . . I *wish* I could talk back to her and tell her——" She caught her breath on a sob.

"Perhaps you should write to Sophia," Mordecai said. "Write everything down, as she did."

Eleanor thought about this for a long moment, while the waves *shush*ed and the breeze fingered its way through the folds of Mordecai's neckcloth. "Perhaps I will."

THEY DUSTED THE sand from their feet and put on their footwear again and walked back to the house, and after luncheon Eleanor Wrotham said, "I'd like to try it, what you suggested: write to Sophia." She sounded diffident and a little embarrassed, as if writing a letter to a dead sister was a foolish thing to do.

Mordecai didn't think it was foolish at all. He showed Eleanor the library, laid sheets of paper, several quills, and an inkpot out on the desk for her, and said, "Take as long as you like. I'll tell the servants not to disturb you."

He spent the afternoon in his study, catching up on neglected business—letters that needed to be replied to, reports from his bailiffs, accounts sent by his man of business. At twilight, Mordecai put the papers to one side and returned the library. He quietly opened the door.

Eleanor Wrotham sat at the desk, but she wasn't writing; she was gazing out the window at the encroaching dusk. She looked pensive.

"Nell?" he said quietly.

She turned her head and smiled faintly.

Mordecai didn't need to ask if writing to her sister had helped. He could tell just by looking her. The stiff misery was gone. By committing her emotions to paper—anger, guilt, regret, grief—Eleanor had found some ease.

He held her that night, and she didn't cry, and the next morning he took her riding. Eleanor wore her new habit. Most riding habits were blue or green, but this one was crimson. So dark a crimson that it was nearly black. The cut was severely elegant—no piping, braiding, epaulettes, frogging, or other embellishments—and for her hat she'd chosen a black, slender-brimmed beaver. Mordecai privately thought that she had never looked so striking.

Eleanor Wrotham's neck-or-nothing riding was one of the things that had first attracted him—so exuberant, such *joie de vivre*—but today they went no faster than a canter. Galloping suited joy, or perhaps anger, but not grief.

Mordecai showed her the whole estate, and then showed her Great Wynthrop estate, too, with its vast dilapidated house. They halted on the edge of the overgrown lawn and gazed at the building. It was bigger than Coombe Regis, and much older. Tudor, not baroque. "I bought it after Father died," Mordecai said. "When I didn't know what to do with all the extra servants. No one's lived in it for a good fifty years. As you can see, it needs a bit of attention." A *lot* of attention.

Eleanor gazed at the building thoughtfully. Her mount was so close to his that Mordecai could have reached across and taken her hand.

"The central part is livable now. The wings will be at least another six months." And then there was the exterior, and the grounds. A good year's work. But at the end of it, Great Wynthrop would be a handsome property.

"What will you do once it's restored?"

Mordecai looked at the wild expanse of lawn, looked at the Hall—huge and old, crumbling slightly at the edges, but with strong bones—and said, "I have absolutely no idea."

BACK AT COOMBE REGIS, he escorted Eleanor to her bedchamber. "Bessie," he said. "Can you please fetch the clothes the tailor sent?"

Bessie disappeared into the dressing room.

"One riding habit is all I need," Eleanor protested.

"It's not a riding habit," Mordecai said, as Bessie returned, a pile of clothing in her arms. "But they are for you to ride in . . . if you wish. Look." He took the topmost item and shook it out and laid it on the bed. A linen shirt. Next was a single-breasted waistcoat, then buckskin breeches, then a pair of linen drawers, and at the very bottom, carefully folded, a tail-coat in the same deep crimson as Eleanor's riding habit. "Made to your measurements. And there are top boots, too."

Bessie darted into the dressing room again and returned bearing a pair of gleaming top boots.

Eleanor stared at the clothes displayed on the bed, she stared at the boots Bessie held. She seemed speechless with astonishment.

Mordecai hoped that she was pleased by his gift, not offended. "Do you like them?" he asked, his tone both more diffident and more hopeful than he'd intended. He had a horrible feeling that he sounded like a child asking for praise.

Eleanor turned her gaze to him. "Yes, Mordecai. I do." And then—despite Bessie standing there—she hugged him. "Thank you."

Bessie, bless her, withdrew to the dressing room, so Mordecai put his arms around Eleanor and hugged her back.

Her elegant beaver hat was in the way. He removed it and tossed it on the bed.

"You can try them out this afternoon," he said, and stroked her soft hair. "But only if you want to. My feelings shan't be hurt if you never wear them."

"Of course I want to wear them." Eleanor rested her forehead on his chest. "How could I ever have thought you autocratic and overbearing?"

"It did puzzle me," Mordecai said.

Eleanor gave a shaky laugh. "It's the fault of that nose of yours."

"My great beak?"

"You have the nose of a Roman emperor."

He stroked her hair again. "I'll take that as a compliment."

Eleanor drew back and met his eyes. "I apologize for saying you were dictatorial."

"Apology accepted," Mordecai said, smiling down at her.

Chapter Thirty-Six

Mordecai didn't take Eleanor riding in her breeches and tailcoat that afternoon because it rained. Fresh, cool rain that washed away the sticky heat of the past month.

Instead of riding, he showed her Coombe Regis, trying to share his delight in the house with her, pointing out his favorite absurdities: the songbirds cavorting across the ceiling in the music room; the gargoyles grinning down from the pelmets in the library; the *trompe l'oeil* panel in the Long Gallery that invited one to step through into a sunlit garden.

He suspected that he talked rather too much, but Eleanor didn't seem to mind. She was even surprised into a laugh when she saw the great, gilded four-poster bed that had been relegated to the very sparest of the spare bedchambers because it was so blindingly gaudy.

Mordecai took her up to the attics last, and they spent an hour opening long forgotten trunks and uncovering paintings wrapped in Holland cloths. They discovered several paintings that Mordecai rather liked, and a trunk of silk brocade gowns that made Eleanor gasp. She knelt on the floor and went through them, turning over the rich fabrics.

"I don't want to wear this," she said, fingering a blue and silver brocade. "But surely it deserves to be *seen*."

"Cushion covers?" Mordecai suggested.

"Slippers, I think." She glanced up at him. "Would you wear slippers made of this?"

"I'll wear anything you make for me," Mordecai said.

Eleanor blushed, and she looked a little bit shy and a little bit flustered and so delicious that if her sister hadn't been dead he would have spread the brocades on the floor and tumbled her on them—but her sister *was* dead, so Mordecai went to have another look at the paintings.

AFTER THE ATTIC, they went down to the library, where it was cool enough to light the fire. Mordecai would have happily passed the rest of the afternoon reading, but Eleanor was restless. She browsed the shelves, pulling books out, flicking through the pages, putting them back, and finally ended up at the tall windows, staring out at the rain, her hands twisting together.

"What is it, Nell? Would you like to go riding?"

"In this weather? No." Eleanor came to sit by the fire. After a moment, she began to fidget, pleating her skirt.

"What is it?" Mordecai asked again.

"I beg your pardon." She flushed, as if embarrassed, and smoothed her skirt hastily.

"For what?"

"Father always said it's unladylike to fidget."

Mordecai snorted. Which was ungentlemanlike, but he didn't care.

Eleanor smiled faintly, and pushed to her feet and crossed to the tall windows again. She stood for a moment looking out, then turned to face him. "It's my cousin's birthday tomorrow. Georgiana."

"Oh?" Mordecai said, wondering what this had to do with anything.

"Her twenty-third birthday."

"Oh," he said again, and put down his book. "Will she receive a . . . a wish?" He gave an instinctive, inward wince. *I can't believe I said that word. I can't believe I believe in magic.*

"Yes." Eleanor's hands twisted together. "I know Georgie wants to find out what happened to Hubert."

Hubert?

And then Mordecai remembered: Hubert was Lord Cathcart's youngest son. The one who'd gone missing four years ago. The one who'd been engaged to Georgiana Dalrymple.

"What if . . . what if . . ."

Mordecai stood and crossed to the windows. He captured Eleanor's hands and stopped their twisting. "What if what, Nell?"

"What if she wishes to be able to find people?" she burst out.

"Do you think she will?"

"She might. It's what I was going to choose. If it hadn't been for the fire I *would* have chosen it."

Mordecai was silent, remembering that blazing stairwell.

"I *want* her to choose it—and I know she might not—and I just wish tomorrow was over. I wish I *knew.*" She leaned into him, resting her forehead against his chest, and sighed deeply. "I'm so full of hope and dread that I can't sit still. I'm sorry."

"Don't be sorry," Mordecai said, stroking the nape of her neck. Her tension was contagious; he felt it himself now.

Tomorrow Georgiana Dalrymple might know where Sophia's baby was.

Or she might not.

"Do the Dalrymples know you're here?"

Eleanor shook her head. "It doesn't matter, does it? If Georgie chooses that wish she'll *know* where I am—and if she doesn't, it's irrelevant."

She was correct. Mordecai brushed his fingers soothingly over her skin and looked out at the streaming rain. Eleanor Wrotham needed a distraction, but it was far too wet for riding. "Come on," he said. "I'll teach you how to fence."

Her head lifted. "What?"

"Or box. Your choice. Run upstairs and change into those breeches of yours."

ELEANOR WROTHAM CHOSE FENCING, and Mordecai spent the next two hours teaching her how to hold the foil and perform a basic lunge step. After dinner, they retired to the library again. She curled up alongside him and he read aloud to her from Wordsworth's poems, and she almost relaxed.

An hour later when he slid into her bed and took her in his arms, she was tense again.

"Thinking about your cousin?" Mordecai asked.

"I'm trying not to."

That night Mordecai made love to Eleanor Wrotham for the third time in his life. He bent his attention to distracting them both. He teased her with his tongue and teeth until she was desperate for release, and then shocked her by asking her to ride him. She was shy at first, hesitant, but then she caught the rhythm and her shyness fell away. She rode him, and it was fierce and urgent and altogether perfect, and when she climaxed Mordecai gritted his teeth and only just managed not to spill his seed inside her. He eased himself from beneath her hastily and ejaculated into his handkerchief, and the pleasure was bittersweet and unfulfilling.

It WAS STILL RAINING the next morning. Eleanor fetched the blue and silver brocade gown down from the attic and set to work cutting up the skirt. For this task, she chose the drawing room, with its view of the long, sweeping driveway. Mordecai elected to stay there, too.

Ostensibly Eleanor was cutting the fabric, but what she was really doing was watching for an express rider. Ostensibly *he* was reading the London newspapers, but what he was really doing was watching Eleanor watch the driveway.

Mordecai knew roughly where the Dalrymple estate was— near Bridport—and he knew roughly how many hours it would take even the fastest rider to cover that distance—and how impossible it was for an express to reach Coombe Regis before noon, but he didn't tell Eleanor that.

He watched her snip the fabric, watched her stare out the window, watched her tension, her anxious hope, her fear. As the morning slowly passed, it infected him. When Walter appeared in the doorway to announce luncheon, Mordecai started so violently that he tore the newspaper he was pretending to read. "Damn it," he said, under his breath, and more loudly: "Thank you, Walter."

Eleanor cast one last glance at the driveway and laid down her scissors.

They were in the great hallway when suddenly a footman hurried past and flung open the front door. A gust of cool air swept in, bringing with it the scent of wet grass and the sound of rain—and rapid hoof beats.

Eleanor's hand clenched convulsively on Mordecai's sleeve.

They arrived at the open door at the same time as two more footmen and the butler. An express rider pull up with a flurry of wet gravel. A footman ran down the marble steps. The rider unbuckled his leather satchel. Ten seconds later, the footman ran back up.

Mordecai took the proffered letter, glanced at the address, and gave it to Eleanor. "For you."

A flare of emotion crossed her face: hope, fear. She tore the seal open.

Mordecai reached into his pocket, but the butler was already counting out a gratuity.

"Triple it," Mordecai told him, and turned his attention to Eleanor.

The door was still open, the express rider still sitting on his horse, the footman running down the stairs again, this time with coins jingling in his hand, but Mordecai ignored these things. He watched Eleanor's face, watched her gaze jump from sentence to sentence.

"Tiverton!" she said, looking up, and he saw tears in her eyes and a fierce, shining joy. "She's in Tiverton. Do you know where that is?"

"Twenty miles the other side of Exeter."

"Can we go there? Now? Today?"

"We can leave in half an hour."

"Thank you!" Eleanor caught up her skirts and turned to the staircase, then swung back and thrust the letter at him. "You may read it."

Mordecai watched her run up the stairs. "I want my traveling chaise ready to leave in half an hour," he told the butler.

"Yes, sir."

"We'll be bringing a child back with us. An infant. Tell Mrs. Putnam we'll need a nurserymaid. And a wet nurse, if she can find one."

"Mrs. Biddle is still nursing her wee boy," his butler said. "And so is Mrs. Clee."

Biddle was a groom, but who the devil was Clee? Mordecai's mind went blank for a moment—and then he placed the name: Clee was one of his groundsmen. "Ask them both, will you? I'll pay any sum they want."

"Yes, sir. And your luncheon?"

"Uh . . . pack it in a basket."

Mordecai read the letter as he hastily climbed the stairs. *Baletongue came at dawn this morning, and I now understand why our great-great-great grandmother made such a grievous mistake with her wish. When one is half asleep and wholly terrified it is very easy to choose the wrong wish! But fortunately I knew what I wanted.*

He skipped down the page.

Hubert is dead of course. I have known that for years. But at least I now know where he lies. By the time you read this, dearest Nell, we shall be on our way to Scotland. Mama and Papa are coming with me and we will be gone at least a month, if not more.

But if Hubert is dead, your little niece is alive. She's in a cottage belonging to a Mrs. Rundle, in Tiverton. A foundling home, I think, or something similar; there are several other infants there. You will know Felicity by the yellow ribbon tied around her wrist.

Georgiana gave precise directions to the cottage. Mordecai read them as he climbed the second flight of stairs.

Good luck, Nell. I look forward to meeting my little cousin when I return from Scotland.

All my love,

Georgie

P.S. Mama says that if Mr. Black does not take good care of you she will turn him into a caterpillar.

Mordecai almost tripped over a step. A caterpillar?

Disconcerted, he folded the letter and tucked it into his pocket.

A caterpillar?

It was a joke, surely.

Chapter Thirty-Seven

COOMBE REGIS TO TIVERTON was only fifty miles, but they were fifty waterlogged miles. Twice the road was flooded and they had to backtrack and find another route. By nightfall they were still twelve miles short of their destination. "I'm sorry, Nell," Black said, when they reached Broadclyst. "We can't go any further tonight."

Nell didn't argue. She knew that trying to reach Tiverton in the dark, on unfamiliar and possibly flooded roads, was far too dangerous.

She climbed down from the carriage, her half-boots splashing in inch-deep water. A footman held an umbrella over her head but even so droplets of rain misted her spectacles. The footman's face was an indistinct blur in the darkness, but she knew who he was: Walter.

Nell looked at him in his dripping greatcoat and then glanced up at Phelps, a dim shape on the box seat. "Mr. Phelps, Walter . . . I'm sorry you're so wet."

"We've been rained on before, ma'am," the coachman said cheerfully. "Didn't harm us then, shan't harm us now."

Nell expected the inn to be overflowing with stranded travelers, but it was almost empty. The innkeeper greeted them with delight. Yes, he had bedchambers for sir and madam, yes, he had bedchambers for their valet and maid, and yes, there was space for a footman and coachman, too. He offered them hot food and hot punch and a private parlor. Black accepted all three. "Hot punch for my coachman and footman as well," he said, shaking rain from his coat. "See that their clothes are dried, will you?"

Nell wiped the rain from the spectacles and perched them back on her nose. Anticipation fizzed in her blood. *Twelve miles to Tiverton.*

The punch came before the food. It was tart and sweet at the same time. Nell tasted lemon, smelled spices. She didn't know what the alcohol was, but it was potent, warming her mouth, warming her chest. She sipped, savoring the heady flavor. *Twelve miles.* The words were drumbeat in her blood. *Twelve miles to Tiverton.*

"We must send an express to Lizzie," she said. "Tell her we've found Felicity."

"I'll send one first thing tomorrow," Black promised.

Nell swallowed another mouthful of hot, spicy punch. "I want Lizzie to be Felicity's godmother, even if she is a . . . a . . ." She tried to find a polite word for it, but there really wasn't one. "Prostitute."

Black nodded, as if he approved of her decision.

"I wish I could give her my portion." If Lizzie had eighty pounds in interest a year, she wouldn't have to be a prostitute.

"No need," Black said. "I've asked my man of business to set up an annuity for her."

Nell stared at him. "You have?"

He nodded again.

Nell didn't need to ask why: Black was helping Lizzie because Lizzie had helped Sophia.

Tears rose in her eyes. She put down her glass and hugged him tightly. "Thank you."

Black's arms came around her. "Lizzie may decide to remain with Mr. Wheatley. She seems very fond of him."

"At least it'll be her choice. She won't have to stay if she doesn't want to. She won't have to sell herself."

"No. She won't."

Nell blinked away her tears and drew back and looked at him. "You're the best man in the world, Mordecai."

He blushed a rosy pink.

NEXT TO ARRIVE WAS the food: thick slices of fried ham and golden-yolked eggs. The innkeeper offered them more punch. Black chose ale. After a moment's hesitation, Nell did, too.

She ate heartily. The ham was salty, the ale bitter, and everything was purely delicious. A rustic meal, but a perfect one. Eagerness and alcohol hummed in her veins. *Twelve miles.*

Nell glanced across the table at Black. Such a striking face, with its formidable nose and slanting cheekbones. Such a strong, beautiful, masculine face.

Mordecai Black was many things. He was a rake. A bastard. A man who could kill. But the most important thing about him wasn't his face, or his birth, or his reputation; it was his heart. Black might be one of the most scandalous men in the *ton*, but he was also one of its kindest.

I love you, Mordecai.

Nell looked down at her plate. Black had asked her to marry him every day until the fire, and not once since.

Had he changed his mind? Was it the magic? Or did propriety hold him silent? Did he feel he couldn't renew his offer because of Sophia's death?

The only way to find out was to ask, but Nell was afraid to.

It took courage to propose marriage—she'd realized that in London—but she hadn't realized quite how *much* courage. Hadn't realized that one could be so afraid of rejection that one's heart raced and one's palms sweated and one felt quite sick with dread.

Some things became easier with practice, but Nell doubted that rejection was one of them—and Mordecai Black had been rejected many times in his life. By his mother. By Cécile. *By me.*

Nine times he'd asked her to marry him. And nine times she had refused.

My poor Mordecai. I'm sorry I hurt you.

Black finished his meal and leaned back in his chair, sipping his ale. He didn't look like a man who was unhappy; he looked relaxed, contented, a little sleepy.

He smiled across the table at her. "Can't finish it all?"

"No." Nell laid her cutlery on her plate, and pushed it to one side. Her heart was beating absurdly fast and her palms were quite damp and a knot was tying itself tightly in her stomach. "Mordecai?"

He lifted his eyebrows.

Nell brushed the coppery ringlets back from her forehead, pushed the spectacles up her nose, and took a deep breath. "Mordecai . . . will you please marry me?"

She saw shock cross his face, saw him blink. He straightened in the chair, put down his tankard, and reached across the table to take hold of her hands. "Nell," he said gently.

"Now isn't the time to be making important decisions. Your grief is too fresh."

"Sophia has nothing to do with this," Nell told him. "I knew I wanted to marry you before I learned of her death."

Black frowned, as if he didn't believe her.

"I knew the day of the fire."

His gaze was intent on her face. He looked as if he was trying to see inside her, trying to tell whether she spoke the truth. His own expression was inscrutable. Nell couldn't tell whether he wished to marry her or not.

"If you would rather not have a wife who can control fire, please say so."

His brow creased. "What?"

"Please be honest, Mordecai. If you don't wish to marry me anymore, *tell* me."

His hands tightened on hers. "Of course I still want to marry you!"

"Even if I can do magic?"

"Of course."

"But . . . if we have any daughters, they'll receive wishes on their twenty-third birthdays."

"Then we shall counsel them to be *very* careful what they choose." Black tightened his grip on her hands until it was almost painful. "Nell, you goose, how could you think I wouldn't want to marry you for such a reason?"

"After Billy English—"

"I didn't understand how things were, then. I do now."

"You still wish to marry me?" Foolish tears welled in her eyes.

"Of course I do." Black released her hands, pulled out his pocketbook, extracted a much-folded piece of paper, opened it, and pushed it across the table. "We can get married tomorrow. Look."

Nell blinked back the tears, and stared. It was a marriage license. A marriage license issued by the Archbishop of Canterbury. A marriage license that looked as if it had been in Black's pocketbook for months, dog-eared, creased. Her dazed eyes found the date: July thirteenth.

She found her name on it, and his. *Mordecai Bamber Evelyn Pontus Pomeroy Pew Black.*

"Bamber Evelyn Pontus Pomeroy?"

"My father's name, exactly—so that no one could doubt I was his son." There was a note in Black's voice that drew her eyes to him. "My mother did it to shame him." He grimaced faintly. "Poor Mother."

Poor Mother? Nell bit her lip, and wondered if she dared ask, and then said, "Do you forgive her for how she treated you?"

"I pity her. She was an unhappy woman."

"And your father? Do you forgive him for not wanting you at first?"

"Father's easy to forgive, because he never forgave himself." Black reached across and took her hands again. "We shall do better with our children. Starting with Felicity."

The foolish tears welled up in her eyes. "Yes."

He saw the tears, and tightened his grip on her hands. "When would you like to marry, love?" he said softly.

"As soon as possible," Nell said. "Tomorrow. Once we've found her."

THAT NIGHT, MORDECAI waited until his servants had retired, then went to Eleanor Wrotham's room. He felt foolish tiptoeing down the corridor in the dark. Tompkin and Bessie both knew about his visits to Eleanor's bed, and yet still he crept around pretending it was a secret. But tomorrow night there'd be no need to pretend; there was nothing scandalous about a husband and wife sharing the same bed.

Mordecai quietly opened her door. The room was shadowy, cozy, lit by one candle. Eleanor sat in her bed, hugging her knees, watching him.

He latched the door behind him, then crossed to her and touched her cheek lightly. She smiled up at him, a smile that lit her eyes, that lit her whole face. She didn't say *I love you,* but he saw it clearly.

Mordecai stood there for a long minute, his fingers resting on her cheek, staring down at her, and neither of them spoke and yet it seemed as if they did, that they said everything that needed to be said, words of love and trust and commitment. Emotion tightened his throat. "Nell . . ." he said, and then stopped, afraid his voice might break.

He snuffed out the candle and climbed into the bed and took Eleanor in his arms. "Mordecai," she whispered, and that whisper held everything, too.

Mordecai found her eyebrows, traced them lightly. He should have left the candle burning. "I wish I could see your face right now."

The candle flickered alight.

Mordecai flinched—and felt Eleanor flinch in response. The candle snuffed out instantly. "I'm sorry," she said.

He found her lips and kissed them. "Light it again, Nell."

The room stayed dark. She was tense in his arms.

Mordecai kissed her again. "Light it, Nell."

"You don't mind?" she asked, and he heard an edge of anxiety in her voice.

"Of course I don't mind," Mordecai said firmly. "It was a little startling, is all."

After a moment the candle lit itself again. This time he didn't flinch.

He gazed at Eleanor. She looked back at him, a little wary, a little uncertain.

"Relax, love," he said, and kissed her temple, kissed her cheek. *My Nell.* "I love your eyelids. I hope our children have them."

He kissed those haughty eyelids, kissed that patrician nose. This woman with the face of a duchess and the soul of a kindred spirit. "Don't wear the wig tomorrow," he told her. Not if they were going to be married. Not if she was going to become Mrs. Black. He kissed her smooth brown hair, kissed his way down the line of her jaw, found her mouth and kissed that, too.

Mordecai made love to Eleanor slowly, reverently, watching her face in the candlelight, and she watched him and touched him and whispered back the words he whispered to her. The clocks seemed to turn back. He felt as if he was making love for the very first time in his life—not with a boy's urgency, but with a man's wonder. And it *was* a first time of sorts—the first time he made love to his wife, because even if they hadn't signed the parish register yet, they *were* man and wife—and so Mordecai didn't hold on to his self-control when she climaxed, didn't withdraw and spill his seed into his handkerchief, but instead let the sensations roll through him, and it was profoundly wonderful: to feel Eleanor's hot, sleek muscles contract around him and to simply let go and allow himself to climax with her.

La petite mort, Cécile had sometimes called this moment. The little death. But there was nothing little about it tonight. It consumed him utterly, went on for an eternity, and it was bliss, pure bliss. *La jouissance. La joie.*

Mordecai slowly floated back to reality. Every muscle in his body was trembling. His breathing was shallow and ragged. He gathered Eleanor in his arms and rolled so that they lay on their sides, legs intertwined. And he was still inside her. Still inside her.

He held her close, and his joy was so great that he didn't know whether to laugh or weep.

Chapter Thirty-Eight

August 9th, 1812
Tiverton, Devonshire

THE DAY DAWNED CLEAR, but the roads were still wet and it was past ten o'clock before the traveling chaise reached Tiverton. Georgiana Dalrymple's directions took them through the town to a cottage on the northern outskirts. Mordecai watched for churches. Tiverton didn't know it yet, but a marriage would take place here today. He took Eleanor's hand as the carriage trundled over the cobblestones, not caring if Tompkin and Bessie saw.

Eleanor didn't seem to mind that they had an audience. She gripped tightly back. He was aware of her trembling, eager anticipation.

Mordecai was eager, too. *By tonight I'll have a wife and a daughter.* A family. His very own family. He felt an upwelling of emotion. His chest constricted. His eyes stung briefly.

The carriage slowed and drew to a halt. Mordecai saw a

small cottage with an apple tree in the front yard, exactly as Georgiana Dalrymple had described.

Eleanor scrambled down from the chaise, not waiting for Walter to let down the steps. Mordecai lengthened his stride to keep up with her as she hurried along the path.

The door had lost most of its paint, the cottage most of its whitewash, and one the windowpanes was cracked and boarded over, but a jar of Michaelmas daisies was bright in the window and the faint, sweet sounds of a lullaby came to Mordecai's ears.

Eleanor knocked.

The lullaby broke off. A few moments later, the door opened. "Mrs. Rundle?" Mordecai asked.

"Yes, sir."

Mrs. Rundle was a tiny, birdlike woman with bright brown eyes and graying hair tucked up in a bun. She reminded Mordecai of a sparrow.

"We understand you have some infants in your care."

"That's right, sir. Six of them. I look after them for the parish." Mrs. Rundle's gown had once been black but was now a faded gray. It was patched at the hem and her apron was neatly darned in two places.

"My niece," Eleanor said eagerly. "You have my niece, Felicity."

"Felicity?" Mrs. Rundle's head cocked to the side. She looked even more like a sparrow. "I've got three girls at the moment, ma'am. I don't know their names."

"She has a yellow ribbon around her wrist."

"Oh, yes." Mrs. Rundle's face broke into a smile. "She came in a fortnight ago. A wee darling, she is. Step inside, won't you? I'm so glad you've come for her."

"How is it that Felicity's here in Tiverton?" Mordecai asked as they followed the woman. The cottage didn't smell of camphor or vinegar; it smelled of stewed apple. "Do you know?"

"The lady that was looking after her didn't want her, so she gave her to her aunt, here in Tiverton, but the aunt didn't want her either. So the parish gave her to me."

"Are all your charges orphans?"

"Orphans, foundlings. No one wants them, the poor wee mites." Mrs. Rundle opened a door and stepped inside.

Eleanor gripped his arm tightly. She vibrated with urgency, with eagerness.

Mordecai glanced around, seeing a small room with bare floorboards and three cots crammed together, side by side. The bedclothes were thin and gray, but the floor was swept clean. Another jar of Michaelmas daisies stood on the windowsill.

The six infants lay two to a cot. One whimpered fretfully; the others slept.

"Felicity?" Eleanor said, and her voice trembled with hope.

"I've been calling her Buttercup, on account of the yellow ribbon." Mrs. Rundle bent over one of the cots. "The babies sometimes do come in with ribbons. I always leave them on, in case the mothers come for them."

"And do they come?" Mordecai asked.

"It's never happened before." Mrs. Rundle gently peeled back a threadbare blanket. "And I've been doing this nigh on fifteen years. Ever since my husband passed away, God rest his soul." She carefully gathered up one of the babies and handed it to Eleanor Wrotham.

Despite Mrs. Rundle's care, the baby woke with a startled wail.

Eleanor took the child and held her close, cradling that downy head in one hand, rocking her, kissing her, soothing her. "Hush, hush, you're safe." And if little Felicity didn't understand the words, she understood the love behind them. The wail died to a whimper. She gave a hiccupping sob and nestled close.

Eleanor turned to Mordecai, tears on her face, joy in her eyes. "Mordecai. Look at her. Isn't she perfect?"

Mordecai looked at the feathery whorls of fair hair, the delicate eyelids, the tiny nose—and as he looked he felt a fierce surge of protectiveness, a visceral emotion centered in his chest. He discovered that tears were leaking from his eyes. He wiped them away. "Perfect," he said, and carefully hugged both Eleanor and Felicity to him. *My wife. My daughter.*

Mrs. Rundle beamed at them. "I can't tell you how it gladdens my heart to know she has a home."

Mordecai looked past her at the cots, at the babies. He felt an unexpected and painful kinship with them—because he was illegitimate himself, because he'd been unwanted for the first eight years of his life. "What will happen to them?"

Mrs. Rundle lost her smile. "The poorhouse, sir." She turned back to the cots. Four of the infants slept, but one still whimpered. She picked it up and began to rock it. "I try to give them as much kindness as I can, poor wee souls. Heaven only knows they won't get any in the poorhouse."

No. That was a certainty. There'd be no kindness for these children once they were old enough for the poorhouse, and very little hope for them. How many of them would reach their fifth birthdays, let alone their tenth? And for those few who did reach that milestone, what bleak future awaited them?

Mordecai glanced around the room, noting the signs of poverty: the bare floor, the threadbare blankets, the chipped jar of daisies. The ceiling was stained with damp in one corner. "How much does the parish pay you?" he asked Mrs. Rundle.

"Sixpence a week for each little one, sir."

"What do you feed them?"

"Gruel," she said. "And stewed apple. And a little milk."

Mrs. Rundle looked as if she survived on gruel and stewed apple and a little milk, too. And she'd be short sixpence a week with Felicity gone. Mordecai released Eleanor and reached for his pocketbook. "I'll compensate you."

"Thank you, sir. That's very kind of you."

Mordecai opened his pocketbook and thumbed through the banknotes, and then looked at the babies, looked at Mrs. Rundle. He thought of Great Wynthrop, with its empty rooms waiting to be filled and its wide, sunlit lawn.

Eleanor glanced up at his face—and then at the three cots. He saw her gaze rest on each infant. She cradled Felicity even closer, one hand protectively cupping that downy head, looked at the cots again, and then at him. "Mordecai?"

Mordecai stared down at her, thinking. He had a vacant house. He had servants to spare. He could give Mrs. Rundle a home that wouldn't leak and the children a place to grow up in that wasn't the poorhouse.

"Mordecai?" Eleanor said again, a note of hope in her voice.

"I think Great Wynthrop is a better place for Mrs. Rundle and these babies," he said. "Don't you?"

A luminous smile lit Eleanor's face. "Yes," she said emphatically. "I do!"

Afterwards

NELL'S TWENTY-THIRD BIRTHDAY had been memorable because of the fire and Baletongue. Whenever she thought back to that day, she remembered her impatience to meet her Faerie godmother, her impatience to find Sophia. She remembered rooftops on fire, a sky dark with smoke, flames cascading from windows. She remembered being terrified that Mordecai might die—and she remembered dying herself for a few moments.

Her twenty-fourth birthday bore no resemblance to her twenty-third. There was no burning city, no streets choked with frantic people, no urgency, no fear.

In the morning, she went riding with Mordecai, coming home via Great Wynthrop, as they invariably did. The house was alive, as it hadn't been a year ago, the main building full of purpose and energy and children's voices. The wings still stood empty, but she knew Mordecai would fill them, too— because that was who he was: a man who rescued people.

In the afternoon, Nell went down to the shore with her

husband and daughter. They paddled in the water. Felicity clung to their hands and tottered unsteadily on her little dimpled feet and laughed at each wave.

Afterwards, they sat on the sand together, enjoying the cool breeze, the warm sunshine. Felicity nestled into Nell's lap and went to sleep.

Nell gathered the little girl closer, and as if in response, Mordecai gathered her closer, too. One of his hands rested on her belly, as it often did these days, guarding the child that grew there.

He brushed a light kiss against her temple. "Happy?"

"Yes." Nell drank in the moment—the sunshine, the breeze, the *shush* of the waves, the child in her lap, Mordecai's arm around her, his hand on her belly. "Right now, I think I must be the happiest person in the world."

"No, that would be me," Mordecai said.

"Shall we argue about it?" Nell asked, stroking the back of his hand, tracing the strong bones.

"Compromise," he said, and Nell laughed and nestled more deeply into his embrace.

"I love you," she said.

"I love you, too."

Altogether, her twenty-fourth birthday was *very* much better than her twenty-third.

Author's Note

In 1809 a woman named Mary Bateman was tried and hanged for witchcraft in Yorkshire, so Nell is right to be scared of being labeled a witch.

A number of cities in England had great fires during their history. Exeter didn't, but it had many smaller fires and was known as the "fiery city" during the 1800s.

A remarkable system of medieval tunnels exist beneath the oldest part of Exeter. The tunnels were used to carry water pipes into the city and were sometimes referred to as "the damps."

I didn't make up *pattes d'araignées,* honestly! The French phrases that Mordecai uses all come from the *Dictionnaire Érotique Moderne,* by Alfred Delvau, which was published in the 1800s.

Coombe Regis doesn't exist, but if you visit Ladram Bay on the Devon coast, you'll see the red cliffs and rock stacks that Mordecai loves so much.

Thank You

Thanks for reading *Ruining Miss Wrotham*. I hope you enjoyed it!

If you'd like to be notified whenever I release a new book, please join my Readers' Group.

I welcome all honest reviews. Reviews and word of mouth help other readers to find books, so please consider taking a few moments to leave a review on Goodreads or elsewhere.

Ruining Miss Wrotham is the fifth book in the Baleful Godmother series. The earlier books are *Unmasking Miss Appleby, Resisting Miss Merryweather, Trusting Miss Trentham*, and *Claiming Mister Kemp*, and the next one is *Discovering Miss Dalrymple*, with more to follow. I hope you enjoy them all!

Those of you who like to start a series at its absolute beginning may wish to read the series prequel—*The Fey Quartet*—a quartet of novellas that tell the tales of a widow, her three daughters, and one baleful Faerie.

The Fey Quartet and *Unmasking Miss Appleby* are available for free when you join my Readers' Group. Here's the link: www.emilylarkin.com/starter-library.

If you'd like to read the first chapter of *Discovering Miss Dalrymple,* please continue . . .

Discovering Miss Dalrymple

September 11th, 1814
Dorsetshire

ALEXANDER ST. CLARE, seventh Duke of Vickery, found his
father's diaries by accident. He was working at the massive oak
desk in the study, reading through the latest report from the
bailiff on his Lincolnshire estate and jotting down notes, when
the tip of the quill split.

"Drain the north paddock," he muttered under his breath,
while he opened the top drawer of the desk and searched for a
penknife. The penknife was at the very back of the drawer.
Alexander groped for it, banged his knuckles against wood—
and then the wood yielded and the penknife skittered out of
reach, deeper into the desk.

Damn. He'd broken the drawer.

Alexander carefully removed it—and discovered that the
drawer wasn't broken at all; the back was hinged, with a little
catch that he must have knocked open.

What the devil?

He got down on his knees and peered into the gaping slot. Was that a secret compartment? In his father's old oak desk?

He reached in and felt carefully. Yes, a secret compartment. The penknife was in there, and . . . books?

Alexander drew the books out. There were six of them, bound with calfskin. He opened one and saw his father's handwriting. *June 17, 1808. The young people all went riding again this afternoon.*

Alexander hastily closed the diary.

He replaced the drawer, stacked the diaries on the farthest corner of the desk, trimmed his quill, and went back to his notes. *Drain the north paddock,* he wrote, and then stared blindly at the bailiff's report.

The young people all went riding again this afternoon.

He could see it in his mind's eye, the four of them cantering along the clifftops: himself and his two best friends, Hubert Cathcart and Oliver Dalrymple, and Oliver's younger sister, Georgiana.

God, what a painful summer that had been. The summer he'd fallen in love with Georgiana. The summer she'd fallen in love with Hubert.

Alexander gave himself a mental shake. He tried to focus on the bailiff's report, on the here and now, but that glimpsed diary entry had dislodged a cascade of memories. His mind took him back six years. He remembered how happy Georgiana and Hubert had been, how they'd glowed with joy, and he remembered congratulating them on their betrothal while in a secret and shameful place deep inside himself he'd been hoping the wedding wouldn't take place.

The wedding *hadn't* taken place, and that had been a thousand times worse. Hubert had gone up to Scotland to visit his godfather and had never returned, vanished somewhere on the road between Edinburgh and Perth. Alexander had hoped and prayed for Hubert's return, he'd got down on his knees in the Thornycombe chapel and *begged* God for it, but weeks had become months, and then years, and then finally Hubert's grave had been found, nowhere near Perth or Edinburgh.

Alexander stared down at the bailiff's report, not seeing the words. *Damn it, Hubert, I wish you had come back.*

"Your Grace?"

Alexander looked up. A footman stood in the doorway to his study.

"It's nearly two o'clock, sir."

Two o'clock. Alexander's thoughts jerked from Hubert to Georgiana. He put down his quill, took the items the footman handed him—hat, riding crop, gloves—and strode from the study. His mood changed as he ran down the stairs two at a time, shedding grief, letting hope take its place. Two o'clock.

Afternoons had always been his favorite time of the day. When he was a boy he'd spent them with Hubert and Oliver, exploring the long, shingly Dorsetshire beaches, climbing the cliffs, hunting for fossils, fishing and eeling and birdnesting, getting wet, filthy, sunburned.

Now his afternoons were special because of Georgiana.

His horse, Sultan, was saddled and waiting in the stable-yard. Alexander suspected that afternoons were Sultan's favorite time of the day, too. Certainly the horse caught his eagerness, lengthening his stride into a canter as soon as they reached the lane.

Thornycombe Hall to Dalrymple Court was less than a mile. Alexander covered that distance in four minutes. Hedgerows flashed past, birds twittered, the Dorsetshire sun shone down, and then he swung into the avenue and there she was: Georgiana Dalrymple, on her bay mare, waiting for him.

Alexander slowed Sultan to a trot, then a walk, and came

up alongside her. A smile broke out on his face, the smile that was only for Georgiana, the one that said, *I love you.*

THEY GALLOPED ALONG the clifftops and then let the horses amble. Alexander looked out at the wide vista of sea and sky, and then let his gaze stray to Georgiana. He loved it when she looked like this, cheeks flushed, eyes bright, curling tendrils of hair escaping from beneath the brim of her hat. It made him want to lean over in his saddle and kiss her.

She was no longer the girl he'd fallen in love with; she was a woman, now, more confident than she'd been all those years ago, more assured, but quieter, too—and still, after all this time, the person he wanted to marry. He let his gaze rest on her—the sparkling brown eyes, the soft brown hair—and thought of the things he loved most about her: her quick mind, her thoughtfulness, her sense of humor, the way they could talk so easily, laugh together, be quiet together.

"Vic?" Georgiana said.

That was another thing he loved about her: that she called him Vic. Not Your Grace, not Vickery, but Vic. *She sees me as a person, not a duke.*

"Vic?" she said a second time.

He knew her almost as well as he knew himself. "You want to gallop again?"

"Yes."

And so they galloped again, the horses' hooves thundering, kicking up clods of turf, and when they pulled up Georgiana was flushed and breathless and laughing, and Alexander felt a painful sensation in his chest, a sensation that combined longing and desire and hope.

The horses came up alongside one another, flanks heaving.

Georgiana grinned at him, and she looked like the girl she'd been six summers ago, vivid, alive, glowing—except that this time the glow in her eyes was for him.

His knee touched hers briefly and their bodies swayed together and there was a moment when they looked into each other's eyes, when a *frisson* shivered over his skin, when Georgiana seemed to hold her breath, when he almost—almost—leaned over and kissed her. And then the horses moved apart and the moment was lost.

THEY RODE SLOWLY back to Dalrymple Court and while they rode Alexander debated his options. It was barely a year since Georgiana had had the strange, prophetic dream that had told her where Hubert's grave was. Was it too soon to pay his addresses? Should he wait a few more months?

Dalrymple Court came into sight: the tall chimneys, the creamy stone masonry half-covered with ivy, the rose garden. They halted side by side in the lane. "Would you like to come in?" Georgiana asked.

Alexander studied her face. Something in her expression, in her eyes, made him think that she felt the same sensation he did: the longing, the hope.

"Yes," he said, "I have something I need to discuss with your parents."

AN HOUR LATER, Alexander ran up the stairs to his study, whistling under his breath. He tossed aside his hat and riding crop, peeled off his gloves, and paced the room, too exhilarated to sit, treading across the Aubusson carpet, backwards and forwards, backwards and forwards. Lord and Lady Dalrymple had said yes. Now he just had to hope that Georgiana would say yes, too.

He crossed to the window and stared out. He would ask her tomorrow. After they'd galloped along the clifftops, when they were windswept and laughing. He felt the words on his tongue, heard them in his ears: *Marry me, Georgie.*

Should he tell her how long he'd loved her? Why he loved her?

Should he mention Hubert?

Alexander considered this for several minutes. No, he wouldn't mention Hubert, not while asking Georgiana to marry him.

He stared out the window and imagined it: Tomorrow afternoon on the clifftops, sunshine, a salty breeze, the thunder of the horses's hooves as they galloped, and then afterwards . . .

He'd wait until they'd both caught their breath and then he'd say, *Georgie, will you please marry me?* And then he'd tell her all the reasons why he loved her.

A MAID CAME to light the candles before dusk. When she'd gone, Alexander sat at his desk and glanced at the bailiff's report, but he was too preoccupied by thought of tomorrow to pay it the careful attention it needed.

His gaze drifted to his father's diaries, stacked on the corner of the desk. What should he do with them?

He picked one up and flicked through the pages, remembering his father's voice, his dry laugh. And then he remembered holding his father's hand while the old man died. Alexander's throat closed for a moment. He blinked several times and turned to the very beginning. There was an inscription on the first page: *Leonard Aubrey St. Clare, Duke of Vickery.* And underneath that: *To be burned in the event of my death.*

Alexander had a flash of memory so strong that he almost smelled his father's deathbed—the camphor, the lavender, the beeswax candles. For a fleeting moment he could have sworn he felt his father's hand in his: the cooling skin, the lifeless fingers. His throat closed again. He needed to blink a few more times, and then he gathered up the diaries and crossed to the hearth. A fire was laid there, but not lit; it had been a warm September.

He kindled the fire, watched the flames take hold—and found himself unable to burn the diaries. His father had been dead for two years, but this felt like a second burial; these pages held his father's thoughts and emotions and experiences.

Alexander examined the diaries. The calfskin was scuffed in places, shiny in others, worn by his father's hands. What could it hurt to read one entry? The day of his birth, nothing more. An entry that bound him to his father. And then he'd burn the diaries and lay the old man to rest again.

He lowered himself into the leather armchair by the fire and thumbed through the diaries until he found the right one, but the entry for January 25, 1785, didn't mention his birth. In fact, it appeared that his father had been in London, not at his wife's bedside in Kent.

Alexander turned the page. On January 26, squeezed between an account of a visit to a *perruquier* and some jotted notes about improvements to make on the Wiltshire estate, were three sentences: *An express came from Kent. Lucretia has delivered a child. A boy, thank God.* And that was it. A disconcertingly short three sentences.

Alexander turned the page, and discovered that his father had traveled to Kent on the twenty-seventh. *The boy looks healthy,* his father had written, *but he has the oddest eyes.* As diary entries went, it was even shorter and more disconcerting.

There was no further mention of his birth. On January 29 his father had gone back to London, where he'd remained until halfway through February, when he'd visited the estates in Cambridgeshire, Northamptonshire, Oxfordshire, and Wiltshire. In May he'd returned to Kent and stayed only long enough to see his son christened before heading back to London.

Alexander frowned at the diary. The writing was his father's, but the man who'd written the entries wasn't the father he remembered.

He flicked further ahead. His father wrote about his estates, about politics, about the war with America, about the latest *on-dits,* but only rarely about his wife, and even more rarely about his son. Every two weeks came an entry that said: *A letter from Kent.* Occasionally an extra sentence was appended. *Lucretia says that Alexander's first tooth has come through. Lucretia says that Alexander is crawling.*

Alexander thumbed through the pages, skimming. As far as he could tell, in the first two years of his life his father had seen him only five times. Five times? In two years?

He put the diary aside, disturbed, and got up to pour himself a glass of brandy. He frowned at the fire while he sipped, frowned at the stack of leather-bound diaries. He didn't know the man the diaries described. Didn't know him at all.

Perhaps he changed when Mother died?

Alexander found the diary for 1788. His father had been in Leicestershire. *An express from Kent. Lucretia is dead. She fell down the stairs and broke her neck.* Alexander turned the page and read further. His father had traveled posthaste back to Kent, seen to his wife's burial, hired a second nurserymaid for his three-year-old son, and gone to Wiltshire.

What? My mother died and you didn't stay with me? You left me with nurserymaids?

Alexander squeezed his eyes shut and rubbed his forehead. He'd loved his father—but he didn't like the man who'd written the diaries.

He opened his eyes and stared at the fire for a moment, and then raised his gaze to the candelabrum on the mantelpiece, where three candles shed golden light. There was a candelabrum on the sideboard, too, alongside the decanters, and another one on his desk. Candles everywhere in the study. Candles and light.

The maid would have lit all the candles in the corridors, too, and the candles in the dining room, the library, the drawing room, the billiard room—any room that he might conceivably wish to enter tonight. It was a huge extravagance, but it was also a necessity.

Because he found it difficult to breathe in the dark.

He'd found it difficult to breathe in the dark ever since he'd been five years old.

Alexander looked at the candles on the mantelpiece—and knew the exact day his father had changed.

He drained the brandy glass, put it to one side, and picked up the diaries again. There was a hard, sick knot in his stomach. He found 1789. Found May. Found June.

Alexander turned the pages reluctantly. *June 8. June 14.* His throat was tight, his shoulders were tight, his chest was tight. He forced himself to inhale, to exhale, to turn the page.

June 20, 1789. An express from Kent. Alexander is missing. The nurserymaids took him into the woods for a picnic and he was abducted by gypsies.

Alexander's heart was beating too fast. There was sweat on

his upper lip. He wiped it away and turned the page and read of his father's hasty journey to Kent, read of men searching the woods and scouring the nearby villages. *I've dismissed the nurserymaids,* his father had written. *How dare they take Alexander into the woods without my permission?* And then an anguished: *Where is my son?*

Alexander thumbed hastily through the next few months, skipping over the details: the advertisements in the newspapers, the posters and the flyers, the search widening beyond Kent into Sussex, into London, into Hampshire.

November, December, January. And there it was:

February 14, 1790. An express from Exeter. One of my men thinks he's found Alexander in the employ of a chimney sweep.

Alexander released the breath he'd been holding and turned the page.

His father had covered the two hundred miles from London to Exeter in two days. *It's Alexander,* he'd written on February 16. *There can be no doubt. Those eyes. But he's shockingly thin. His cheeks are quite hollow and he has bruises where he's been beaten.*

He hasn't said a word yet. Not one. He flinches whenever anyone touches him, even me. He doesn't recognize me as his father, but how could he? It's been almost a year since I last saw him, and then only for five minutes. I wouldn't recognize him myself, but for those eyes.

I won't have a nurserymaid near him. I have sworn an oath to that: No nurserymaids, ever again. It was I who fed him tonight, who bathed him and put him to bed and sat with him until he slept. I stroked his hair once he was asleep, and he didn't flinch, and then I held his hand.

I'm holding it now as I write. I don't ever want to let it go.

Alexander put down the diary. He crossed to the decanters and poured himself another glass of brandy. He gulped a mouthful, coughed, and swallowed a second more cautious mouthful. Then he went back to the diaries and read into

March and April. It didn't surprise him to learn that he'd been terrified of the dark, terrified of small spaces, that he'd had nightmares every single night, but it did surprise him to learn that he'd been mute for months.

May 10, 1790. Alexander spoke for the first time today. One word only, but that word was "Father." I didn't know whether to laugh or cry, so I did both.

May 14, 1790. He spoke a full sentence this morning.

June 1, 1790. Alexander laughed today. And I laughed, too, and then afterwards I cried with relief, because I know he's going to be all right. If he can laugh, he's going to be all right.

June 17, 1790. He's chattering all the time now. I never thought it would give me such joy to hear a child's voice.

The diary ended in 1791. Alexander picked up the next one. He turned the pages slowly, carefully. This was the father he remembered, the father who'd read him to sleep every night, who'd sat at his bedside when he was sick, who'd always had time for him, who'd never once said, *Not now, Alexander. I'm too busy.* The father who had loved him. The father he had loved.

He saw himself grow up through his father's eyes.

April 10, 1792. I can't bear to send him to Eton yet. He's still too thin. I've decided to take him to Dorsetshire instead. The sea air will do him good.

August 3, 1793. Dorsetshire agrees with us both. Alexander is a sturdy wee fellow now and as brown as a berry. I've taken his name off the Eton roll.

March 16, 1798. He's only thirteen and yet he's already as tall I am. He quite dwarfs his cousins. I have no doubt that he'll dwarf me before the year is out.

December 8, 1801. Alexander has grown out of his clothes again. He's over six foot, now. If his shoulders grow any broader he'll not fit through a door. I told him that and he laughed. He laughs a lot, my boy.

July 30, 1803. It's time to think of sending Alexander to Oxford. I hate to let him go, but he's a man now and he needs to find his feet in the world. I have no doubt that he'll enjoy university. He has a gift for making friends.

January 25, 1806. Alexander is twenty-one today. Perhaps it's a father's partiality, but I truly believe there's no finer man in England. It's a comfort to know I can pass the dukedom to him. He'll bear that burden far better than I have. He's so level-headed. And despite what happened when he was a child he has a merry heart.

May 11, 1807. A letter from Lucretia's brother telling me it's past time that I arranged a marriage for Alexander. Damned impertinence. I refuse to do to Alexander what my parents did to me. He will choose the bride he wants, when he wants.

The next diary covered 1808 to 1812. Alexander skipped over the first two years. He didn't want to read about Georgiana's betrothal or Hubert's disappearance. He thumbed through 1810 and 1811, reading the odd entry, and slowed when he reached 1812. The handwriting grew spidery, shaky. He turned the pages gently, feeling grief well in his chest, remembering his father's decline, the way he'd spent less time in the study and more in his bed.

August 26, 1812.

A terrible thing happened today. Alexander came to sit with me after my nap and for a moment I didn't recognize him. "Who are you?" I asked, and he said, "Your son," and I looked at him and knew that he couldn't possibly be, not with that face, not with those shoulders. A terrible fear grew in me. What if I had rescued the wrong boy all those years ago?

I asked Alexander to take me to the Long Gallery, and we spent half an hour looking at the portraits together. I couldn't find anyone who looked like him. Where did he get his height from? Those eyebrows? That chin? They're not mine, and they're certainly not Lucretia's.

Alexander saw I was distressed. He took both my hands in his and asked what was wrong, and I looked into his eyes and knew myself for a foolish old man. Those are my son's eyes. There can be no doubt.

But now, without those eyes looking at me, the doubt has returned and I can't sleep for fear that I rescued the wrong child.

Alexander is my son. He has to be. If my boy is still lost out there I couldn't bear it.

Alexander stared at the entry for a long time, and then turned the page. There was no mention of his shoulders or his eyebrows in the next entry, or the next. The journal advanced a few more days, and then abruptly stopped.

He sat still for a moment, then turned back to August 26. He read what his father had written. *I can't sleep for fear that I rescued the wrong child.*

Like to read the rest?
Discovering Miss Dalrymple is available now.

Acknowledgments

A number of people helped to make this book what it is. Foremost among them is my sterling developmental editor, Laura Cifelli Stibich, who made this story immeasurably better. (Seriously, she did.)

I also owe many thanks to my eagle-eyed copyeditor and proofreader, Martin O'Hearn.

The cover and the series logo are both the work of the talented Kim Killion, of The Killion Group. Thank you, Kim!

And last—but definitely not least—my thanks go to my parents, without whose support this book would not have been published.

Emily Larkin grew up in a house full of books—her mother was a librarian and her father a novelist—so perhaps it's not surprising that she became a writer.

Emily has studied a number of subjects, including geology and geophysics, canine behavior, and ancient Greek. Her varied career includes stints as a field assistant in Antarctica and a waitress on the Isle of Skye, as well as five vintages in New Zealand's wine industry.

She loves to travel and has lived in Sweden, backpacked in Europe and North America, and traveled overland in the Middle East, China, and North Africa.

Emily enjoys climbing hills, yoga workouts, watching reruns of Buffy the Vampire Slayer and Firefly, and reading.

She writes historical romances as Emily Larkin and fantasy novels as Emily Gee. Her websites are www.emilylarkin.com and www.emilygee.com.

Never miss a new Emily Larkin book. Join her Readers' Group at www.emilylarkin.com/newsletter and receive free digital copies of *The Fey Quartet* and *Unmasking Miss Appleby*.

OTHER WORKS

THE BALEFUL GODMOTHER SERIES

The Fey Quartet (Series Prequel)
Maythorn's Wish ~ Hazel's Promise
Ivy's Choice ~ Larkspur's Quest

Original Series
Unmasking Miss Appleby
Resisting Miss Merryweather
Trusting Miss Trentham
Claiming Mister Kemp
Ruining Miss Wrotham
Discovering Miss Dalrymple

Garland Series
(Coming soon)

OTHER HISTORICAL ROMANCES

The Earl's Dilemma

My Lady Thief

Lady Isabella's Ogre

The Midnight Quill Trio

The Countess's Groom

The Spinster's Secret

The Baronet's Bride

FANTASY NOVELS

(Written as Emily Gee)

Thief With No Shadow

The Laurentine Spy

The Cursed Kingdoms Trilogy

The Sentinel Mage ~ The Fire Prince ~ The Blood Curse

Printed in Great Britain
by Amazon